Praise for the novels of
#1 bestselling author Debbie Macomber

"Macomber is a skilled storyteller."
—*Publishers Weekly*

"Debbie Macomber writes characters who are as warm and funny as your best friends."
—#1 *New York Times* bestselling author Susan Wiggs

"It's easy to see why Macomber is a perennial favorite: she writes great books."
—*RomanceJunkies.com*

"[Debbie Macomber] demonstrates her impressive skills with characterization and her flair for humor."
—*RT Book Reviews*

"When God created Eve, he must have asked Debbie Macomber for advice because no one does female characters any better than this author."
—*Bookbrowser Reviews*

"Macomber's storytelling sometimes yields a tear, at other times a smile."
—*Newport News, VA, Daily Press*

"Debbie Macomber is one of the most reliable, versatile romance authors around. Whether she's writing lighthearted romps or more serious relationship books, her novels are always engaging stories that accurately capture the foibles of real-life men and women with warmth and humor."
—*Milwaukee Journal Sentinel*

"Popular romance author Debbie Macomber has a gift for evoking the emotions that are at the heart of the genre's popularity."
—*Publishers Weekly*

January 2015

Dear Friends,

There's a saying (it actually comes from General Douglas MacArthur) that old soldiers never die. I'm grateful to say that this appears to be the case with the early-in-my-career books, too. They take on whole new lives in these repackaged sets. *Together Again* contains two such books— *The Trouble With Caasi* and *Reflections of Yesterday*, both originally published in the 1980s.

My readers are often curious as to how I choose my characters' names. Because names are important to the story, I will often search for a week or two before I find the appropriate name for my character. In one book, I actually changed the name of the hero four times until I found one that was the perfect fit. Caasi's name in *The Trouble With Caasi* is a somewhat unusual one; it's her father, Isaac's, name spelled backward.

This story takes place in Alaska where my husband worked as an electrician one winter. He fell in love with the natural beauty and later he brought me north so I could experience it myself. Like Wayne, I, too, fell in love with Alaska.

Reflections of Yesterday is one of my favorite early stories. I've always felt that there's something so tender in the love Simon and Angie shared. This is a classic kind of story, about young lovers torn apart by parents and obligation, and then finding each other again years later.

You can reach me through my website at debbiemacomber.com or on Facebook. If you prefer to write a letter, mail it to PO Box 1458, Port Orchard, WA 98366. I love hearing from readers and I value your opinions!

Warmest wishes,

Debbie Macomber

DEBBIE MACOMBER

Together
Again

MIRA®

Recycling programs
for this product may
not exist in your area.

ISBN-13: 978-0-7783-1514-8

Together Again

Copyright © 2015 by Harlequin Books S.A.

The publisher acknowledges the copyright holder of the individual works as follows:

The Trouble With Caasi
Copyright © 1985 by Debbie Macomber

Reflections of Yesterday
Copyright © 1986 by Debbie Macomber

www.MIRABooks.com

Printed in U.S.A.

This book is dedicated to the enduring friendships
of two beautiful women in my life—
Maryanne Gardner and Marti Siler.
Thank you, dear friends.
—Carol Virak.

Also by Debbie Macomber

More books by Debbie Macomber listed on page 7

Midnight Sons

VOLUME 1
(*Brides for Brothers* and
  The Marriage Risk)
VOLUME 2
(*Daddy's Little Helper* and
  Because of the Baby)
VOLUME 3
(*Falling for Him,
  Ending in Marriage* and
  Midnight Sons and Daughters)

This Matter of Marriage
Montana
Thursdays at Eight
Between Friends
Changing Habits
Married in Seattle
  (*First Comes Marriage* and
  Wanted: Perfect Partner)
Right Next Door
  (*Father's Day* and
  The Courtship of Carol Sommars)
Wyoming Brides
  (*Denim and Diamonds* and
  The Wyoming Kid)
Fairy Tale Weddings
  (*Cindy and the Prince* and
  Some Kind of Wonderful)
The Man You'll Marry
  (*The First Man You Meet* and
  The Man You'll Marry)
Orchard Valley Grooms
  (*Valerie* and *Stephanie*)
Orchard Valley Brides
  (*Norah* and *Lone Star Lovin'*)
The Sooner the Better
An Engagement in Seattle
  (*Groom Wanted* and *Bride Wanted*)
Out of the Rain
  (*Marriage Wanted* and *Laughter in the Rain*)

Learning to Love
  (*Sugar and Spice* and
  Love by Degree)
You...Again
  (*Baby Blessed* and
  Yesterday Once More)
Three Brides, No Groom
The Unexpected Husband
  (*Jury of His Peers* and
  Any Sunday)
Love in Plain Sight
  (*Love 'n' Marriage* and
  Almost an Angel)
I Left My Heart
  (*A Friend or Two* and
  No Competition)
Marriage Between Friends
  (*White Lace and Promises* and
  Friends...And Then Some)
A Man's Heart
  (*The Way to a Man's Heart* and
  Hasty Wedding)
North to Alaska
  (*That Wintry Feeling* and
  Borrowed Dreams)
On a Clear Day
  (*Starlight* and
  Promise Me Forever)
To Love and Protect
  (*Shadow Chasing* and
  For All My Tomorrows)
Home in Seattle
  (*The Playboy and the Widow*
  and *Fallen Angel*)

*Debbie Macomber's
Cedar Cove Cookbook*
*Debbie Macomber's
Christmas Cookbook*

CONTENTS

THE TROUBLE WITH CAASI

One

The majestic beauty of white-capped Mount Hood was unobstructed from the twentieth floor of the Empress Hotel in downtown Portland. Caasi Crane stood in front of the huge floor-to-ceiling window, her arms hugging her slim waist. Blake Sherrill's letter of resignation was clenched tightly in one hand.

Blake was the best general manager she'd ever hope to find. His resignation had caught her off guard. As far as Caasi knew he had been perfectly content. His employee file was open on her computer, and Caasi moved across the plush office to study the information.

His salary was generous, she noted, but Caasi believed in paying her employees what they were worth. And Blake earned every cent. Maybe he'd reconsider if she offered him a raise. But according to the file, he'd received a healthy increase only three months earlier.

Scrolling down through the information Caasi paused to read over the original employment application that included his photograph. He was six three and at her guess around a hundred and eighty pounds. Dark hair and brown eyes. None of that had changed.

She knew him to be single and thirty. Certainly she would know if he'd married. He hadn't she was sure of that. Had Blake been with Crane Enterprises that long? Funny she didn't remember that.

Caasi pushed the wide-rimmed glasses up from the tip of her nose and sat in the cushioned white leather chair.

Her assistant buzzed, interrupting her thoughts. "Mr. Sherrill's here to see you."

Caasi released the intercom lever. "Please send him in." Mentally she prepared herself. Her father had groomed her well for this position. If Blake was displeased about something, she'd soon discover what it was. Employee performance and customer satisfaction were the name of the game. But an employee, even one as good as Blake, couldn't perform if he was unhappy. If so, Caasi wanted to know the reason. She pretended an interest in his computer file when the door opened. Looking up, she smiled brightly. "Sit down, Blake." Her hand indicated a chair on the other side of her desk.

He wasn't a handsome man. His features were rough and rugged, too craggy to be considered attractive. His chin projected stubbornly and the shadow of his beard was heavy. Caasi didn't doubt that he had to shave twice a day. He wore a dark business suit and silk tie, and his hair was coal dark. Could he be Italian with a name like Sherrill? Funny how she'd never really noticed Blake. At least, not the toughness in the lean, hard figure that stood in front of her.

"If you don't mind, I'd rather stand." With feet braced slightly apart, he joined his hands.

"Honestly," Caasi admonished with a soft smile, "you look like a recruit standing at attention."

"Sometimes I feel that way." The words were hardly above a whisper.

"Pardon?" Caasi looked up again.

"Nothing." The small lines about his eyes and mouth creased in a mirthless smile. "You're right. I'll sit down."

"How long have you been with us, now, Blake?"

"Eight years, six months, and five days," he replied dryly

"You counted the days?"

He shrugged. "Maybe I was hoping to gain your attention."

Caasi gave him a troubled look. Clearly something was troubling him? Not in the five years since she'd taken over the company had Blake behaved like this.

"You have my attention now." She held up the resignation letter. "What's the problem?"

He looked away. "There's no problem. The time has come to move on, that's all."

"Is it the money?"

"No."

"Have you got another job offer?" That was the scenario that made the most sense.

"Not yet." This wasn't going well and she was fast losing her grip on the situation.

"All right, Blake, tell me what's up."

"Do you want a full report submitted? There's one due at the end of the month as usual."

"I don't mean that and you know it." Angrily she glared at him.

"I thought you read every report," he muttered with an edge of sarcasm.

Caasi paused. "I've never known you to be cynical," Caasi cut in.

"But then, you've never known me, have you?"

Caasi didn't know how to answer him. Maybe if she'd dated more often she'd be able to deal with men more effectively. That was one area in which her father had failed to instruct her. Sometimes she felt like a bungling teenager, and just as naive.

"Take the rest of the week off, Blake. I would like you to reconsider this letter."

"I'm not going to change my mind." There was a determined look about him, unyielding and confident.

She didn't want to lose Blake. "Take it anyway, and let's talk again the first of the week."

He gave her a mocking salute. "As you wish."

Blake's resignation weighed heavily on Caasi the rest of the day. By the time her assistant left, she was in a rotten mood. It was due to far more than Blake, she recognized that. That night was the monthly get-together with Edie and June, her two BFFs.

The months passed so quickly that sometimes it seemed that they were meeting much too often—and at other times it wasn't nearly enough. Yet the two were her best friends…her *only* friends, Caasi admitted grudgingly as she slid the key into the lock of her apartment door.

The penthouse suite on the twenty-first floor had been Caasi's home for as long as she could remember. She must have been eight before she realized that milk came from a cow and not the busboy who delivered all of the family's meals.

Daddy's little girl from the beginning, Caasi had known from the time she could walk that someday she would be president of Crane Enterprises and the string of hotels that ran down Oregon's coast and into California. Isaac Crane had tutored her for the position until his death five years earlier.

Daddy's little girl… The thought ran through her mind as Caasi opened her closet and took out a striped dress of teal, plum and black. Everything about her reflected her father. A thousand times in her twenty-eight years Caasi had explained that her name hadn't been misspelled but was Isaac spelled backwards.

Soaking in a bubble bath a few minutes later, Caasi lifted the sponge and drained the soothing water over her full breasts and flat stomach. Her big toe idly played with the faucet spout. Her medium-length chestnut hair was piled on top of her head as she lay back and let the hot water refresh her.

Steam swirled around the huge bathroom as Caasi wrapped a thick cotton towel around herself and moved into her bedroom. She didn't feel like going out tonight. A quiet dinner and television would be more to her liking, but she knew Edie and June well enough to realize they wouldn't easily let her forgo their monthly dinner.

An hour later, Caasi entered Brasserie Montmartre, a French restaurant Edie had raved about the previous month. Caasi didn't mind checking out the competition. The Empress's own small French restaurant served—in her opinion—some of the best food in town.

Edie waved when she saw Caasi. June apparently hadn't arrived yet, and Caasi wondered if she would, since June's baby was due any time.

"Greetings, fair one," the pert brunette said as Caasi pulled out a chair and sat down. It was a standard joke between them that, of the three, Caasi was the most attractive. She accepted their good-natured teasing as part of the give-and-take in any friendship. They were her friends, and heaven knew she had few enough of those these days.

"You look pleased about something," Caasi said. Edie was grinning from ear to ear.

"I am." Edie took a sip of champagne and giggled like a sixteen-year-old. "I should probably wait until June's here, but if I don't tell someone soon, I think I'll bust."

"Come on, give," Caasi urged and nodded at the waiter, who promptly delivered another glass and poured for her. Good service, she mused.

"I'm pregnant!"

Caasi nearly choked on the bubbly liquid. "Pregnant!" she spat back. Not both friends at the same time. It was too much!

"I don't think I've ever seen Freddy more excited."

"But you're the one who said—"

"I know, but I changed my mind. It's crazy, but I'm really happy about it. The doctor said there's no reason for me to lose my figure, and he's already put me on a high-protein diet. Freddy's agreed to the natural childbirth classes. From what we've read it's the best way for the baby. June's taking them now, and I'm hoping she can let me sit in on one of her sessions. And then there's the nursery to do. I think Freddy may make the cradle."

"Slow down," Caasi said with a light laugh. "My head's spinning already."

"What do you think?" Edie scooted back her chair and arched her shoulders.

"Think about what?" Caasi shook her head.

"Do I show?"

"Show? For heaven's sake, Edie, you can't be more than a couple of months along!"

"You're right." She giggled, her dark eyes dancing. "And no more than a sip of champagne for me. I'm completely off alcohol and caffeine. I was just hoping…"

"Hoping what?" A tall blonde waddled up behind them. June's protruding stomach left little conjecture as to her condition. One hand rested against her rib cage as she lowered herself into the third chair. "Champagne?" Round blue eyes sought those of the others. "What are we celebrating?"

"Babies, in the plural," Edie supplied with a wide grin that lit up her whole face.

June looked blank for a minute.

"It seems our Edie has found herself with child," Caasi informed her.

"Edie?" June whispered disbelievingly. "Not the same Edie who marched in a rally for zero population growth when we were in high school?"

"One and the same." Edie laughed and motioned for the waiter, who produced a third glass.

"We're talking about the girl who was afraid to eat lettuce because it could ruin her perfect figure."

"Not the one who said 'Lips that touch chocolate shall never touch mine'?" June's eyes rounded with shock.

"'Fraid so," Caasi said with an exaggerated sigh.

"Would you two quit talking about me as if I wasn't here?" Edie demanded.

"A baby." Caasi looked from one to the other and shook her head. "Both of you. Wasn't it yesterday that I was your maid of honor, June? And, Edie, remember how we argued over who got which bed our freshman year?"

"I always thought you'd be the first one to marry," June said to her in a somber tone. "Caasi the beauty. Gray eyes that were to die for and a figure that was the envy of every girl in school."

"The fair one," Edie added.

"The aunt-to-be," Caasi murmured in a poor attempt at humor. "Always the bridesmaid, never the bride."

"I find it more than just ironic," Edie said with conviction. "It's high time you came down from the lofty twentieth floor and joined us mortals."

"Edie!" June snapped. "What a terrible thing to say!"

"It's the champagne," Caasi said, excusing her friend.

"In this instance it's a case of loose lips sinking ships."

"Ships?" Edie inquired.

"Friendships!"

"To friendship." Edie raised her glass and their former good mood was restored.

"To friendship." June and Caasi gently clicked their delicate crystal glasses against Edie's.

"By the way, who's paying for this?" June questioned.

"I don't know," Caasi joked, "but I'm only paying one fifth, since both of you are drinking for two."

They all laughed and picked up their menus.

As Edie had promised, the food was superb. With observant eyes, Caasi noted the texture and quality of the food and the service. Such scrutiny had been ingrained in her since childhood. Caasi doubted that she could dine anywhere and not do a comparison.

"What about next month?" Caasi eyed June's stomach.

"No problem. Doc says I've got a good five weeks."

"Five weeks?" Edie looked shocked. "If I get that big, I'll die."

"You know, Edie, if your shoes are a little too tight, don't worry," Caasi teased.

"My shoes?" Edie looked up with a blank stare.

"After being in your mouth all night, they should fit fine."

Edie giggled and stared pointedly across the table. "I swear, the girl's a real wit tonight."

They divided up the check three ways. Although Caasi wanted to treat her friends, June and Edie wouldn't hear of it.

Sitting back, she watched as the waiter took their checks. No matter what her mood at the beginning of these gatherings, Caasi always felt better afterward. Even Edie's remark had flowed off her like water from an oily surface. These two were like sisters. She accepted their faults and loved them none the less.

Large drops of rain pounded against the street as the three emerged from the restaurant.

"How about an after-dinner dessert?" Edie suggested. "I'm in the mood for something sweet."

June and Caasi eyed one another and attempted to disguise a smile.

"Not me." June bowed out. "Burt's at home, anxiously awaiting my return. He worries if I'm out of his sight more than five minutes."

Edie raised both brows, seeking Caasi's response.

Caasi shrugged. "My feet hurt."

"I thought I was the one with tight shoes," Edie teased, looping her arm through Caasi's. "Come on, be a sport. If you're extra nice I'll even let you take me up to your penthouse suite."

Caasi sighed. "I suppose something light and sweet would do wonders toward making me forget my problems."

"What about you, June? Come on, change your mind."

June shook her head and patted her rounded stomach. "Not tonight."

The hotel lobby at the Empress was peacefully quiet when Edie and Caasi came through the wide glass doors. The doorman tipped his hat politely, and Caasi gave him a bright smile. Old Aldo had been a grandfather when the hotel hired him twenty years before. Other employers would have retired him by now, but Caasi hadn't. The white-haired man had a way of greeting people that made them feel welcome. That quality wouldn't easily be replaced.

The sweet, soulful sounds of a ballad drifted from the lounge, and Edie paused to hum the tune as they waited for the elevator.

"Nice," she commented.

"The piano player's new this week. Would you rather we have our dessert down here?"

Edie's nod was eager. "I think I would. I'm in the mood for romance and music."

Caasi's laugh was sweet and light. "From the look of things, I'd say it's been a regular occurrence lately." Her eyes rested on her friend's still smooth abdomen. They chose to sit in the lounge in order to listen to the music.

The hostess seated them and saw to their order personally. The crowd was a good one. Caasi looked around and noted a few regulars, mostly salesmen who stayed at the hotel on a biweekly basis. The after-work crowd had thinned, but there were a few die-hards.

The middle-aged man at the piano was good. A portion of the bar was built around the piano, and Caasi watched as he interacted with the customers, took requests and cracked a few jokes. She'd make sure he was invited back again.

Edie's spoon dipped into the glass of lemon sorbet while Caasi sampled hers. They didn't talk. They didn't need to. The piano music filled the room. A young couple at the bar started to sing and were joined by several others.

Edie's hand squeezed Caasi's forearm. "I'm sorry about what I said earlier."

"No need to apologize." Edie's gaze faltered slightly under Caasi's direct look. "I understand."

"I worry about you sometimes, Caasi."

"Worry about me? Whatever for?"

"I love you. You're more like a sister to me than my own. I don't know how you can be happy living the way you do. It's not natural."

"What's not natural?" Caasi realized she was beginning to sound like a worn echo.

"Your life."

Mildly disconcerted, Caasi looked away. "It's the only way I've ever known."

"That doesn't make it right. Haven't you ever yearned for someone to share your life? A man to cuddle up against on a cold night?"

Caasi's laugh was forced. "I've got my electric blanket."

"What about children?"

Although content with her lifestyle, Caasi had to admit that seeing both June and Edie pregnant was having a peculiar effect on her. She'd never thought much about being a mother, but, strangely, she found the idea appealing. "I...I think I'd like that, but I'm not so keen on a husband."

"If it's a baby you want, then find yourself a man. You don't need a wedding ring and a march down the aisle to have a baby. Not these days."

Caasi tugged a strand of hair behind her ear, a nervous habit she rarely indulged. "I can't believe we're having this conversation."

"I mean it," Edie said with a serious look.

"What am I suppose to do? Find a good-looking man, saunter up, and suggest children?"

Edie's full laugh attracted the attention of others. "No, silly, don't say a word. Just let things happen naturally."

How could Caasi explain that she wasn't into casual affairs? Had never had a fling, and at twenty-eight remained a virgin? Edie would be sick laughing. Lack of experience wasn't the only thing holding her back; when would Caasi find the time for relationships and/ or motherhood? Every waking minute was centered around Crane Enterprises. Even if she did find herself attracted to a man, she'd have to squeeze him in between meetings and conferences. Few men would be willing to accept that kind of relationship. And what man wouldn't be intimidated by her wealth? No, the die had been cast and she...

"Caasi." Edie's hushed whisper broke into Caasi's thoughts. "What you need is a man like the one who just walked in."

Caasi's gray eyes searched the crowd for the newcomer. "Where?" she murmured.

"There, by the piano. He just sat down."

The blood exploded in Caasi's cheeks, rushing up from her neck until she felt her face shining like a lighthouse on a foggy night. Blake Sherrill was the man Edie had pointed out. Pressing a tentative hand to her face, Caasi wondered at her reaction.

"Now, *that's* blatant masculinity if ever I've seen it."

"He's not that good-looking," Caasi felt obliged to say, grateful that Edie hadn't noticed the way the color had invaded her face.

"Of course not. His type never is. There's a lean hardness to him, an inborn arrogance that attracts women like flies to honey."

"Oh, honestly."

"Notice his mouth," Edie continued.

Caasi already had. Blake looked troubled about something, a surprising occurrence, since he'd always presented a controlled aura when he met with her. She watched as he ordered a drink, then emptied the shot glass in one gulp. That wasn't like Blake either. As far as she knew, he stayed away from liquor.

"See how his lips are pressed together? The tight, chiseled effect. Women go for that."

There was a slight tremor in Caasi's hands as her friend spoke. "Maybe some women. But not me."

"Caasi." Edie groaned. "You can't be *that* oblivious. You're staring at an unqualified hunk. Good grief, my blood's hot just looking at him."

"He's not my type," Caasi muttered under her breath, at the same time thinking she'd never really seen Blake. For years they'd worked together, and not once had she ever thought of him except as an exceptionally good general manager.

"That man is every woman's type. I've seen women threaten to kill for less."

Caasi knew her friend was teasing and offered a half-hearted smile. "Maybe he is my type, I don't know."

"Maybe?" Edie shot back disbelievingly. "Go over and introduce yourself. It can't hurt, and it may do you a lot of good."

"Do you think I should?"

"I wouldn't have said so if I didn't."

"This is crazy." Caasi shoved back her chair. Really, what did she hope to accomplish? Blake *was* more man than she'd ever recognized before, but the idea of a casual affair with him was crazy. More than crazy, it was ludicrous.

"Hurry up before he leaves," Edie whispered encouragingly.

Caasi didn't know why she didn't want her friend to know she was already well acquainted with Blake.

Edie stood with her.

"Are you coming too?" Caasi cast her a challenging glare.

"Not this time, although I'm tempted. I just noticed the time. Freddy will be worried. I'll call you tomorrow."

"Fine." Caasi's spirits lifted. She could leave without saying a word to Blake and Edie need never know.

"I'll just wait by the door to see how you do. Once you've made the contact, I'll just slip away."

Caasi's spirits plummeted.

The stool beside Blake was vacant. Caasi strolled across the room, her heart pounding so loudly it drowned out the piano man. As casually as possible she perched herself atop the tall stool.

Blake looked over at her, surprise widening his eyes momentarily. He turned back without a greeting.

"Evening," she muttered, shocked at how strange her voice sounded. "I thought you were taking the rest of the week off."

"Something came up."

Caasi straightened. "What?"

"It's taken care of—don't worry about it."

"Blake." Her tone was crisp and businesslike.

Pointedly he turned his wrist and looked at his watch. "I was off duty hours ago. If you don't mind, I'd like to leave the office behind and enjoy some good scotch." He raised his shot glass in a mocking toast.

Caasi's throat constricted. "I've had one of those days myself." She didn't mention that his letter had brought it on, but that understanding hung oppressively in the air between them.

The bartender strolled past and braced both hands against the bar. "Can I get you anything?" He directed the question at Caasi.

Obviously he didn't know who she was, which was just as well; she could observe him at work. "I'll have the same as the gentleman."

Blake arched both brows. "It must have been a harder day than I thought."

"It was."

His lips came together in a severe line. "Drink it slowly," he cautioned.

"I can hold my liquor as well as any man," she said, surprised by how defensive she sounded. She didn't want to be. What she wanted was an honest, frank discussion of the reason or reasons he'd decided to leave Crane Enterprises.

"As you say." The corners of his mouth curved upward in challenge.

When Caasi's drink arrived she raised it tentatively to her lips and took an experimental sip. To her horror, she started coughing and choking.

"You all right?" he questioned with a rare smile.

As if she wasn't embarrassed enough, his hand pounded vigorously against her back.

"Stop it," she insisted, her eyes watering.

"I thought you said you could handle your scotch."

"I can!" she choked out between gasps of air. "It just went down wrong, that's all."

Blake rotated the stool so that she was given a profile of his compelling features. She turned back around, aware that half the lounge was watching her. "I'm fine, I'm fine," she felt obliged to say.

"So you are," Blake murmured.

"Aren't you worried about leaving your job?" she asked, even though he'd basically said he didn't want to discuss business. He turned to her then, his eyes dark and glittering as his taut gaze ran over her. "No, as a matter of fact, I'm not."

"Why not?" she queried, her hand curling around the small glass. "At least you owe me the courtesy of telling me why after all these years you want out."

"It's not a marriage, Cupcake."

Caasi bristled. "Don't call me that. Don't ever call me that." Cupcake had been her father's pet name for her. Only Isaac Crane had ever called her that. "I'm not a little girl anymore."

His laugh was short and derisive. "That you're not."

She took another sip of her drink. It burned all the way down her throat and seared a path through her stomach. But she didn't cough and felt pleased with herself.

"What do you want from me?" he asked as he shoved the empty scotch glass aside.

Feeling slightly tipsy and more than a little reckless, she placed her hand gently over the crook in his elbow. "I want to dance."

His head jerked up, and the color seemed to flow from his face. "Not with me."

"Yes, with you," she said softly, surprised at how angry he sounded. Who else did he think she meant? The piano player?

"No."

The word was issued with such force that Caasi felt as if he'd physically struck her. How embarrassing and humiliating. All at once Caasi knew she had to get out of there before disgracing herself further. "Thanks anyway."

Her hands trembled as she slid off the stool. Wordlessly she turned and walked out of the lounge. She made it as far as the elevator before she felt her entire body start to shake.

The penthouse was dark. Very dark. Even the million lights of the city couldn't illuminate the room. Leaning against the door, Caasi heaved her shoulders in a long shuddering sigh. She'd had too much to drink that night, far more than normal. That was what was wrong. Not Edie. Not Blake. Not even her. Only the alcohol.

Undressing, she pulled the long nylon gown over her head. Accidentally, her hand hit against her abdomen and she paused, inhaling deeply. Lightly her fingers traced her breasts, then fell lifelessly to her sides as she hung her head in defeat.

"I am a woman," she whispered. "I am a woman," she repeated, and fell across the bed.

Two

Caasi's head throbbed the next morning when the alarm rang. She rolled over and moaned. She'd made a complete idiot of herself the night before. She couldn't believe that she'd actually suggested that Blake dance with her. Heavens, she hadn't been on a dance floor since her college days. The temptation was to bury her head under a pillow and go back to sleep, but the meeting with Pacific Contractors was scheduled for that morning, plus a labor relations conference for that afternoon.

Laurie, the paragon of virtue who served as Caasi's secretary, was already at her desk when Caasi arrived.

"'Morning," Caasi greeted her crisply.

"Schuster's been on the phone twice. He said it's important." Laurie held out several pink message slips.

Caasi groaned inwardly. Every time Schuster phoned it was important. She didn't want to deal with him. Not today. Not ever, if she could help it.

"Is Mr. Sherrill in yet?" Caasi would give the pesky troublemaker to Blake to handle. He'd deal with Schuster quickly and efficiently. Caasi almost groaned out loud when she remembered that she'd given Blake the rest of the week off.

"He's been in and out," Laurie announced, following Caasi into the inner office. "He left something on your desk."

A silver tray with a large pot and cup rested on the clean surface of her desk. Beside the cup was a large bottle of aspirin. Caasi managed just a hint of a smile.

"Thanks, Laurie," she murmured and waited until the short, plump woman left the office.

A folded piece of paper lay on the tray beside the aspirin. Slowly, Caasi picked it up, her heart hammering wildly. A single note and her heart was reacting more to that than any profit-and-loss statement.

The large, bold handwriting matched the man. How often had she read his messages and not noticed that his penmanship personified him? The note read: *Thought you could use these this morning. B.*

Caasi realized that she could. Snapping the cap off the bottle, she shook two tablets into the palm of her hand and poured the steaming coffee into the cup. She lifted her hand to touch the chestnut hair gathered primly at the base of her neck as she lazily walked across the carpet.

Everything last night hadn't been a fluke. Edie had raised questions that Caasi had long refused to voice. She was a woman, with a woman's desires and a woman's needs. Home, husband, children—these were things she had conveniently shelved. Seeing June and Edie happily married, in love and expecting children, was bringing all these feelings to an eruptive head. Her father hadn't counted on that. Caasi was the only child, the last of the Cranes, who were now an endangered species. With Isaac gone, there was only Caasi. Alone. Against the world.

Caasi wanted to be protected and loved, cherished and worried about. Like Edie and June. But at the same time, she wanted to be proud, independent, strong… everything her father had worked so hard to ingrain in her. Sometimes she felt as though a tug-of-war were going on inside her, with her heart at stake. Some days she looked in the mirror only to discover that a stranger was staring back at her.

The phone buzzed, interrupting her musings. Another day was about to begin, and her doubts would be pushed aside and shelved again.

Saturday morning Caasi woke, sat up in bed, and sighed heavily. The past two days, she'd crawled out of bed more tired than she'd been the night before, as if she hadn't slept at all. Now her eyes burned and she felt as if the problems of the world were pressing against her shoulders.

The company copter was flying in that day, and Caasi was scheduled to officiate at a ground-breaking ceremony at Seaside. Another Empress Hotel, the tenth, was about to be launched. She should be feeling a sense of pride and accomplishment, yet all she felt was tired and miserable. The day would be filled with false smiles and promotional hype.

She dressed in a navy-blue linen suit, double-breasted. Her father would approve.

Her breakfast tray was waiting for her, but she pushed it aside. The silver pot of coffee reminded her of Blake. Absent two days and she missed him like crazy. He was scheduled to have gone with her on this little jaunt. Somehow, having Blake along would have made the outing far more endurable.

Caasi was back at her suite by four. Exhausted, she kicked off her shoes and pulled the pins from her hair. The weather was marvelous, a glorious, sunny April afternoon. How could she have felt anything but exhilarated by the crisp ocean breeze? Everything had run smoothly—thanks to Blake, who had been responsible for setting up the ceremony.

The instant his name floated through her mind, the heaviness she'd experienced that morning returned. For years she'd taken him for granted. In rethinking the situation, Caasi realized that he had cause to resign. But he was invaluable to her. He couldn't leave; she wouldn't let him. The sooner he understood her feelings, the better.

Slouching against the deep, cushioned couch, Caasi propped her feet on the shining surface of the glass coffee table. She'd talk to him. Explain Crane Enterprises' position. And the sooner, the better. Now. Why not?

After changing into a three-piece pantsuit, Caasi sailed into her office to look through his personnel file. They'd worked together for years and she didn't even know where he lived. There were so many things she didn't know about Blake.

She scanned the computer file until she located the Gresham address, several miles outside of Portland.

Her silver Mercedes had been a gift from her father. Caasi had little need to drive it. Usually she made a point of taking it for a spin once a month. It had been longer than that since she'd last driven it, but the maintenance men kept it tuned and the battery charged for her.

It took almost thirty minutes to find the address. She

drove down a long, winding road that seemed to lead nowhere. Although there were several houses around, they were separated by wide spaces. Blake...in the country. The mental image of him tilling the fields flitted into her mind. The picture fit.

She stopped at the side of the road and, before pulling into Blake's driveway, checked the nearest house number against the one she'd scribbled down in her office. The house was an older two-story with a wide front porch, the kind Caasi would picture having an old-fashioned swing. A large weeping willow tree dominated one side of the front yard. Caasi had always loved weeping willows.

By the time she opened the car door and climbed out, Blake had come out of the garage, wiping his hands on an oily rag.

"Caasi." His voice was deep and irritated.

"Afternoon," she replied, sounding falsely cheerful. "This is beautiful country out here."

"I like it." He came to a halt, keeping several feet distant from her.

"Everything went fine today."

"I knew it would."

Caasi untied the lemon-colored chiffon scarf from her throat and stuffed it in her purse. "Can we talk?"

His gaze traveled over her before he lifted one shoulder. "If you like."

Caasi felt some of the tension ease out of her. At least he was willing to discuss things.

"Go in the house; I'll wash up and be there in a minute."

"Okay," she agreed.

"The back door's unlocked," he called to her as he returned to the garage.

Caasi let herself into the rear of the house. An enclosed porch and pantry contained a thick braided rug, on which she wiped her feet. The door off the porch led into a huge kitchen decorated with checkered red-and-white curtains on its large windows.

The glass coffeepot resting on the stove was half full, and Caasi poured herself a mug, hugging it to keep her hands occupied.

Her purse clutched under her arm, she wandered out of the kitchen. A large formal dining room contained built-in china cabinets. An array of photographs filled the open wall space. Caasi stopped to examine each one. They left her wondering if Blake had once been married. A small frown of nervous apprehension creased her brow. Several pictures of children who vaguely resembled Blake dominated the grouping. Another of an older couple, dark and earthy, captured her attention. Caasi lifted the wooden frame to examine the two faces more closely. These must be his parents. They both had round, dark eyes—wonderful eyes that said so much. Warm, good people. If Caasi ever had the opportunity to meet them, she knew she would enjoy knowing them. They were the salt of the earth.

Another picture rested behind the others; this one was of a large family gathering outside what appeared to be the very house she was in. The willow tree was there, only smaller. The two adults were shown with six children. Blake's family. He stood out prominently, obviously the eldest.

"My parents," he explained from behind her.

Caasi hadn't heard him come in and gave a startled

gasp, feeling much like a child caught looking at something she shouldn't. Her hand shook slightly as she replaced the photograph.

"The children?" she asked hesitatingly.

"My nieces and nephews."

"You've never married?"

Blake's mouth thinned slightly. "No." He ran a hand through his dark hair. "You said you wanted to talk?"

"Yes." Her head bobbed. "Yes, I do."

"Sit down." His open palm gestured toward the living room.

Caasi moved into the long, narrow living room. A huge fireplace took up an entire wall, and she paused momentarily to admire the oil painting above the mantel. Mount Hood was richly displayed in gray, white and a forest of green, against a backdrop of blue, blue sky.

"Wonderful painting," she commented casually, looking for the artist's name and finding none.

"Thanks."

Caasi sat in a chair where she could continue to study the mountain scene. On closer inspection she found minute details that weren't readily visible on casual notice. "I really like it. Who's the artist?"

The small lines about Blake's mouth hardened. "Me."

"You!" Caasi gasped. "I didn't know you did anything like this. Blake, it's marvelous."

He dismissed the compliment with a short shake of his head. "There's a lot you don't know about me."

"I'm beginning to find that out," she said on a sober note.

His eyes pinned her to the chair.

Uncomfortable, she cleared her throat before continuing. "As I mentioned, the trip to Seaside went without a hitch. But it didn't seem right, not having you there."

"You'll get used to it."

"I don't want to have to do that."

Blake propelled himself out of the overstuffed chair he had sunk into and stalked to the far side of the room. "My decision's been made."

"Change it."

"No."

"Blake, listen." She set her coffee aside and stood. "Today I realized how inconsiderate I've been the last few years. Putting it simply, I've taken you for granted. You were Dad's right-hand man. Now you're mine. I don't know that I can do the job without you."

His laugh was sarcastic, almost cruel. "I have no doubts regarding your ability. More than once I've been amazed at your insight and discernment. You're a magnificent businesswoman, and don't let anyone tell you different."

"If I'm so wonderful, why am I losing you?"

He didn't answer her.

"I'm prepared to double your salary."

"You overpay me as it is."

She clenched her fist at her side and stared at the oil painting, searching for some clue to the man she once thought she knew. "Then it isn't the money."

"I told you it wasn't."

"Then clearly someone else has made you a better offer. Holiday Inn? Hilton?"

"No." His voice was loud and abrupt.

Don't yell at me, she wanted to shout back but held her tongue. They'd never argued. For months on end they'd worked together without saying more than a few necessary words to one another. And suddenly everything had changed.

"Caasi." Her name was issued on a soft groan. "I wouldn't do that to you. I don't know what I'm planning yet, but I won't go to work for the competition."

"What is it you want?" Angrily she hugged her stomach with both arms and whirled around. "I've never known you to be unreasonable."

He was silent for so long, she didn't know whether he intended answering her.

"You can't give me what I want."

"Try me." She turned back to him, almost desperate. Blake was right; she could manage without him. A replacement could come in, be trained, and suffice, but she wanted him. Trusted him.

His dark gaze fell to her mouth. They stood so close that Caasi could see the flecks of gold in his dark irises. A strange hurt she didn't understand seemed to show in them. A desire welled in her to ease that pain, but she didn't know how. Wasn't that a woman's job, to comfort? But then, she was a complete failure as a woman.

He reached out and gently touched the side of her face. A warmth radiated from his light caress. "I was planning to take the summer off. Do some hiking. I've always wanted to climb mountains, especially Rainier."

Sadly, Caasi nodded, her eyes captured by his. "I've never hiked." She laughed nervously. "Or climbed."

"There are lots of things you haven't done, aren't there?" His soft voice contained a note of tenderness. He dropped his hand.

Caasi forced her eyes away. Blake didn't know the half of it. Her gaze fell on the rows of family pictures.

"Do...do you like children?" What a ridiculous question and yet it was one she'd asked of him.

"Very much."

"Why haven't you married and raised a houseful? You've got the room for it here."

"The same reason you haven't, Cupcake."

Caasi bit her tongue to keep from reminding him not to call her that. The name itself didn't bother her. Nor did she care if he reminded her of her father. What she didn't like was Blake thinking of her as a child.

"For the last several years," he elaborated, "the two of us have been married to Crane Enterprises."

"But you could have a family and still work for me." She was grasping at straws and knew it.

"I'm a little too old to start now."

"Old," she scoffed. "At thirty-six?"

Blake looked surprised that she knew his age.

"I don't want to lose you."

His expression hardened as if her words had displeased him. "I'll walk you to your car."

Perplexed, she watched him move across the room and pull open the front door.

"You're angry, aren't you?"

He forced a long breath. "Yes."

"But why? What did I do?"

"You wouldn't understand."

Her hand sliced through the air. "You keep saying that. I'm well above the age of reason. I have even been known to exhibit some intelligence."

"And in other ways you're incredibly stupid," he interrupted. "Now go before I say something I'll regret."

Caasi sucked in her breath. Her shoes made a clicking rattle against the wooden steps as she hurried to her car. She couldn't get away from Blake fast enough.

Thirty minues later still angry and upset, Caasi let herself into the penthouse suite and threw her purse on the bed. Her shoes went next, first the right and then the left. She felt like shouting with frustration.

Dinner arrived and she stared at it with no appetite. No breakfast, a meager lunch, and now dinner held no appeal. She should be starved. Steak, potato and baby white asparagus, eaten alone, might as well be over-baked, dried-out macaroni and cheese. Eating alone hadn't bothered her until that night. Why it should now remained a mystery.

The portrait of Blake's parents came into her mind. How easy it was to picture his mother standing in the kitchen with fresh bread dough rising on the counter. Kids eating breakfast and laughing. How could something she'd never known bother her so much? *Children. Family. Home.* Each word was as foreign to her as the moon. Yet she felt a terrible, gnawing loss.

Determinedly she took the crusty French roll and bit into it. Hard on the outside, tender inside, exactly right. It was the only thing in her life that was exactly right.

The phone buzzed, which usually meant trouble. Caasi heaved an irritated sigh and lifted the receiver.

"Mr. Sherrill's on his way up," the hotel receptionist informed her cheerfully.

"Thank you," Caasi answered in a shaky voice. Blake coming here? He'd never been to her private quarters. Maybe when her father was alive, but not since she'd taken over.

Hurriedly she rushed into the bathroom and ran a brush through her hair. Halfway out the door, she whirled around and added a fresh layer of light pink gloss to her lips. Her hands shook, she was rushing so much. She unscrewed the cap from a perfume bottle and added a touch of the expensive French fragrance behind each ear and to the pulse points at her wrists.

Caasi started at the sound of his knock. Pausing to take in a deep, calming breath, she sauntered to the door.

"Why, Blake, what a pleasant surprise," she said sweetly.

He didn't look pleased. In fact, he looked much the same as he had when she'd left him earlier.

The feeling of happy surprise drained out of her.

"Go on, change."

"Change?" She stared at him blankly as he walked inside.

"Clothes," he supplied.

"You're not making any sense."

"Yes I am," he refuted. "What you had on last night will do."

"Do for what?" His attitude was beginning to spark her anger.

"Dancing. That's what you said you wanted."

Hot color extended all the way down her neck. "That was after several drinks."

"You don't want to dance? Fine." He lowered himself onto the long couch. "We can sit and drink."

The dark scowl intimidated her. She'd stood up to angry union leaders, pesky reporters and a thousand unpleasant situations. Yet one dark glower from Blake and she felt as though she could cry. Her gaze was centered on the carpet, and she noted that in her rush she'd forgotten to put on shoes.

"Caasi?" His voice pounded around the room like thunder.

"I don't know how to dance," she shouted. "And don't yell at me. Understand?" she said. "The last time I went to a dance I was a college sophomore. Things…have… changed."

She moved to the window and pretended an interest in the city lights.

Blake moved behind her and gently laid a hand on her shoulder. "What you need is a few lessons."

"Lessons?" she repeated softly. The image that came to her mind was of the times the hotel had booked the ballroom for the students of several local dance studios.

"I'll be your teacher." The words were husky and low-pitched. The gentle pressure of his hand turned her toward him.

Submissively, Caasi's arms dangled at her sides. "What about music?"

"We'll make our own." He began to hum softly, a gentle ballad that the piano man had played the night before. "First, place your arms around my neck." Lightly his hands rested on the curve of her hip just below her waist.

Caasi linked her fingers behind his neck. "Like this?"

Their eyes met and he nodded slowly—very slowly, as if the simple action had cost him a great deal. The grooves at the sides of his mouth deepened and he drew her close. His hands slid around to the small of her back, his touch feather-light.

Caasi had to stand on the tips of her toes to fit her body to his. When she eased her weight against him he went rigid.

"Did I do something wrong?" she asked in a whisper.

"No." His breath stirred her hair. "You're doing fine."

"Why aren't we moving?"

"Because it feels good just to hold you," he said in a strange, husky voice.

A flood of warmth filled every pore, and when she raised her eyes she saw that his angry look had been replaced by a gaze so warm and sensuous that she went completely still. She didn't breathe. She didn't move. She didn't blink.

He moved his hand up her back in a slow, rotating action that brought her even closer, more intimately, against him.

"Blake?" Her voice was treacherously low.

His other hand slid behind her neck, and he wove his fingers into her hair. "Yes?" Slowly, Blake lowered his mouth, claiming the trembling softness of hers.

His lips were undemanding, the pressure light and deliciously seductive. But soon the pressure deepened, as if the gentle caress wasn't enough to satisfy him.

Caasi's body surged with a warm, glowing excitement. She'd been kissed before, but never had she experienced such a deep, overwhelming response. Her arms locked around his neck.

"Caasi…" He ground out her name on a husky breath. He kissed her again, and she parted her lips in eager welcome. Their mouths strained against one another, seeking a deeper contact.

Blake tore his mouth away and buried his face in her soft throat.

Caasi sighed softly. "My goodness," she whispered breathlessly, "that's some dance step."

Blake shuddered lightly and broke the contact. "Go change, or we'll be late."

"Be late?" she asked, and blinked.

His fingers traced the questioning creases in her brow, then slid lightly down the side of her cheek and under her chin. "My cousin's wedding is tonight. If we hurry we'll make it to the dance."

"Will I meet your family?" Somehow that seemed important.

"Everyone. Even a few I'd rather you didn't know."

"Oh, Blake, I'd like that," she cried excitedly. "I'd like that very much."

Blake smiled, one of those rare smiles that came from the eyes. He had beautiful eyes, like his parents, and Caasi couldn't move. His look held her softly against him.

"Hurry," he urged in a half groan.

Reluctantly she let him go and took a step in retreat. "Are you sure what I wore last night will be all right? I have plenty of more formal outfits."

"It's fine. But whatever you wear, make sure it has a high neckline."

"Why?" she asked with a light laugh.

"Because I don't want any of my relatives ogling you." He sounded half angry.

Hands on her hips, her mood gay and excited, Caasi laughed. "Honestly, there isn't that much to ogle at."

Boldly, his gaze dropped to the rounded fullness as he studied her with silent amusement. "You have ten minutes. If you haven't appeared by that time, I'll come in and personally see to your dress."

The threat was tempting, and with a happy sigh, Caasi hurried out of the room.

Sorting through her wardrobe, she took out a pink-and-green skirt and top. The blouse had a button front, so the option of how much cleavage to reveal was left strictly to her. Purposely she left the top three buttons unfastened, blatantly revealing the hollow between her breasts. Caasi realized she was openly flirting with Blake, but she hadn't flirted with anyone in so long. The desire to do so overrode her usual modesty.

Blake was standing at the window looking out when she appeared. He turned and froze, his gaze meeting hers.

"Will I do?" Suddenly she felt uncertain. Idly her fingers played with the buttons of her blouse, fastening the most provocative one.

"Dear sweet heaven, you're beautiful."

Caasi felt a throb of excitement pulsate through her. "So are you."

The intensity of his look deepened, and he glanced at his watch. Caasi had the impression he couldn't have told her the time if she'd asked.

"We'd better go."

"I'll get a jacket." Cassie returned to her bedroom and took a velvet jacket from the hanger.

Blake took it out of her hand and held it open, gliding the soft material up her arms. His hands cupped her shoulders and brought her back against him. His breath stirred the hair at the crown of her head.

The sensations Blake was causing were new. So new that Caasi hadn't time to properly examine them. Not then. Not when his hand held her close to his side as they took her private elevator to the parking garage. Not when he opened the passenger door of the '57 T-Bird

with the convertible top down. Not when he leaned over
and lightly brushed his mouth across hers.

The dance was held in a V.F.W. hall off Sandy Boulevard. The lot was full of cars, the doors to the huge
building open while loud music poured into the night.

"Once you meet my relatives you might consider
yourself fortunate to be getting rid of me."

Caasi wished he hadn't mentioned his resignation
but forced herself to smile in response. "Do you think
I could find your replacement here?"

Either he didn't hear the question or chose to ignore it.

"Hey, Blake, who's the pretty lady?" A couple of
youths strolled toward them. Caasi could remember
trying to walk in the same "cool" manner.

The boy who had spoken was chewing a mouthful
of gum.

"You toucha' my lady and I breaka' your head."
Blake's teasing voice carried a thread of warning.

Caasi doubted that either boy took him seriously.

"These two are my baby cousins."

"Baby cousins." The boys groaned. "Hey, man, give
us a break."

"You taking your lady to Rocky Butte?" The second youth was walking backward in front of Blake and
Caasi, his arms swinging at his sides.

"Rocky Butte?" Caasi glanced up at Blake.

"The local necking place." His hand found hers, and
Caasi enjoyed the sensation of being linked to this powerful man. "You game?"

"No," she said, teasing. "I want more dancing lessons first."

His chuckle brought an exchange of curious glances between the youths.

"You're not going to dance, are you, Blake? That's for sissies."

"Wait a few years," he advised. "It has its advantages."

They paused in the open doorway. The polished wooden floor was crowded with dancing couples. A five-piece band was playing from a stage to the far right-hand side of the hall. Long tables containing food were against another wall, and several younger children were helping themselves to the trays of sweets. Older couples sat talking in rows of folding chairs.

A sense of wonder filled Caasi. This was a part of Blake. A part of life she had never experienced. "Are you related to all these people?"

"Most of them."

"But you know everyone here?"

"Everyone." He looked down at her and smiled. "Come on, I want you to meet my parents."

As soon as people were aware that Blake had arrived, there were shouts of welcome and raised hands. He responded with his own shouts, then gave Caasi a whispered explanation as to various identities.

"How many uncles do you have?" she asked, astonished.

"Ten uncles and twice as many aunts. I gave up counting cousins."

"It's marvelous. I love it." Her face beamed with excitement and the laughter flowed from her, warm and easy.

Blake stopped once and turned her around, placing

a hand on each shoulder. "I don't think I've ever heard you laugh. Really laugh."

She smiled up at him. "I don't know that I have. Not in a long time."

The bride, in a long, white, flowing gown, the train wrapped around her forearm, giggled and hurried to Blake. "I didn't think you'd ever get here," she admonished and stood on tiptoes to kiss his cheek. "Now you have to dance with me."

Blake laughed and cast a questioning glance at Caasi. "Do you mind?"

"No, of course not." She stepped aside as Blake took the young woman in his arms. A wide path was cleared as the couple approached the dance floor. People began to clap their hands in time to the music.

Someone bumped against Caasi, and she turned to apologize. "Sorry," she murmured.

The dark eyes that met hers were cold and unfriendly. The lack of welcome surprised Caasi.

"So *you're* the one who's ruined my brother's life!"

Three

"Ruined your brother's life?" Caasi repeated incredulously. "I'm Caasi Crane." The girl obviously had her confused with someone else. A curious sensation attacked the pit of Caasi's stomach at the thought of Blake with another woman.

"I know who you are," the woman continued in angry, hissing tones. "And I know what you've done."

What she'd done? Caasi's mind repeated. Those same wonderful eyes that had mesmerized her when she had studied the photo of Blake's parents were narrowed and hard in the tall woman beside her. Blake's own eyes darkened with the same deep intensity when he was angry.

"Are you sure you're talking to the right woman?"

"Oh, yes, there's no doubt. I'd know you…"

Loud applause prevented Caasi from hearing the rest of what the woman was saying.

Caasi watched as the young bride, laughing and breathless, hugged Blake. His eyes were full of amusement, but when his gaze found Caasi and saw who was with her, the humor quickly vanished. He kissed the bride, handed her to the waiting groom, and hurried across the crowded dance floor to Caasi's side.

"I see Gina has introduced herself to you," Blake said as he folded an arm around Caasi's shoulders. He smiled down at her, but there was a guarded quality in his gaze.

The eyes of the two women clashed. Something unreadable flickered in Gina's. Surprise? Warning? Caasi didn't know.

"We didn't get around to exchanging names," Caasi said as she held out her hand to Blake's sister. It was important to clear away the misconception Gina had about her.

The hesitation was only minimal before Gina took her hand and shook it lightly.

"If you'll excuse us," Blake said, directing his comment to his sister, "I want to introduce Caasi to Mom and Dad."

"Sure," Gina said, her voice husky. She cleared her throat and shook her head as if to dispel the picture before her. Her look was confused as she glanced from her brother to Caasi. "I'm sure they'd like that."

"I know I would." Caasi didn't need to be a psychic to feel the finely honed tension between brother and sister. That Gina adored him was obvious just by the way she looked at him. That same reverence had been in the eyes of the young bride. Blake was an integral part of this family, loved and respected. Caasi, on the other hand, belonged to no one; her life had never appeared so empty—just a shell. She'd give everything she owned—the hotels, her money, anything—to be a part of something like this, to experience that marvelous feeling of belonging.

Blake was watching her, his look curious. "You look a hundred miles away."

"Sorry," she answered with a feeble smile.

He escorted her to a row of folding chairs. Several older women were gathered in a circle and were leaning forward, chatting busily.

"Mother." Blake tapped one of the women gently on the shoulder and kissed her cheek affectionately.

"Blake!" his mother cried in a burst of enthusiasm as she stood and embraced her son. "You did come! I knew you wouldn't disappoint Kathleen."

The gray-haired woman had changed little from the photo Caasi had seen. Although several years older and plumper, Blake's mother was almost exactly the same. Warmth, love, and acceptance radiated from every part of her. Caasi had recognized those wonderful qualities in the photo; in person they became even more evident.

"Mother." Blake broke the embrace. "I'd like you to meet Caasi Crane." He turned to Caasi. "My mother, Anne Sherrill."

"Miss Crane." Two large hands eagerly enveloped Caasi's. "We've heard so much about you. Meeting you is a long-overdue pleasure."

"Thank you," Caasi replied with a wide smile. "I feel the same way." She couldn't take her eyes from the older woman. "You're very like your photo."

Anne Sherrill looked blank.

"I should explain," Caasi inserted quickly. "I was at Blake's house this afternoon."

"Where's Dad?" Blake's arm continued to hold Caasi to his side. She enjoyed the feeling of being coupled with him, the sense of belonging.

Anne Sherrill clucked with mock displeasure. "In the parking lot with two of your uncles."

Fleetingly Caasi wondered what they were doing in the parking lot but didn't ask.

Blake's rich laughter followed. "Do you want me to check on him for you?"

"And have you abandon Miss Crane?" Mrs. Sherrill sounded outraged.

"Please, call me Caasi," was Caasi's gentle request. "I don't mind." The latter comment was directed at Blake. "I'll stay here and visit with your mother. I wouldn't mind in the least."

"I'll only be a few minutes," Blake promised. "Mom, keep Caasi company, and for heaven's sake, don't let anyone walk away with her." He kissed his mother on the cheek and whispered something about lambs and wolves. With a knowing smile, his mother nodded.

Caasi had to bite her tongue to keep from asking what the comment had been about.

"Have you eaten?" Anne wanted to know. "With that son of mine, you probably haven't had a chance to breathe since you walked in the door. Let's fix you a plate. Not fancy food, mind you."

Caasi started to protest but realized she *was* hungry. No, starved. "I'd like that," she said as she followed Blake's mother to the row of tables against the wall. The variety of food was amazing, and all home-cooked, from the look of the dishes. It was probably a pot-luck supper, with each family contributing. Thick slices of ham, sausage and turkey and a dozen huge salads were set out, along with several dishes Caasi didn't recognize.

Anne handed Caasi a plate and poured herself a cup of punch.

"This looks fantastic," Caasi murmured as she surveyed the long tables. She helped herself to a slice of ham and a couple of small sausage links. The German-style potato salad was thick with bacon and onions, and Caasi spooned a small serving of it alongside the ham. "This should be plenty."

"Take as much as you like. There's always food left over, and I hate having to take anything home with me."

"No, no, this is fine. Thank you."

They sat down again. Caasi balanced her plate on her knees and took a bite of the potato salad. "This is really delicious." The delicate blend of flavors wasn't like anything she'd ever tasted.

"Anne's German potato salad is the best this side of heaven," the middle-aged woman on the other side of Caasi commented.

"You made this?" Caasi looked at Anne.

Anne nodded with a pleased grin. "It's an old family recipe. My mother taught me, and now I've handed it down to my daughters."

Anne Sherrill's heritage to her daughters included warmth, love and recipes. Caasi's was a famous father and a string of hotels, but given the chance she'd gladly have traded.

"No one makes German-style potato salad like Anne," the other woman continued. When she paused, Anne introduced the woman as Blake's cousin's wife.

"What's in it?" Caasi questioned before she lifted the fork to her mouth. Her interest was genuine.

Anne ran down a list of ingredients with specific instructions. Nothing was listed in teaspoons; it was all in dashes and sprinkles. Caasi doubted that the family recipe had ever been written down. Caasi had never

known her own mother and at times when growing
up had felt a deep sense of loss—but never more than
right now. Her father had tutored her so thoroughly in
the ways of business and finance. It was only at times
like this that Caasi realized how much she missed a
mother's loving influence.

"It's best to let the flavors blend overnight."

Caasi picked up on the last bit of information and
nodded absently, her thoughts a million miles away.

"You must come to dinner some Sunday."

"I'd like that," Caasi said. "I'd like it very much."

"This is the first time Blake's brought a woman to
a family get-together, isn't it?" The cousin's comment
came in the form of a question. "Handsome devil, Blake
Sherrill. I've seen the way women chase after him. Yet
he's never married."

"No, Blake's my independent one."

Caasi paid an inordinate amount of attention to cutting the ham slice. "Why hasn't he married?"

The hesitation was slight. "I'm not really sure," Anne
supplied thoughtfully. "He loves children. I think he'd
like a wife and family, but he just hadn't found the right
woman, that's all."

Caasi nodded and lifted a bite of meat to her mouth.

"Is tomorrow too soon?" Anne questioned and at
Caasi's blank look continued, "For dinner, I mean."

Mentally Caasi went over Sunday's schedule. It
didn't matter; she could change whatever had been
planned. "I'd enjoy nothing more. What time would
you like me?"

Anne wrote the address and time on the back of one
of Caasi's business cards. She wasn't sure why Blake's
mother had invited her, but it didn't matter—she was

going. Being with his family, Caasi couldn't help but learn more about the enigmatic man who was leaving her just when she was beginning to know him.

"I think I see Blake coming now," Anne murmured with a tender smile. "With his father in tow."

Caasi studied the gentle look on the older woman's face before scanning the room for Blake. She could barely make out his figure through the crowd of dancers. The faint stirrings of awareness he awakened within her surprised Caasi. She was proud to be with Blake, to meet his family, to be included in this celebration.

Their eyes sought one another when he stepped into full view. Hers were soft and welcoming; his, slightly guarded.

"Dad, this is Caasi."

Blake's father reached down and took Caasi's hand, his dark eyes twinkling. "Pretty thing." The comment was made to no one directly.

"Thank you," Caasi murmured and blushed.

"Fine bone structure, but a little on the thin side. Always did like high foreheads. It's a sign of intelligence."

"Dad." Blake's low voice contained a thin note of warning.

"George." Anne slipped an arm around her husband's waist. "His tongue gets loose after a beer or two," Blake's mother explained to Caasi.

"Would you like to dance?" A corner of Blake's mouth tilted upward. He looked as if dancing was the last thing he wanted.

"If you like." Caasi would have preferred to stay and talk more with his parents, but she recognized the wisdom of following Blake onto the polished floor.

The band was playing a polka, and with a quick turn, Blake pulled her into his arms.

Caasi let out a small cry of alarm. She didn't know how to dance, especially the polka.

"Just follow me," he instructed. "And for heaven's sake, don't step on my toes with those high heels."

"Blake," she pleaded breathlessly. "I can't dance. I don't know how to do this."

"You're doing fine." He whirled her around again and again until she was dizzy, her head spinning with the man and the music.

They stopped after the first dance, and Blake brought her a glass of punch. Caasi took one sip and widened her eyes at the potency of the drink.

"Rum?" she quizzed.

"And probably a dab of this and that."

"Old family recipe," she said with a teasing smile. "I'm getting in on several of those tonight. Oh, Blake, I like your family."

"They're an unusual breed, I'll say that." His voice was lazy and deep.

"Is Sherrill a German name?"

"No. Dad's English, or once was. Mom's the one with the German heritage."

The band started playing a slow waltz, and Caasi's eyes were drawn to the dance floor again.

Blake took the cup from her and set it aside. "Shall we?" His eyes met hers, the laughter gone, as he skillfully turned her into his arms.

A confused mixture of emotions whirled in her mind as he slid his arms around her waist, the gentle pressure at the small of her back guiding her movements.

A warmth flowed through her, beginning at his touch

and fanning out until she could no longer resist and closed her eyes to its potency.

Caasi placed her head on his shoulder, her face against his neck. The scent of his aftershave attacked her senses. She was filled with the feel and the smell of Blake. It seemed the most natural thing in the world for her tongue to make a lazy foray against his neck, to taste him.

"Caasi." He groaned. "You don't know what you're doing to me."

"I do," she said with a deep sigh. "And I like it. Don't make me stop."

He brought her closer to him, the intimate feel of his body sensuously moving with hers enough to steal her breath.

"This is insane," Blake ground out hoarsely, as if her touch was causing him acute pain.

Gently his mouth nibbled at her earlobe, and red-hot sensations shot through her like a bolt of lightning. "Blake," she pleaded. "Oh, Blake, this feels so good."

Abruptly he broke the contact and led her off the dance floor. "Just how much have you had to drink?" he demanded roughly.

Caasi was too stunned to answer. She opened her mouth but found herself speechless. Angrily she clamped it closed. The embarrassment that filled her face only served to anger her more.

"Apparently not nearly enough." She didn't know why Blake was acting like this. She didn't know how he could turn from a gentle lover to a tormenting inquisitor in a matter of seconds either.

They stood only a few feet apart, glaring at one another. Neither spoke.

"Hey, Blake, when are you going to introduce me to your lady?" A low masculine voice broke into the palpable silence that stretched between them.

A tall, good-looking man with a thick mustache over a wide smile came into view. He was about Blake's age and good-looking in a stylish sports coat. His tie had been loosened, revealing curling black hairs at the base of his throat.

"Johnnie—Caasi. Caasi—Johnnie. My cousin."

Johnnie chuckled, his eyes roaming over Caasi with obvious interest. "You don't sound so thrilled that we're cousins." The comment was directed at Blake, but his eyes openly assessed Caasi.

"I'm not," Blake stated bluntly. "Now, if you don't mind, Caasi and I are having a serious discussion."

"We are?" she interrupted sweetly. "I thought we were through. I was just saying how thirsty I am and how delicious the punch is."

Johnnie cocked his head in gentlemanly fashion. "In which case, allow me to escort you to the punch bowl."

"I'd like that."

"Caasi." Blake's low voice was filled with challenge. "I wouldn't."

"Excuse me a minute, Blake," she returned, ignoring his dark, narrowed look. She placed her arm through Johnnie's offered elbow and strolled away. She didn't need to turn around to see that Blake's eyes were boring holes into her back.

"Like to live dangerously, don't you?" Johnnie quizzed with a good-natured grin.

Caasi's lower lip was quivering, and she drew in a shaky breath. "Not really."

"Then I'd say you enjoy placing others in terminal

danger. My life wouldn't be worth a plugged nickel if Blake could find a way of getting hold of me without causing a scene."

The thought was so outrageous that Caasi felt her mouth curve with amusement. "Then why are you smiling?" she asked. Johnnie was obviously a charmer, and she found that she liked him.

"I have to admit," he said with a low chuckle, "it feels good to do one up on Blake. He's the family hero. Everyone looks up to him. Frankly, I'm jealous." Johnnie said it with such devilish charm that Caasi couldn't prevent a small laugh.

"Are you thirsty, or was that an excuse to put Blake in his place?" he queried.

"An excuse," she murmured wickedly.

"Then let's dance."

Caasi hesitated; dancing with Johnnie was another matter altogether. "I'm not sure."

"Come on," he said encouragingly. "Let's give Blake a real taste of the green-eyed monster."

By this time Caasi was beginning to regret her behavior. She was acting like a spoiled child, which undoubtedly confirmed what Blake thought of her.

"I don't think so. Another time."

"Don't look now," Johnnie whispered, "but Blake's making his way over here, and he doesn't look pleased. No," he amended, "he looks downright violent."

Caasi shifted restlessly. The sound of Blake's footsteps seemed to be magnified a thousand times until it was all she could do not to cover her ears.

"Excuse us," Blake said to Johnnie and gripped Caasi's upper arm in a punishing hold, "but this dance is ours."

Caasi glanced at him nervously, resisting the temptation to bite into her bottom lip as he half dragged her onto the dance floor.

When he placed his arms around her the delicious sensations didn't warm her, nor did she feel that special communication that had existed between them only a few minutes previously.

Caasi slid her arms around his neck, her body moving instinctively with his to the rhythm of the slow beat. She studied him through a screen of thick lashes. His mouth was pinched. The dark eyes were as intense as she'd ever seen them, and his clenched jaw seemed to be carved in stone.

Swallowing her pride, Caasi murmured, "I've only had the one glass of punch. I apologize for going off with your cousin. That was a childish thing to do."

Blake said nothing, but she felt some of the anger flow out of him. His arm tightened around her back. "One drink?" he retorted, his mouth moving disturbingly close to her ear.

"Honest."

"You were playing with fire, touching me like that. The way your body was moving against mine…" He paused. "If you aren't drunk, then explain the seduction scene." The harshness in his voice brought her head up and their eyes met, his gaze trapping hers.

"Seduction scene?"

"Come on, Caasi, you can't be that naive," he muttered drily. "The looks you were giving me were meant for the bedroom, not the dance floor."

Her eyes fell and she lost her rhythm, faltering slightly. "Let me assure you," she whispered hotly, hating the telltale color that suffused her face, "that was not my intention."

"Exactly," Blake retorted. "You don't need to explain, because I know you."

"You know me?" she repeated in a disbelieving whisper.

"That's right. You're a cool, suave, sophisticated businesswoman. Primed from an early age to take over Crane Enterprises. It's all you know. That isn't red blood that flows in your veins—it's ink from profit-and-loss statements."

They stopped the pretense of dancing. Caasi had never felt so cold. A myriad of emotions came at her from every direction.

Wordlessly she dropped her hands and took a few steps in retreat. Her knees were trembling so badly she was afraid to move. The silence between them was charged like the still air before a storm. It was all she could do to turn away and disguise her reaction to his cruel words. Blindly she walked off the dance floor.

Somehow she made her way into the ladies' room. Her reflection in the mirror was deathly pale, her blue-gray eyes haunted.

Her hands trembled as she turned on the faucet and filled the sink with cold water. A wet paper towel pressed to her cheeks seemed to help.

Blake was right. She should have recognized as much herself. She wasn't a woman, she was a machine, an effectively programmed, well-oiled machine. Her father had repeatedly warned her against mixing business with pleasure. He'd said it often enough for her to know better than to become involved with Blake. Even now she wasn't sure why had she agreed to accompany

Blake. She had to ask herself where the common sense her father had instilled in her was. Furthermore she wanted to know why the truth in Blake's accusations hurt so much. The sound of someone coming into the room caused Caasi to straighten and make a pretense of washing her hands. She didn't turn around, not wanting to talk to anyone.

"I'm glad I found you." The soft, apologetic voice spoke from behind.

Caasi raised her head and her eyes met Gina's in the mirror. The dark-haired girl looked embarrassed and disturbed. Caasi looked away; she wasn't up to another confrontation.

"I'd like to apologize for what I said earlier," Blake's sister said softly. "It was unforgivable."

Caasi nodded, having difficulty finding her voice. "I understand. It's forgotten." She forced a wan smile.

"Mom said you're coming to dinner tomorrow."

Caasi's eyes widened; she'd forgotten the invitation. "Yes, I'm looking forward to it."

"I hope we can be friends. Maybe we'll get a chance to visit more tomorrow." Gina offered her a genuine smile as Caasi dried her hands.

With most of her poise restored, Caasi returned to the crowded hall. She saw Blake almost immediately. He stood by the exit. Caasi made her way across the room to Blake's mother. Anne looked up and a frown marred her brow.

"I enjoyed meeting you, Mrs. Sherrill."

"Anne," the woman corrected softly. "Call me Anne."

"I'd be honored."

"Is something wrong, Caasi?"

Caasi had always prided herself on her ability to

disguise her emotions. Yet this woman had intuitively known there was something troubling her.

"I'm fine, thanks. I'll be at your home tomorrow if the invitation's still open."

"Of course it is."

"Say good-night to your husband for me, won't you?"

Anne's eyes were bright with concern. "You do look pale, dear. I hope you're not coming down with something."

Caasi dismissed the older woman's concern with a weak shake of her head. "I'm fine."

Blake had straightened by the time she came to the front door.

"You're ready to go?" he asked, his tone curt.

"Yes," she said primly. "I'm more than ready."

He led the way to his car, opened her door, and promptly walked around the front and climbed into the driver's side. The engine roared to life even before Caasi could strap her seat belt into place.

The night had grown cold, and Caasi wrapped her arms around herself to ward off the unexpected chill. Maybe it wasn't the night, Caasi mused, but the result of sitting next to Blake. If this cold war continued, she'd soon get frostbite.

They hadn't said a word since they'd left the reception. Caasi couldn't bear to look at him and closed her eyes, resting her head against the seat back.

The wind whipped through her hair and buffeted her face, but she didn't mind—and wouldn't have complained if she had.

The car slowed and Caasi straightened, looking around her. They were traveling in the opposite direction from the Empress. The road was narrow and curving.

"Where are we going?" she asked stiffly.

"To Rocky Butte."

"Rocky Butte?" she shot back incredulously. "Are you crazy?"

"Yes," he ground out angrily. "I've been crazy for eight years, and just as stupid."

Caasi watched as his eyes narrowed on the road. "You're taking me to the local necking place? Have you lost your senses?"

Blake ignored her.

"Why are you bringing me here?" she demanded in frustration. "Do you want to make fun of me again? Is that how you get your thrills? Belittling me?"

Blake pulled off to the side of the road and shoved the gears into Park. The challenge in his chiseled jaw couldn't be ignored.

"Remember me?" she said bravely. "I'm the girl without emotions. The company robot. I don't have blood, that's ink flowing through me," she informed him as unemotionally as possible. To her horror, her voice cracked. She jerked around and folded her arms across her breast, refusing to look at him.

Blake got out of the car and walked around to the front, apparently admiring the view of the flickering lights of Portland. Caasi stayed exactly where she was, her arms the only defense against the chill of the late night.

Blake opened her car door. "Come on."

Caasi ignored him, staring straight ahead.

"Have it your way," he said tightly, slamming the door and walking away.

Stunned, Caasi didn't move. Not for a full ten seconds. He wouldn't just leave her, would he?

"Blake?" She threw open the door and hurried after him. Running in her heels was nearly impossible.

He paused and waited for her.

"Where are you going?" she asked once she reached him.

"To the park. Come with me, Caasi." The invitation was strangely entreating. Would she ever understand this man? She should be screaming in outrage at the things he'd said to her and the way he'd acted.

A hand at her elbow guided her up two flights of hewn rock steps to a castlelike fortress. The area was small and enclosed by a parapet. There were no picnic tables, and Caasi wondered how anyone could refer to this as a park. Even the ground had only a few patchy areas of grass.

The light of the full moon illuminated the Columbia River Gorge far below.

"It's beautiful, isn't it?" Caasi whispered, not really sure why she felt the need to keep her voice low.

"I love this place," Blake murmured. "It was too dark for you to notice the rock embankment on the way up here. Each piece fits into the hillside perfectly without a hair's space between the rocks. That old-world craftsmanship is a lost art. There are only a few masons who know how to do that kind of stonework today."

"When was it built?" Caasi questioned.

"Sometime during the Depression, when President Roosevelt implemented the public-work projects."

Despite her best efforts, her voice trembled slightly. "Why did you bring me here...especially tonight?"

He shot her a disturbing look, as if unaware he'd said as much. "I don't know." He spoke softly, his smoldering gaze resting on her slightly parted lips. He turned toward her, his eyes holding her captive. "I suppose I should take you home."

Caasi's heartbeat soared at the reluctance in his voice. She didn't want to go back to the empty apartment, the empty shell of her life. Blake was here and now and she wanted him more than she'd ever wanted anything in her life.

"Blake…" His name came as a tormented whisper.

A breathless, timeless silence followed as he slipped his arms around her. Ever so tenderly, with a gentleness she hadn't expected from him, Blake fit his mouth over hers. Again and again, his mouth sought hers until Caasi was heady with the taste of him.

He moaned when her tongue outlined the curve of his mouth, and his grip tightened. Caasi melted against him as his hands slid down her hips, holding her intimately to his hard body.

Her hands were pressed against the firm wall of his chest and his heartbeat drummed against her open palm, telling her that he was just as affected as she. He felt warm and strong, and Caasi wanted to cry with the wonder of it.

Reluctantly, he tilted his head back, and his warm gaze caressed her almost as effectively as his lips had.

"Shall we go?"

Caasi fought the catch in her voice by shaking her head. If it was up to her they'd stay right there, exactly as they were, for the rest of their lives.

His hand at her waist led her back to the parked car. He lingered a moment longer than necessary after opening her door and helping her inside.

Blake dropped her off in front of the Empress. "I won't see you inside," he stated flatly.

"Why?" She tried to disguise the disappointment in her voice.

His fingers bit into the steering wheel. "Because the way I feel right now, I wouldn't be leaving until the morning. Does that shock you, Caasi?"

Four

Caasi checked the house number written on the back of her business card with the one on the red brick above the front door. Several cars were in the driveway as well as along the tree-lined street. Caasi pulled her silver Mercedes to the curb, uneasily aware that her vehicle looked incongruous beside the Fords and Volkswagens.

This was a family neighborhood, with the wide sidewalks for bicycle riding and gnarled trees meant for climbing. Caasi looked around her with a sense of unfamiliarity. Her childhood sidewalks had been the elevators at the Empress.

Children were playing a game of tag in the front yard; they stopped to watch her curiously as Caasi rang the doorbell, her arms loaded with a huge floral bouquet.

"Hi," a small boy called out. His two front teeth were missing and he had a thick thatch of dark hair and round brown eyes.

"Hi," Caasi said with a wide smile.

"I'm Todd Sherrill."

"I'm Caasi."

"Are you coming to visit my grandma?"

"I sure am."

The door opened and Gina called into the kitchen, "Mom, it's Caasi." Gina held open the screen door for her. "Come on in, we've been waiting for you."

"I'm not late, am I?" Caasi glanced at her watch.

"No, no."

Anne Sherrill came into the living room from the large kitchen in the back of the house. She was wiping her hands on a flowered terrycloth apron. "Caasi, we're so pleased you could come."

"Here." Caasi handed her the flowers. "I wanted you to have these."

Anne looked impressed at the huge variety of flowers. "They're beautiful. Thank you."

For all the cars parked in the front of the house, the living room was empty. Caasi glanced around as Anne took down a vase from the fireplace mantel. The decor was surprisingly modern, with a sofa and matching love seat. The polished oak coffee table was littered with several magazines.

"Come back and meet everyone," Anne said encouragingly. "The men are involved in their card game and the women are visiting."

"Which is a polite way of saying we're gossiping," Gina inserted with a small laugh.

Caasi followed both women into the kitchen, immediately adjacent to which was a family room filled to capacity. Children were playing a game of Monopoly on the floor while the men were seated at a table absorbed in a game of cards.

A flurry of introductions followed. Caasi didn't have trouble remembering names or faces; she dealt with so many people in a hundred capacities that she'd acquired the skill for such things.

Five of the six Sherrill children were present. Only Blake was missing. Caasi talked briefly with each one and after a few questions learned who was married to whom and which child belonged to which set of parents. Blake and Gina were the two unmarried Sherrill children. But Gina proudly displayed an engagement ring. Caasi's eyes met Gina's. Whatever animosity had existed between them in the beginning was gone. Several grandchildren crowded around Anne and Caasi, following them as Anne led the way outside so that she could show off her prize garden.

"Roses," Gina supplied. "My mother and her roses. Sometimes I swear she cares as much about them as she does about us kids."

"Portland is the City of Roses," Anne said as she strolled through the grounds pointing out each bush and variety of rose as if these, too, were her children.

The bigger grandchildren followed them, while Gina carried a two-year-old on her hip. Young Tommy had just gotten up from his nap and was hiding his sleepy face against his aunt's shoulder.

Todd, the eight-year-old who had introduced himself at the front of the house, linked his hand with Caasi's.

"You're pretty," he commented, watching her closely. "Are you my aunt?"

"Does this mean only pretty girls are your aunts?" Caasi teased him, enjoying the feeling of being a part of this gathering.

Todd looked flustered. "Aunt Gina's pretty, and Aunt Barbara's pretty."

"Then you can call me Aunt if you want to," Caasi told him tenderly. "But I'll have to be a special aunt."

"Okay," he agreed readily. They heard another boy calling him, wanting Todd to play. Todd looked uncertain.

"It's all right, you can go," Caasi assured him. "I'll stay with your grandma, and you can come see me later."

The brown eyes brightened. "You'll be here for dinner?"

"Yup."

"Will you play a game of Yahtzee with me afterwards?"

"If you like."

"'Bye, Aunt Caasi."

Todd's words sent a warm feeling through her. She watched him run off and her heart swelled. This was the first time anyone had ever called her aunt.

The baby in Gina's arms peeked at Caasi, eyeing her curiously.

"Do you think he'll let me hold him?" she asked Gina, putting her hands out to the baby. Immediately, Tommy buried his face in Gina's shoulder.

"Give him a few minutes to become used to you. He's not normally shy, but he just woke up and needs to be held a few minutes."

"Is Donald coming?" Anne asked Gina.

"He'll be here, Mom—you know Donald. He'll probably be late for his own wedding, but I love him anyway."

"Have you set a date?" Caasi questioned as they strolled back to the house.

"In two months."

"The wedding shower's here next month, Caasi. We'd be honored if you came." Anne extended the invitation with an easy grace that came from including everyone, as she probably had all her life, Caasi realized.

"I'd love to. In fact, if you'd like, I could arrange to have the shower at the hotel. I mean, I wouldn't want to take over everything, but that way…" She hesitated; maybe she was offending Anne by making the offer.

"You'd do that?" Gina asked disbelievingly.

"We wouldn't want you to go through all that trouble." Anne looked more concerned than dismayed that Caasi would take on the project.

"It's something I'd enjoy doing, and it would be my way of thanking you for today."

"But we can't let you…"

"Nonsense," Caasi interrupted brightly, enthusiasm lighting up her expression. "This will give Gina and me a better chance to get acquainted."

"Oh, Mom," Gina said and sighed happily. "A wedding shower at the Empress."

"We'll get together one day soon and make the arrangements," Caasi promised.

Tommy was studying her more intently now. "Can you come and see me, Tommy?" Caasi asked encouragingly, holding out her hands to him. The little boy glanced from Caasi to Gina, then back to Caasi, before holding out both arms to her.

"You are such a good boy." Caasi lifted him into her arms. She was sure that at one time or another in her life she'd held a small child, but she couldn't remember when, and she thrilled to the way his tiny hands came around her neck.

"I think you've got yourself a friend for life." Anne

laughed and held open the back door for Caasi to come inside. Donald had arrived, and Gina hurried into the living room to greet her fiancé.

Tommy's mother was busy making the salad at the sink, and she smiled shyly when Caasi entered the house carrying Tommy.

"Here." Anne pushed out a tall stool for Caasi to sit on while she put the finishing touches on the meal.

Although Caasi joined in the conversation around her, she was enjoying playing peekaboo and pattycake with Tommy. The little boy's giggles rang through the house.

Her face flushed and happy, Caasi glanced up and saw Blake standing in the doorway of the kitchen. He was watching her, and her breath caught in her throat at the intensity of his gaze. At first she thought he was angry. His eyes had narrowed, but the glint that was shining from them couldn't be anger. A muscle worked in his jaw and his eyes seemed to take in every detail of her sitting in his mother's kitchen, bouncing a baby on her lap.

One of his brothers slapped Blake across the back and started chatting, but still Blake didn't take his eyes off her.

She broke the contact first as Tommy reached for her hair, not liking the fact that her attention had drifted elsewhere. Suddenly a dampness spread through her linen skirt and onto her thighs. She gave a small cry when she realized what had just happened. Laughing, she handed Tommy to his embarrassed mother, who was apologizing profusely.

Anne led Caasi into the bathroom and gave her a dampened cloth to wipe off her teal blue skirt. Someone called Anne and she left Caasi standing just inside the open bathroom door. Caasi couldn't keep from smiling.

"What are you doing here?" Blake was leaning against the doorjamb. That warm, sensuous look was gone, replaced with something less welcoming.

"Your mom invited me last night," she told him, her eyes avoiding his as she continued to rub at her skirt. "Do you mind? I'll leave if you do. I wouldn't want to interfere with your family. I'm the outsider here."

He was silent for a long moment.

"No," he murmured at last, "I don't mind."

Some of the tension eased out of her. "If you'll excuse me, I'll see if I can help in the kitchen." She laid the cloth on top of the clothes hamper and started out the door. But Blake's arm stopped her.

"How'd you sleep last night?" A strange smile touched the curve of his mouth.

Caasi didn't know what he wanted her to say. "Fine. Why?" she asked tightly.

He shrugged, giving the impression of nonchalance. "No reason." But he didn't look pleased with her response and turned abruptly to leave her.

Anne gave her the job of dishing up the home-canned applesauce, dill pickles and spicy beets. All the women were in the kitchen helping in one capacity or another. Laughing and joking with everyone, Caasi didn't feel the least like a stranger. She was accepted, she was one of them. It was the most beautiful feeling in the world.

After the meal, everyone pitched in and helped with the dishes. As promised, Caasi played Yahtzee with Todd and a couple of the other children. Blake was playing cards with his father and brothers and future brother-in-law.

While the children watched TV, Caasi joined the women, who were discussing knitting patterns and recipes. Caasi listened with interest, but her studied gaze was on Blake. He looked up once, caught her eye, and winked. Her heart did a wild somersault and she hurriedly glanced away.

"What game are the men playing?" Caasi asked Gina, who was sitting beside her.

"Pinochle. Have you ever played?"

Card-playing was unheard of in the Crane family; even as a child Caasi had never indulged in something her father considered a waste of valuable time.

"No." Caasi shook her head with a sad smile.

"You've never played pinochle?" Gina repeated incredulously. "I thought everyone did. It's a family institution. Come on, let Dad and Blake teach you."

"No...no, I couldn't."

"Sure you could," Gina insisted. "Donald, would you mind letting Caasi sit in? She's never played."

Blond-headed Donald immediately vacated his chair, holding it out for Caasi.

Standing, Caasi looked uncertain. Her eyes met Blake's, but he ignored the silent entreaty. He didn't want her to play, and his eyes said as much. He scooted out of his seat, offering to let another of his brothers take his place.

Caasi felt terrible. The other women hadn't played.

"Come on. I'll coach you," Gina persisted and straddled a chair beside Caasi's at the table.

The other men didn't look half as obliging as Donald, but one look told her he had been losing. Slowly she lowered herself into the vacant seat opposite Blake's father, who was to be her partner.

The cards were dealt after a thorough review of the rules. Gina wrote down the necessary card combinations on a piece of paper as a ready reminder for Caasi. The bid, the meld and the passing of cards were all gone over in careful detail until Caasi's head was swimming.

They played a practice hand to let Caasi get the feel of the game. Her eyes met Gina's before every move. Once she threw down the wrong card and witnessed her partner's scowl. Caasi's stomach instantly tightened, but George glanced up and offered her an encouraging smile. They made the bid without the point she had carelessly tossed the opponent, and all was well again.

Soon Caasi found herself relaxing enough to enjoy the game. Although playing cards was new to her, the basic principle behind the game was something she'd been working with for years. She studied her opponent's faces when they bid and instinctively recognized what cards were out and which ones she needed to draw. By the time they finished playing, almost everyone else had left—including Blake—and it was almost midnight.

Anne and George walked Caasi to her car, extending an open invitation for her to come again the next week.

"You do this every Sunday?"

"Not everyone makes it every week," Anne was quick to inform her. "This week was more the exception. Everyone was home because of Kathleen's wedding."

Caasi was glad Anne had reminded her. She snapped open her purse and took out an envelope. "Would you give this to Kathleen and her husband for me?" She had written out a check and a letter of congratulations.

"You didn't need to do this," Anne said, fingering the envelope.

"I know," Caasi admitted freely, "but I wanted to."

"I'll see that she gets it."

Caasi could see the elderly couple in her rearview mirror as she drove away. Their arms were around one another as they stood in the light of the golden moon as if they had always been together and always would be. A love that spanned the years.

Caasi was humming as she walked into her office the following morning. Laurie, her secretary, gave her a funny look and handed her the mail.

Caasi sorted through several pieces as she sauntered into her portion of the office. Pivoting, she came back to Laurie's desk.

"I'd like you to make arrangements for a wedding shower in the Blue Room a week from Thursday. Also, would you send the chef up here? I'd like to talk to him personally about the cake and hors d'oeuvres."

Laurie looked even more perplexed. "I'll see to it right away."

"Thanks, Laurie," Caasi said as she strolled back into her office.

The morning passed quickly, and Caasi ate a sandwich for lunch while at her desk. She hadn't seen Blake all morning, which wasn't unusual, but she discovered that her thoughts drifted to him. She wondered what he'd say when she did see him. Would he be all business, or would he make a comment about her visit with his family?

She stared down at the half-eaten sandwich and nibbled briefly on her bottom lip. His mother and sister had been discussing a quiche recipe that had been in Wednesday's paper. Caasi hadn't thought much about it at the time, but the urge to bake something was suddenly overwhelming. She'd taken a cooking class with Edie once simply because her friend didn't want to attend the session alone, but that seemed a hundred years ago. There was a kitchenette in her suite, although she'd never used the stove for much of anything. The oven had never been used, at least not by her. There hadn't been any reason to. And even if she did make the quiche she'd be eating it all week.

Still…

Impulsively she buzzed her secretary. "Laurie, please get me last Wednesday's paper."

Laurie returned twenty minutes later looking slightly ruffled as she handed Caasi the newspaper.

Caasi spread it across her desk and pored over it until she found what she wanted. Reading over the list of ingredients, she realized that not only would it be necessary to shop for the groceries, but she would need to buy all the equipment, including pots, pans and dishes. Quickly she made out a list and handed it to Laurie, who stared at it dumbfounded.

"What you can't find and have delivered to my suite, get from Chef," Caasi instructed on her way out the door to a meeting.

Laurie opened and just as quickly closed her mouth, then nodded.

"Thanks," Caasi said.

She was late getting back to her office. Laurie had left for the day, but Caasi wanted to check over the list of phone messages before heading upstairs. She was shuffling through the pink slips when she walked into her office and found Blake pacing the floor.

He took one look at her and frowned.

"Hello, Blake." She smiled nervously, avoiding his piercing glare. "Is something the matter?" The atmosphere in the room was cool. He turned away, his back rigid. "Blake, what's wrong?"

He spun around, obviously angry as his blazing gaze seared over her. "I got a call from my mother this afternoon. She dropped off the card you gave her for Kathleen." His words were harsh. "What is the idea of giving them a check for two thousand dollars?" The challenge in his eyes was as hard as flint.

Caasi swallowed tightly. "What do you mean?"

"They're strangers to you."

"They're not strangers," she contradicted him sharply. "I met them when I was with you Saturday night. Don't you remember?"

"Kathleen and Bob don't need your charity." His eyes were as somber as they were dark.

"It wasn't charity," she returned. Her hands shook, and she clenched them into hard fists at her sides. "I have the money. In fact, I have lots of money. What does it matter to you what I do with it?"

"It matters," he shouted in return. "Do you think you can buy yourself a family? Is that it? Are you so naive as to believe that people are going to love and respect you because of your money?"

Caasi blanched, her hand shooting out behind her to grip the edge of her desk. She suddenly needed its support to stand upright. From somewhere she found the courage to speak. "I don't need anyone, least of all you. Now I suggest you get out. I'll send a letter of apology to your cousin. It wasn't my intent to offend her or you or anyone. Now kindly leave."

He hesitated as if he wanted to say something more, but then he pivoted sharply and stalked out of the room.

Caasi lowered herself into her desk chair and covered her face with her hands. She took several deep breaths and managed to keep the tears stinging the back of her eyes at bay. It mortified her that Blake thought she was looking to buy herself a family. His family. The thought was too humiliating to consider. She wouldn't go to the next Sunday family dinner. Maybe keeping her away had been Blake's intent all along.

She stayed a few minutes longer in her office, but any thoughts of returning her phone messages had been sabotaged by Blake's anger. She leaned against the elevator wall on the ride to the penthouse suite, weary and defeated. Blake was right in some ways. That was what hurt so much. No matter how much she tried, she wasn't going to fit into the homey family scene with love and acceptance. She didn't belong. A lump had formed in her throat by the time she let herself into the empty suite. What she needed was a hot bath, an early dinner, and bed.

Dinner… Her mind stumbled over the word. She'd canceled her meal for the evening because she'd planned to bake the quiche. The laugh that followed was brittle. Well, why not? She could cook if she wanted to. Who was to care?

Laurie had done her job well, and the kitchen was filled with the necessary equipment. After a quick survey, Caasi slipped off her high heels and tucked her feet into slippers. Fearing she'd spill something on her suit, she used an old shirt as an apron, tying the sleeves around her waist. Rolling her sleeves up to her elbows, she braced both hands on the counter and read over the recipe list a second time. Lastly, she lined the ingredients up on the short countertop in the order in which she was to use them.

The pie crust was going to be the most difficult; everything else looked fairly simple.

Blending the flour and shortening together with a fork wasn't working, so Caasi decided to mix it with her fingers, kneading the shortening and flour together in the palms of her hands.

The phone rang; she stared at the gooey mixture on her hands and decided to let it ring. Ten minutes later, just as she'd spread a light dusting of flour across the counter and was ready to roll out the dough, there was a loud knock on her door.

"Come on, Caasi, I know you're in there."

Blake.

Panic filled her. He was the last person she wanted to see, especially now.

"Aldo says you haven't left. Your car's in the garage and there's no one in the office, so either let me in or I'll break down the door."

He didn't sound in any better mood than he had when she'd last seen him.

"Go away," she shouted, striving—vainly—for a quiet firmness.

"Caasi." His low voice held a note of warning.

"I'm…" She faltered slightly with the lie. "I'm not decent."

"Well, I suggest you cover yourself, because I'm coming through this door in exactly fifteen seconds."

She caught her lower lip in her teeth and breathed in deeply. Why was it that everything in her life had to end up like this?

"It's unlocked," she muttered in defeat.

Blake let himself in, then stopped abruptly when he saw her framed in the small kitchen. A smile worked its way across his face, starting with crinkling amusement at his eyes and then edging up a corner of his chiseled mouth.

"What are you making?" he asked, hands on his hips.

"What do you think you're doing, coming up to my suite like this? I should have security toss you out."

"Why didn't you?" he challenged.

"Because…because I had dough on my hands and would have gotten it all over the phone."

"That's a flimsy excuse."

Caasi released a low, frustrated groan. "Listen, Blake, go ahead and laugh. I seem to be an excellent source of amusement where you're concerned."

"I'm not laughing *at* you." The humor drained out of his eyes, and he dropped his hands.

"Then say what you came to say and be done with it. I'm not up to another confrontation with you." Her voice trembled and her eyes had a wild look. Blake had the ability to hurt her, and that was frightening.

"To be honest," he murmured gently as he took several deliberate steps toward her, "I can't recall a time I've seen you look more beautiful."

For every step he advanced, she took one in retreat, until she bumped against the oven door. The handle cut into the backs of her thighs.

"There's flour on your nose," Blake told her softly.

Caasi attempted to brush it aside and in the process spread more over her cheek.

His gaze swept over her and he shook his head in dismay. "Here, let me."

"No." She refused adamantly. "Don't touch me, Blake. Don't ever touch me again."

He looked as though she'd struck him. "I've hurt you, haven't I, Cupcake?" he asked gently.

"You can't hurt me," she lied. "Only people who mean something to me have that power."

He frowned, his dark eyes clouding with some unreadable emotion. *Surely not pain,* Caasi mused.

"For what it's worth," he said quietly, "I came to apologize."

She shrugged, hoping to give the impression of indifference.

"I got halfway home and couldn't get that stricken look in your eyes out of my mind."

"You're mistaken, Blake," she said pointedly, struggling to keep her voice steady. "That wasn't shock, or hurt, or anything else. It was…" She stopped abruptly when he placed the tips of his fingers over her lips. Helplessly, she stared at him, hating her own weakness. By all rights she should have him thrown out after the terrible things he'd said.

His hands slid around her waist and she tried to push him away, getting dough on his suit jacket.

"I told you not to touch me," she cried. "I knew something like this would happen. Here, I'll get something to clean that."

"There's only one thing I want," Blake murmured softly, pulling her back into his arms. His mouth settled hungrily over hers.

Caasi's soft body yielded to the firm hardness of his without a struggle. His arms tightened around her waist until every part of her came into contact with him. For pride's sake, Caasi wanted to struggle, but she was lost in a swirling vortex of emotion. She could feel the hunger in him and knew her own was as strong.

His teeth gently nibbled on her bottom lip, working his way from one corner of her mouth to the other. Caasi wanted to cry at the pure sensuous attack. No one had ever kissed her like that. What had she missed? All these years, what had she missed? Her breath came in quick, short gasps as she broke out of his arms. Tears filled her eyes until he became a watery blur.

"Don't," she whispered achingly and jerked around, her back to him as she placed her hands on the counter to steady herself.

His ragged breathing sounded in her ear as he placed a comforting hand on her shoulder. "That's the problem," he said quietly. "Every time I touch you it nearly kills me to let you go. Someday you won't send me away, Cupcake."

"Don't call me that. I told you before not to call me that."

The phone rang and she glanced at it guiltily, not able to answer it with her dough-covered hands.

"Aren't you going to answer it?" Blake demanded.

She waved a floury hand in his direction.

"Wash your hands. I'll get it for you."

Because the water was running in the sink, Caasi didn't hear what Blake said or who was on the line.

"It's someone by the name of June. She sounded shocked that a man would answer your phone."

Caasi threw him an angry glare and picked up the receiver. "Yes, June."

"Who was that?" June demanded in low tones.

"My general manager. No one important." Caasi smiled at Blake sweetly, hoping the dig hit its mark.

"I just got out of the doctor's office and he said that everything is looking great. He also said that I could have someone in the delivery room with me when my time came, and I was wondering if you'd like to be there."

Caasi didn't even have to think twice. "I'd love to, but what about Burt?"

"Oh, he doesn't mind. I can have two people with me, and I wanted you to be one of them."

"I'm honored."

"I'm going to be touring the hospital facilities on Friday. Could you come?"

"Yes, that shouldn't be any problem. I'll phone you in the morning once I've had a chance to check my schedule."

"I'll let you get back to that unimportant, sexy-sounding manager."

Caasi laughed lightly, knowing she hadn't fooled her intuitive friend. "Talk to you tomorrow," Caasi promised and hung up.

When she returned to the kitchen, she discovered that Blake had taken off his jacket, rolled up his sleeves, and was placing the pie crust into the pan with the ease of an expert.

"Just what do you think you're doing?" she demanded righteously.

"I figured you couldn't possibly eat all this yourself and you'd probably want to invite me to dinner."

"You have a high opinion of yourself, Blake Sherrill."

His boyish smile would have disarmed a battalion. "And if you plan to invite me to dinner, the very least I can do is offer a hand in its making."

Five

"Well, don't just stand there," Blake insisted. "Beat the eggs."

Caasi hesitated, her feelings ambivalent. She wanted to tell Blake to leave, to get out of her life. He had hurt her in a way she had never expected. But at the same time he had awakened her to what it meant to be a woman, and she wanted him with her. He made her laugh, and when he touched her she felt more alive than she had in all her twenty-eight years.

Not fully understanding the reasons why, Caasi decided to swallow her pride and let him stay. She took the eggs and cracked them against the side of the bowl one by one. Silently they worked together. Caasi whipped the eggs until they were light and frothy while Blake chopped onion and green pepper and sliced zucchini.

"I'm going to the hospital Friday," Caasi mentioned casually.

Blake paused and turned toward her. "Is something wrong?"

"No," she assured him quickly. "It's one of the most natural things in the world. Babies usually are."

A stunned silence crackled in the tension-filled room. "Did you say 'baby'?"

Caasi was enjoying this. "Yes," she murmured without looking up, pouring the milk into the measuring cup.

"Are you trying to tell me you're pregnant?" Blake demanded.

Caasi had trouble keeping a smile from forming. "I'm not trying to tell you anything. All I did was make a casual comment about going to the hospital Friday."

"Because of a baby?"

Caasi nodded. She could see the exasperation in his expression.

Blake's eyes raked over her, and she noticed the way the paring knife was savagely attacking the green pepper. "Who's the father?"

"Burt."

"Who's Burt?"

"June's husband."

"But that was June on the phone and..." Blake stopped in midsentence, as comprehension leapt into his eyes. "You little tease," he said deeply, "I should make you pay for that."

"Tease? Me?" Caasi feigned shock. "How could you accuse me of something like that? You have to remember, I'm not a real woman, with real blood."

Blake linked his arms around her waist and nuzzled her neck. "I don't know, you're becoming more womanlike by the minute."

"You think so, do you?" A throb of excitement ran through her at his touch. Fleetingly Caasi wondered why she hadn't experienced these sensations with other men.

"Yes, I do." He turned her into his arms, linking

his hands at the small of her back. Hungrily, his gaze studied her.

Caasi gave a nervous laugh and broke free. These feelings Blake was creating within her were all too new, too strong. They frightened her.

"I want you to know," Caasi began, taking a shaky breath, "I thought about what you said at the dance—about having ink in my veins."

A silence seemed to fill the small kitchen. "And?" Blake asked her softly.

"And I think you're probably right. Ever since Dad died, I've been so busy with Crane Enterprises that I've allowed that role to dominate my life." She slipped the onion and other vegetables he had chopped into the egg mixture and poured it over the thinly sliced zucchini already in the pie crust. "June and Edie tried to tell me the same thing," she said and gave a weak laugh. "Edie said what I needed was an affair."

"An affair," Blake repeated slowly, his dark eyes unreadable. "So that's what this is all about."

"What?"

"You heard me. What happened then? Did you suddenly look at me and see the most likely candidate?" His words went cold.

"Of course not. I thought Edie was nuts. I'm not the type of woman who would have an affair. Do you honestly think I'd do something like that?"

"Why not? I won't be around much longer. You can have your fling and be done with me."

Words momentarily failed her as she struggled to control her outrage. "Why do you do this to me? I started out by telling you that you were right in what you'd said about me and suddenly I'm on the defensive again." One hand gripped the oven door, and she knotted the other until the long nails bit into her palm. "June and Edie had noticed that I have no life except the business. All I'm saying is that I'm trying to change that." Irritated with her inability to explain herself in simpler terms, Caasi walked across the suite to stand in front of the large picture window. Her arms hugged her stomach. These changes made her vulnerable to Blake. If these changes only brought pain, then she wanted no part of it.

He came to stand beside her but made no attempt to touch her. "Have you noticed how we can't seem to be together anymore without disagreeing about one thing or another?"

"Oh, yes, I've noticed." Her hands dropped to fists at her side.

"By all rights you should throw me out."

Caasi knew that, but she didn't want him to leave. He might have the power to wound, but just as strong was his ability to comfort and heal.

"I can't do that." A wry smile twisted her mouth. "You made half the dinner." It didn't make sense, Caasi realized, but she wanted him there, liked having him around.

"Truce, Caasi?" His voice was soft and gruff at the same time.

"For how long?" They hadn't gone without fighting for more than a few minutes lately.

"Just tonight. We can get through one night without arguing."

Caasi resisted the temptation to slip her arms around him. "Working together, we can manage it." They'd been a team for years—but soon that, too, would change. The thought was a forceful reminder that Blake had turned in his resignation and would be leaving her soon. She wondered if she'd ever see him again after he left the Empress. The realization that she might not produced a painful sensation in the area of her heart. Blake had always been there. She relied on him. Nothing would be the same after he left. But she couldn't mention that now. Not when they'd agreed on a truce. Every time she said something about him leaving, they argued.

"The quiche has to bake for an hour. Would you like to listen to some music?"

"And have a glass of wine."

Caasi kept a supply of her favorite Chablis available and brought down two crystal glasses. While she poured, Blake reached for his phone.

Music filled the suite as Caasi brought their drinks into the living room.

Blake sat on the couch, holding out his arm to indicate he wanted her at his side. Caasi handed him the wine and sat next to him on the plush leather sofa, leaning her head against his shoulder. A hand cupping her upper arm kept her close. Not that Caasi wanted to be anyplace else.

The music was mellow and soft, the ballad a love song. Oftentimes, after a long day, Caasi would sit with her feet propped up on the coffee table, close her eyes, and let the music work its magic on her tired body. But the only magic she needed that night was Blake.

"June asked me to go into the delivery room with her when her baby is born," Caasi said, elaborating on the earlier conversation. "That's why I'm going to the hospital this Friday. They want to familiarize the three of us with the procedures."

"Three of you?"

"Four, actually," Caasi said, correcting herself. "Burt, June, baby, and me."

"You're sure you want to do this?" Caasi felt his gaze wandering over her as if in assessment. "From what I understand, labor is no picnic, and for someone who's never had a baby it may be more than you can handle."

Caasi stiffened, biting back angry words. "I want to be there and nothing's going to stop me."

Blake glanced at his wristwatch. "Twenty minutes."

"What's twenty minutes?"

"How long we lasted without arguing."

"We didn't fight. I was tempted, but being the mature woman I am, I managed to avoid telling you that I found that remark unnecessarily condescending."

Blake chuckled and took a sip of his wine. "I'm glad. Because then I can admit that sometimes I say things purposely just to see the anger spark in your eyes. You're beautiful when you let that invisible guard down, and sometimes anger is the only thing that lowers it."

Every part of her was conscious of Blake. Pressed close to his side, she ached for the urgent feel of his arms around her and the hungry taste of his mouth. But their truce wasn't limited to arguments, although they hadn't stated as much. They needed to find a level plane, a happy medium between the fighting and the loving.

"I'm working to change that about myself," Caasi admitted softly. "When Dad was in charge he was firm in his belief about mixing business with pleasure. When he was in the office he was one man and outside the office, another. In some ways I'm a lot like my father. We've worked together five years, Blake, but I never saw you as anything more than my general manager."

"And you do now?"

Her voice was becoming huskier as she strove to keep the emotion out of it. "Yes."

"Because I'm leaving?"

"Say…" She laughed shakily. "Why am I doing all the talking? Shouldn't you make some deep revelation about yourself?"

Blake's answering grin was dry. "I like fine wine—" he raised the glass to his lips and took a sip "—and the challenge of climbing mountains. I love the Pacific and enjoy walks along the beach in the early hours of the morning before the sun rises. Sometimes when the mood comes over me, I paint." He paused. "Does that satisfy your curiosity?"

"In some ways." But he didn't offer to reveal more, and the point was well noted.

The timer on the stove rang and Caasi reluctantly broke from his arms. "I'll check our dinner."

She set the quiche on top of the stove to cool and returned to the living room. Blake was looking out the window at the view.

"Some nights, especially when things are troubling me," Caasi admitted softly as she joined him, "I'll stand here and think."

"So that's why there's a worn spot in the carpet," Blake teased.

"I've been here frequently of late."

"Why?" Blake turned and took a step toward her. Only a few inches separated them.

Caasi lowered her gaze to the floor and shrugged. "Lots of things."

"Anything in particular?"

She ignored the question. "The quiche is ready if you are."

Blake brushed a strand of hair from her face. When his hand grazed her cheek, Caasi was forced to stifle an involuntary gasp of pleasure.

"No," Blake said slowly, his words barely audible. "I'm not ready." His hand worked its way around the back of her neck, his fingers twining into her hair as he brought her mouth up to meet his.

With a small sigh of welcome, Caasi swayed into him, melting against him, her arms reaching instinctively for him. Her response was so automatic she didn't have time to question it.

As his mouth plundered hers, Caasi felt as though she were on fire, the burning heat spreading down her legs until she was weak and clinging.

This wasn't supposed to happen, they'd promised one another it wouldn't, but they were like two climbers waiting to explore a mountain and would no longer be denied the thrill of the challenge.

Her roaming hands reveled in the feel of the hard muscles and smooth skin of his back. A delicious languor spread through her, and her breath came in sharp gasps.

Blake buried his face in the hollow of her throat and shuddered. "Let's eat," he whispered, and Caasi smiled at the husky timbre of his voice as she realized he was experiencing the same sensations she was.

Neither showed much interest in the meal. Blake commented that she'd done a good job and Caasi was pleased with her efforts, but her mind wasn't on the food.

They hardly spoke, but each intuitively seemed to know what the other was thinking. Caasi wished she had her wine, and without a word Blake stood and brought it to her.

Simultaneously they set their forks across half-full plates, their interest in food entirely gone. Blake stood and held out his hand to her.

Heedless of where he was taking her, Caasi realized she would have followed him to Mars. She placed her hand in his. Blake reached for his phone and once more the music played as he led her back to the sofa.

Caasi slid an arm around him and rested the side of her face close to his heart. Blake rubbed his jaw against the top of her head in a slow, rotating action that was faintly hypnotic. His fingers were in her hair.

Caasi didn't need to look to know that his eyes were closed. This was like a dream, a trance from which she never wanted to wake. The barriers were down.

Caasi didn't know how long he held her. The music had faded long ago, but they made their own. Blake had made that comment to her when he'd given her the dancing lesson, but she hadn't understood him then. Now she didn't even need to close her eyes to hear the violins.

Blake shifted and Caasi was shocked to look at her watch and see that it was almost midnight.

"Walk me to the door," he whispered and kissed the crown of her head, his breath stirring her dark hair.

She nodded, not finding the words to release him readily.

"Our truce lasted," she said softly and added, with a warm smile, "sort of."

"If we're going to fight, let's do it like this. Agreed?" He took her in his arms, gazing down at her upturned face with a warmth that reached all the way to the soles of her feet.

"Yes, I agree." Her hand lovingly stroked his thick, unruly hair. "Are you really going to leave me, Blake?"

He went completely still. "How do you mean?"

Did he think she was asking him to spend the night? If she was honest, she would admit the thought wasn't an alien one. But she had been sincere when she explained that she wasn't one to indulge in casual affairs. She wanted Blake; Caasi couldn't deny it. But she wanted him forever.

"The Empress," she explained. "You're not going to leave, are you?" The minute the words were out she knew she'd said the wrong thing.

Blake looked as if she'd physically struck him. He pulled her arms away, severing the contact. "So that was what this was all about." Impatience shadowed his face.

"Blake, no!" But he wasn't listening as he sharply turned, opened the door and left.

"There's a Gina Sherrill to see you," Laurie announced over the intercom the following Monday.

"Send her in," Caasi replied. "And, Laurie, could you see to it that we're not disturbed?"

"Of course."

Gina stepped into the office a moment later.

"Hi, Caasi." She looked uncertain, her eyes taking in the expensive decor of the room. "Wow, you've got a great view from up here, haven't you? How do you ever get anything done?"

"It's hard, especially on a sunny day like today when it seems that the whole world is outside this window and ready to be explored."

"We missed you Sunday."

Caasi rolled a pencil between her palms. "I had a previous engagement." The lie was only a small one.

"Everyone likes you, and we were hoping you'd come again."

"I will," Caasi assured her but secretly doubted that she could. Not with Blake in his present state of mind. Another confrontation with him was to be avoided at all costs. They treated one another like polite strangers. Blake had hired his replacement and was training the middle-aged man now. Caasi liked Brian Harris and had recognized almost instantly that she wouldn't have any trouble working with him.

Blake's last day was scheduled for the end of the month, less than ten days away.

"Let's go down to the Blue Room and you can tell me what kind of decorations you want. Are the other women coming?" Caasi asked. Gina had asked to include her maid of honor and bridesmaids in the shower planning.

"They're in the lobby. We didn't feel like we should all descend on you."

"Why not?" Caasi asked, setting the pencil aside. "I'm looking forward to meeting them."

"Blake's leaving, isn't he?" Gina's question came as a surprise.

Caasi nodded with forced calm. "Yes, he handed in his resignation not long ago."

"I'm surprised." Gina wrinkled her nose. "I didn't think Blake would ever leave you."

That was the crux of the problem—Caasi hadn't thought so either.

"Shall we go now?" Caasi wanted to divert the conversation from Blake.

"Sure," Gina answered eagerly.

Riding the elevator down to the lobby Gina announced, "All the invitations have been mailed. Everyone is impressed that the shower's at the Empress. I'm still having problems believing it myself."

"I'm glad to do it." Caasi meant that.

"You'll be there, won't you? I know it's in the middle of the day and everything, but you wouldn't have to stay long and I'd really like everyone to meet you."

Caasi hesitated. There was an important meeting scheduled with some architects the afternoon of the shower, and if past experience was anything to go by, she could be held up for hours.

"I won't make any promises, but I'll see what I can do."

"Great," Gina enthused.

They met the others in the lobby, and the small party took the broad, winding stairs built against a mirrored wall to the second floor where the Blue Room was situated.

"Oh." Gina sighed with excitement. "It's perfect, just perfect."

Caasi stayed only a few minutes longer. She wanted to have some time to herself before she had to leave for a luncheon engagement that was scheduled with the Portland Chamber of Commerce; they would be discussing plans for a basketball players' convention that winter.

Briefly Caasi explained to Gina that she'd ordered the flowers delivered Thursday morning and had asked the chef to provide a sketch of the cake.

"The cake," Gina said happily, "is larger than the one for the wedding."

Glancing at her wristwatch, Caasi sighed. "I've got to run, but I'll see you Thursday afternoon."

"Oh, thanks, Caasi. I can't tell you how excited I am about this."

"To be honest, I'm having as much fun as you, doing it."

Caasi took the elevator back to her office. As the huge doors glided open, Caasi stepped into the wide hallway—and nearly bumped into Blake.

His hands shot out to help her maintain her balance and their eyes clashed. "Are you all right?"

Caasi couldn't take her eyes from his face. For the first time in days there was a faint flicker of something more than polite disregard. Every angle of his jaw was lovingly familiar, and she longed to ease the lines of strain from his eyes and mouth.

"Caasi," he said sharply.

Her eyes studied the floor, and she struggled to maintain the thin thread of her composure. "I'm fine."

He released her slowly. "Will you have time this afternoon to go over the Wilson figures?"

"Yes, that shouldn't be any problem. I'll be back around two."

"Fine," he said in clipped tones. "I'll send Harris into your office then."

"Harris." She repeated the name. She knew the man was replacing Blake, but she had yet to deal with him directly. "Yes." Her voice faltered a bit. "That'll be fine."

Caasi stepped into her office and retrieved her purse. "I'm leaving now."

Laurie looked up at her blankly. The luncheon wasn't scheduled for another hour. "But Mr. Gains is due to see you in twenty minutes."

"Send him in to Blake," Caasi said curtly. "You know where to reach him."

Caasi took the Mercedes, heading east down Sandy Boulevard until she located Broadway. She drove around for several fruitless minutes. It had to be around here somewhere. Finally she recalled seeing that small mom-and-pop grocery and knew she was headed in the right direction. For all her years in Portland, she'd been to Rocky Butte only once. With Blake, the night of his cousin's wedding.

She parked her car in the same area Blake had. The scene was all the more magnificent during the day. The snow-capped mountain peaks of the Cascade range, the flowing Columbia and Willamette rivers, could all be seen from there. Washington State was just on the other side of the Columbia River Gorge, and once powerful Mount Saint Helens was in full view. No wonder Blake loved it up there so much.

The park itself was a different matter. Someone had broken beer bottles against the steps, and Caasi avoided the sharp pieces of glass as she climbed the flights of rock-hewn stairs for the second time. Walking to the parapet, she studied the view again. Faint stirrings of love and appreciation for what lay before her brought an involuntary smile. Caasi, born and raised in Portland, Oregon, was unaware of her city's charm and beauty. A shame, she mused dejectedly.

Caasi sauntered into the office a little after two, having decided to send Harris to the luncheon. Laurie glanced up at her nervously.

"Mr. Sherrill's in your office."

"Thanks, Laurie." Her assistant's tone told her Blake wasn't in a mood to exchange pleasantries.

"Problems, Blake?" she quizzed as she entered.

He swiveled and jammed his hands into his pockets. His gaze hardened. "Gains had the appointment with you. Where were you?"

"Out," she snapped.

"You don't give important people like Gains the brush-off like that. The banker was furious, and with good reason."

Perfectly calm, Caasi sat at her desk and glared at him. "Do you presume to tell me how to run Crane Enterprises now? Criticizing my personal life isn't enough?"

Blake clamped his mouth closed. "You're in no mood to discuss this rationally."

Caasi's laugh was sarcastic and brittle. "This is getting better every minute," she said, refusing to let him talk down to her. "Send Harry in with the Wilson figures, please."

"The man's name is Harris."

The contempt in Blake's eyes was enough to make her cry. Maybe tears would dissolve the lump of loneliness within her. Maybe tears would take away the pain of what Blake was doing. But somehow Caasi doubted it.

Thursday afternoon, fifteen minutes before her scheduled meeting with the architects, Caasi took the elevator to the Blue Room, where Gina's wedding shower was in progress.

She stood in the entry watching the young girl open her gifts. The turnout was a good one, and Caasi recognized several people from Kathleen's wedding.

The bouquets of blue and white flowers harmonized

beautifully with the room's decor. The chef had outdone himself with the huge sheet cake.

Gina saw Caasi just inside the doorway and gave a squeal of delight. The young bride-to-be hurried to proudly introduce Caasi to her friends.

Caasi's appearance was only a token one, and she made her farewells, sorry to learn that she'd missed Anne. She would have enjoyed seeing Blake's mother again.

Laurie smiled when Caasi returned to the office. "There was a Mrs. Sherrill here to see you. I told her you'd gone down to the Blue Room."

Caasi smiled sadly. She'd just missed Anne again. But that was the way her life was headed. Always close but never close enough.

She'd barely sat down at her desk when Blake slammed into her office, nearly taking her door off the hinges when he closed it.

"What was my mother doing here?" he demanded.

"Your mother was here because of Gina's shower," Caasi replied calmly.

"Gina's wedding shower?" He was pacing the floor like a caged lion eager for the opportunity to escape and hunt the closest victim.

"Yes. It's in the Blue Room."

"My family can't afford the Blue Room."

"But I can. I'm doing this for Gina."

Blake froze, and his anger burned from every pore. "You did what?"

"I would have said something earlier if we'd been on better terms. Everything I do lately angers you. There are only a few days left until you're free of me. Must you fight me at every turn?"

Blake marched to the far side of the office and raked

his hand through his hair. "I want you to add up every cent that this fiasco has cost and take it out of my next paycheck."

"What?" Caasi exploded, bolting out of her chair.

"You heard me. Every cent."

Tears sprang into her eyes, blinding her. She lowered her gaze so Blake wouldn't notice.

"Why?" she asked, amazed that her voice could remain so steady when she felt as though the world was crumbling apart beneath her.

"I told you before that you couldn't buy yourself a family. Least of all mine."

"Yes, of course." She swallowed at the painful hoarseness in her throat. "Now, if you'll excuse me."

She nearly walked into Laurie. "Conference Room A is ready for…" Laurie stopped sharply. "Miss Crane, are you all right? Do you need a doctor?" The woman looked flabbergasted to see Caasi in tears. Hurriedly she supplied Caasi with a tissue.

"Cancel the meeting, Laurie." Her voice trembling, Caasi fought down a sob. "Please extend my sincere apologies." With as much self-possession as she could muster, Caasi walked out of the office.

Blake came up behind her. "Caasi." Her name was issued grimly.

She ignored him and stepped into the elevator. When she turned around their eyes met. The tall, lean figure swam in and out of her vision.

"You have so much, Blake. Is it that difficult to share just this little bit with me?" The huge metal doors swished shut and Caasi broke into sobs that heaved her shoulders and shook her whole body.

Six

Caasi leaned against the penthouse door, her face buried in her hands as her shoulders shook. If this horrible ache was part of being a woman, she wanted none of it. Ink in her veins was preferable to the pain in her heart. But it was too late and Caasi recognized that.

Arms hugging her stomach, she tilted her face to the ceiling to keep the tears from spilling. She was tired. The weariness came from deep within.

Blake was leaving; why shouldn't she? She hadn't been on a real vacation in years, not since she took over Crane Enterprises.

Wiping the moisture from her cheeks, she took a quivering breath and stood at her favorite place by the window. She'd be fine. All she needed was a few days away to gain perspective.

Her leather luggage was stored in the bedroom closet. Caasi wasn't exactly sure where she'd go. It would be fun just to drive down the coast. Oregon had some of the most beautiful coastline in the world.

The soft knock on the door surprised her. Probably Laurie. The secretary had been shocked to see Caasi cry…and little wonder. Caasi wasn't the weeping female type.

"Yes," Caasi called softly, striving to sound composed and confident. "Come in."

When Blake strolled into the living room, Caasi felt ice form in the pit of her stomach. "These are my private quarters," she told him in a voice that was dipped in acid. "I don't know who or what has given you the impression that you may come up here, but that has got to change. Now, get out before I call security." She marched out of the room and into her bedroom, carelessly tossing her clothes into the suitcase.

"Caasi, listen." There was an unfamiliar pleading quality to his voice as he followed her. "Let me apologize."

"Okay," she said without looking up. "You're sorry. Now leave."

"What are you doing?" His eyes followed her as she moved from the closet to the suitcase, then back to the closet.

"That's none of your business."

"If you're going someplace, I need to know."

"I'll leave the details of my trip with Laurie." She didn't look at him; she was having enough trouble just keeping her composure intact.

"Isn't this trip a bit sudden?"

"Since when do you have the authority to question me?" She whirled around, placing her hands challengingly on her hips.

"Since you started acting like an irrational female," he returned sarcastically.

"Me?" Caasi exploded. "Of all the nerve!" She

stormed across the room and picked up the phone. "Security, please."

"I'm not leaving," Blake threatened. "Call out the National Guard, but I'm not leaving until we understand one another."

"Understand?" Caasi cried. "What's there to understand? I'm the boss, you're the employee. Now get out."

"No."

"Yes." Caasi spoke into the receiver. "This is Miss Crane. I'm having a problem here. Could you send up security?" She hung up the phone and tossed Blake a hard look. "Oh, before I forget," she said and gave him a saccharine smile, "be sure and have accounting give you an employee discount on the Blue Room." She slammed the lid of her suitcase closed and dragged it off the top of the bed.

Taking a smaller case, she entered the master bathroom and impatiently stuffed brush, comb, shampoo, hair dryer, and an entire cupboard of cosmetics into it. When she whirled around, Blake was blocking the doorway.

"Will you kindly step out of the way?"

"Not until we talk."

Expelling a long sigh to give the impression of boredom, Caasi crossed her arms and glared at him. "All right, you win. Say what you want to say and be done with it."

Blake looked surprised but determined. He paused and ran his hand over his jaw.

"What's the matter, has the cat got your tongue?" she taunted unfairly.

Confusion flickered across his brow. "There's something about you, Caasi, that makes me say and do things I know are going to hurt you. Yet I do them."

"This is supposed to be an apology?" She faked a yawn.

Blake's thick brows drew together in a pained, confused expression. Caasi doubted that her feigned indifference could create a fissure in the hard wall of his defenses.

The phone rang, diverting her attention to the other room.

"If you'll excuse me."

"No, not now." His arm across the door prevented her from leaving.

"Blake." She groaned in frustration. "This is ridiculous. Look at you. Now, for heaven's sake, will you let me out of the bathroom so I can answer the phone?"

He didn't budge.

"Please," she added.

Blake dropped his hand and turned his back to her. As she hurried past him, Caasi noted fleetingly that he looked as weary and defeated as she felt.

"Hello," she answered on the fourth ring, her voice slightly breathless.

"Caasi?" The male voice on the other end was only faintly recognizable.

"Burt?" Caasi felt all the blood drain from her face.

"It's June. She's in labor. She said I should phone you now."

"Now?" Caasi repeated with a sense of unreality. "Isn't this early?"

"Only ten days. The doctor assured us it wasn't anything to worry about. I'm at the hospital; the nurse is checking June and said she'd prefer I stepped out for a few minutes." Burt sounded worried and unsure.

"I'll be there in five minutes." Caasi's heart was singing with excitement as she replaced the telephone receiver.

"Who was it?"

Caasi had forgotten Blake was there. "Burt. June's in labor." She grabbed her purse from the end of the bed and hurried out of the suite. A security man met her just outside the door.

"You wanted me, Miss Crane?"

"Yes," she shouted and shot past him to the elevator. "I mean, no, everything's been taken care of. I'm sorry to have troubled you."

"No trouble, miss." He touched the brim of his hat with his index finger.

"Caasi," Blake called as he followed her out of the suite. "I'll meet with the architects and we can talk about it in the morning."

"Fine." She'd have agreed to anything as long as it didn't delay her.

The car engine roared to life when she turned the key. Caasi wondered if June was experiencing this same kind of exhilarated excitement. Burt and June wanted this baby so much and had planned carefully for it. For *her,* Caasi corrected her thoughts. June's deepest desire was for a little girl.

The visitors' parking lot was full, and Caasi spent several frustrating minutes until she found a space on the street. On her visit the previous Friday, she had learned that once Burt phoned she was to go directly to the labor room on the third floor. Stepping off the elevator, her shoes clapped against the polished, squeaky-clean floor.

"I'm Caasi Crane," she announced at the nurses' station. "Can you tell me which labor room Mrs. Kauffman is in?"

The uniformed nurse with white hair and a wide smile glanced at the chart. "Number 304. I believe her husband is with her."

"Thanks," Caasi said with a smile.

The room was the second one on the left side of the hall. The door was closed, so Caasi knocked lightly.

Burt opened it for her, looking pale and worried.

"Is anything wrong?" Caasi asked anxiously.

"No, everything's fine or so I've been assured." He ran his hand through his hair. "June's doing great."

Caasi smiled. "How come you look like *you're* the one in labor?"

"I don't know, Caasi, I can hardly stand to see June in pain like this."

"Caasi?" June looked flushed against the white sheets. "Is that you?"

"I'm here."

"I suppose I got you out of some important meeting."

"Nothing I wasn't glad to escape from," Caasi assured her and pulled up a chair so she could sit beside the bed. "I've read that babies aren't particularly known for their sense of timing."

June laughed weakly. "At least not this one. The pains woke me up this morning, but I wasn't really sure this was the real thing. I didn't want to trouble you if it wasn't."

Burt came around to the other side of the bed and took his wife's hand in both of his. "How do you feel?"

His eyes were filled with such tenderness that it hurt Caasi to look at him. Would any man ever look at her like that? The only thing she'd seen in Blake's eyes lately was disdain.

"I'm fine, so quit worrying about me. Women have been having babies since the beginning of time."

Burt looked up at Caasi. "I'll say one thing; having a baby is a lot different than I thought."

Caasi smiled reassuringly. "I don't imagine it's much what June thought either." She glanced down to note that June's face was twisted with pain. Instinctively, Caasi gave June her hand. Her friend gripped it the way a drowning man would a life preserver. The young face relaxed.

"The pains last about thirty seconds, but it's the longest thirty seconds of my life," June whispered.

"The last time the nurse checked, she'd dilated to five centimeters. She has to get to ten centimeters in the first stage of labor."

Caasi had been reading the book the doctor had given her in preparation for the big event. Once June was fully dilated, the second stage of labor, when the baby entered the birth canal, would begin.

"The nurse said that won't be for hours yet," June told her.

"Not to worry, I've got all day. What about you?"

"Well, if the truth be known, I'm missing a big sale at Lloyd Center," June admitted with a weak smile.

The hours passed quickly. Caasi was shocked to look up from timing a contraction to note that it was after seven, and she hadn't eaten lunch. But she was too busy to care about food.

When the hard contractions came, Burt coached his

wife, while Caasi, her hand on June's abdomen, counted out the seconds. Time and again Caasi was astonished at her friend's fortitude. June and Burt had decided in the beginning that they wanted natural childbirth, and although the pains were excruciating, June's resolve didn't waver. Burt didn't look as confident.

When the time came to move into the delivery room, Caasi and Burt were asked to don surgical gowns.

"I didn't realize I would have to dress for the occasion," Caasi joked as June reached for her hand.

A small cry slipped from June as the pain crescendoed. As it ebbed, June lay back on the pillow, panting.

Burt carried June's fingers to his lips. Then, tenderly, he wiped the moisture from her brow.

"I love you," June whispered, the soft light of love shining in her eyes.

Strangely, Caasi didn't feel like an intruder on the touching scene; she felt she was a part of it—a wonderful, important part.

"I've never loved you more than I do right this minute," Burt whispered in return.

Another pain came and June bit into her lip with the grinding agony, panting and breathless when it waned.

"One more pain and you should be able to see the head," the doctor told them. A round mirror was positioned near the ceiling, and all eyes focused on the reflection as another pain came and passed. June gave Caasi a happy but weak smile.

The baby started crying once the head was free of the birth canal, the doctor supporting the tiny skull.

"Good pair of lungs," Burt said excitedly. "It must be a girl."

One final contraction and the baby slipped into the doctor's waiting hands.

"It's a girl," he announced.

June gave an exhilarated cry. "Oh, I wanted a girl so badly. Burt...a girl." Laughing and crying at the same time, she threw her arms around her husband's neck, hugging him fiercely.

"Seven pounds, twelve ounces," the nurse said as she lifted the squalling baby from the scale.

Unabashed tears of happiness flowed down Caasi's cheeks. She had never felt such wondrous joy in her life. To have had even a small part in the baby's birth produced warm emotions that touched the softest core of her heart.

"Caasi." June gripped her hand. "You're crying. I don't think I've ever seen you cry."

"It's all so beautiful. And your daughter's beautiful."

"Should I tell her?" Burt looked down with love at his wife. At June's confirming nod, he glanced up. "June and I decided if we had a daughter we would name her Cassi—two *s*'s, one *a*."

"After a lifelong friend we both love and respect," June added.

Caasi couldn't push the words of love and appreciation past the lump of happiness in her throat.

"And, of course, we want you to be her godmother," Burt continued.

"Of course," Caasi confirmed, tears winding a crooked path down her face.

An hour later, Caasi walked to her car parked on the deserted street. A look at her watch confirmed that it was almost ten. She felt like skipping and singing. Tiny, sweet baby Cassi was adorable, and Caasi couldn't love her any more if she were her own.

Caasi pulled onto the avenue and merged with the flow of traffic. She felt wonderful and rolled down the window, singing as she cheerfully missed the turn that would lead her back to the downtown area and the Empress.

Before she could reconsider, she took the turnoff for Gresham and Blake's house. He'd said something about wanting to talk to her after the meeting that afternoon, but that wasn't the reason she had to see him. If she didn't tell someone about the baby, she'd burst.

There wasn't a streetlight to guide her as she drove down the winding road. She had to pull over to the side of the road a couple of times, having difficulty finding her way in the night. Finally she pulled into the driveway, the old weeping willow the only reminder she required.

The kitchen lights were on, and Caasi paused before climbing out of the car and slowly closing the door. Maybe coming to Blake's wasn't such a good idea after all. They'd been fighting when she left.

The back door opened and Blake came down the steps. "Caasi." He sounded shocked. "Is anything wrong?"

She shook her head. "June had a baby girl."

"That's wonderful. Come inside and I'll make you a cup of coffee."

"I'd like that."

A hand at her elbow guided her up the stairs. The coffeepot was on the kitchen counter. Caasi glanced into the living room and saw an open book lying across the arm of an overstuffed chair. Blake had been spending a quiet evening at home reading.

He handed her a mug and Caasi took it, leaning against the kitchen counter as she hugged the coffee cup with both hands.

"June and Burt are naming her Cassi—two *s*'s, one *a*. She's so beautiful, all pink and with the tiniest hands. She's perfect, just perfect. Before they moved her out of the delivery room, the nurse let me hold her for a few minutes. It was the most incredibly marvelous feeling I've ever experienced, holding this new life. I still can't believe it," she finished breathlessly.

A warm smile appeared on his face and was reflected in his eyes as he watched her. "Come and sit down in the living room. You can tell me all about it."

"I don't even know where to start." She sat in the chair opposite his and lifted the lid from a candy jar nearby, popping a couple of pieces of hard candy into her mouth. "I'm starved. I hope you don't mind if I help myself."

"Didn't you eat dinner?"

Caasi shook her head. "Not lunch either. No time," she explained while sucking the lemon drops. The sugary sweetness filled her mouth, making her hunger more pronounced.

"Let me fix you something."

"No, I'll be fine, really," she asserted.

Blake ignored her, returning to the kitchen and opening the refrigerator as Caasi trailed after him. "There are leftover pork chops, eggs, bacon. What's your pleasure?"

Caasi bit into the side of her mouth to keep from saying: *You.* The thought nearly squeezed the oxygen from her lungs. Never had she wanted a home and husband more than she did at that moment. They even looked like an old married couple, standing in the kitchen, roaming through the fridge and looking for leftovers.

"Caasi?" Blake glanced up, his look questioning.

She shook her head. "Anything's fine. Don't worry about a meal, a sandwich would do as well."

"Bacon and eggs," he decided for her, taking both from the refrigerator and setting them on top of the counter.

Caasi pulled out a chair and sat at the table while Blake peeled off thick slices of bacon and laid them across a skillet.

"June was marvelous," Caasi continued. "She was a real trouper. Burt and June had decided they wanted natural childbirth and she did it. She refused to give up. The doctor tried to encourage her to use the anesthesiologist a couple of times—it would have made his job easier. But June refused." She paused and smiled. "It's a good thing the doctor didn't ask Burt. He could barely stand to see June suffer. Instead of watching, he closed his eyes along with her. Don't get me wrong— he was wonderful too. I don't know how any woman can have a baby without her husband's help. I know I couldn't." Caasi swallowed tightly. But then, she probably wouldn't have a child. Some of the enthusiasm left her and she stared into the coffee mug.

A disturbing silence filled the kitchen.

"The meeting with Schultz and Son went fine. But they'd like you to make a trip to Seaside next Tuesday, if you can."

"I don't see why not." Eagerly Caasi picked up the conversation. "I don't remember that anything's scheduled. I'll check with Laurie in the morning." Her index finger made a lazy circle on the tabletop. "Will you be coming?" Blake sometimes traveled with her, depending on the circumstances.

"It looks as if I'll have to. We'll leave Harris in the office, which will be good experience for him."

"Sure," she agreed, feeling somewhat guilty. Not once in the past week had she made an effort to meet or talk to Brian Harris. The man only served to remind her that Blake was leaving, and she hadn't accepted that. *Couldn't* accept it. Not yet.

The bacon grease was sizzling in the frying pan when Blake cracked two eggs against the side and let them slide into the hot fat. With the dexterity of an accomplished chef he flipped down the toaster switch.

"Hey, I didn't realize you were that skilled in the kitchen," Caasi murmured, uneasy with the fact that he could cook and she couldn't.

"Practice makes perfect, and I've cooked plenty of solitary meals in my time," he said as he slid the fried eggs onto a plate. He set the meal in front of her and straddled a chair, drinking his coffee while she ate.

Everything was delicious and she said as much. "I don't remember a time I've enjoyed a meal more." At his skeptical look, Caasi laughed and crossed her heart with her finger. "Honest."

"Then I suggest you have a talk with that expensive chef you imported."

Blake had never approved of her hiring the Frenchman who ran the Empress kitchen.

"I'd be willing to do away with the whole kitchen staff if you'd agree to stay."

Forcefully Blake expelled his breath, and Caasi realized that she'd done it again.

Lowering her gaze to the empty plate, she tore a piece of crust from her toast. "That was a dumb joke. I didn't mean it." For once, just tonight, when she was so happy, she didn't want to say or do anything that would start a disagreement.

"Didn't you?" he asked in a low, troubled voice.

Caasi peered at him through thick lashes. "Well, it's true I don't want you to go, but my reasons are entirely selfish."

"You don't need me anymore."

Oh dear heaven, if only he knew. "I guess not," she agreed reluctantly, "but you've always been there, and it won't be the same when you're gone."

"Sure it will."

How could he sound so casual about leaving the place that had been his second home for eight years? Apparently she didn't mean much to him. Instead of seeking answers to the nagging doubts, Caasi scooted out of her chair and stood.

"I'll do the dishes. Anyone who does the cooking shouldn't have to do the dishes."

"Caasi Crane doing dishes," Blake said mockingly. "This I've got to see."

"Well, just who do you think did them the night we baked the quiche?" she declared righteously. "I am a capable person, Blake, whether you care to admit it or not."

She washed while he dried and put away. Wordlessly they worked together, but it wasn't a strained silence.

When they finished, Caasi noted that it was very

late…they both had to be at work in the morning. There wasn't any reason to stay, but she didn't want to go.

"I suppose I should think about heading back," she murmured as she dried her hands on a kitchen towel.

Blake agreed with a curt nod, but he didn't look as though he wanted her to leave either.

Caasi glanced at the oil painting over the fireplace. "Have you done any artwork lately?" Maybe some small talk would delay her departure.

"Not much to speak of." He shrugged his shoulders. "I'm thinking about concentrating more on my painting after the first of the month."

After the first—when he would no longer be at the Empress and wouldn't be troubled with her anymore.

"Let me know; I'd like to buy something from you."

Blake laughed outright. "I only dabble in art. The Empress displays paintings from some of the best in the country. Those artists would be insulted to have my work hanging beside theirs."

Caasi hadn't been thinking of hanging it in the hotel, but in her suite. It would give her something tangible to remember him by. But rather than admit it, she said nothing.

"We did it," Caasi murmured as they strolled toward her car.

"Did what?"

"Went the whole night, or at least a portion of it, without fighting. That's a record, I think."

"You mentioned my resignation only once."

"I won't admit how many times I've had to bite my tongue," Caasi teased.

"Is my leaving that difficult for you to accept?"

Blake leaned against the front of her car and folded his arms across his chest.

Caasi shrugged both delicate shoulders. "Yes," she admitted starkly. "But I'm beginning to understand how selfish I'm being toward you. There's something about having you with me.... I trust you, Blake—sometimes more than I do myself. Looking back, I can see the mistakes I've made in my enthusiasm to live up to Dad's expectations. I allowed Crane Enterprises to become everything to me."

For a long second he looked at her. "But not anymore?"

"I don't know," she admitted honestly. "But I'd do anything if you'd change your mind."

Indecision flickered in his narrowed gaze. "You're handing me a powerful weapon; you know that, don't you, Caasi?"

"You're worth it."

"To Crane Enterprises?"

She nodded. "And me," she told him softly.

He was silent for so long that Caasi wasn't sure if he'd heard her.

"Let me think about it," Blake said. Looking away, he took a deep breath, as if struggling within himself.

"How soon before you can give me an answer?" Her heart was beating double time. If Blake stayed she would have the opportunity to explore the relationship that was developing between them. The thought of losing him now—just when she was discovering Blake, the man—was intolerable.

"I'll let you know by the first of the week."

"Great," Caasi agreed. At least there was a chance.

Seven

Monday morning Caasi strolled into the outer office and greeted her secretary with a cheerful, "Good morning."

Laurie glanced up. A frown drove deep grooves into her wide brow. "Good morning, Miss Crane."

Caasi was sure Laurie didn't know what to think of her anymore. Her secretary probably attributed the wide swings in her moods to Blake's resignation. Not immune to office gossip, Caasi was aware that there was heavy speculation as to his reasons.

Today she would know his decision. How could he refuse her after all that they'd shared recently? How could he walk away from her on a day as gorgeous and sunny as this one? He wouldn't, Caasi was sure of it.

In her office, she buzzed the intercom. "Laurie, would you ask Mr. Sherrill to come to my office when he arrives?"

"I think he's in now."

"Good."

Caasi released the switch and sauntered to the far side of the room. So much had changed between her and Blake in such a short time. Mostly there was Blake to thank for that. And he'd see that she was changing and that would be all the incentive he'd need to stay.

Friday she'd watched him, studied his body language as well as his speech. He didn't want to leave, she was sure of it. Her father had warned her of the hazards of being overconfident, but she didn't feel the necessity to heed his counsel this morning. Not this glorious morning.

Caasi had spent Sunday with June, Burt, and baby Cassi. June had come home from the hospital, and while Burt had fussed over his wife, Caasi had sat and held the baby. Cradling the tiny being in her arms had filled her heart with love. This was what it meant to be a woman, whole and complete. The overwhelming tenderness she'd experienced holding the baby lingered even now, a day later.

Sunday night Caasi had lain awake staring at the ceiling, unable to sleep. So much depended on Blake's decision. Her father had taught her to hope for the best but plan for the worst. She'd asked herself over and over again what would change if Blake decided to leave. Ultimately nothing. Brian Harris seemed capable enough of assuming Blake's duties.

But losing Blake the man would be more than Caasi could bear. Not now, not when she was just coming into her own. Surely he'd see the changes in her and withdraw his resignation.

"Good morning," Blake said as he entered the room. "You wanted to see me?"

"Yes." Caasi nodded, standing at her desk. One look at Blake and a nauseous feeling attacked her stomach. He looked terrible. "Blake, are you ill?"

"No," he denied with an abrupt shake of his head. "I suspect you want to hear my decision."

"Of course I do," she said somewhat sharply. What she wanted to do was scream at him to say what she needed to hear: the promise that he'd never leave her, that he'd stay with her all her life.

Blake rubbed a hand over his eyes. "This decision hasn't been easy," he said softly.

"I know," she whispered in return. *Dear God,* her mind screamed, *don't let him leave me.*

"I can't stay, Cupcake."

Caasi slumped into her chair, fighting to disguise the effect of his decision by squaring her shoulders and clamping her hands together in her lap. "Why?"

Blake lowered himself into the chair on the other side of her desk. "Not for the same reasons I originally resigned," he explained.

"I see," Caasi replied stiffly. "In other words—"

"In other words," Blake interrupted, "things have changed between us."

"For the better," she inserted, not easily dissuaded. "I've tried so hard."

"Too hard, Cupcake."

Caasi couldn't respond as the continued waves of disappointment rippled over her.

"In light of my decision, maybe it would be best if Brian Harris accompanied you tomorrow."

Somehow, with a determined effort, Caasi managed to nod.

"My last day is Wednesday, but if you think you'd like me to stay a few more days…"

"No," she whispered. "No," she repeated softly, a bit

more in control of her voice now. "If you've made your decision, then don't prolong the inevitable."

"You're beginning to sound like your father again."

"Again?" Caasi asked with a dry smile. "I've always sounded like Dad. Why shouldn't I? After all, I am his daughter."

"Caasi…" Blake sounded unsure.

"If you'll excuse me, I've got a meeting to attend." She spoke crisply and centered her gaze just past him on the seascape hanging on the wall.

The door clicked and Caasi realized that Blake had left. Taking deep breaths helped to calm her pounding heart. She was stunned, completely and totally shocked.

"Laurie." Her hand was surprisingly steady as she held down the intercom switch. "Do I have anything pressing this morning?"

Her secretary ran down a list of appointments.

"Would you reschedule them at a more convenient time, please? I'm going out for a while."

"Going out?" Laurie repeated disbelievingly. "But there's the meeting with Jefferson at nine."

"I'll be here for that, but cancel everything else."

"The whole day?"

"No." Caasi pressed a hand to her forehead. She was overreacting. She had to come to grips with herself. "Just this morning."

An hour later Caasi couldn't have repeated one word of the meeting with Jefferson. The accountant seemed to be aware of her lack of attention and called their time short. Caasi didn't return to her office but went directly to the parking garage and took out her Mercedes.

The drive to the Lloyd Center was accomplished in only a matter of minutes. Leaving her car in the underground parking garage, she took the escalator to the second-floor shopping level. Standing at the rail, she looked down at the ice-skating rink situated in the middle of the huge complex.

A sad smile touched her eyes as she watched the figures circle the silvery ice. Most of the skaters were senior citizens, loving couples with their arms around one another as they skillfully glided around the rink. Thirty years from now she could picture June and Burt skating like that. Thirty years from now and she would remain an observer, standing on the outside of life— exactly as she was now.

In the mood to spend money, Caasi went from store to store, buying whatever took her fancy. She bought baby Cassi enough clothes to see her into grade school. She also bought toys, blankets, shoes—whatever attracted her attention. Caasi held up one frilly outfit after another and understood why June had wanted a baby girl.

Returning to the hotel garage, she left instructions for the packages to be taken to her quarters. The last thing she needed was for Blake to see what she'd bought and accuse her of buying herself another family.

Laurie glanced up and smiled when Caasi stepped into the outer office.

"Happy Monday," Caasi said and handed her secretary a small box.

"What's this for?" Laurie pulled the gold elastic ribbon off the box.

"Just a thank you for rearranging the day."

Her announcement was followed by a short gasp of pleasure from Laurie. "Chocolates from How Sweet It Is. But they're fifty dollars a pound."

"You deserve only the best."

For the first time in years, Laurie looked completely flustered. "Thank you, Miss Crane."

"Thank *you,* Laurie," Caasi stated sincerely.

The stack of phone messages was thick. Caasi shuffled through them and paused at the one from Dirk Evans from The International Hotel chain. He'd phoned several times in the past few years, eager to talk to her about acquiring the Empress. International was interested not only in the Portland Empress but also in several others in California and along the Oregon coast.

She stared at the pink slip for several moments while pacing the floor. Pausing at the window, she examined her options. Her father would turn over in his grave if she were to sell. But why did she need the hotels? Why did she need any of this? Even without the hotels she was a wealthy woman. No, the thought of unburdening herself was tempting at the moment, but the Empress was her family, the only family she'd ever known, the only family she would ever know. She couldn't throw that away, not on a whim.

Laurie buzzed and broke into her thoughts. "Call from Edie Albright on line one."

"Thanks, Laurie." Caasi released one button and pushed down another. "Edie, how are you?"

"Fine."

"You don't sound fine. What's wrong?"

"Freddy's in New York and I'm bored. I don't suppose you'd be interested in dinner with me tonight? Nothing fancy. I could come to the Empress if you'd like."

"I'd like it very much. I'm feeling a little down myself." That was a gross understatement, but if she admitted as much they'd both be crying in their salads.

"Great." Edie cheered up immediately. "What time?"

"Any time you like."

Edie paused. "My goodness, you're accommodating today. I expected an argument at the very least. You don't go out that often."

Caasi smiled drily. "And how would you know that?"

"Honestly, Caasi, June and I are your best friends. We know you."

"Apparently not well enough," Caasi couldn't resist adding. "I'll meet you at seven in the main dining room."

"Wonderful. You don't know how much I appreciate this," Edie said with a sigh. "I've got lots to tell you. This pregnancy stuff isn't all it's cracked up to be."

Caasi replaced the receiver a few minutes later and stared into space a while longer. Seeing Edie that night was just what she needed. Her friend, scheming and crazy, had a refreshing way of helping her see the bright side of things. And she'd need a lot of talking to see the pot of gold at the end of the rainbow as far as Blake's leaving was concerned.

The afternoon passed in a whirl of appointments and phone calls. By six Laurie had left, and although there were several items on Caasi's desk that needed her immediate attention, she decided to deal with them Wednesday. The next day she'd be flying to Seaside with Brian Harris to meet with the architects. The time spent with Harris would help her become acquainted with the man. They'd be working closely in the future, and there was no reason to delay knowing one another.

No reason, her mind repeated, and a curious pain attacked her heart.

Wednesday would be Blake's last day. As she pushed the elevator button, Caasi wondered how or where she would get the courage to relinquish him as unemotionally as possible.

Her living room was filled with packages from that morning's shopping spree. Caasi decided to ignore them until after her bath. She didn't want to keep Edie waiting.

The bathwater was running when there was an abrupt knock on her door.

Caasi wasn't sure it was someone at her door until the sound was repeated. "Just a minute," she called and hurried to turn off the water. She was grateful that she hadn't completely undressed. Grabbing a housecoat, she tied the sash as she walked across the living room carpet.

"I thought I said seven in the dining room," Caasi murmured good-naturedly as she opened the door. Her jaw must have sagged.

"Can I come in?" Blake looked at her, his eyes sparkling with amusement as he surveyed her appearance.

"I... I'm not dressed for visitors," Caasi stammered, her heart pounding wildly.

"Get dressed then, if it'll make you feel more comfortable."

Numbly, she stepped aside, swinging open the door.

"I'll only take a minute of your time," Blake promised with a half smile.

"I think I'd prefer to be dressed even if it is only for a minute," she said. Naturally she was curious as to why he'd come. She wasn't ready to deal with him. Not that night, not after he'd announced his decision. "If you'll excuse me." She turned around and nearly choked. The packages from her shopping spree covered the sofa and chair. She closed her eyes and groaned inwardly. The only thing she could do was ignore them now. If she called Blake's attention to the parcels and boxes that covered the sofa it would only invite comment.

Her fingers shook as she hurriedly donned her blouse, fumbling with the tiny buttons. Stuffing the silk tails into her skirt, she returned to the living room.

"Yes," she said crisply. "What is it?"

Blake turned around with a slightly guilty look. "I'd say this is a little small, wouldn't you?" He held up one of the dresses she'd purchased for June's baby.

"It's not for me," she said stiffly, refusing to meet his laughing eyes.

"I'd guessed as much," he returned seriously. "Is all this for little Cassi?"

Caasi jerked the dress out of his hands and stuffed it back into its paper sack. "That's none of your business," she told him. "And don't you dare…" She paused to inhale a quivering breath. "Don't you *dare* say I'm buying myself a family."

"You *are* their family, Cupcake," Blake said gently.

Caasi jerked her face up and their eyes met. His were warm and oddly indulgent. She wanted to yell at him not to look at her like that. How could he do this when only hours before, he'd told her he wanted nothing more to do with her or the Empress. He was the one who wanted out, not her. Heaven knew she didn't want him to go.

Abruptly, Caasi turned away. "Was there something you wanted to tell me?" she asked in a clipped, businesslike tone.

"Yes." Blake walked to the other side of the room and ran his hand through his hair. "Harris won't be able to go with you tomorrow. His son's involved in a high-school championship baseball game. So it looks like you're stuck with me for one last trip."

Terrific, her mind threw out sarcastically.

Some of her thoughts must have shown in her expression. "Don't look so pleased," Blake chided. "We'll be back by afternoon. I assume after all these years that we can manage to get along for a few hours."

"Sure." The word nearly stuck in her throat, then came out sounding scratchy and weak. "Why not?"

"You tell me," Blake said in a low voice.

Caasi pivoted sharply and walked to her favorite place by the window. "No reason," she said and shrugged her shoulders.

"I'll see you in the morning, then."

Without turning around, she answered, "It looks that way." She stood poised, waiting for the click of the door. When it didn't come, she turned to find Blake watching her.

"Caasi?"

"Was there something else?" she asked politely.

His searching eyes narrowed on her, and Caasi had the impression he wanted to say something more. "No." He shook his head. "I'll see you tomorrow."

"Fine."

Edie was already seated in the dining room when Caasi arrived. Caasi returned her small wave as she entered the room.

"You look positively…" Edie paused and sighed longingly. *"Skinny."*

Caasi laughed. "You always did have a smooth tongue."

"The only reason I'm so candid is that for every ounce you've lost, I've gained three." Elbows on the table, Edie leaned forward. "I'm telling you, Caasi, I'm going crazy."

"What's wrong?" Edie had always been the dramatic one, so Caasi wasn't overly concerned.

"Well, for one thing, I can't stop eating peanut butter. I woke up at two this morning and ate it straight out of the jar. Freddy couldn't believe it and for that matter neither could I."

"At least peanut butter is a high source of protein."

Edie groaned and closed her eyes. "That's what Freddy keeps telling me."

"Why the worry?"

"My dear Caasi, have you any idea how fattening peanut butter is?"

"I haven't checked out any calorie counters lately," Caasi responded and fought to hide the smile that teased the corners of her mouth.

"Well, it's fattening, believe me. The shocking thing is I've hated the stuff since I was a kid."

"There are worse things." Caasi attempted to soothe a few of Edie's doubts.

"Okay," Edie agreed and took a sip from her cocktail. "Listen to *this*. I was watching the Blazers play basketball the other night. The center missed two free throws at the foul line and all of a sudden tears welled in my eyes and I started crying. Not just a few silent tears, but gigantic sobs. Freddy didn't know what to think. He was finishing up a report in his den and came rushing in. I'm sure he thought the telecast had been interrupted and someone had just announced that my mother had died or something."

The small laugh could no longer be contained. "Listen, Edie, I'm no expert on the subject, but isn't this all part of being pregnant?"

"Dear sweet heaven, I hope so," Edie said fervently.

"Have you talked to June? She'd probably be more help than me."

"June," Edie repeated and shook her head dramatically. "You know June; she's the salt of the earth. The entire time she was pregnant she acted as if she was in heaven. June's the kind of woman who would deliver her baby and go back to work in the fields an hour later. *I'm* going to need six months' rest on the Riviera to recover."

The maître d' handed them the menu and gave Caasi a polite nod of recognition.

Edie opened the menu, took one look, moaned, and folded it closed.

"What's the matter?" Caasi asked.

"I was afraid this would happen. Everything looks divine. I want the first four entrées and chocolate mousse for dessert."

"Edie!" Caasi couldn't prevent her small gasp of shock. Of the three, Edie had always been the most weight-conscious.

"I can't help it," Edie hissed.

"If you eat that much, *I'll* get sick."

"All right, all right," Edie said, "you choose for me. I don't trust myself."

The waiter took their order and filled their water glasses.

"Enough about me." Edie took a sip from the steaming cup. "I want to hear what's been going on in your life. I don't suppose you've picked up any tall, dark, handsome men lately, have you?"

Caasi shrugged and looked away uncomfortably. "Not recently. You know I went into the delivery room with June and Burt, don't you?"

"Don't tell me a thing about it. I don't want to hear." Edie shook her head and squinted her eyes closed.

"It was one of the most beautiful experiences of my life," Caasi reminisced softly.

"Sure—it wasn't *you* going through all that pain."

Caasi didn't bother to try to explain. Edie wouldn't understand. At least, not until her own baby was delivered.

"Have you had any thoughts about what I was saying the last time we were together?" At Caasi's blank look, Edie continued, "You know, about having an affair and maybe getting pregnant yourself?"

Caasi nearly choked on her coffee. "Edie, I wish you wouldn't talk like that."

"Maybe not, but it's what you need. I bet you've lost five pounds since the last time I saw you. Believe me when I tell you a man can do wonders."

"Maybe," Caasi conceded, feeling the color seep up her neck.

"I take it that it didn't work out with the hunk you met here the last time?"

Caasi's hands surrounded her glass of water. She stared at the melting ice and felt the cold move up her arm and stop directly at her heart. "No. It didn't work out."

"It was only your first try, so don't let it discourage you. Would you like me to pick out someone else?"

"No," Caasi returned forcefully. "I'm perfectly capable of finding a man myself. If I want one."

"If?"

Their dinner arrived, and thankfully Caasi was able to steer the conversation from Edie's questions to the light banter they normally enjoyed.

After their dinner they decided to visit the lounge although Edie wouldn't drink. The same piano player was at the keyboard and a fresh crowd was gathered around the bar.

The cocktail waitress brought Caasi a drink and Edie cranberry juice. They sat listening to the mellow sounds of a love song.

"Hey," Edie whispered excitedly. "Don't turn around now, but guess who just came in!"

"Who? The Easter Bunny?"

"No," Edie remarked seriously. Her eyes didn't waver. "Mr. Incredible."

"Who?" Caasi whispered.

"The same guy who was here the other night. You remember—you've got to," Edie admonished, her voice dipping incredulously.

Caasi moved her chair so that she could look at the newcomer. She didn't need a second guess to know it was Blake.

Edie's eyes widened appreciatively. "He really is something, isn't he?"

"If you go for that type," Caasi replied with a flippancy she wasn't feeling.

"He's everyone's type," Edie said without taking her eyes off Blake. "Did you notice how every woman here perked up the minute he walked in?"

Caasi certainly had. Her stomach felt as if a hole was

being seared through it. The burning sensation didn't lessen when a tall, attractive blonde slid onto the empty stool beside Blake. Caasi's eyes narrowed as the woman leaned close and whispered something to Blake.

"Watch," Edie advised. "This blonde knows what she's doing. You might be able to pick up a few pointers."

Caasi smiled weakly, her fingers linked into a hard fist in her lap. For one crazy moment she felt like screaming in outrage. Blake was hers! But he wasn't, not really—he had made that clear that morning. Rather than watch the exchange between the two, she lowered her gaze to her fruity drink.

"Well, I'll be," Edie murmured unbelievingly.

"What?" Caasi demanded.

"Weren't you watching?"

"No," Caasi whispered, her voice shaking.

"As slick as a whistle, Mr. Incredible gave the blonde the brush-off. I wouldn't have believed it. This fellow is one tough character. Little wonder you didn't have any luck."

"Little wonder," Caasi repeated.

Edie continued to study Blake. "You know, just watching Mr. Incredible I'm getting the distinct impression he's hurting."

"Hurting?" Caasi asked and swallowed tightly.

"Yes. Look at the way he's leaning against the counter. See the way his elbows are positioned? He doesn't want to be disturbed and his body is saying as much, discouraging anyone from joining him."

"Why doesn't he just sit at a table?" Caasi whispered, revealing her curiosity.

"Because that would be an open invitation for company. No, this man wants to be left alone."

"Just because he wants his own company doesn't mean he's eating his heart out."

Thoughtfully, Edie shook her head. "That's true. But he's troubled. Look at the way he's hunched over his drink. He looks as if he's lost his best friend."

Caasi felt Edie's slow appraisal turn to her. "So do you, for that matter."

"So do I—what?" Caasi feigned ignorance on a falsely cheerful note.

"Never mind," Edie murmured thoughtfully.

"I was looking through some travel brochures the other day…." Caasi quickly changed the subject before Edie managed to stumble onto something she could only escape by blatantly lying. "Do you realize I haven't had a vacation, a *real* vacation," she amended, "in over five years? I was thinking of a cruise."

"I'll believe it when I see it." Edie tilted her chin mockingly. "You wouldn't know what to do with yourself with empty time on your hands."

"Sure I would," Caasi argued. "I'd take a few classes. I've always wanted to learn how to do calligraphy. And get back to reading. I bet there are a hundred books I haven't had time to read in the last five years. They're stacked to the ceiling in my bedroom just waiting for me. I'd bake, and learn how to sew, and volunteer some time at the local—" She stopped abruptly at the peculiar look Edie was giving her.

"I can't believe this is Caasi Crane speaking!" Edie looked shocked.

Caasi laughed, hoping to make light of her own enthusiasm and squelch Edie's growing curiosity. "It's been on my mind a lot, that's all."

"What's been on your mind?" Edie asked. "Those weren't things you'd do on vacation. They're things an everyday housewife does."

"A housewife?" She gave Edie a surprised look. "And what's wrong with a housewife and mother?"

"Nothing." Edie was quick to amend her attitude. "Heavens, June's one, and I'll be one shortly. Think about it, Caasi. You, a housewife? A baby on each hip, diapers that need to be changed with dinner boiling on top of the stove. Can you picture yourself in that scene?"

Caasi pressed her mouth tightly closed. She longed to cry out that she'd never wanted anything more. If she could run ten hotels effectively, she could manage a single home. The only condition her mind demanded was that Blake share that loving picture with her.

Her eyes drifted across the room to the dejected figure sitting at the bar. It took everything within her not to go to him. But she couldn't see that it would do any good. She'd bared her heart and he'd rejected her. Just remembering the shock she'd felt at hearing his decision caused her to bite into her bottom lip.

"Caasi?" Edie's soft voice broke into her musings.

Gently Caasi shook her head. "Sorry." She turned her attention back to Edie. "What were you saying?"

Edie's attention was focused in the direction of the bar. "Look who's coming our way," she whispered in shocked disbelief.

Blake strolled to their table and nodded politely at Edie. "We didn't set a time for tomorrow morning. Is eight too early?"

"Fine." Caasi managed to answer with some difficulty.

"I'll see you then."

Edie looked stunned as Blake turned and walked away. "All right, Caasi Crane," she whispered in a shocked voice, "you've got some explaining to do."

Eight

The whirling blades of the helicopter stirred the early morning air. With her purse clutched under her arm and her head bowed, Caasi rushed across the landing pad. Blake supported her elbow as she climbed aboard.

The volume of swirling sound made conversation impossible, which was just as well. There was little Caasi had to say to Blake. Not anymore. A week before, even less, she would have been excited about this trip with him. It would have been a chance to talk, another opportunity to learn more about this man who had been invaluable to her for the past several years. Now it would be torture to sit beside him and know that the next day he would be walking out of her life.

"Caasi."

Blake's hand against her forearm recalled her from her musings.

"It's not too late. We can make the drive in less than—"

"No," she interrupted him and, closing her eyes, leaned her head back against the seat cushion. When they'd met at eight that morning, the first thing Blake had done was propose that they drive instead of taking the helicopter. Caasi couldn't understand why he would make such a suggestion. He wasn't any more eager to spend time alone with her than she was to endure the stilted silence that would have existed in the comparative quiet of a car.

When they didn't take off immediately, Caasi opened her eyes and noted that Blake was talking to the pilot. A frown creased his brow before he nodded abruptly and climbed back aboard.

"Is everything all right?" she asked.

"Nothing to worry about," Blake assured her.

A wobbly sensation attacked her stomach as the helicopter rose. To hide her anxiety, Caasi clenched her hands, closed her eyes, and turned her head as if she were gazing out the window.

Blake placed his hand over hers; Caasi sat up and shook her hand free. She didn't want his comfort or assurance or anything else. The day was torture. If he was going to get out of her life, then he should go. Why prolong the agony?

They didn't say a word as Portland disappeared. A small smile flickered across Caasi's face at the memory of Edie's reaction when Blake had stopped at their table the night before. Her friend had been stunned speechless. Caasi couldn't remember a time in all the years they'd known each other that Edie didn't have an immediate comeback.

"You sly fox," Edie had gasped a full minute after Blake had sauntered away from the table.

"Don't get excited," Caasi returned with a nervous smile. "Blake works for me. He's been around for eight years."

Edie shook her head in disbelief. "You have worked with that hunk all these years?"

"His last day is Wednesday." Something in Caasi's voice must have revealed the pain she felt at the thought.

Edie's look was thoughtful. "I noticed something was different almost from the moment you came into the dining room tonight. At first I was sure I was imagining things. Somehow, you're…softer. It's in your eyes, even in the way you walk, if that's possible. You have, my dear, dear Caasi, the look of a woman in love."

Caasi tried to laugh off Edie's announcement. "Who, me?"

"Yes, you!" Edie declared adamantly. "Now tell me, why is Blake leaving?"

Sadly Caasi shook her head. "I don't know. I've tried everything I know to convince him to stay."

"Everything?"

Hot color suffused Caasi's face and she lowered her gaze, unable to meet Edie's probing eyes. "It wouldn't do any good. Blake's mind is set."

"Is there any chance of you two getting together?"

Caasi shook her head, unable to answer with words. A terrible sadness settled over her heart. The pain was as potent as it had been at her father's death. In some ways, the hurt was the same. Blake would be lost to her. Just as she would never have her father again, she would never have Blake.

"What about your baby hunger?" Edie asked.

"My what?" Caasi jerked her head up.

"The last time we were together we talked about you and a baby, don't you remember?"

"Yes, but a baby usually requires a father."

Edie gave a sophisticated shrug. "Not always. You're

a successful career woman. You're strong, independent, and financially capable. Any child would be lucky to have you as a mother."

"I can't believe what I'm hearing." Caasi gripped her hands in her lap so that Edie wouldn't see how her fingers were trembling. "You're not really suggesting I get pregnant with Blake's child?"

"Of course I am. He's leaving, isn't he? You want a baby, not a husband. As far as I can see, the setup is perfect."

Even now, with Blake sitting beside her, Caasi couldn't help shaking her head in disbelief at her friend's suggestion. Sometimes it was astonishing that two women so completely different could be such good friends.

An hour later, with a cup of coffee in front of her, Caasi reviewed the architects' plans. The piece of beach was prime property, and Caasi realized how fortunate she was to have obtained it. No, she had Blake to thank for that. He was the one who had handled the negotiations.

Seaside was a tourist town. The economy depended on the business of travelers. With only a few weeks left until summer and a flux of vacationers, the community was preparing for the seasonal traffic.

The morning passed quickly. Leaving the architects' office, Caasi donned a hard hat and visited the building site. Everything was ahead of schedule; where she had pitched a shovelful of dirt only a few weeks before now stood the empty shell of the latest Empress Hotel.

Caasi walked around, examining each area. Once she would have experienced an intense satisfaction at the venture; now she was surprised to feel nothing. The lack of emotion shocked her. What did she care if there were ten or a hundred Empress Hotels? Would breaking ground for another hotel bring her happiness? Perhaps at one time it would have. But no longer. Blake was responsible for that. He was responsible for a lot of things.

Her smile felt frozen as she entered the restaurant where the chamber of commerce was holding its luncheon.

After they ate, Caasi stood before the group and spoke a few introductory words before turning the presentation over to Blake. As he was talking, Caasi observed the way the men in the room responded to him. In some ways their reactions were like those of the women in the cocktail lounge the night before. Blake was a man's man. The magnetism about him defied barriers.

Caasi's fingers were tender from all the handshaking she'd done by the time they returned to the copter. The pilot, a middle-aged man with a receding hairline, removed his hat as they approached. He shook his head, seeking Blake's eyes.

"Is something wrong?" Caasi asked Blake.

"I don't know, but I'll find out."

Blake and the pilot talked for several minutes and when Blake returned, his jaw was tight, his look disturbed.

"Well?"

"There's something wrong with the chopper. Dick noticed that one of the gauges was malfunctioning when he revved it up this morning. That was why I suggested we drive."

Caasi closed her mouth tightly to bite back bitter words. Blake hadn't been eager for her company that morning. Had she been fooling herself with the belief that he would have enjoyed an intimate drive from Portland?

"How long will it take to check it out?"

"An hour, two at the most."

Unwilling to spend an extra minute in Blake's company, Caasi announced, "I'll wait for you on the beach, then."

Blake didn't acknowledge her as she turned and walked the block or so to the ocean.

Wind whipped her hair about her face as she stood looking out over the pounding surf.

A flight of concrete stairs led to the beach. Caasi walked down to the sand, removed her heels, and strolled toward the water until her nylons felt the moisture.

Once, when she was a little girl, her father had taken her to the ocean. A business trip, Caasi was sure. Very little in Isaac Crane's life had been done for pleasure. Caasi could recall vividly how the thundering surf had frightened her and how she'd clung to her father's leg.

Funny, Caasi mused, she hadn't thought about that in years. She couldn't have been more than two, maybe three, at the time. The incident was her earliest memory.

Swinging her high heels in her hands, Caasi walked for what seemed like miles, enjoying the solitude, the fresh, salt-scented air, and the peace that came over her. Blake would go and she'd hurt for a time, suffer through the regrets for the love they could have shared. But the time would come when that, too, would pass. And she'd be better for having loved him.

When she turned around to return to the street, she noticed Blake standing at the top of the concrete steps watching her. He was a solitary figure silhouetted against the bright sun, hands in his pockets and at ease with the world. That disturbed her somehow. He was leaving her without a second thought, without regrets, without looking back.

As she neared the steps, Blake came down to meet her. "I just talked to Dick."

"And?" she prompted.

"The problem is more extensive than he thought. It looks as if we'll have to spend the night."

"Spend the night?" she cried in frustration. "I won't do that."

"There isn't much choice," Blake returned with limited patience.

"Rent a car. And if you can't do that, then buy one! I'm not spending the night here."

"Caasi." Blake drew in a slow, angry breath.

"You're still my employee," she said bitterly and glanced at her watch. "For another twenty-three and a half hours I expect you to do what I ask. After that, I don't care what you do."

Caasi regretted the words the minute they slipped out. She watched Blake's struggle to hide his anger. His fists knotted at his sides until his knuckles were white.

"I didn't mean that," she said in a low voice and released her breath slowly. "Make what arrangements you can. I'll phone Laurie and answer any necessary calls from here."

Fifteen minutes later Caasi walked across her hotel room, carrying her cell with her as she spoke. A knock on her door interrupted the conversation.

"Could you hold a minute, Laurie?" she asked before

unlocking the door and letting Blake into the rented quarters.

"It's Blake," she said into the receiver. "I'll give you a call in the morning before we leave." She hung up and turned to him. "Yes?"

"I thought you might need a few things." He handed her a small sack that contained a toothbrush and toothpaste.

"Thanks." She smiled her appreciation. "But what I could really use is a good martini."

"Dry, of course."

"Very dry," Caasi agreed.

The cocktail lounge was deserted; it was too early for the predinner crowd and too late for the business-luncheon group.

It amazed Caasi that they could sit companionably at a minuscule table and not say a word. It was almost as if they were an old married couple who no longer needed words to communicate. Caasi focused her attention on the ocean scene outside the window. The view was lovely, but she had seen so much breathtaking scenery in her life. That day it failed to stir the familiar chord of appreciation.

Without asking, Blake ordered another round of martinis for them. Slowly, Caasi sipped her drink. The bitter liquid seared its way down her throat. The lounge was quickly filling now; after two martinis Caasi could feel the coiled tension ease out of her.

"Are you ready for dinner?" Blake asked.

"Sure," she agreed readily, "why not?"

His hand cupped her elbow as he escorted her into the dining room. The food was good, though not excellent.

"I should have Chef share some of his recipes," Caasi remarked as she set her fork aside.

"You and that chef. I don't know when I was more upset with you than when you imported him."

Caasi's smile didn't quite reach her eyes. "Oh, I can tell you. Several times you've looked as if you wanted to wring my neck, all within the last couple of weeks too."

Blake's expression was weary and he conceded her observation with a short shake of his head.

The soulful sounds of a singer drifted into the dining room from the lounge.

"Shall we?" Blake asked softly.

Caasi couldn't find an excuse to refuse. All there was to do in her room was watch television. "All right," she agreed, somewhat reluctantly. When they reentered the lounge, she saw that a few couples occupied the tiny dance floor, which was little bigger than a tabletop.

They sat for a long time, so close their thighs touched, listening to the music and not speaking. For the first time Caasi admitted to herself how glad she was that the helicopter needed work. The repairs afforded her this last chance to be with Blake. She didn't speak for a long time, fearing words would destroy the moment.

"Caasi."

Their eyes met and she drew a shaky breath at the intensity of his look.

"Dance with me, Blake," she whispered urgently. "Hold me one last time."

He answered her by standing and giving her his hand. They didn't take their eyes from one another as Caasi slid her arms around his neck, her body's movement joining his in a rhythm that was uniquely theirs.

His fingers were pressed against the small of her

back as he molded her body to him. His mouth was mere inches from hers as his warm breath fanned her cheek.

The music stopped—but they didn't. If Blake released her now, she'd die, Caasi mused.

She released an uneven breath when the singer began again. A love song. Caasi bit into the corner of her bottom lip and sighed. Tomorrow Blake would go—but for tonight he was hers.

Caasi lost track of how long Blake held her, how many songs they danced to, barely moving, oblivious to the world surrounding them.

When the music stopped, Caasi led the way off the dance floor, but instead of stopping at their table she continued out of the lounge and down the wide hall to their rooms, which were opposite one another.

Her hands shook as she inserted the key and opened the door to her room. It was dark and silent.

Blake's dark eyes bored into hers as she stepped inside the room and extended her hand to him. A look of indecision passed across his face. Caasi's eyes pleaded with him, and gradually the expression on his face softened as his look became potent enough for her to drown in.

He took one step inside and Caasi released a deep sigh of relief. He couldn't turn away from her. Not now. Not tonight.

She slid her arms around his neck and stood on the tips of her toes as she melted against him.

He groaned her name, reaching out to close the door as she fit her body to his.

She wouldn't let him talk, her open mouth seeking his. He hadn't kissed her in so long, so very long.

"Caasi." He groaned, repeatedly rubbing his mouth

over hers. "You don't know what you're doing." His voice was husky and hungry.

"I do," she insisted in a low murmur. "Oh, Blake, I do."

Again and again his mouth cherished hers, eager, hungry, seeking, demanding, giving, taking. The soft, gentle sounds of their lovemaking filled the silence. They whispered phrases of awe as passion took control of their bodies.

Caasi paused long enough to tug the shirt free at Blake's waist. Her eager fingers fumbled with the buttons until she could slip her palms over his chest. The sensations were so exquisite she wanted to cry.

"Caasi, no," Blake whispered gruffly. "Not now, not like this." The shirt fell to the floor.

"Yes, like this," she pleaded. "Only tonight, it's all I want." She felt the tears well in her eyes. Her body trembled wildly against his, and Blake released an anguished groan as he swung her off her feet and carried her across the room.

Caasi wanted him so desperately, she could no longer think. Pressing her face to his neck, she gave him tiny, biting kisses and felt his shudder as he laid her on the bed.

Her arms around his neck, Caasi refused to release him, half lifting herself as she kissed him long and hard, her mouth slanting under his.

His eyes looked tortured in the golden glow of the moon as he pulled her arms from his neck. "Caasi," he whispered in a voice she hardly recognized. "Are you drunk? Is this the liquor?"

"Yes, I'm drunk," she whispered, "but not from the martinis. You do this to me, Blake. Only you."

"This isn't the way I wanted it, but heaven knows I haven't got the strength to let you go," he murmured, his lips above hers. His hands ran down her smooth body, exploring, touching, until Caasi was sure she would die if he didn't take her. She arched against him and sighed with a longing so intense that it sounded like a mournful cry.

Impatiently he worked at her clothing, freeing her from the constricting material. The feel of his hands against her bare skin was an exquisite torture.

"Tonight," she whispered in a quivering breath. "For tonight, I'm yours."

"Yes," he agreed, his mouth seeking hers again.

"I'm freeing you from any...consequences." She stammered slightly.

He froze. For a moment he didn't even breathe. "You're what?" He sat up, holding her away from him, a rough hand against each bare shoulder.

"I'm freeing you from any responsibility," she murmured, confused. What had she said that upset him so much? Wasn't that something a man wanted to hear?

Sitting on the edge of the bed, Blake leaned forward and buried his face in his hands as if he needed time to compose himself.

"Blake," she pleaded in a soft whisper, "what did I say?"

He didn't answer as he reached for his shirt and rammed his arms into the sleeves. Not bothering to fasten the buttons, he started across the room.

"Blake," she begged, "don't do this to me. Please don't do this to me."

He turned to her in the moonlight. She had never

seen a man look more upset. His face was contorted with anger, his mouth twisted, his eyes as hard as flint.

Caasi sagged against the bed, closing her eyes against the pain that went through her heart, a pain so deep that it was beyond tears.

For hours Caasi lay exactly as she was, staring dry-eyed at the ceiling. She had offered Blake everything she had to give and he had rejected it all.

Even her makeup couldn't camouflage the dark circles under her eyes the next morning. The mirror revealed pale, colorless cheeks, as if she were recovering from a long illness. Caasi doubted that she would ever recover. Not really. She'd go on with her life, would probably even laugh again, but something deep inside her had died last night. In some respects she would never be the same.

It gave her little satisfaction to note that Blake looked as if he hadn't slept either.

Dick was at the helicopter when they arrived, assuring them that everything was fixed and ready to go.

Blake didn't offer her his hand when she climbed inside, which was just as well, since she would have refused it. They sat as far apart from each other as possible.

The atmosphere was so thick that even Dick was affected, glancing anxiously from one to the other, then concentrating on the flight.

As Caasi ran the bathwater in her quarters back at the Empress, she realized there was nothing about the short flight home that she could remember. The pain of being so close to Blake was almost more than she could bear. Her mind had blotted it from her memory.

Blake had stepped out of the helicopter and announced stiffly that he was going home to change and would be back later to clear out his desk and pack up what remained of his personal items. It was Wednesday. His last day with Crane Enterprises.

Caasi hadn't bothered to answer him but had turned and gone directly to her suite.

Some of the staff had planned a small farewell party for Blake, but she hadn't contributed anything. Not when seeing him go was so painful. There would be an obligatory statement of good wishes she would make. Somehow she'd manage that. Somehow.

A hot bath relieved some of the tiredness in her bones, but it had little effect on her heart.

Dressed in a prim business suit, Caasi walked briskly into the office and offered Laurie a short nod before entering her own.

Her desk was stacked with mail, telephone messages, and a variety of items that needed her immediate attention.

"Laurie," she called to her secretary, "send in Brian Harris."

"Right away."

If the man was there to take Blake's place, she had best start working with him now.

By noon Caasi's head was pounding. She wasn't one to suffer from headaches, but the pain was quickly becoming unbearable.

"Are you all right?" Laurie asked as she came into Caasi's office for dictation.

"I'm fine," Caasi said with a weak smile. She stood at the window, her fingertips massaging her temples as she shot off one letter after another, scarcely pausing between items of correspondence.

Laurie sat on the edge of her chair, her glasses delicately balanced on the bridge of her nose as her pencil flew across the steno pad.

"That'll be all." Caasi paused. "No, get me Dirk Evans of International on the phone."

Laurie returned to her office and buzzed Caasi a minute later. "Mr. Evans is on line two."

"Thanks, Laurie," Caasi said with a sigh. "Would it be possible for you to find me some aspirin?"

"Of course."

"Thanks." Five years since she took over for her father, and this was the first time she'd ever needed anything to help her through the day.

The aspirin had little effect on the pounding sensation that persisted at her temples well into the afternoon.

Laurie came into her office around four to tell her that the farewell party for Blake was in progress.

"I'll be there in a minute," Caasi said without looking up, her fingers tightening around her pen.

Hands braced against the side of her desk, Caasi inhaled deeply, closing her eyes and forcing herself to absorb the silence for a couple of moments before rising and going to join the party.

Someone had opened a bottle of champagne. Caasi stood on the outskirts of the small crowd and watched as everyone toasted Blake and wished him success. One of the women had made a farewell cake and was serving thin slices. Caasi recognized her as Blake's personal assistant but couldn't recall her being so attractive.

Caasi felt far removed from the joking banter that existed between Blake and his staff. There wasn't one who didn't regret his leaving. Yet he had chosen to do exactly that.

Someone slapped him across the back and he laughed but stopped short as his eyes met hers.

Quickly Caasi looked away. A hush fell over the room as she walked to the center, Blake at her side.

"I think we can all agree that you'll be missed," she said in a voice that was surprisingly steady. "If my father were here I'm sure he would say how much he appreciated the excellent job you have done for Crane Enterprises for the past eight years. I'm sure he'd extend to you his personal best wishes."

"But not yours?" Blake whispered for her ears alone.

Stiffening, Caasi continued somewhat defiantly, "My own are extended to you in whatever you pursue. If there's ever a time you feel you'd like to return, you know that there will always be a place for you here. Goodbye, Blake."

"What? No gold watch?" he mumbled under his breath as he stepped forward and shook her hand. "Thank you, Miss Crane." Those dark, unreadable eyes stared into hers, and Caasi could barely breathe.

Grateful for the opportunity to escape, she nodded and stepped aside as Blake's assistant approached with a small wrapped package. Hoping to give the impression she was needed elsewhere, Caasi glanced at her watch. "If you'll excuse me, please."

"Of course." Blake answered for the group.

Without another word, she turned and walked away, not stopping until she reached her desk.

Caasi forced herself to eat dinner. For two days she hadn't been able to force down more than a few bites of any meal.

The headache was now forty-eight hours old. Nothing seemed to relieve the throbbing pain. She hadn't slept well either. After several hours of tossing fitfully she would fall into an uneasy slumber, only to wake an hour or two later more tired than when she'd gone to bed.

The phone rang Saturday when she returned from a spot check at the Sacramento Empress.

"Hello," she said, with little enthusiasm.

"Is this Caasi?"

Faintly Caasi recognized the voice over the phone. Her home phone had a private listing and she seldom gave out the number.

"Yes, it is."

"Caasi." The young voice sounded relieved. "This is Gina. Gina Sherrill."

"Hello, Gina. What can I do for you?" Caasi's hand tightened around the receiver. The girl had phoned three times in the last few days, and Caasi hadn't returned the calls. She had completely severed herself from Blake and wanted every painful reminder of him removed from her life.

"I'm sorry to bother you like this, but I haven't been able to get hold of you at your office."

"I've been busy lately." She hoped the tone of her voice would effectively convey the message. She didn't want to be purposely rude to the girl.

"I knew that, and I hope you'll forgive me for being so forward, but I did want to tell you that everyone would like it if you could come to dinner on Sunday."

Everyone but Blake, Caasi added silently. "I'm sure I'd like that very much, but I'm sorry, it's impossible this week. Perhaps another time."

Caasi heard a sigh of disappointment come over the line. "I understand."

Maybe she did, Caasi mused.

"I'd like to talk to you someday when you've got the time."

"I'd enjoy that, Gina, but I really am busy. Thank you for calling. Give my love to your family."

"I will. Goodbye, Caasi."

Caasi heard the drone of the disconnected line sound in her ear. Replacing the receiver, she walked to the window and studied the view of miniature people and miniature cars far below.

Someone knocked on her door, and she wanted to cry out in irritation. Why couldn't people just leave her alone? Everything would be fine if she could have some peace and quiet in her life.

"Just a minute," she answered shortly as she strode across the floor. She opened the door to discover... Blake. Her heart leapt into her throat, and she was too stunned to move.

"I hope you haven't eaten yet. By the way, where were you all afternoon?" he asked as he walked past her into the living room.

Nine

"Where was I?" Caasi repeated, nonplussed. What was Blake doing here? Hadn't he left her, decided to sever his relationship with her and Crane Enterprises?

"Yes—I've been trying to get you all day."

Her hand on the doorknob, Caasi watched his relaxed movements as he sauntered to the sofa, sat back and positioned his ankle on his knee.

"I do have a business to run." She hated the telltale way her voice shook, revealing her shock.

"Yes, but it wasn't business that kept you out. I know, because I checked."

"You checked?" Caasi demanded. "Then I suggest you question your sources, because it most certainly *was* business."

"Instead of standing all the way over there and arguing, why don't you come and sit with me?" He held out his hand invitingly. "I certainly hope you're hungry, because I'm starved."

Caasi closed the door but didn't sit with him as he requested. Instead she walked to the window, her arms cradling her waist.

"What you're wearing is fine," he assured her. "Don't bother to change."

Her gaze shot to him. The friendly, almost gentle light in his eyes was enough to steal her breath. His ready smile was warm and encouraging.

"I thought you wanted out of Crane Enterprises."

"I did."

"Then why are you here? Why come back? Don't you know how hard it was for me to let you walk away? Are you really that insensitive, Blake? I don't want you flitting in and out of my life when the mood strikes you. I haven't seen you in…"

"Three days," he supplied. "I know. I wanted you to have time to think things through, but I can see you haven't figured anything out yet."

Caasi's hands became knotted fists and fell to her sides. "I hate it when people play these kinds of games with me. If you have something to say, then for the love of heaven just say it."

Blake released a frustrated sigh. "Are you really so dense you can't see?"

"I don't need to stand in my own home and be insulted by you, Blake Sherrill." She stalked across the room and opened the door. "Perhaps it would be best if you left."

"Caasi." A hint of anger reverberated in his husky voice. "I didn't come here to argue."

"Well, you seem to be doing a bang-up job of it."

He stood and rammed his hands into his pockets. He strode to the window, his back to her as he gazed at the panorama.

Caasi could see and feel the frustration in the rigid set of his shoulders. She didn't want to fight. The desire to walk to him and slip her arms around his waist and press her face to his back was almost overwhelming. The headache that had persisted since Blake left was her body's method of telling her how miserable she had been without him.

A hundred times since Wednesday she'd had to stop herself from consulting him, remembering that Blake was no longer available to ask. Softly she exhaled and closed the door.

At the sound of the click, Blake turned around. "Can we start again, Cupcake? Pretend I'm an old friend who's come to town for the weekend."

Caasi lowered her gaze. "Don't call me Cupcake," she murmured stiffly. "I'm not a little girl. That's the last way I want you to think of me."

The sound of his robust laugh filled the room. "There's no worry of that."

Indecision gripped Caasi. All her life she'd been in control of every situation. She had always known what to expect and how to react. But not with Blake and this new ground he seemed to want to travel with her. Of one thing Caasi was sure: she couldn't tolerate much more of the pain he inflicted when he walked away.

"Dinner, Caasi?" His arched brow contained a challenging lift.

Her compliant nod was as weak as her resolve. She would accept what little Blake was willing to offer and be grateful.

His smile crinkled the lines at his eyes. "Come on. I've got fat steaks ready for the barbecue."

Caasi took a light jacket out of the closet. "Where are we going?"

"To my place."

"Your place?"

"Then after dinner I thought we'd try our luck at the horse races."

"Horse races?" she repeated.

Blake looked around, stared at the ceiling, and shook his head. "This room seems to have developed an echo all of a sudden."

Caasi smiled. It was the first time she could remember smiling since Monday, when Blake had announced he would be leaving her and Crane Enterprises.

They rode in his T-Bird convertible with the top down. The wind ruffled her sleekly styled curls, and Caasi closed her eyes to savor the delicious sensations that flowed through her. She was with Blake, and it felt right.

The barbecue could be seen in the backyard, a bag of briquets leaning against its base, when Blake pulled into the driveway. He came around and opened her car door for her. Leaning over the rolled-down window, he lightly brushed his mouth across hers. He straightened and his eyes looked deeply into hers. With a groan his arms surrounded her, half lifting her from the car as she arched against the muscular wall of his chest. Caasi slipped her arms around his neck and surrendered fully to his kiss. Gradually his grip relaxed and he tenderly brushed the tangled hair from her temple. "I've missed you."

Still caught in the rush of emotion he could evoke, Caasi didn't speak. A happy smile lifted the corners of her mouth in a trembling smile. "I've missed you too."

"I'll cook the steaks if you fix the salad. Agreed?"

Eagerly, Caasi nodded. He helped her out of the car,

his arm cupping her shoulders as he led her up the back stairs and into the kitchen.

"I'll get the barbecue going and leave you to your task," he instructed.

Almost immediately he was out the back door. Taking off her jacket, Caasi draped it over a chair and looked around. She really loved this house. A gentle feeling warmed her. Any woman would be proud to be a part of this.

The ingredients for the salad were in the refrigerator, and she laid them on the counter. Next she searched through the cupboards for a large bowl. A salad shouldn't be difficult, she mused happily. Her culinary skills were limited, but a salad would be easy enough.

She was at the cutting board chopping lettuce when Blake came back for the steaks and a variety of spices.

He paused, watching her as she slid the knife across the fresh lettuce.

"Is something the matter?" She tensed and looped a strand of hair behind her ear. What could she possibly be doing wrong in making a salad? It was the simplest job he could have given her.

"No. It's just that it's better to tear apart the lettuce leaves instead of cutting them."

"Okay." Feeling incredibly naive in the kitchen, Caasi set the knife aside.

"Did you wash it?" Blake asked her next.

Caasi swallowed at the painful lump that filled her throat. With tight-lipped grimness she answered him with a negative shake of her head. Dumping the cut lettuce into the bowl, she carried it to the sink and filled the bowl with water. Pure pique caused her to pour dishwashing liquid over the green leaves. "Like this?" She batted her long lashes at him innocently.

Not waiting for his reaction, she moved into the living room and stared sightlessly out the front window. A hand over her mouth, she took in several deep breaths. What was she doing here with Blake? This wonderful homey scene wasn't meant for someone like her. She was about as undomesticated as they came.

The sound of footsteps told her Blake had moved behind her. His hand on her shoulder sent a silky warmth sliding down her arm.

"I apologize," she whispered. "That was a stupid thing to do."

"No—I should be the one to apologize." The pressure of his hands turned her around. Gently he pulled her into his arms, his chin resting against the top of her head.

"It's just that I'm so incredibly dumb." Her voice was thick with self-derision.

"You, stupid?" Soft laughter tumbled from his throat, stirring the hair at the crown of her head. "Maybe you won't be competing in the same class as Chef, but not because you lack intelligence. You've just never learned, that's all."

"But will I ever?"

"That's up to you, Cupcake."

Caasi winced. "You're using that name again when I've asked you repeatedly not to."

He didn't comment for several tense moments. "I don't think I'll ever forget the first time I saw you. I'd been working with your father for several months. Isaac didn't talk much about his private life. I think I was at the Empress six months before I even knew he had a daughter. We were in his office one day and you came floating in as fresh as spring and so breathtakingly beautiful I nearly fell out of my chair." He stopped and gently eased her away so that he could look at her as he spoke. "I watched this hard-nosed businessman light up like a sparkler on the Fourth of July. His eyes softened as he held out his arms to you and called you Cupcake. I've never thought of you as anything else since."

"I was only twenty."

A finger under her chin lifted her face to his. "The amazing part is that you're even more beautiful now." Ever so gently, he placed his mouth over hers.

No kiss had ever been so incredibly sweet. Caasi swayed toward him when he released her and sighed with all the love in her heart. "I hope you've got another head of lettuce. I'm afraid I've ruined the first one."

"I'll start cooking the steaks now." He kissed her on the tip of her nose and released her. "How do you want your steak cooked? Rare?"

"No, medium."

Blake looked dissatisfied. "You honestly should try it cooked a little less sometime."

"Blake." She placed her hands on her hips and shook her head. "We seem doomed for one confrontation after another. I happen to prefer my meat medium. If you'd rather, I can cook my own."

"I'd like to see that."

"Steak," she asserted, "I can do. There's nothing to it but flopping it over the grill a couple of times."

"It's an art."

"You overrate yourself," Caasi insisted. "How about I cook the steaks and you make the salad?"

Blake chuckled, shaking his head. "I hate to see good meat wasted, but it'll be worth it just to prove my point."

Caasi was in the backyard readjusting the grill so that it was closer to the fire when Blake walked out.

"I thought you were making the salad."

"I did," he said teasingly, his eyes twinkling. "I slapped a hunk of lettuce on a plate, added a slice of tomato, and poured dressing over the top. What's happening to my steak is of much more interest to me."

"On second thought…" Caasi moistened her dry lips. "I'd hate to ruin your meal. Why don't we each cook our own?"

"That sounds fair," Blake agreed with a smile.

The thick steaks sizzled when placed across the grill, flames curling around the edges of fat.

"Who lowered this? It's too close to the fire," he said irritably.

Guiltily, Caasi handed him the pot holders she was holding. "Sorry," she muttered.

Blake didn't look pleased. He obviously took his barbecuing seriously. He'd flipped his steak over before Caasi had a chance to add salt and pepper to hers.

When he lifted the barely warmed meat from the grill, Caasi dropped her jaw in disbelief. "That couldn't possibly be done."

"This is a rare steak."

"That's not rare," she declared with tight-lipped insistence. "It's raw. A good vet would have it back on its feet in fifteen minutes."

What had been a light, teasing air was suddenly cold and sober.

"You cook your meat the way you like it and I'll have

mine my way. As far as I can see, you're not in any position to tell me what's right or wrong in the kitchen."

Caasi felt the color drain out of her face. Quickly she averted her eyes.

"Caasi," Blake said, forcefully expelling his breath. "I didn't mean that."

"Why not?" She gave a weak smile. "It's true. You go and eat. I'll join you in a few minutes."

Caasi ate little of her dinner and noted that Blake didn't either. Her steak was burned crisp around the edges and was far more well-done than she normally enjoyed. The whole time they were eating she waited for Blake to make some sarcastic comment about her cooking. She was grateful that he didn't.

Blake didn't say anything when she left the table and took her plate to the sink. The bowlful of sudsy lettuce leaves was there to remind her of her childish prank. This new relationship Blake apparently wanted to build wasn't going to work; she couldn't be with him more than ten minutes without fighting. She didn't know how to respond to him on unfamiliar ground. Crane Enterprises had been a common denominator, but now that was gone.

Gathering the wilted greens in her hands, she dumped them into the garbage.

"You could use the disposal instead of..."

"I think I've had enough of your 'instead ofs' to last me a lifetime." She made a show of glancing at her watch. "On second thought, maybe we should forgo the races for another time."

"I couldn't agree with you more," he snapped. He stood abruptly, almost knocking over his chair in the process. Pointedly he took the car keys from his pocket.

They didn't say a word during the entire drive back to the Empress. Caasi sat upright, her arms crossed determinedly in front of her. The entire evening had been a fiasco.

Blake pulled up to the curb in front of the hotel. His hands clenched the steering wheel as he stared straight ahead. "We need to talk, but now isn't the time. Neither one of us is in the mood for a serious discussion."

Caasi released a pain-filled sigh. "What do you want from me, Blake? When you worked for the hotel I knew exactly where we stood, but now all I feel is an uncertainty I can't explain." She watched as Blake's hand tightened on the wheel until his knuckles were white.

"You haven't figured it out yet? After all these years you still don't know, do you?" He was so angry that Caasi knew any kind of response would only fuel his irritation. "Maybe it is too late, maybe you're so impossibly wrapped up in Crane Enterprises that you'll never know." A resolute hardness closed over his features.

She'd barely closed the car door before he drove away. As the car sped down the street, she stood alone on the deserted sidewalk. Blake was always leaving her.

Later that night, as she lay in bed staring at the dark ceiling, Caasi thought about his parting comment. Obviously she had been horribly wrong not to recognize his motives.

Rather than suffer through another day of self-recrimination over her relationship with Blake, Caasi drove to June and Burt's on Sunday afternoon.

"Welcome," June said and gave Caasi a hug after letting her in the screen door. "I'm glad you came. The first pictures of Cassi have arrived. You wouldn't believe how much she's changed already."

"Sure I would." Caasi walked into the house and handed June a small gift she'd picked up for the baby while in Sacramento.

"Caasi," June protested, "you've got to stop buying Cassi all these gifts. Otherwise, she'll grow up and not appreciate anything."

"Let me spoil her," Caasi pleaded and lifted the sleeping baby from the bassinet. "She's probably the closest thing I'll ever have to a daughter. And I love her so much, it's hard not to."

"I know." June sighed and shook her head in defeat. "But try to hold it down. There isn't any more room in her bedroom to hold all your gifts."

"I hope that's not true."

"Almost," June said. "She's due to wake up any minute and will probably want to eat. I'll get you a cup of coffee now. Burt's working in the back, building one of those aluminum storage sheds."

Cradling the sleeping baby in her arms, Caasi sat in the rocking chair. Her eyes misted as she watched the angelic face. It never failed to materialize, the powerful, overwhelming surge of love she experienced every time she held this child. If this was what she felt with June's baby, how much more would she feel for her own? The question had been on her mind ever since her dinner with Edie. What had Edie called it? Baby hunger. But it was more than that, far more than a passing fancy because her two best friends were having children. When June and Edie had married she hadn't had the urge to go out and find herself a husband. These feelings were different.

A home and family would be worth more than all the accumulated riches of Crane Enterprises. Her father had worked himself into an early grave, and for what reason? All those years he had slaved to build a fortune for her. But she didn't want wealth. The greatest desires of her heart were for a simple life. A home and family, maybe a dog or two. Certainly, money alone couldn't provide all that.

The baby stirred and, opening her tiny mouth, arched her back and yawned.

"Diaper-changing time," Caasi announced as she carried little Cassi into the bedroom and laid her across the changing table. Within a matter of minutes Caasi handed the baby to her mother.

June sat in a rocking chair and unbuttoned her blouse to nurse. "Every time I see you with the baby I'm amazed at how natural you are with her," June said as she smoothed the soft hairs away from her daughter's face. "To be honest, I was afraid you wouldn't do well around children, but I was wrong. You're a natural. I wish you'd marry and have children of your own."

The coffee cup sat on the end table, and Caasi's hand tightened around it. "I've been giving some serious thought to exactly that."

"Caasi, that's wonderful!" June exclaimed. "You don't know how glad I'll be to see you get away from that hotel. It's dominated your life. I swear, it's been like a monster that's eaten away at you more and more until you were hardly yourself. Who's the lucky man?"

Caasi shifted uncomfortably, crossed and uncrossed her legs, then set her cup aside. "I wasn't thinking of getting married."

June's eyes widened incredulously. "You mean…" She stopped and looked flustered. "You're just going to have a baby?"

"Something like that," Caasi explained cheerfully. "A husband is a nice extra but not necessary."

"I don't get it. Why not marry? You're an attractive woman, and you have so much to offer."

"Maybe," Caasi returned flippantly, "but in this case a husband would be an encumbrance I can live without."

"What about the baby? Doesn't he—or she—have a right to a father?"

"That's something I'm thinking about now."

"This whole idea doesn't even sound like you. Where did you come up with…" June stopped, a knowing look lighting her eyes. "Edie. This sounds exactly like one of her crazy schemes."

"Maybe." A smile tugged at Caasi's mouth. "And when you think about it, the idea isn't all that crazy. Single women are raising children all the time."

"Yes, but…" Slowly June shook her head, her eyes narrowing with concern. "Have you chosen the father? I mean, have you said anything to him?"

"Not yet."

"Then you *have* chosen someone?"

"Oh, yes. You've never met him, but he…" Caasi paused and swallowed. "He used to work for me. Actually, I think my method is a better idea than Edie's. She suggested I pick up someone in a bar. I swear, that woman is looney sometimes."

"I'm going to have a talk with her," June muttered between tight lips.

"Don't. To be honest, I think she was only kidding. She didn't expect me to take it all so seriously, but I have and I am."

"You know, Caasi, I've never advised you about anything. You've never needed my advice. There's confidence in everything about you—the way you talk, the way you stand, the way you look. Think about this, think very seriously before you do something you might regret all your life."

"I will," Caasi assured her with a warm smile. "I've never done anything haphazardly in my well-ordered existence, and I'm not about to start now."

Monday's mail included an invitation to Gina and Donald's wedding. She felt badly at having snubbed Blake's sister the past Saturday. Gina was a warm and loving young woman. Caasi took her checkbook and wrote out a generous amount. Staring at the amount, she pictured her confrontation with Blake after she'd sent his cousin a wedding gift. She could imagine what he'd accuse her of if he saw this. Defeated, Caasi tore the check in two and wrote another for half the amount of the first.

"What the heck," she muttered with frustration. What gave Blake Sherrill the right to dictate the amount or kind of gift she gave anyone? Angrily she tore out another check and wrote it out for the amount of the original one. After scribbling an apologetic letter declining the invitation, she added her congratulations and hoped the couple could put the money to good use.

The letter and money went out in the afternoon mail.

Tuesday Caasi met with her lawyer. If he thought her request was a little unusual he said nothing, at least not to her. He did admit, however, that he hadn't handled anything like that in the past and would have to get back to her. Caasi told him there wasn't any rush. She hadn't heard from Blake since their Saturday-night clash.

Wednesday morning Caasi was in her office giving dictation to Laurie when Blake burst in.

"There'd better be a good explanation for this." He slapped a newspaper on top of her desk.

Completely calm, Caasi turned to Laurie. "Maybe it would be best if you excused us for a few moments, Laurie. It seems Mr. Sherrill has something he'd like to say."

The secretary stood up, left the office and closed the door behind her. Blake waited until they were alone.

"Well," he demanded and stalked to the far side of the room.

"I knew this would happen." Her hand gestured impatiently. "I knew the minute I put the money in the mail that you'd come storming in here as if I'd done some terrible deed. Quite frankly, Blake Sherrill, I'm growing weary of your attempts to dictate my life."

"Dictate your life!" he repeated and rammed both hands into his pants pockets, then just as quickly pulled them out again and smoothed back his hair. Even when angry, Blake was a fine male figure. His body was rock hard as he continued to pace the carpet. "I couldn't believe it. I still am having trouble." He stared at her as if he'd never seen her before. "Caasi, what would your father say?" He was deadly serious as his narrowed gaze captured hers.

"My father?" She shook her head in bewilderment. "My father has been dead for five years. I don't think he'd care one way or another if I sent your sister a generous wedding present."

"My sister?" he said, confused. "What has Gina got to do with this?" He spread the newspaper across her desk and pointed to the headlines in the business section: International Rumored to Buy Empress Hotels.

"Oh, *that*." Caasi sighed with relief. "I thought you were talking about…"

"I know what you thought," he shouted. "I want to ask you about this article. Is it true?"

She gestured toward the chair on the other side of her desk. "Will you sit down?" she requested calmly, her even words belying her pounding heart. "We need to talk, and there's no better time than the present."

Blake lowered himself into the soft leather chair, but he sat on the edge of the seat as if ready to spring up at the slightest provocation.

"Well?" he demanded again. "Is it true?"

"Yes," she said, confirming his suspicions. "But I'm only selling eight hotels. I'm keeping the Portland Empress and the Seaside Empress."

"Caasi." He groaned in frustration. "Do you know what you're doing?"

"Yes." She nodded. "I've never been more sure of anything in my life. I don't have the time to manage the hotels and everything else."

"Everything else? What?" he demanded. "What could possibly be more important to you than Crane Enterprises?"

Sitting opposite him, Caasi watched his face intently as she spoke. "A baby," she murmured softly.

"A baby," he exploded and shot to his feet.

Caasi closed her eyes and emitted a bittersweet groan. "Blake, I wanted to have a nice logical discussion with you. But if you insist on overreacting like this, then I'm simply going to have to ask you to leave."

"You don't say things like that and expect me to react as if you've asked for the sugar bowl."

"Okay, okay," she agreed with limited patience. "When you've cooled down I'd like to have a calm, rational discussion."

He said nothing for several moments as though trying to calm himself. After a while he asked, "Are you pregnant?"

"Not yet."

"Not yet?" Impatience showed in the set of his mouth.

Caasi lowered her gaze and struggled to keep a firm grip on her composure. "I've met with a real estate agent and have started looking at houses. I don't want my baby growing up in a hotel the way I did."

Blake straightened in the chair, his back ramrod stiff.

"I've also talked with an attorney, and he's drawing up the necessary papers. I think…the father…should have some rights, but I'd be foolish not to protect myself and the baby legally."

Blake's face was hard, his eyes blazing. Yet he was pale, as if his grip on his temper was fragile. "And the father?" he asked curtly.

"Yes, well…" Caasi felt the muscles of her throat tighten as the words slipped out. "I'd like you to be my baby's father."

Ten

Blake's razor-sharp gaze ripped into her. "What did you say?"

Caasi had trouble meeting his eyes. "You heard me right."

Blake propelled himself out of the chair and stalked to the far side of the room. "Have you seen a doctor?" He ground out the question, his back to her.

"No, not yet. I didn't feel that would be necessary until I was fairly certain I was pregnant," she explained tightly.

Blake swiveled around, his brow knit with questioning concern. "I'm not talking about that kind of doctor."

"Honestly, Blake. Do you think I need a psychiatrist?" Her smile was tense and nervous.

"Yes," he insisted, "quite frankly, that's exactly what I think. You've been working too hard."

Caasi's spirits sank and she lowered her head. Her fingers toyed with a stack of papers on her desk. "I'm not working any harder now than I have for the past five years."

"Exactly." His hand sliced through the air.

"Blake, the Empress has nothing to do with this. I woke up, that's all. I've decided I want something more out of life than money and an empty suite." She didn't elaborate that he was the one responsible for awakening her. "I'm a woman with a woman's desires. Is it so wrong to want to be a mother? I can assure you I'll be a good one." She inhaled deeply. "June says I'm a natural with the baby and I'd make—"

"Why pick me?" he interrupted, a grim set to his jaw.

"Why not?" she said and shrugged. The heat seeped into her face, reddening her cheeks. "You're tall, good-looking, and possess certain characteristics I admire." Nervously she stood up and walked around to the front of the desk. Leaning her thighs against the flat top, she crossed her arms.

"Just how do you propose to get pregnant? By osmosis?" Blake taunted.

"No...of course not," she stammered. "Listen, Blake, I'm not doing a very good job of explaining this. I really wish I hadn't said anything. At least, not until I'd heard from the lawyer. But aside from anything else, I'd like you to know I'm willing to make this venture worth your while."

His mouth twisted into a cynical smile. "You don't have enough money to pay me for what you're asking. I'd like to tell you what to do with your proposition, Cupcake, but your face would burn for a week." Slowly he turned and walked to the door.

"Don't go, Blake. Please."

His hand on the doorknob, he turned; his gaze was concentrated on her, disturbing her even more. "There's nothing you can say. Goodbye, Cupcake."

Just the way he said it made her blood run cold. His

voice expressed so many things in those few words. Frustration. Disappointment. Contempt. Disbelief.

Caasi sagged against the desk as the door closed. Blake couldn't be feeling any more confused than she was. He had been angry. Blazingly angry. She'd seen him express a myriad of emotions over the years. And plenty of anger. But never like this. This kind of anger went beyond raised voices and lost tempers. This time it came from Blake's heart.

The thought of working was almost impossible. Caasi tried for the remainder of the morning, but her concentration drifted, and every page seemed to mirror Blake's look as he walked out the door. At lunchtime she announced to Laurie that she didn't know when she'd be back. Laurie rounded her eyes with frustration but said nothing.

Caasi let herself into the penthouse suite and slowly sauntered around the empty quarters. She shouldn't have approached Blake that day. Even the most naive business graduate would have recognized that this wasn't the time to propose anything to him. He'd been upset even before she'd opened her mouth. Her sense of timing couldn't have been more off-kilter. That wasn't like her. She knew better.

Staring out the window, Caasi blinked uncertainly. She needed to get away. Think. Reconsider.

After changing out of her smart linen business suit into capris and a pink sweater, she took her car out of the garage and drove around for a while. It was true that she wanted a baby. But what she hadn't realized until that morning was that she wanted Blake's child. If he wouldn't agree, then she would have to abandon the idea completely.

She had to talk to Blake and make him understand. All the way to Gresham, she practiced what she wanted to say, the assurances she would give him. Nothing in her life had ever been so important.

His driveway was empty when she turned into it. She had counted on his being there. Just as she climbed out of her car, it started to rain. Staring at the skies in defeat, Caasi raised the collar of her jacket and hurried up the back steps, pounding on the door on the off chance he was inside. Nothing.

Rushing back to her car, she climbed inside and listened to the pelting rain dance on the roof. An arc of lightning flashed across the dark sky. *Wonderful,* she reflected disconsolately. Even nature responded to Blake's moods.

Ten minutes passed and it seemed like ten years. But Caasi was determined to stay until she'd had the chance to explain things to Blake.

Half an hour later, when the storm was beginning to abate, she got out of the car a second time. Maybe Blake had left his back door unlocked and she could go inside.

The door was tightly locked, but Caasi found a key under a ceramic flowerpot. It looked old and slightly rusted. Briefly Caasi wondered if Blake even knew it was there. After several minutes spent trying to work the key into the lock, she managed to open the door.

Wiping her feet on the mat, she let herself into the kitchen. Blake's dirty breakfast dishes were on the table and she carried them to the sink. It looked as if he'd been reading the morning paper, found the article about the rumored sale of the Empress, and rushed out the door, newspaper in hand.

To fill the time, she leafed through several magazines. But nothing held her interest, so she straightened up the living room and ran warm, sudsy water into the kitchen sink to wash the breakfast dishes. She had just finished scrubbing the frying pan when she heard a car in the driveway.

Her heart thumped as though she'd just run a marathon when Blake walked in the door. Turning, her hands braced on the edge of the sink behind her, Caasi smiled weakly.

"Who let you in?"

Involuntarily, Caasi flinched at the cutting edge in his voice.

"There was a key under the flowerpot." Her voice nearly failed her. Turning back to the sink, she jerked the kitchen towel from the drawer and started drying the few dishes she'd washed. At least she could hide how badly her hands were shaking.

"Okay, we'll abort that how and go directly to why. Why are you here?" The dry sarcasm in his voice knotted her stomach.

"Would you like a cup of coffee?" she asked brightly. "I know I would."

"No!" he nearly shouted. "I don't want any coffee. What I'd like is a simple explanation." His narrowed gaze swung to her as she took a mug from the cupboard and helped herself to the fresh pot of coffee she'd made.

"Caasi." The tone of his voice as he spoke her name revealed the depth of his frustration.

Pulling out a chair, she sat down, her eyes issuing a silent invitation for him to do the same.

He ignored her and leaned against the kitchen counter.

She didn't look at him as she spoke. "You once accused me of having ink in my veins. At the time you were right. But the ink is gone and there's blood flowing there now." Briefly her gray eyes slid to him. His stance didn't encourage her to continue.

"So?" His arms were crossed as if to block her out. He drew his head back, pride dictating the indifference he so vividly portrayed.

"So?" she repeated with bitter mockery. "*You* did this to me. You're the one responsible…."

Blake straightened slightly. "Does that make it my duty to fall in with these looney plans of yours? Do you have any idea of how crazy you sound? You want to pay me to father your child, so you can be a mother. What in heaven's name do you have against marriage?"

"Nothing. I…I think marriage is wonderful."

"Then if you're so hot for a family, why don't we get married?"

She stiffened with angry pride as she met his glare. "Is this a proposal?"

"Yes," he snapped.

Caasi felt as if someone had punched her in the stomach, effectively knocking the oxygen from her lungs. Tears brimmed in her eyes.

"Well?" His voice softened perceptibly.

One tear slid down her drawn face and she wiped it aside with the tips of her fingers. "Every girl dreams about having a man ask her to marry him. I never thought my proposal would be shouted at me from across a kitchen."

"I'm not exactly in a romantic mood. Do you want to get married or don't you?" he barked. "And while we're on the subject, let's get something else straight. We'll live right here in this house and on my income.

Whatever money is yours will be put into a trust fund for the children."

A soft curtain of hair fell forward to cover her face as she stared into the steaming coffee. "My mother died before I knew her," she began weakly. "Maybe if she'd lived I would know a better way to say these things. To me, marriage means more than producing children. There's love and commitment and a hundred different things I don't even know how to explain. The quiet communication I witnessed between your mother and father. That look in Burt's eyes as June was delivering their child. Do you see what I'm trying to say?"

Blake was quiet for so long, she wondered if he'd heard her. "Maybe as time goes by you could learn to love me," Blake said with slow deliberation. "I think we should give it a try."

"Learn to love you?" Caasi repeated incredulously. "I love you already." She raised her eyes to his, her gaze level and clear. "I don't want any baby unless it's yours. I don't want any other man but you...ever."

In the next instant, she was hauled out of the chair and into his arms. "You love me?" Roughly he pushed the hair from her eyes, as if he had to see it himself, couldn't believe what she was saying and had to read it in her face.

Her hands were braced against his chest. "Of course I do. Could I have made it any more obvious in Seaside?" Her lashes fluttered closed as she struggled to disguise the pain that his rejection still had the power to inflict. "But you...you..."

"I know what I did," he interrupted, a grim set to his mouth. "I walked out. It was the hardest thing I'd ever done in my life, but I turned away and left you." He released her and twined his fingers through his hair. "I was half a breath from telling you how much I loved you. Then I heard you say that you were absolving me from any responsibility. Here I was ready to give you my heart and you were talking to me like a one-night stand."

"Oh, Blake." She moaned, lifting the hair from her forehead with one hand. "I wanted you to understand that I didn't expect anything of you. You didn't have to love me, not when I loved you so much."

Tenderly, his eyes caressed her. "How can any two people misunderstand each other the way we have?"

Sadly, Caasi shook her head. "Why did you resign? Why did you leave when I wanted you so desperately to stay?"

He took her back into his arms, and his lips softly brushed her cheek. "Because loving you and working with you were becoming impossible. I've loved you almost from the moment you floated into your father's office that day. I kept waiting for you to wake up to that fact. Then one day I realized you never would."

"Why didn't you say something? Why didn't you let me know?"

"Caasi, I couldn't have been any more obvious. All the times I made excuses to touch you, be with you. Anything. But you were so caught up in Crane Enterprises you didn't notice. And, to be truthful, your money intimidated me. One day I decided: why torture myself anymore? You were already married to the company, and I was never going to be rich enough for you to believe I wasn't attracted to you for your money."

"But, Blake, I didn't think that. Not once."

"But then, you didn't guess I loved you either."

Smiling, Caasi slid her arms over his shoulders and looked at him with all the love in her heart shining from the blue-gray depths of her eyes. "But now that I know, Blake Sherrill, I'm not letting you go. Not for a minute."

Tenderly he kissed her as if she were a fragile flower and held her close as if he'd never release her.

"I love you so much." She curled tighter into his embrace. "And, Blake, we're going to have the most beautiful children."

"Yes," he murmured, his lips seeking hers. "But not for a year. I want you to myself for that long. Understood?"

"Oh, yes," she agreed eagerly, her eyes glowing with the soft light of happiness. "Anything you say."

Five months later Caasi stood on the back porch as Blake drove into the driveway. Even after three months of marriage, just seeing her husband climb out of the car at the end of the day produced a wealth of emotions.

"Hi—how was your afternoon?" she greeted him, wrapping her arms around his neck and kissing him ardently. She worked mornings at the Empress but gradually was turning her responsibilities over to Blake so that the time would come when she could pursue some of the things she wanted.

Lifting her off the floor, Blake swung her around, his mouth locating the sensitive area at the hollow of her throat, knowing the tingling reaction he'd evoke.

"You're being mighty brave for five-thirty in the afternoon," she teased.

"It doesn't seem to matter what time of the day it is, I don't think I'll ever stop wanting you," he whispered in her ear. "Fifty years from now, I'll probably be chasing you around the bedroom." His voice was deep and emotion-filled.

"I don't think you'll have to chase too hard."

"Good thing," he said as he set his briefcase aside so he could hold her tightly against him. "Your cooking is improving, because whatever it is smells delicious."

"Yes—that reminds me." Caasi groaned and broke from his embrace. "I have good news and bad news. Which do you want first?"

Blake's eyes narrowed fractionally. "Knowing you, I think I'd better hear the bad news first."

"Promise you won't get angry?"

"I'm not making any promises." He pulled her back into his arms and nuzzled her throat playfully.

Giggling and happy, Caasi blurted out, "The bad news is I burnt the roast. The good news is I went out and got Kentucky Fried Chicken."

"Caasi, that's twice this month." Blake groaned, but there was no anger in the way his eyes caressed her.

"That's not all," she added, lowering her eyes. "Honey, I tried, but I can't make Ekalb into a decent name for a boy or a girl."

Blake laughed. "What are you talking about now?"

"Your name spelled backwards, silly. I wanted to name the baby after you, and Ekalb just isn't going to do it."

A stunned silence fell over the room. "Baby?" Blake repeated. "What baby?"

"The one right here." She took his hand and pressed it against her flat stomach. "I know you said a year, but eight months from now it will be almost that long."

"Caasi," Blake murmured as if he couldn't believe

what he was hearing. "Why didn't you say something sooner?"

"I couldn't. Not until I was sure. Are you upset?"

"Upset?" He chuckled. "No, never that. Just surprised, that's all." His smile was filled with an intense satisfaction as he pulled her into his arms.

Closing her eyes, Caasi slid her arms around her husband's neck and released a contented sigh as she drew his mouth to hers.

* * * * *

REFLECTIONS OF YESTERDAY

Prologue

An iridescent moon lit up the sky above Groves Point, South Carolina. Simon Canfield sat in his Mercedes, opening one aluminum can after another until he'd downed the six-pack. Beer cooled the burning ache in the pit of his stomach. Beer helped him remember. For three hundred and sixty-four days of the year he successfully curtailed thoughts of Angie. Only on June 7 did he pull out the memories, roll them around in his tortured mind and relive again the golden days of his abandoned youth.

After ten years it astonished him that the memory of Angie's passionate young body under his held such power. Closing his eyes produced a flood of images, and a sensation of almost painful pleasure. He hated her, and in the same breath realized that he'd go to his grave never having loved another woman the way he'd loved Angie. Only thoughts of her were capable of reducing him to this pensive melancholy. Rarely did he indulge himself the way he had tonight.

Normally, Simon Canfield lived his life as a respected citizen, vice-president of the local bank, the man who made decisions that set the course of an entire community.

Tonight he drank beer instead of whiskey sours. Tonight he wore jeans instead of a pin-striped suit. Tonight he yearned for a time long past, and the young man who had loved with a passion he never hoped to recapture.

Simon's grip compressed around the hard steering wheel. The pleasure of those youthful days had been swept away by the pain that had followed in the backwash of her deception.

A turn of the key fired the car engine to life. Simon drove carefully, his sleek 450 SL cruising through the dark streets unnoticed. His first stop was outside the Catholic church, St. Elizabeth's. His figure hadn't darkened the doorway in ten years. Fleetingly he wondered if the priests kept the church doors locked these days.

Without conscious direction he headed through town, ignoring the changing message of the time and temperature flashing from the sign above the bank. In the still, silent streets he drove over the railroad tracks until he was parked outside of Angie's old house. The white paint had peeled and the flower beds were sadly neglected, the once well-groomed lawn forsaken. A string of toys and a tricycle on the sidewalk assured him the house wasn't empty. Somehow, Simon doubted that the halls rang with music as they once had.

A surge of anger rose within him until the taste of bitterness erupted in his mouth. He'd wanted children even then. They'd talked about what they would do if Angie were to have a baby. Ironically, their last conversation had been over the possibility of her being pregnant. He could picture her as clearly today as he had ten years before; her long brown hair had been pulled away from her face and tied back with a red chiffon scarf, her brown eyes as round as a deer's, mirroring her troubled heart. She'd looked so unhappy, but had quietly assured him that there wasn't any need to worry, she wasn't pregnant. Dear heaven, he wished she had been.

Now there would be no children for him. He was thirty and with one disastrous marriage in his wake, he wasn't about to try again. He'd like to blame Angie for that fiasco. But he was the one who'd been fool enough to marry a woman he didn't love, and he had paid dearly for the mistake. He wouldn't marry again.

The ache grew within him until his chest hurt with the intensity of it. Dear sweet heaven, he'd loved Angie.

Simon drove around for what seemed like hours, not surprised that his unplanned route led to the backwoods. His parents had owned these twenty acres. Simon had purchased the land after his divorce from Carol was final. He'd built the house a year later. But it wasn't the welcoming of his home he sought now. Instead, Simon drove down the long driveway that stretched from the road to the back of his house. The harsh slam of his car door echoed through the quiet night. Enough was enough. The ax was stored in the garage and with an impatience he couldn't understand, Simon fetched it, then carried it deep into the twenty acres to the small clearing. He hadn't come here in years, and the memories this land evoked were bittersweet. But Simon had neither the patience nor the desire to explore its significance.

He located the large pecan tree with some difficulty. The only light was the silken rays of a distant moon, slowly creeping toward the horizon.

On the first swing, the ax met the tree's bark with

an unrestrained violence. The second and third that followed were born of anger and frustration. Blow followed blow, and he paused only once, to remove his shirt. Uncaring, he tossed it aside and resumed his task until his muscles quivered with the effort and his shoulders heaved with exertion.

The huge tree began to fall, and a panting Simon stood back. His lungs hurt as he sucked in huge gulps of air. His naked torso glistened with perspiration in the glow of the moonlight.

"It's over," he mumbled, chest heaving, as the mighty pecan slammed against the earth.

One

The day was flawless as only Groves Point could be in the summer. The golden sun shone brightly from a sky as clear as the Caribbean Sea. Angie Robinson stood outside the hotel. Her fingers toyed nervously with the room key in her pocket as she glanced down Main Street.

Nothing was different, but everything had changed. A traffic signal had been added in front of Garland Pharmacy, and the J.C. Penney store had installed a colorful awning to shade the display windows. The beauty shop was in the same location, but the neon sign flashed a new name—Cindy's.

Drawing in a deep breath to calm herself, Angie walked toward the bakery at the end of the block. A quick survey inside revealed that the small Formica tables and the ever-full, help-yourself coffeepot were still there. But Angie didn't recognize the middle-aged woman behind the counter. The clerk caught her eye through the large front window and smiled. Angie's smile in return felt stiff and unnatural.

She crossed the street and was halfway down the

second block before she noticed that the bank had put up a sign that alternately flashed the temperature and the time of day. For a full minute she stood in a daze, watching as if it could tell her what would happen once she walked inside the double glass doors.

Angie had expected to feel a surging wave of anger, but none came. Only a blank, desolate feeling. A hollow emptiness that was incapable of echoing in the dark emotion that had dictated her life these past twelve years.

She took a step in retreat, swiveled and walked away. Not yet, she thought. She'd been in town only a few minutes. A confrontation so soon would be unwise.

Crossing the street at the light, Angie's quick-paced steps led her to the beauty salon. Cindy would tell her everything she needed to know. Cindy had been her friend. Her best friend.

"Can I help you?" A blue-eyed blonde at the reception desk glanced curiously at Angie. The girl transferred a wad of gum from one side of her mouth to the other as she waited for Angie's response.

"Is Cindy available?" she asked, trying to keep her voice even.

"Sure, she's in the back room. If you'll wait a minute, I'll get her."

"Thank you."

The girl slid off the stool and headed for the back of the salon. Empty chairs and a stack of magazines invited Angie to sit down, but for now she preferred to stand.

The bead curtain that covered a rear doorway made a jingling sound as a tall brunette appeared. Two steps into the room she paused in midstride. "Oh, my heavens, Angie." A rumbling laugh followed. "Oh, heavens, girl, where have you been all these years?" Before another moment passed, Angie was hauled into open arms and hugged as if she were a lost child returned to a worried mother. "I don't believe it." A hand gripping each shoulder pushed Angie back. "Let me look at you. You haven't changed at all."

A smile lit up Angie's soft, brown eyes. Cindy was one person she could always count on welcoming her. "Neither have you."

The musical sound of Cindy's laughter followed. "When did you get in town?"

"Just a few minutes ago." Angie felt breathless and a little giddy. Her friend looked wonderful. Cindy had been the tallest and thinnest girl in class; now she possessed the womanly curves that rounded out her height.

"Can you stay?"

"I'm only here for a couple of days."

"Dear heaven," Cindy murmured and released a long, slow sigh, "it's good to see you."

Her friend's unabashed enthusiasm for life had always been infectious. Angie had often thought that if someone could tap into Cindy's knack for seeing the bright side to everything, the world would be a much happier place. "Tell me about everyone. I'm dying to know what's been going on in Groves Point."

"Filling you in on the last…twelve years…has it really been that long?" Cindy shook her head in slow amazement. "Mimi, I'll be at the King Cole's. Call me if something disastrous comes up."

Mimi smiled. "Don't worry, I'll hold down the fort."

King Cole's was one of three restaurants in town. The food had always been moderately good and relatively cheap. Angie's father used to take her there for dinner once a month on payday. She'd never told him that she would have preferred hamburgers at the A & W on the outskirts of town.

"Bernice," Cindy cried out as they slid into the upholstered vinyl booth. "Bring us a pair of javas."

"You got it." The slim waitress in the pink uniform brought out two cups of coffee.

"You remember Bernie, don't you?" Cindy prompted. "She was a couple of classes behind us."

For the life of her, Angie didn't, but she pretended to, smiling up at the waitress who looked as blank as Angie. "Good to see you again, Bernice."

"You too." She set the beige mugs on the Formica tabletop. "You want cream with this?"

"No, thanks."

With a slow gait, Bernice returned behind the counter. "We tried to get hold of you for the ten-year reunion," Cindy said with a hint of frustration. "But no one knew where you were."

"Charleston."

"Really? Bob and I were there just this summer."

"You married Bob." That deduction wasn't one of her most brilliant, she thought. Cindy and Bob had dated exclusively their senior year.

"Going on eleven years now. We've got two boys. B.J.'s ten and Matt's eight."

"Wonderful." Angie couldn't have meant that more. Her childhood friend deserved a life filled with happiness. "Bob was in the service for a time and I went to beauty school in Fayetteville and lived with my aunt." Her finger made lazy circles around the rim of the mug as she spoke. "What about you? The last thing I remember is that you were working as a clerk at the pharmacy."

Angie stared into the dark depths of the coffee cup. "Dad and I moved the February after graduation." Neither mentioned that she had left Groves Point without a word or a forwarding address. Not in twelve years had she contacted anyone.

"Remember Shirley Radcliff?"

Angie wasn't likely to forget her. Simon's mother had been furious when he'd asked Angie to the Senior Prom instead of Shirley.

"Whatever became of Shirley?" The muscles of her stomach knotted. If Mrs. Canfield had gotten her way Shirley would have married Simon.

"She married a guy in real estate. From what I understand, they're living high off the hog in Savannah. No kids, mind you. It would ruin their lifestyle."

A smile tugged at the corner of Angie's mouth. No, Shirley wouldn't be the type to appreciate children.

"Gary Carlson's a lawyer in Charlotte. He's married and has a daughter. And Sharon Gleanson's a flight attendant."

"I don't believe it." Angie couldn't control a soft laugh. Sharon had always been overweight and extremely shy.

"What about you, Angie? Are you married? Do you have children?"

For an instant, one crazy instant, she hesitated. "No to both." Averting her gaze, fearing what her eyes would reveal, Angie asked, "What about Simon? Whatever happened to him?"

"You two were really thick for a while, weren't you?" She didn't wait for Angie to reply. "He married a girl from college, I can't recall her name offhand… Carol, I think. It didn't last long, two, three years. Simon's kept to himself since."

"Is he at the bank?" The question was unnecessary, Angie already knew without having to ask, but she had to do something to disguise the pain. So he had married. She'd known it, in her heart she'd always known it. Angie had assumed that after all these years what Simon did couldn't hurt her anymore. But she was wrong. "His daddy's the president and Simon's the vice-president. But these days I think Simon runs most everything. He's gotten to be a real stuffed shirt, if you know what I mean."

Angie did. Simon had become the mirror image of his father in spite of his best intentions.

Cindy downed the last of her coffee. "Listen, I've got to get back to the shop. Mrs. Harris, my two o'clock appointment, just arrived. Can you come to dinner tonight? I'll see if I can get a few of the ol' gang together."

"That'd be great. But don't go to any trouble."

"Are you kidding, I haven't got time. Come around six-thirty. We're in the old Silverman place across the street from the park."

"Sure, I remember it. I'll see you tonight."

Cindy pulled some change from her pocket. "Coffee's on me."

"Thanks."

Angie left King Cole's with a sense of exhilaration. After everything that had happened in the past twelve years, she had thought she'd hate Groves Point. But it wasn't in her. The best times of her life had happened in this small community. As much as she'd wanted to blot out the past, it was impossible. Glenn had tried to explain that to her, but she hadn't understood. Now she did. He had been right to tell her she had to confront the past before looking to the future. She'd known that, too, but the past was so painful that it had seemed simpler to ignore the hurt and go on with her life.

The urge to talk to Glenn directed her back to the hotel. Her room was clean, but generic. A double bed, nightstand, dresser and chairs made up the room's furnishings. The one window looked over Main Street, and from where she stood, Angie could see the sign above the bank. An indescribable pain flashed through her. Angie reached for her phone.

"Glenn Lambert."

The warm familiarity of his voice chased the chill from her blood. "Angie Robinson here."

"Angie," he said softly. "How was the trip?"

"Uneventful."

"And Groves Point?"

She smiled gently. "The same. I looked up an old friend who clued me in on what's been happening. The class brain's a lawyer and the shyest girl at Groves Point High is a flight attendant."

"I thought you were the class brain," he said with a chuckle.

"Gary and I shared the honors."

A short silence followed. "I miss you, babe."

Angie always felt uncomfortable when he called her that, but she'd never told Glenn. "I miss you too."

"I wish I could believe that." A trace of impatience tinged his voice, but he disguised it behind a cheerful invitation. "When you come home I'm going to cook you the thickest steak in Charleston."

"I'll look forward to that."

"Good. Have you finished...your business yet?"

Glenn didn't know exactly what it was she had to do in Groves Point, and Angie had never explained. That lack of trust had hurt Glenn, and she felt a twinge of guilt. Glenn was the best thing to happen in her life in twelve years. "I've only been in town an hour." But it had to be today. The banks were closed on weekends.

"Will you call me tomorrow?"

"If you want."

"I want you for the rest of my life, Angie. I love you."

"I love you, too," she echoed softly. "I'll talk to you tomorrow." Gently, she ended the call. Talking to Glenn reinforced her determination to be done with the purpose of her visit. A quick check in the mirror assured her that she was now a composed, mature woman. Simon Canfield, Sr., would be incapable of destroying her as he had so long ago.

Not once on the walk to the bank did Angie hesitate. Her heart leaped to her throat as she pushed the glass door that opened into the interior. That, too, hadn't changed. Marble pillars, marble floors, marble hearts.

The teller gave no indication that she recognized her, but Angie remembered Mrs. Wilson, who had been with Groves Point Citizens Federal for years.

"I'd like to see Mr. Canfield," she announced in a crisp voice.

Mrs. Wilson's lined face revealed nothing. "Do you have an appointment?"

"No, but I'm confident he'll see me." She wasn't the least bit sure, but Mrs. Wilson didn't know that. "Tell him Angie Robinson is here."

Again Mrs. Wilson's features remained stoic. "If you'll wait a moment." She left Angie standing on the other side of the counter as she walked the length of the bank and tapped against a frosted glass door. She returned a minute later, her face a bright red hue. "Mr. Canfield suggests…" she started, then swallowed with difficulty. "He would prefer not to see you, Ms. Robinson."

How dare he! Angie fumed inwardly, but gave a gracious smile to the teller. "Thank you for your trouble."

The older woman gave her a sympathetic look. "Nice seeing you again, Angie."

"Thank you."

Her heels made sharp, clicking sounds against the marble floor as she turned and walked toward the exit. How dare he humiliate her like this! He had no right. None. With one hand against the metal bar on the glass door, Angie forcefully expelled her breath. She wasn't scum he could walk over. She wouldn't let him.

With an energy born of anger and pride, she pivoted sharply and walked the length of the bank lobby, her chin tilted at a proud angle. She wasn't a member of the country club, nor had she been a member of the upperclass, but she was going to have her say to Simon Canfield, Sr., whether he wanted to hear her or not.

Not bothering to knock, Angie let herself in to the office. "Excuse me for interrupting…" She stopped and swallowed back the shock. It wasn't Simon's father who rose from the large oak desk to confront her, but Simon. Time had altered his dark good looks. The gray eyes that had once warmed her with his love were now as cold and grim as the storm-tossed North Sea. Tiny lines fanned from them, but Angie was convinced he hadn't gotten them from smiling. He was so cold that in his gray flannel suit he resembled a stone castle whose defenses were impenetrable. Cold and cruel. The edge of his hard mouth twisted upward. "Hello, Angie."

"Simon." The oxygen returned to her lungs in a deep breath.

Neither spoke again. The chill in the room was palpable, Angie mused, and a smile briefly touched her eyes. It hadn't always been that way with them. Years ago, the temperature had been searingly high, and they couldn't stay out of each other's arms.

"Something amuses you?"

"No." If anything, the thought should produce tears. But Angie hadn't cried in years. Simon had taught her that. She lowered her gaze to the desk top. Crisp, neat, orderly.

"You wanted to see me?" he began in starched tones.

"I wanted to see your father."

"He isn't well. I've assumed most of his duties."

They were speaking like polite strangers.... No, Angie amended the thought. They were facing each other like bitter adversaries.

"I'm sorry to hear about your father."

"Are you?" He cocked a mocking brow.

"Yes, of course." She felt flustered and uneasy.

"I'd have thought you hated him. But then, it must be difficult to dislike someone who has been so generous with you in the past."

Simon's biting comment was a vivid reminder of the reason for her being in Groves Point. The color flowed from her face, leaving her sickly pale. "Taking that money has always bothered me," Angie confessed in a weak voice that she barely recognized as her own.

The pencil Simon was holding snapped in two. "I'll

just bet it did. Ten thousand dollars, Angie? I'm surprised you didn't want more."

"Want more?" she repeated, her heart constricting painfully. "No." Slowly, she shook her head from side to side. She wouldn't bother to explain that it'd nearly killed her to accept that.

Her fingers fumbled at the snap of her purse and were visibly shaking as she withdrew the narrow, white envelope. "I'm returning every penny, plus ten percent compounded interest. Tell your father that I…" She hesitated. "No. Don't tell him anything."

"I don't want your money." Simon glared accusingly at the envelope on the edge of his desk.

"It was never mine," Angie said, her voice laced with sadness. "I took it for Clay."

"My, my, aren't you the noble, self-sacrificing daughter?"

The words hurt more than if he'd reached out and slapped her. Involuntarily, Angie blanched. "It bought you your freedom," she managed awkwardly. "I would have thought you'd treasure your marriage more. You paid enough for it."

It looked for a moment as if Simon wanted to physically lash out at her. His fists knotted at his sides, the knuckles whitening.

"I didn't mean that," she whispered, despising their need to hurt each other. "I know you won't believe this, but I wish you well, Simon."

He didn't answer her, instead his troubled gaze narrowed on the envelope.

"If you don't want the money," she murmured, her gaze following his, "then give it to charity."

"Maybe I will," he said and his lip curved up in cynical amusement. "I believe that was my father's original intent."

To her dismay, Angie sucked in a hurt gasp. Slowly the ache in her breast eased so that she could speak. "Oh, Simon, you've changed. What's made you so bitter?"

His short laugh was mirthless. "Not what, but who. Leave, Angie, before I do something we'll both regret."

With an inborn dignity and grace, Angie turned and placed her hand on the doorknob. But something deep within her wouldn't allow her to walk out the door.

"Go ahead," he shouted.

"I can't," she murmured, turning back. "It's taken me twelve years to come back to this town. Twelve years, Simon." Her voice was raised and wobbled as she fought to control the emotion. "I refuse to have you talk to me as though I did some horrible deed. If anyone should apologize it's you and your family."

"Me?" Simon nearly choked. "You're the one who sold out, so don't play Joan of Arc now and try to place the blame on someone else."

"I did it for you," she cried.

His harsh laugh was filled with contempt. "Only a moment ago you did it for Clay, or so you said."

Angie swallowed back the painful lump that tightened within her throat. Sadly she shook her head. "I'm sorry, Simon, sorry for what happened and sorry for what you've become. But I won't accept—"

"Our love had a price tag—ten thousand dollars," he shouted. "It was *you* who took that money and left. So don't try to ease your conscience now." Leaning forward, he rested the palms of his hands on the edge of the desk. "Now I suggest that you leave."

"Goodbye, Simon."

He didn't answer but turned and faced the window that looked out onto the parking lot.

The door made a clicking sound as she let herself out. Several pairs of eyes followed her progress across the marble floor. Undoubtedly her sharp exchange with Simon had been heard by half the people in the bank. A rush of color invaded her pale face, but she managed to keep her unflinching gaze directed straight ahead as she returned to the hotel.

The key to the hotel room wouldn't fit into the lock as Angie struggled to keep her hand steady. She felt as if her legs were made of rubber. By the time she'd manipulated the lock, she was trembling and weak.

A soft sob erupted from her throat as she set her purse on the dresser. Angie's hand gripped the back of the chair as another cry followed the first. Tears blurred her eyes so that the view from the third-story window swam in and out of her vision.

At first she struggled to hold back the emotion, disliking the weakness of tears. Her fingers wiped the moisture from her cheek as she began to pace the room, staring at the ceiling. Soon every breath became a heart-wrenching cry for all the pain of a love long past. She fell across the bed and buried her face in the pillow, crying out a lifetime of agony. She cried for the mother she had never known. And the weak father whom she loved. She cried for the empty promises of her father's dreams, and the Canfield money that had given him the chance to fulfill them. And she cried for a town divided by railroad tracks that made one half unacceptable to the other and had doomed a love from the start.

Fresh tears filled her eyes. Glenn loved her enough

to force her to settle the past. He loved her enough to want her for his wife.

Twisting around, Angie stared out the window at the blue sky. She wept for Glenn, the man she wasn't sure she could marry.

And for Simon, the man she had.

Two

The gleaming white envelope remained on the corner of Simon's desk as he rolled back his chair and stood. For Angie to come to Groves Point had taken courage. To confront him and return that money had cost her a lot of pride. One thing Simon remembered vividly about Angie was that she might not have had two pennies to rub together, but when it came to pride, she had been the richest lady in town.

When he'd told her to leave, she'd turned for the door and hesitated. Her small shoulders had stiffened with resolve as she refused. In that minute it was as if twelve years had been wiped out and she was seventeen again. She'd been so beautiful. And heaven help him, she was just as beautiful today. Naturally, several things about her were different. No longer did her silky brown hair reach her waist. Now it was shoulder length and professionally styled so that it curled around her lovely oval face.

Her graceful curves revealed a woman's body, svelte and elegant beneath a crisp, linen business suit. There had been a time when Angie hated to wear anything but washed-out jeans and faded T-shirts.

Angie had been his first love and he had been hers. Together they had discovered the physical delights of their bodies. With excruciating patience they had held off as long as they could, because it had been so important to Angie that they be married first.

Discipline might well have been their greatest teacher. In restraining their physical desires, they had learned the delicate uses of kissing and the exquisite pleasure of exploring fingers. Their hearts beat as one and they were convinced their love could overtake convention, prejudice and everything else that loomed in their path.

Only it hadn't. Angie had prostituted herself. Simon had loved her so much he would have willingly given his life for her. And now he wanted to hate her with the same intensity and discovered he couldn't.

The bank was empty when Simon left his office. The envelope remained on his desk. He would do as Angie suggested, and give it to charity. Money meant little to him. He'd had it all his life and had never been happy. The only real contentment he'd ever known had been those few months with Angie. Now it seemed that she, too, had discovered money's limitations.

The Mercedes was parked in the side lot, and Simon was on Main Street before Angie drifted into his thoughts again. He wondered where she was staying and if she had come to town alone. She had used her maiden name, but he hadn't thought to look for a diamond on her ring finger. If she hadn't married, it would be a shock. One glance at the woman she had become revealed a rare jewel. Angie was a prize most men wouldn't ignore.

Engrossed in his thoughts, Simon automatically took a left turn off Main onto Oak Street on his way to the country club. Tonight he needed a long workout. A flash of color captured his attention and he glanced across the green lawn of the city park. Cindy and Bob Shannon were in the front yard firing up a barbecue. Dressed in blue shorts and a faded T-shirt was Angie. She sat on the Shannons' porch with a beer bottle in her hand, chatting with her friends as if she hadn't been away more than a week. Charlie Young, the school's football hero and new owner of the hardware store, came out the screen door and plopped down beside her. He said something to Angie, who threw back her head and laughed cheerfully. The musical sound of her mirth drifted through the park to Simon, assaulting him from all sides.

The muscles of his abdomen tensed. Angie was where she belonged. She was with her friends.

The sleek white Mercedes caught Angie's eye as it peeled down the narrow street. Simon. It had to be. She didn't know of anyone else in town who could afford such an expensive car. The ten thousand she'd brought was petty cash to a man like Simon, but to her it represented five years of scrimping and not building up her business as she'd wanted. Returning it was a matter of pride. She hadn't touched a dime of it. Clay had spent it chasing dreams. Her father had insisted that the Canfields owed her that money. As far as Angie was concerned, the Canfields owed her nothing.

"You have to remember we're rubbing elbows with the upper echelon," Bob teased, twisting off the cap of a beer bottle. "Ol' Charlie is now a member of the Groves Point Country Club."

"Charlie!" Cindy gave a small squeal of delight. "That's really something."

Angie thought it revealing that a city would decide Charlie unacceptable one day and welcome him the next.

"I knew there was a reason I bought that hardware store."

With the agility of a man well acquainted with the art of barbecuing, Bob flipped over the hamburgers as if he were handling hotcakes. "And tell us mere serfs, your worship, what's it like to mingle with the Canfields and the Radcliffs of our fair city?"

Casually Charlie shrugged one shoulder. "Why not find out yourselves? There's a dinner tomorrow night and I'd like the three of you to come as my guests."

Cindy tossed her husband a speculative glance. "Oh, Bob, could we? I've always wanted to know what the inside of the country club looks like."

Uneasy now, Bob cleared his throat. "I suppose this means I'll have to wear a suit and tie."

"Honey, you've got the blue one we bought on sale before Easter," Cindy argued. The burst of excited happiness added a pinkish hue to her face. "Of course I'll need to have something new," she said and shared a conspiratorial smile with her friend.

Admirably, Angie refrained from laughing. From the sound of them they were all seventeen again and discussing prom night.

"What about you, Angie? Can you come?" Charlie was regarding her with an eager expression. From the minute Charlie had arrived he'd made it plain that he liked what he saw. His divorce was final, and he looked as if he was ready to try his hand at love again. In an effort to steer clear of his interest, Angie had taken pains to mention Glenn.

"Like Cindy, I'm afraid I haven't a thing to wear," Angie explained and lifted her palm in a gesture of defeat.

"We'll both go shopping!" Cindy exclaimed with enthusiasm. "I know the perfect shop in Fairmont."

"Fairmont!" Bob choked. "Just don't go using any credit cards."

Slowly shaking her head, Cindy tossed her husband a playful look. "Robert, Robert, Robert. I've always said if the shoe fits, charge it."

Angie woke with the first light of dawn. Sunlight splashed through the open drapes and spilled over the bed and walls. Sitting up, she rubbed the sleep from her face and stood. Her watch announced that it was barely six, hardly a decent hour to be up and about on a Saturday. Cindy wasn't expecting her until ten. With four hours to kill, Angie dressed in old jeans and an Atlanta Braves T-shirt.

A truck stop on the outskirts of town was the only place open where she could get a cup of coffee. She'd hoped to avoid that area of town because the Canfields' twenty-acre property was in that direction.

As Angie climbed inside her small car, she realized coffee was only an excuse. Yes, she'd pull over at the truck stop, but her destination was the small clearing on the Canfield property. Something inside her needed to return there. The thought was a sad reflection of her emotional state. Twelve years had passed, and she

hadn't been able to forget the love she'd shared with
Simon in that small clearing in the woods. The physical aspect of their relationship still had the power to
inflict a rush of regret and sorrow. They'd been wrong
to steal into the church that night. Wrong to have gone
against convention and the wishes of his parents. A
few words whispered over her mother's Bible had never
been legally binding. But Angie had felt married even
if Simon hadn't.

The years had changed the land, and Angie nearly
missed the turnoff from the highway. A long, sprawl-
ing house had been built, and the paved road led to the
back and a four-car garage.

Hesitating, Angie decided to ignore the house and
go on. The morning was young, and it wasn't likely
that she'd wake anyone. The road went deep into the
property, and she could steal in and out without anyone
knowing she'd ever come.

Leaving the car, Angie took care to close the door silently, not wanting the slightest sound to betray her presence. With her hands stuffed deep within her jeans, she
climbed over a fallen tree and ventured into the dense
forest. A gentle breeze chased a chill up her arm, but
the cold wasn't from the wind. Her breathing had become shallow and uneven, and for a moment she wasn't
sure she could go on. Only once had she felt this unnerved, and that had been as a child when she'd visited
her mother's grave.

There were similarities. In this clearing she was returning to a time long past and a love long dead. But
from the way her nerves were reacting, nothing about
this time and place had been forgotten. Every tree, every
limb was lovingly familiar.

To someone who didn't know these woods, the clearing would come as a surprise. The climb up the hill was steep, and just when she felt the need to pause and rest, the quiet meadow came into view. Even now, the simple beauty of this small lea caused her to stop and breathe in the morning mist. The uncomplicated elegance had been untouched by time. As she walked down the hill to the center, Angie felt like a child coming home after a long absence. The urge to hold out her arms and envelop this feeling was overwhelming. She wanted to swing around and sing, and laugh…and cry.

It had been here that Simon had held her in his arms and assured her that heaven and earth would pass away, but his love wouldn't. It had been here that they'd talked of the children to come and the huge house he planned to build her.

She'd laughed when he'd taken a stick and drawn out the plans in the fertile ground. They'd have lots of bedrooms and a large kitchen with plenty of cupboard space. He'd build it himself, he claimed. And remembering the skill he had with wood, Angie didn't doubt him.

Then that night in June, he had brought her to their imaginary home, lifted her in his arms and carried her over the threshold. Drunk with happiness she'd looped her arms around his neck and kissed his face until he demanded she stop.

"Just where are you taking me?" Angie had murmured, playfully nibbling on his earlobe with her teeth.

"To the master bedroom, where else, Mrs. Canfield?"

Angie tossed back her head and laughed. "Oh, Simon, I do love you. I'll make you the best wife in all South Carolina."

"I'm holding you to that," he said and kissed her

until she was weak with longing. His tenderness had brought tears to her eyes as he unbuttoned her blouse and slowly slipped it from her shoulders. Her long hair fell forward as she bowed her head. Tears filled her dusky, dark eyes.

"Angie, what's wrong?"

"Nothing," she whispered. "I love you so much. It's just..."

"What?" Gently, he had brushed the hair from her face and kissed the corner of her eyes, stopping the flow of tears. "Angie, I'd do anything in the world for you."

"I'm being silly to cry over a silly piece of paper. I don't need it. Not when I have you. But, Simon, do you think we'll forget our anniversary?"

"I'll never forget anything about you, or this night," he vowed. Straightening, he had taken the knife from his pocket and crossed the meadow to a huge pecan tree. It stood regal and proud, the tallest tree on the edge of the clearing. With painstaking effort he'd engraved the date and their names in the bark. The tree would stand for all time as their witness.

A distant sound of a barking dog shook Angie from her reverie. The tree. That was what was missing, gone. Sadness overwhelmed her when she located the stump. From the look of it, the tree had been crudely chopped down years ago. Simon had done this, cutting her out of his world as ruthlessly as the ax had severed the life of the mighty pecan. It shouldn't hurt this much, she told herself. But it did. The pain dug as deep as the day Simon's mother had come to her with the money.

Her legs felt as though they would no longer hold her upright, and she slumped down, sitting on the stump as the strength drained from her. Gone was the outrage, vanishing as quickly as it came. Her tears were those of sorrow and for what they had lost. There was no more fight left in her. Simon had appointed himself judge and divorced her with an ax. If their marriage had been a document instead of bark she at least would have had the advice of counsel. Without conscience he had cast their love aside as though it had no meaning.

A dog barked again and the sound was noticeably closer. Brushing the hair from her forehead, Angie straightened. A black Labrador raced into the clearing, barking, his tail and ears alert.

A sad smile touched Angie's eyes. "Oh, Blackie, is it really you?" Simon had trained the dog from a pup.

The angry dog ignored her, intent only in voicing his discovery.

"Blackie, don't you remember me?" Crouched as she was, Angie held out her hand for him to smell. Blackie had once been her friend as well.

"That isn't Blackie."

Simon's gruff voice from behind startled Angie. She sprang to her feet, her eyes wide and fearful as they fell on the rifle in his hands.

"This is Prince, Blackie's son." He lowered the gun at his side so that the muzzle was angled toward the ground.

Prince continued to voice his displeasure, but one sharp word from Simon silenced him.

"What happened to Blackie?"

"He died," Simon answered starkly.

"I'm sorry.... I know how much you..."

"You're trespassing."

The sun was high enough now so that it invaded the

clearing, its brightness peeking through the limbs and bathing the earth with a gentle glow.

"Am I?" she asked in a voice so soft it could barely be heard. "Once it was my home."

"Don't try to make this place something it wasn't." A withdrawn look marked his features. His calm declaration chilled her more than angry words. "There was only one room here and that was the bedroom."

"Oh, Simon," she pleaded. "Don't ruin that, too."

"Too?" His intense gray eyes narrowed and a bitter laugh escaped his throat. "If anything was ruined, it was your doing, Angie."

Their gazes clashed for a long moment, and Angie swallowed back an angry retort.

"Look at us, treating each other this way." She tucked the tips of her fingers in her jeans pockets and looked past him into the clearing. There had always been a special magic to this place, a calming reassurance she hadn't found elsewhere, even in church. Here, the love they shared had sheltered and protected them from the influence of the outside world. "At one time we were best friends, and…and a lot more. There wasn't anything we couldn't share."

Simon tensed. "That was a long time ago." Again bitterness coated his words.

"I've hurt you, and oh, dear Simon, I'm deeply sorry for that. But you need to realize that I was hurt, too. It nearly killed me to leave you and Groves Point."

"Did the money help soothe the pain?"

Stinging tears welled in her eyes, but she blinked them away, turning her hurt, questing gaze to him. She'd come to Groves Point to make her peace with

Simon, but he seemed intent on lashing out at her with a storehouse of twelve years' resentment.

The curve of his mouth quirked in a derisive frown. "Tears, Angie? Believe me, I'm too old and too wise for that female trick."

Her heart wanted to cry in anguish, but no sound came from her parched throat. Proudly, she lifted her trembling chin. "It's taken me so long to come back. This place has haunted me all these years. But I never thought to find you so cold and bitter." The hard lump in her throat caused her to swallow before continuing. "I'm sorry for you, Simon. Sorry for what you've become, but I can't accept the blame." Her gaze swept the meadow, and again she was soothed by its peacefulness.

Turning away from him, she started down the steep slope toward her car. She felt Simon's presence looming above her. Proud, bitter, hurtful...hurting. A part of her yearned to ease that pain, but she doubted that anything she could do would touch Simon now.

Once inside the car Angie risked a look into the trees, but Simon and his dog were gone. Her hands gripped the steering wheel until the grooves made deep indentations into her palms. This wasn't the way she'd wanted things to be. Deep in her heart she'd expected to find Simon married...and happy.

The sudden need to escape was almost overwhelming. Glenn was right, she had needed to come back to Groves Point, but it wasn't working out as either of them had anticipated.

The turn of the car key produced a dull, grinding sound. Angie tried again. There shouldn't be anything wrong, she thought. She'd driven there without a problem. Again she tried the ignition, but only a sickly coughing sound returned.

"Oh, great." She slammed her fist against the steering wheel and groaned angrily. She didn't know a thing about the internal workings of a motor. Pulling back the hood release, she climbed out of the car. The hood was cracked open and she inserted a finger to release it fully. A full three minutes later, her finger hurt and she had yet to loosen the hood latch.

"What's the problem?" Simon's gaze impaled her, grim displeasure thinning his mouth.

"My car won't start." She felt like an idiot, standing there massaging her finger.

"Why not?"

"Go ahead, car, tell me why you won't start." She turned and mockingly questioned the Ford. "How am I supposed to know? Believe me, Simon, I want out of here just as much as you want me gone."

A brittle smile cracked his mouth. "I sincerely doubt that. Here, let me take a look." He handed the rifle to Angie. "Hold this."

Doing her best to disguise her uneasiness, Angie accepted the gun.

"It isn't loaded," he said with his back to her as he released the latch and lifted the hood. "Has this car been giving you problems?"

"No. I drove from Charleston without a hitch."

"Charleston," he repeated.

"I live there now."

The hesitation was barely noticeable. "It's a beautiful city."

Angie was holding her breath. This brief exchange was the first civil one she'd had with Simon. His dog was eyeing her again, his sleek ebony head tilted at a curious angle. Crouching down, Angie held out her hand to him a second time.

"I remember your daddy," she told him softly.

The long, black tail began to move as his cold nose smelled her fingers.

"How long have you had Prince?" Angie asked, more to carry the conversation than any desire to know the dog's age.

"Must be five, six years now." Simon's voice was muffled, his upper body folded over the side of the car. "I'm going to need a couple of tools."

"Can I get them for you?" Angie's voice was faintly high in her eagerness to help. "Believe me, car problems were the last thing I expected." She gave a small, tight laugh. "If the truth were known I was hoping to make a grand exit."

A hint of a smile came and went. "My tools are in the garage."

The house had to be a good quarter mile down the gravel road.

Simon's gaze followed Angie's. "You can wait here if you prefer."

"I'd like to come with you." It felt so good to talk to Simon again without a decade of bitterness positioned between them like a brick wall. There was so much she wanted to say, and just as much she had hoped to ask. Tomorrow she'd be gone.

His gray eyes brushed over her speculatively. "If you like."

Fingertips tucked in her pockets once again, Angie matched his stride as they walked toward the house. Covertly, she studied him. The sprinkling of gray hairs at his temple gave him a distinguished look. His hair was shorter now than she recalled. But little about Simon was the way she remembered.

Her mind searched for something to say and came back empty. They were strangers. But intimate strangers. She doubted that others in this world knew Simon as well as she had at seventeen. He lived behind a stone mask now, closing himself off from the world. It hadn't taken much to discern from her conversation with Cindy and Bob that Simon had become an entity unto himself. He needed no one and had made that plain to the citizens of Groves Point.

"What do you think's wrong with my car?" she asked after a long moment, disliking the silence.

"I'm not sure."

Angie's shoes kicked up the gravel as they walked. Her usual pace was somewhat slower, but she wanted to keep even with Simon. Undoubtedly, he wanted to be rid of her as quickly as possible. But this unexpected reprieve was a welcome respite. Prince marched at his master's side, content to be with Simon, rather than run ahead.

Angie's gaze roamed over the trees and flowers that grew in abundance there. Once, years ago, she had been as young and fresh as the wildflowers, pushing through the fertile ground and seeking out the sun. Now she felt as old as the earth and not nearly as wise.

Glancing at Simon, she witnessed the proud defiance in the tilt of his head. Even the beauty of this land had been tarnished by his hate.

"I've always loved it here," she said quietly.

The subdued tone of her voice drew his gaze. "Then why did you leave?"

"Oh, Simon, if I could change our past, rectify all my mistakes, don't you think I would? I left Groves Point because I felt I was doing the best thing for us. Don't you realize that it hurt me too?"

His jaw was clenched and tight, but he said nothing as he stared unfalteringly at her.

A strained silence followed.

"Then why did you come back?"

Angie didn't know how to put into words the emotion that had driven her to Groves Point. "I wanted to return the money." An uncomplicated answer seemed best.

"You could have mailed it."

Her hand burrowed deeper into her jeans pockets. "Yes, I could have."

They approached the back of the property, giving Angie a moment to study the house. Briefly, she wondered if the interior was anything like the plans Simon had drawn for her. Excitement flashed through her and died as quickly as it sprang. Feeling the way he did about her, Simon would have gone to great lengths to avoid a house that would even faintly resemble their dream one.

"This way," Simon spoke, holding a door for her that opened into the three-car garage. The gloomy interior was filled with shadows, the open door dispersing slivers of light into the dark.

Angie's gaze fell beyond the sleek white Mercedes to the turquoise convertible.

"Simon," she whispered unsteadily as she moved into the room. "You still have the car." Reverently her hand brushed the polished fender. Some of the best times of her life had been in this old convertible. Their first kiss had taken place in this '51 Chevy. Simon had come to her house so she could help him study for a science test. Afterward he'd taken her to the A & W for a root beer. And later still, he'd nervously leaned over and lightly brushed her mouth with his. Their first kiss hadn't been much more than that, but with time their technique had greatly improved.

On countless summer evenings they'd driven up to Three Tree Point and gazed at the stars. Some evenings the heavens loomed so close that it seemed that all they had to do was reach out and pluck the stars from the sky. Simon had cradled her in his arms and whispered that if it were in his power, he'd weave moonbeams as a crown for her hair.

"I've been meaning to sell that old thing for years," he said flatly. "It doesn't run and hasn't in years. All it does is take up space in the garage."

Angie dropped her hand to her side. "It brings back a lot of memories." The corners of her mouth lifted with a sad smile.

He didn't speak for a minute. "Yes, I suppose it does," he said as though the thought hadn't occurred to him.

Simon would like her to think the old Chevy convertible was a useless piece of junk, but Angie wasn't easily fooled. There had been too many hot summer days when she'd helped him smear the car wax over a spotless surface, her reflection shining like glass from the polished hood. Simon loved this old car. The fact that it was in his garage said as much.

"I'm ready to go." His eyes had narrowed into silver slits as he paused at the door, toolbox in hand. "Are you coming or not?"

Reluctantly, Angie left the car. She would have liked

to look inside the glove compartment, to see what secrets it held.

They were several yards down the road before Simon spoke again. "How's Clay?"

The question surprised her. Clay and Simon had never been close. They had tolerated each other. Clay's dislike of the Canfields had been as strong as Simon's distrust of her now. "He's doing well," she said and didn't elaborate.

Simon breathed in deeply. "What about you, Angie, are you happy?"

Her throat went dry and a bubble of hysterical laughter choked off a reply. For twelve years her life had been in limbo. Could anyone be content there? She hadn't thought about being happy, not really, not in years. Happiness was relative to her circumstances. "I suppose."

"You must enjoy Charleston, it's a beautiful city."

Each question was a gentle prod. He cared enough to be curious and that pleased her. "I own a flower shop."

Simon nodded, seemingly unsurprised. "You always did love flowers. Business must be good." He was referring to the envelope she'd given him.

She lifted one shoulder in a delicate shrug. "I can't complain."

Idly she picked up a stick and threw it for Prince. Playing catch had been Blackie's favorite game, and his son was sure to appreciate it, too. Immediately the Labrador kicked up his feet and shot into the woods. Angie's musical laughter followed him.

Simon stopped and studied her, their gazes clashing. "Your laugh is the same."

Angie dropped her eyes first. "I wouldn't like to think much about me was different."

"Why not? We all change in twelve years."

"That's not what I meant." She wasn't quite sure what she was trying to explain. Simon was right, there were several things different about her. She was a mature woman now, not a naive teenager.

Proudly, Prince returned with the stick, and bending over to retrieve it gave Angie a moment to compose her thoughts. "In some ways, I'm looking to recapture that enchanted summer of my life. That summer with you."

"You can't." Simon's words cut at her as painfully as a slashing knife. "That time is gone forever."

Angie paused and felt a compelling urge to reach out and touch him. Tightening her hand around the stick, Angie threw it again. "I know."

"Why did you come back?" Simon demanded harshly. "Why now, after all this time?"

Slowly, she turned toward him. "I had to come, I've wasted too many years as it is."

Panting, Prince returned with the stick, but when Angie bent over to take it from his mouth Simon stopped her. Gripping her left hand he raised his eyes to hers.

His dark brows furrowed together. "You've never married?"

Angie swallowed, but her voice wavered emotionally. "I couldn't. I married at seventeen."

Three

Simon went pale, his hand dropping hers. "Are you saying that you never married because of what we did?"

Her head drooped. Angie couldn't find the words to explain. "No. I realized when your mother gave me the check that whatever commitment you felt toward me was over."

"Haven't you got that turned around?"

"How do you mean?" Angie asked, missing the gist of his question. She remembered vividly how Georgia Canfield had come to her and explained that Simon had found another girl at college.

"I wasn't the one who asked to be free." His mouth tightened grimly.

"Not technically," she argued. "You sent your mother to do it for you."

"What?" he exploded. He opened his mouth, then closed it again as if to cut off what he was about to say. "I think we'd better talk." Pivoting sharply, he headed toward the house, leaving a confused Angie to follow in his wake.

He was so far ahead of her that by the time she

reached the back of the house, he was already inside and the door was left open, waiting for her.

The back door led to a porch with a matching washer and dryer. Angie wiped the mud from her shoes on the braided rug just inside. Rounding the corner she paused in the doorway of the kitchen. The room was huge with bright countertops and shining appliances. Apparently, Simon had someone come in to do the housekeeping.

His hip was leaning against the long counter, his arms crossed over his chest. "Now say that again?"

"What? That your mother asked for your freedom?"

"Yes." His eyes were measuring her with an accusing glint. "How could you have believed such a thing?" He looked as if he wanted to strangle her.

"I didn't!" she shouted in her defense. "Don't you remember I took the Greyhound bus to the university. I asked you myself."

"You couldn't have." He straightened and began pacing the polished tile floor like a tormented beast trapped in the close confines of a cage. Suddenly, as if he needed to sit down, he pulled out a chair. "I think we had better start at the beginning."

Angie joined him at the round oak table, her hands clasped in her lap. The confrontation with his mother might have taken place twelve years ago, but she vividly remembered it as if it had happened yesterday. And now Simon was acting as if none of this were true.

"Don't lie to me, Simon. Not now, after all these years."

"I swear before everything I hold dear that I never asked to be free from you, Angie." Every facet of his face was intent, imploring.

Slowly, Angie shook her head, not knowing what to believe.

"Start from the beginning," he urged, his gray eyes wide and rapt.

"You'd left for the university that September."

He nodded. "I wrote to you practically every day and phoned almost that often. How could you have possibly believed there was someone else?"

Her nails cut painfully into her palms. She couldn't deny that in the beginning he'd contacted her daily. Being separated like that had been miserable for them both. But Simon seemed to have adjusted more quickly than she. "At first you did."

"What does that mean?" His eyes narrowed defensively.

"I...noticed that around November your letters became less frequent." She lowered her eyes to the quilted placemat on the tabletop. "You didn't phone nearly as often either."

"I was saving money so I could buy you a Christmas present. The phone bill for October had taken nearly all my allowance."

She had known that, too. But at the time, she'd been so unhappy without him that every day apart had seemed an eternity. "I knew you were involved with basketball so I didn't say anything. But whenever we talked, you were always in such a hurry, and even your letters were getting shorter and shorter."

"Angie, I was about to flunk out of two classes because I spent so much time writing and talking to you."

It all sounded so petty now. She wanted to tear her eyes away from him but found she couldn't. His smoldering gaze held her captive, demanding that she continue.

"The second week in February your mother came into the pharmacy and said she needed to talk to me." Nervously her fingers toyed with the fringe around the orange-and-brown plaid placemat. "She...she said that she'd noticed over the holidays that you were unhappy." This was hard, so much harder than she had ever imagined it could possibly be. Each word was wrenched from her until her voice wavered. "She said you'd found another girl at school, but you felt guilty about me. She didn't want me to be hurt and offered me the...money to leave town."

Simon's hand reached for hers, gripping it so tightly that it felt as though he had cut off the flow of blood to her fingers. "Angie, I hadn't."

Tears shimmered in her eyes and she bit into the corner of her bottom lip. "I didn't want to believe her. That's why I took the bus to see you. If you were going to be rid of me, then you'd have to tell me yourself."

Leaning his elbow on the table, Simon wiped a hand over his bloodless features and pinched the bridge of his nose. "You were walking in front of the fraternity." Simon's own memory of that last meeting was strikingly clear. Her long, shining dark hair had been tied back and her mournful, troubled eyes had searched his. He had known she needed him at that moment, but couldn't stand the pressure of another demand.

"I'd been waiting outside your fraternity for an hour, pacing," Angie inserted, caught in her own reminiscence. "I wanted so badly to believe it wasn't true. But you took one look at me and said you hoped to God I wasn't pregnant. A pregnancy would ruin everything."

Simon turned his head and stared out the kitchen window with unseeing eyes. That day had to have been the worst of his life. His grades had been so poor that he was kicked off the basketball team. He'd found Angie after leaving the coach's office, where he'd gotten the lecture of his life. His father had been to the university earlier that week, berating him. The last thing he needed was to have Angie show up and tell him she was pregnant.

"And you assumed from what my mother said that everything was true."

"It made sense at the time," she murmured, the tremble in her low voice barely noticeable any longer. "It had been weeks since you'd seen me and when you did, you acted like…"

"I know how I acted." Rising to his feet, Simon crossed the room. "So you returned to Groves Point, took the money and moved out of town."

She hadn't wanted that ten thousand dollars. Clay was the one who'd insisted they take it. Simon owed her that much, he had argued. All Angie had cared about was the desperate need to escape Groves Point, and the Canfields. "Yes, I took the money and left." She offered no excuses. None were needed.

"So much for trust and vows spoken before God." Tears stung the back of her eyes. This wasn't a time for accusations, but for understanding and forgiving. In her hurt anger she lashed back at him with a vengeance. "I notice it didn't take you long to seek solace." Her nerves felt threadbare. "How many women warmed your blood before you married Carol?"

Simon raked his fingers through his dark hair. "Three years, Angie. For three years I waited for you to come back." His mouth was pinched, the bracketing grooves, white.

He'd waited for her to return. Shock waves rippled over her as her eyes widened in painful astonishment. "Even when I'd taken the money, you waited?" Blinking back the ready flow of emotion, she stared up at him. "Oh, Simon…"

He took a step toward her and paused uncertainly. If he touched her, he wasn't sure he'd ever be able to let her go again. A myriad of emotions raged through him like a wildfire on a sun-scorched field. Anger. Surprise. Regret. But paramount was a burning sense of betrayal by the ones he loved and trusted most.

Impulsively, Angie raised her hand and reached out, lightly touching his forearm. Moisture shimmered in her eyes as she raised her gaze to him.

He caught her hand and gripped it as though it were a lifeline to sanity. "Angie, how could we have let this happen to us?"

"I don't know," she whispered, her voice wavering and unsteady. "It was all so long ago."

"I could kill them."

"No, no, don't even think such a thing." Vaulting to her feet, she forcefully shook her head. "There's been enough hate and misunderstanding. Your parents did what they thought was best for you."

The pinched look about his mouth didn't relax. "They had no right—"

"No, they didn't," she agreed readily. "But who's to say what the future held for us? We were both incredibly young…."

"And stupid," Simon inserted. "But it doesn't change what they did."

The cold ruthlessness was back in Simon. At seventeen she'd never seen that side of him. Their world had been filled with high ideals and warm promises. Who could have said that their love would last less than a year?

"I'm leaving in the morning," she said softly, her hand reaching for his and clasping it tightly. "And when I do I want to look back on these past few days as a time of healing. I came back to Groves Point to make my peace, not to stir up grief. I bear no one malice, least of all your family. We need to forgive your parents and my dad. But most of all, we need to forgive each other."

Simon expelled an angry breath as his gaze narrowed on her upturned face. "I don't know that I can," he ground out. Without warning he reached for her, bringing her into the tight circle of his arms.

Having Simon hold her like this was like returning safely home after fighting a twelve-year battle. With her ear pressed against his chest, she heard the steady drumbeat of his heart. He released a sigh of contentment and she felt him rub his unshaved chin across the crown of her head. They had shared the most beautiful part of their youth together. Simon would always be someone special in her life, but the love they shared was over. She was free now. Free to return to Charleston and Glenn. Free to love.

A surge of happiness brought an excited bubble of laughter from her throat. "I'm so relieved."

"I don't know what I feel," he confessed in a strained voice. All the emotions remained, most of which he would need to deal with privately. But Angie was here, in his arms, and he had to find a way to keep her there. "Angie," he murmured her name as he loosened his grip. A hand on each of her shoulders pushed her gently back so he could study her. She was beautiful. Even her tear-streaked face couldn't mar the natural beauty of her perfect features. The lovely mouth drew his attention, and he struggled to align his thoughts. "I don't want you to leave tomorrow." Not when he'd just found her again. Not when he'd been offered a second chance at life. Holding Angie was like stepping into the freshness of a newborn spring after suffering through the bitter cold of winter.

Angie was stunned. Simon's asking her to remain in Groves Point was the last thing she'd expected. "I have to go. My home, my business…everything's in Charleston." Suddenly it was vitally important that she get back to Glenn. There was so much she was burning to tell him.

"Stay longer—only a few more days," he pleaded, his fingers tightening their grip on the slender curve of her shoulders. "Just until we have things worked out."

"I can't." Her eyes implored him to understand. She was afraid of what would develop if she did. Simon and Groves Point were a part of her life that belonged in the past. Glenn and Charleston were her future. "In fact," she murmured, glancing at her wristwatch, "I need to be leaving right away. Cindy's expecting me." It was on the tip of her tongue to mention that she'd be at the country club dance that evening. But it wasn't an event she was looking forward to attending.

"Your car." Simon straightened as his gaze shifted to the tools lying on the top of the counter. A near-smile touched his mouth. "Since we're speaking honestly here, I guess I should own up. I pulled your hot wire."

"My what?" Angie stared up at him blankly.

"Your car. That's why it wouldn't start."

She was flabbergasted. "But why?" She'd have thought he would have gone to any lengths to be rid of her.

"I didn't know the car was yours when I did it. If someone was trespassing on my property, I didn't want them running off until I knew the reason."

"Oh." The logic in that was irrefutable.

"And later, when I discovered it was you——" he paused and smiled wryly "——I was happy to have an excuse for you to stay."

"I'm so glad you did," she admitted, keeping her voice low.

By unspoken agreement they left the kitchen, walking into the sunlight that shone down on them like a healing balm.

His hand rested lightly at the base of her neck as if he needed to touch her. How different their steps on this same bit of road had been only a short time ago.

Simon repaired her car within minutes by simply reconnecting the wire. When he lowered the hood, an awkward silence hung between them.

After wiping his fingers clean on a white handkerchief, Simon stuffed it in his back pocket. "I want to see you again."

Her heart was going crazy, its beat accelerating to an alarming rate. Part of her was crying out to explore the unbelievable tenderness they had once shared. Maybe if so much time hadn't elapsed, she would have been more willing. But the worlds that separated them twelve years ago had widened even more. She couldn't come back.

Her eyes were sad when they met his. She was angry

because he asked and angry because she knew what her answer must be. "I'm sorry, so sorry, but no."

He looked for a moment as if he didn't believe her. "Why not?"

"Because what we shared was a long time ago. We can't recapture our youth. Nor can we alter the past. The time has come to go on."

His brow furrowed in a thick frown, Simon shook his head, and captured her hand with his. "Angie, listen to me. I love you. I can live a hundred years and never feel this strongly about another woman."

"Simon, don't," she pleaded, feeling guilty and increasingly miserable. "What you love is a memory."

"No," he argued with a warm gentleness that nearly undid her. "I love *you*."

"You don't know me," she shouted desperately in a half sob, reaching inside the car for her purse. Her fingers fumbled with the clasp, as she struggled to remove her car keys.

"I'm not going to push this." His fingertips brushed a stray tear from her ashen cheek. A dry grin twisted his mouth. "But I think it's a sad commentary on our lives if, after twelve years, you suggest we need more time."

Angie's laugh escaped on the swell of a broken sob. "You're going to start me crying all over again. Oh, Simon. I've cried more these past few days than I have in years."

"Good," he murmured, taking a step closer, "let those tears be an absolution." He placed his hand on the curve of her neck, his long fingers sliding into the length of her hair. His other hand wiped the moisture from her cheek. Unhurried, his mouth made a slow descent to her trembling lips.

As the distance lessened, Angie closed her eyes. She should break away, she thought guiltily, but the curiosity to discover his kiss again was overpowering. They weren't teenagers anymore, but adults, curious after a long absence.

His lips warmly covered hers, his touch firm and experienced. The tension eased from Angie as she slid her hands over his rib cage, feeling his hard muscles through the material of his shirt.

The pulse point in her neck throbbed against his fingers, betraying his overwhelming effect on her. Her hold tightened as her mouth clung to his.

"Oh, Simon," she whispered as his mouth released her.

Slowly he lifted his head, awed by the power an uncomplicated kiss held over him. Angie's eyes were wide and faintly puzzled. This overpowering response was just as much of a surprise to her. She resembled a frightened doe, unsure of her footing. His first reaction was to reach out and hold her secure. But he couldn't. As difficult as it was at this moment, he had to let her go. In some ways, it had been easier the first time. He dropped his hands to his side and took a step in retreat.

"Goodbye, Simon," she said in a choked, unhappy voice.

He couldn't answer her. For him the kiss wasn't a farewell, but a welcoming. He opened the car door for her and closed it once she'd climbed inside.

The car engine roared to life without a problem. Her eyes glistened with tears as Angie shifted the gears, backed the car around and drove away. Not once did she glance in her rearview mirror, although everything within her was demanding that she take one last look at Simon.

* * *

A blazing orange sun was greeting the horizon when the two couples pulled into the country club parking lot.

"I'm as nervous as a virgin on her wedding night," Cindy confessed as Bob gave her his hand and helped her out of the backseat of Charlie's Lincoln Continental.

"How do I look?" Cindy nervously asked Angie as her fingers brushed at a small crease in the front of her dove-gray silk dress.

"Gorgeous," Angie said and winked. "We both do." After spending the morning and most of the afternoon shopping she wouldn't admit to anything else. Cindy did look lovely. Even Bob's jaw had dropped in surprise when his wife had appeared.

Bob inserted a finger in the starched white collar of his shirt. "Are you sure there isn't going to be a problem?" His question was directed at Charlie.

"I'm sure," Charlie returned confidently. "Everyone's entitled to bring guests."

As he'd promised, there wasn't so much as a raised eyebrow as they entered the foyer. Charlie signed in for them, and with a hand cupping Angie's elbow, he led the way into the dining room.

Each round table was covered with a pure-white linen tablecloth. An expertly folded red napkin was standing at attention at each place setting. The lights had been lowered and flickering candles cast a festive glow across the room. The hardwood dance floor was toward the front, and the band instruments were set up and waiting.

Cindy was whispering excitedly to Bob, who was walking behind Angie, but she couldn't hear her friend. Perhaps she would have been more in awe of the fancy club if Simon hadn't brought her here all those years ago. Once for a birthday dinner, and again for a dance. But his parents had objected strenuously to Simon taking Angie to the club. They had fought, and Angie, not wishing to be a source of problems for Simon at home, had refused to come again.

Charlie pulled out the high-backed chair for Angie, and Bob followed suit. The two women exchanged happy smiles.

"I guess I have to come to the country club for Bob to pull out my chair," Cindy teased her husband affectionately.

Within minutes they were studying an oblong menu, a gold tassel hanging from the top.

The women ordered veal picatta and the men chose steak au poivre. Charlie insisted on paying for their meal, but Bob picked up the tab for the domestic wine, a delicious Chardonnay.

Nostalgia flowed as freely as the wine, and an hour later while they lingered over freshly brewed coffee, the five-piece band started up.

Only a few couples took to the floor.

"Do you dance, Angie?" Charlie leaned toward her and asked.

"It's been a while," she admitted. Her lifestyle didn't take in many evenings like this one. She and Glenn shared many quiet evenings alone, but he was a lumberjack of a man and had never suggested they go dancing.

"My feet are itching already," Cindy confessed and pointedly batted her curved lashes at her husband.

As Angie recalled, Bob and Cindy made quite a couple on the dance floor. They proved her memory correct as they took to the floor with an ease that produced a sigh of admiration from Angie.

"Shall we?" Charlie held out his hand to her.

"Why not?" Angie answered with a warm smile. "But forgive me if I step on your toes. It's been a long time."

"I'll come up with some penance," Charlie teased, drawing her into his arms when they reached the outskirts of the floor.

Angie felt stiff and a little awkward as Charlie tightened his hold. "You're still as beautiful as ever," he whispered. "I always thought you were the prettiest girl in class."

Angie managed to hide a soft smile. Charlie had dated a long succession of cheerleaders. In four years of high school, she doubted that he'd ever given her more than a second glance.

"You were dating Canfield and he let it be known in no uncertain terms that you were his."

A part of her would always be Simon's, Angie mused, a thoughtful frown creasing her brow. She didn't want to have to think about Simon.

"You've done well for yourself, Charlie." Early in the evening, Angie had realized that Charlie enjoyed talking about his success. It was easier to listen to self-proclaimed accolades than discuss her relationship with Simon.

The music was slow, and as they turned Angie caught sight of a silver-haired woman with delicate features sitting at a table against the window. Georgia Canfield, Simon's mother. Angie's heart stopped cold. The older woman had changed dramatically. In twelve years, she'd aged thirty. One look confirmed that life hadn't been easy for Simon's mother and a rush of unexpected compassion filled Angie. She had often wondered what she'd feel if she saw Mrs. Canfield again. The bitterness had been with her a lot of years, just as it had been with Simon.

"Excuse me a minute," she said as she broke loose from Charlie. "There's someone I'd like to see."

Charlie dropped his arms, surprised. "Sure."

Making her way across the crowded dance floor, Angie formulated her thoughts. This was possibly the worst thing she could do, but the opportunity was here and she wouldn't allow it to escape.

"Hello, Mrs. Canfield," she spoke softly as she stood before the older woman who was sitting alone at the small table.

A network of wrinkles broke out across her face as she turned, unable to disguise her shock. "Angela."

"I hope you'll forgive me for being so brash as to intrude on you this evening."

"All young people are brash," Mrs. Canfield said, recovering quickly. "What are you doing here? As I recall, my husband and I paid a steep price to keep you out of this town."

Angie's fingers laced in front of her, tightened. "I realize that. I've only come for a visit."

"I didn't know you had relatives in the area," Mrs. Canfield said stiffly.

"I haven't." Angie eyed the empty chair across from Simon's mother. "Would you mind if I sat down? I'd like to talk for a moment."

Georgia Canfield answered with a polite nod, but Angie noted that her shoulders were arched and her back was uncomfortably straight.

"I won't stay long," Angie promised as she took the seat. Her insides were tied in a double knot, but she knew she appeared outwardly calm, as did Mrs. Canfield. "First, I want to ask your forgiveness for taking that money. There hasn't been a day since that I haven't regretted it."

Gray eyes, so like Simon's, widened perceptively.

"By accepting your offer," Angie continued relentlessly, "I confirmed every bad thing you wanted to believe about me."

"I realized at the time that it was more your father's doing than yours."

"That's no excuse." Both were aware that Clay Robinson was a weak man, but Angie refused to lessen the blame on herself.

"Have you seen Simon?" Georgia Canfield gave no indication that she was concerned, and Angie marveled at her composure.

"Yes, I talked to him at the bank yesterday when I returned the money."

"Returned the money..." The piercing eyes held Angie's for a long moment. "Are you planning to move back?"

An intense sadness settled over Angie. Simon's mother was more concerned that she was going to intrude on their lives. The fact they might discover her subterfuge didn't appear to concern her.

"No," she answered simply. "I'll be leaving town in the morning."

The older woman looked relieved. "It was good to see you again, Angela. Although you may think differently, I do wish you well."

Their eyes met and held over the top of the table. "I

bear you no ill will," Angie said and, placing her hand against the edge of the table, stood. "Goodbye, Mrs. Canfield."

The silver-haired woman lowered her gaze first. "Goodbye, Angela."

Angie inserted the key into her apartment door, turned the latch and reached inside for the switch. A flood of light filled the room. She blinked and lowered her suitcase to the floor. Charleston seemed a different world from Groves Point. Here there was an elegance and grace that had all but vanished from the rest of the South, or at least what she'd seen of it.

Reaching for her cell she called Glenn.

"Glenn," she said, barely giving him time to answer. "Listen to me."

His husky laugh met her. "Angie, of course I'll listen to you. Are you back?"

"Yes, yes, I just walked in the door and I'm dying to see you."

"I'm on my way, babe."

The phone clicked in her ear, and with a sigh of contentment, Angie carried her suitcase into her bedroom. The drive would take Glenn a good twenty minutes; she would have time to shower and look her best.

The doorbell chimed exactly eighteen minutes later and she crossed the floor quickly, flinging open the door. "Glenn," she whispered, "oh, Glenn." She reached for him, faintly aware that he was taller and more muscular than Simon. Her arms slid around his neck as she met his mouth in a fierce kiss.

With his arms wrapped around her waist, Glenn

lifted her from the carpet and swung her around, closing the door with the heel of his shoe.

"If that's the kind of warm welcome I get, I just may send you away more often."

"And I'd go." Angie smiled up into dark eyes. Glenn was a dear, dear man. There were few in all the world whom she trusted more. He wasn't handsome, not in the way Simon was. His brow was wide and intelligent, his mouth a little too full and his nose a trifle too pronounced. But at this moment, Angie couldn't recall a man more wonderful.

"Glenn, dear, sweet Glenn." Leaning back, she held both his hands with her own. "You've asked me this question a hundred times and finally I can answer you."

The teasing, happy glint left his eyes and Angie watched as they grew dark and intense.

"Yes, Glenn, I'll marry you."

Four

With Prince trotting at his side, Simon rounded the last curve in the road that led him back to the house. The sun was rising, bathing the earth in the golden light of early morning. Sweat rolled off Simon's face as a surge of energy carried him the last quarter mile.

Just inside the driveway Simon paused, his hands on his knees as he leaned forward and dragged deep gulps of oxygen into his heaving lungs. He hated these early morning runs and did them only as a means of self-discipline. But this morning had been different. With every foot that pounded the pavement, he filled his mind with thoughts of Angie. For the first time in more years than he cared to remember, his thoughts of her weren't tainted with bitterness. Unbridled, his mind roamed freely over their early days and the little things that had attracted him to her. His heart hammered and with every beat it repeated her name: Angie, Angie, Angie. He remembered the first time he'd ever really noticed her. She'd been standing by her locker in their high school, laughing with a friend. Her long straight hair had reached her waist and shone as if blessed by a benevolent sun god. The musical sound of her laughter had caught him by surprise, and he paused to see what was so amusing. His gaze had found hers and the feelings he had experienced when he viewed this slim dark-haired girl had enthralled him. This was a girl from Oak Street. Simon hadn't even been sure he remembered her name.

From that moment on, he began to notice little things about Angela Robinson. His classmates often sought her out, pausing to say a few words to her on their way to class. Her smile had a way of lighting up her entire face. Her eyes were the darkest shade of brown he'd ever seen, a mysterious deep color. The girls came to her with their problems, knowing Angie was never too busy to listen. Even the guys set her aside in their minds. Subtly Simon had tried to find out what he could about her and discovered that where the guys were usually loose-tongued about girls, they weren't about Angie. Even his best friend, Cal Spencer, seemed reluctant to talk about her.

"What do you want to know for?" Cal had insisted.

"I hadn't noticed her before, that's all. Is she new?" Simon knew she wasn't. Faintly he could recall seeing her there sophomore year.

"No. She's been around a while."

"Who's she dating?" Simon pressed.

"Hey, man, she's a nice kid, leave her alone. Okay?"

Cal's words had irritated Simon. Why did Cal care anyway? he had thought. This girl who had captured his attention lived on Oak Street. The truth was, she wasn't even that pretty. Not in the way Shirley Radcliff was, and he'd been dating her for weeks. The way things were going he'd be sleeping with Shirley by summer.

Most of the guys had already been physically active and took pride in recounting their experiences. Simon was sixteen and he felt it was high time he shared his own conquests.

"If you must know," Cal cut in abruptly, "Angie looked over my term paper before I handed it in to that old biddy Carson."

"You mean she wrote it for you, don't you?" Simon teased, nudging his friend with an elbow.

"No. I offered to pay her, but she refused. She said that she'd be happy to help, but she wouldn't do it for me."

"Did she?"

"Yeah, and she's helped me and a lot of the others having trouble, too."

"What do you mean?" Simon didn't like the sound of that.

"She's got brains and isn't a snob about it."

From then on, Simon had found that he watched her even more. Angie wasn't the cheerleader type, nor was she outgoing and vivacious. But she was the heart of their junior class. She was loved and respected, and there wasn't a person in all Groves Point High who had a bad thing to say about her. It wasn't that Simon was attracted to her. He had Shirley. But he was captivated by this long-haired girl with the shy smile and the warm heart. The longer he studied her the more he realized that people were comfortable around her. Nothing about her was manufactured.

It had taken Simon a week to gather up enough courage to approach Angie. He had started by passing her in the hall and talking to her as if he'd been doing it for years. "Hello, Angie."

The first time she had looked shocked. "Hi..." It hadn't occurred to him that she might not know his name. Everyone knew the Canfields.

Other meetings, supposedly by accident, followed. He had just happened to be driving by one day when she was walking home from school alone.

"Hi." He pulled his shining turquoise convertible to the curb and looped an arm over the seat. "I'm going your way. Can I give you a lift?"

Angie had tucked a piece of hair around her ear and shaken her head. "No, thanks, it's only a few blocks."

Her refusal vexed him. This was Simon Canfield she had just turned down. The boy who scored the most points on the basketball team, son of the banker, and the richest kid in town. Who did she think she was anyway?

Another week passed before Simon approached her again. This time they both were in the city library. Simon played it cool and didn't say a word. He did, however, nod in her direction once when he had caught her eye. She smiled in return and glanced down at her books.

Simon picked up a book on archeology and sat at the table across from her. For a full twenty minutes neither said a word. Simon pretended to be reading, but his gaze was drawn unwillingly to her several times. The feeling of being this close to her was euphoric. But for all the attention she gave him, he thought, he might as well have been a pillar of salt.

Even now he couldn't remember who spoke first. What he did recall was that they sat and talked until the library closed. Simon discovered that he loved to hear Angie speak. Her voice was low and melodic. It wasn't her voice so much as what she said; her insights were refreshing. She made him feel intelligent and awakened a sense of humor in him he'd never known he possessed. He liked Shirley and had even thought he loved her, but after an hour with Angie he found Shirley utterly boring.

Although it was dark when they left the library, Angie again insisted on walking home. Simon remembered that he tried to sound casual about meeting her again sometime and had even made an excuse about needing help with one of his subjects. Undoubtedly she saw through that. He was an honor student himself.

After that they met nightly at the public library. With each meeting, Simon tasted a little more of the secret beauty that attracted Angie to his friends. She was lovely without being beautiful. Intelligent without being shrewd. And shy without being docile.

At school she smiled at him in the halls, but never sought him out. Since they didn't share any classes, Simon had to go out of his way to see her. He did so willingly, not caring who saw him or what they said.

Two weeks after he first started meeting Angie at the library, Shirley announced that she'd decided to start seeing another guy. If she'd expected Simon to argue, she was disappointed. Actually Simon was grateful. He wanted to ask Angie to the dance after the game Friday night and would have felt obligated to Shirley.

Angie turned him down flat.

For two nights he didn't show up at the library. Nor did he make a point of passing her in the halls. He wasn't stupid; he'd gotten the message.

The Wednesday before the game, Simon stayed after school shooting baskets in the basketball hoop beside the tennis courts. Almost everyone had gone home.

He didn't know how long he had continued to drive to the hoop...long after his muscles had protested the exercise...long after his throat felt dry and his stomach ached...long after Angie had walked over to watch him. Even when he did notice her, he pretended he hadn't.

"Simon."

"Yeah." He continued bouncing the ball, took aim and shot from the free-throw line. The ball swished through the net.

"About the dance..."

Bouncing the ball, Simon drowned out her words, shot, missed, made a rebound and slam-dunked the basketball.

"Simon...I..." She hesitated, and her voice became small.

He tucked the ball under his arm and wiped the sweat from his face with the back of his hand. "Listen, I got the picture. You don't want to go to the dance with me. Fine, there are plenty of other girls who would jump at the chance." His throat felt as dry as sandpaper. Without a backward glance he walked to the water fountain and drank enough to ease the parched feel.

Angie followed him. "Would you consider taking me if—" she swallowed "—if I met you there?"

"Met you there?" Simon repeated, astonished. "Listen, Angie, I know you live on Oak Street. I do drive in that part of town. It isn't any crime to live where you do."

"I know, it's just that my dad, well... Would it be all right if I met you at the gym?"

"No," he repeated calmly, "it wouldn't be all right. If I ask a girl out then I expect to pick her up and take her home. Understand?"

Slowly Angie nodded. Her arms tightened around her books, crushing them to her chest. "That's the kind of thing you should do."

"Are you coming with me or not?" Simon shifted his weight to his left foot, the basketball tucked under his arm. He tried to give the appearance that it didn't matter to him either way. If she went with him, fine. If not, he'd ask another girl. The choice was hers.

"Thank you for asking me, Simon. I'll always remember that you did." With that she turned and walked away.

A long minute passed before Simon ran after her. "Angie."

She hesitated before turning around. Her face was so pale that her dark eyes were in sharp contrast to her bloodless features. "Yes."

She looked so miserable that he immediately wanted to comfort her. "I could pick you up at the library."

"Would you?" Her voice grew even softer.

"I don't want to go to the dance with anyone but you."

She looked for a moment as if she wanted to cry. Biting her lower lip, she gnawed on it before forcing a smile. "There's no one else I'd want to take me."

"Can I carry your books?"

She nodded and when he reached for her hand she gave him that, too.

That night they'd shared a tentative kiss. For the first time Angie let Simon drive her home from the library. They stopped at the local drive-in for something to drink, and sat and talked until Angie glanced at her watch and looked startled. She had Simon drop her off a block before Oak Street. Her fingers were on the doorknob when Simon stopped her by placing a hand on her shoulder. Surprised, she looked back. Simon said nothing as he leaned forward and gently brushed his mouth over hers. He'd experienced far more passionate kisses, but none so sweet.

By the time he arrived home, Simon was whistling.

"You've got it bad," Cal had commented a month later.

"What do you mean?" Simon decided to play dumb.

"You and Angela Robinson."

"Yeah, so what's the big deal? She's terrific, I like her."

"I like Angie too. Everyone does, but you know what kind of problem you'll face if you ask her to the prom."

Simon did know. It'd been in his mind all week. Angie hadn't mentioned it, but the biggest dance of the year loomed before them like D-Day. For all his parents knew he was still dating Shirley. Neither his mother nor his father would appreciate him asking a girl from Oak Street to the country club dinner scheduled for after the prom. For that matter, Angie had never mentioned her home or family, either.

They'd continued to see each other nightly, with Simon dropping her off a block from Oak Street and sitting in the car until she was safely inside her house. A couple of times he'd driven down her street without her knowing it and had been surprised at how meticulous the yard and flower beds were. As far as he could see there was nothing to be ashamed of. He worried about Angie and wondered if her father was abusive or alcoholic. She had given him no clues, but he couldn't press the subject, since he hadn't taken her to meet his parents, either.

A week before the dance Simon had made his decision. "We're going," he announced that night. They were parked at Three Tree Point, sitting in the convertible with the top down. Angie sat close to his side, her head resting on his chest. Simon's arm was looped around her shoulder and he pressed her close.

Angie hadn't made the pretense of not knowing what he was talking about. "There'll be trouble."

"We'll face it together." Slowly, reassuringly, his hand stroked the length of her arm. "And this time I won't pick you up at the library or anyplace else. I'm coming to your front door with the biggest corsage this town has ever seen."

"Oh, Simon," she had whispered, uncertainty in her voice, "I don't know."

"And with you on my arm, I'm going to introduce you proudly to my parents."

Simon felt the tension building in her. "You're sure?"

"I've never been more positive of anything in my life."

The evening had been a disaster from beginning to end. As he said he would, Simon picked Angie up at her house. He had barely knocked when the door was opened. Simon wasn't sure what he expected, but it wasn't the tall, gray-haired man who stood before him. Simon introduced himself and shook hands with Angie's father, Clay Robinson. Clay was dressed in a suit, his hair slicked down. From listening around school, Simon knew that Angie's father worked at the mill. Weekends he played banjo at a local tavern.

"You've come to take my Angie to the prom?"

"Yes, sir."

"You're that rich kid from on the hill, ain't you?"

"Yes, sir."

"I don't suppose you and your daddy like good blue-grass?"

"Daddy, please," Angie pleaded, her face red with embarrassment.

"We enjoy music." All Simon wanted to do was get Angie out of that house.

"Me and my band play good, you say something to your daddy, you hear, boy?"

"Yes, sir."

Angie didn't say a word until Simon had parked the car in the parking lot. The music drifted from the open door of the school gymnasium. "I'm sorry, Simon," she mumbled, her chin tucked against her collarbone.

"What for?"

"Dad. He shouldn't have asked you to do that."

"Angie, it doesn't matter. Okay?" A finger under her chin lifted her eyes to his. They were so dark and intense that he leaned forward and kissed her. "Have I told you how beautiful you are tonight?" She was, incredibly so. Her hair was piled high upon her head, and small flowers were woven into the design. The dress was new, a light blue thing with an illusion yoke of sheer lace. Angie had designed it herself and he was astonished at her skill.

For the first time that evening, she smiled. "No."

"Then let me correct the oversight." He chuckled. "You are incredibly beautiful tonight, Angie." He said it with all the emotion he was experiencing and gazed deep into her fathomless eyes.

Her smile revealed the happiness his words produced. "Thank you, Simon."

They should have been able to enjoy the dance, but

they didn't. Instead they both were anticipating the confrontation that awaited them at the country club. Simon's mother hadn't disappointed him.

"Mom," he said, tucking his arm around Angie's waist. "This is Angela Robinson."

"Hello, Angela." Politely Mrs. Canfield shook Angie's hand, but her eyes had turned questioningly to her son. His mother was far too refined to say anything at the moment, but Simon knew he'd hear about his choice of a date later.

Simon escorted Angie to a dinner table in the front of the room where they were joined by Cal Spencer and his date. No sooner were they seated when Simon's father approached the table, expecting an introduction. He asked the group to excuse Simon and took him across the room, where he proceeded to demand to know exactly what kind of game his son was playing.

"Trouble?" Cal asked when Simon returned.

"No." Simon reached for Angie's hand under the table. "Everything's fine." Only it hadn't been and they both knew it.

Some time later, when Simon was away from the table exchanging polite inanities with a friend of the family, Cal came for him.

"Angie's left."

Simon looked around him in disbelief. "What happened?"

"Someone came up and said her kind wasn't welcome here."

Anger filled every fiber of his being. "Who?" He was ready to swing on the bastard.

"It doesn't matter, does it?" Cal murmured. "Shouldn't you be more concerned about Angie?"

It amazed him how far she'd gotten in so short a time. "Angie," Simon called, running after her. A hand on her shoulder stopped her progress down the hill. Her dark lashes were wet and he knew she'd been crying.

"Oh, Angie." He pulled her into his embrace and wrapped his arms around her. She sniffled once and broke free, pausing to wipe her cheek, but kept her face lowered, refusing to meet his gaze.

"I'm sorry, running away was a childish thing to do, but I couldn't stay there another minute with everyone looking at me and whispering." Her voice was so muted he could hardly hear her.

"Angie, it was my fault." He brought her back into his arms and breathed against her hair, taking in the fresh fragrance. "I should be the one to apologize."

"No." She kept her head down. "I don't think we should see each other again."

Simon was utterly stunned. "You don't mean that."

She shook her head. "We'll talk about it later."

"No, we won't." He held her at arm's length, a hand on each shoulder. "We'll talk about it now. I love you, Angie Robinson. Do you understand me?"

"Oh, Simon, please don't say that."

"I love you," he repeated.

"Don't, Simon, this isn't funny."

"I tell a girl how I feel and she accuses me of joking? You have a lot to learn about me."

She sniffled and wiped the tears from her face. "Stop it, right now, you hear?"

"I love Angie," he shouted, tossing back his head. He wanted the world to know. Loving Angie wasn't an embarrassment; she was the best thing that had ever happened in his life.

"Simon."

"I love you," he whispered, drawing her into his arms.

"I won't go back there," she whispered defiantly.

"Don't worry, I wouldn't put you through that." With their fingers entwined they walked to the parking lot. From there they drove to their favorite drive-in and ate thick hamburgers.

That summer Angie had gotten a part-time job working at Garland Pharmacy. Simon picked her up in the morning and dropped her back home when she was finished. He sometimes worked at the bank, but he didn't recall that he did much of anything worthwhile.

"Are you going to be working there after college?" Angie asked one night. They were parked in their favorite spot at Three Tree Point.

"I'll probably take over for my dad someday," Simon answered, more interested in kissing Angie's earlobe than talking.

"Is that what you want to do?"

Simon grinned and straightened. Angie had a way of doing this whenever their kissing became too hot and heavy. With any other girl he would have pressed her, but not Angie. He didn't want to do anything she wasn't ready to try. It wasn't easy not to touch her. Some nights he thought the frustration would kill him.

"I've never thought about doing anything else but working in the bank. Why?"

"No reason."

She was quiet after that and didn't resist when he turned her lips to his and kissed her long and hard, pulling her lower lip between his teeth and sucking on it. Angie had a beautiful mouth: wide, soft, passionate.

Simon loved the feel of it under his own. But then he loved everything about her.

As usual he dropped her off a block before Oak. She sat for a moment staring at her hands. "Lloyd Sipe was in Garland's today."

"And?"

"He asked me to a movie this weekend."

Simon felt a lead balloon sink in his stomach. "You're not going, are you?"

"I told him I wouldn't."

Simon relaxed.

"But I think it might be a good idea if we didn't see so much of each other for a while."

"Why?" he exploded.

"I'm afraid," she whispered. "Afraid because I love you so much. I…I want us both to start seeing others. Just until school starts. We can talk about things in September."

Simon's immediate reaction had been to argue, but eventually she had worn him down. They stopped dating. The separation nearly drove Simon crazy. He loved her, it was only natural that he wanted to be with Angie. But in the months that they'd been seeing each other, something else, something more far-reaching had happened. Angie had become his best friend. Nothing seemed right without her. His life had been ripped open, leaving a gaping hole exposed. Even Cal, who had been Simon's friend since grade school, couldn't fill the gap. For a long time Simon didn't date. He couldn't see that it would do any good. When Angie realized he wasn't seeing other girls, she started dating Lloyd Sipe. Simon got the message and asked out Kate Holston. He found her even more boring than Shirley. Later that summer his mother arranged a date for him with the visiting niece of one of her Garden Club friends. Jill Something-or-other had hidden a pint of vodka in her purse and proceeded to get smashed. By the end of the evening, Simon couldn't drive her back to Auntie fast enough. Laughing, her hair in a wild disarray, Jill had placed her hand high on his thigh and claimed she wasn't in any hurry to get home. If he knew "someplace private" there were lots of things she could think of to do to kill time.

The first day of their senior year, Simon had stopped Angie in the hall. "You said we'd talk. Are you ready?"

She smiled and nodded.

They met outside the library and drove to Three Tree Point. Simon parked the car, turned off the engine and reached for Angie. He held her so hard that for a moment he feared he might have hurt her. "It's not the same," he whispered into her hair. "It'll never be right unless it's you in my arms."

Her own words were muffled as she buried her face in his shoulder, but the strength of her hold told him everything he needed to know.

With Angie, Simon was on the same intellectual and spiritual plane. By early the next spring they were a hairsbreadth from exploring the sexual plane.

"Angie, I love you, I want to marry you."

"Don't ask me," she pleaded, spreading eager kisses across his face. "Please don't ask."

Simon was so inflamed that controlling himself took a superhuman effort. "We've got to stop, Angie. Right now. Do you understand?"

"Yes," she repeated, her voice soft and willing. "I understand."

He leaned his head against the back of the car seat and took in deep, agonizing breaths.

"Can...can you hold me, Simon?" she pleaded. "Just for a few minutes."

"Oh, Angie. This does it," he muttered. "I'm talking to my dad tomorrow."

Angie turned stricken eyes to him. "About what?"

"Us."

"Simon, they're not going to let us get married."

"They can't stop us. I love you. After last summer I know I don't ever want to be without you again."

The confrontation with his parents had been the worst thing Simon had ever faced. Angie had wanted to go with him. Later he thanked God that he hadn't let her. The first thing his mother asked him after he announced that he wanted to marry Angie was if she was pregnant.

Simon couldn't believe that his mother would even suggest such a thing. It only proved that Georgia Canfield didn't know Angie.

"Of course she isn't. We haven't even made love. Angie doesn't want to until we're married."

"Can't you see what she's after?" his father had demanded. "This little girl from Oak Street isn't stupid. Of course she doesn't want to do 'it' until after you're married. Men don't like to pay for what they can get free."

It took all of Simon's restraint not to shout at his parents that it wasn't like that with him and Angie. The taste of gall filled his mouth at the thought that the two people who supposedly loved him so much would try to take the beautiful relationship he shared with Angie and make it into a sordid, ugly thing.

"You're only seventeen," his mother pleaded.

"And in this state you need our permission to marry," Simon, Senior, interjected. "And as far as I'm concerned you don't have it."

His father had come to Simon's bedroom later and sat on the mattress beside him. He draped a fatherly arm over his shoulder and assured him that Angie was the type of girl for Simon to sow his wild oats with. No need to marry her kind. Later, he suggested, another girl would come along from the right kind of people, and Simon would feel just as strongly about her. At seventeen, Simon wasn't ready for the responsibilities a wife and possible family would entail. He should have fun with Angie, but be careful that she didn't get pregnant. Simon's jaw had been clenched so tight that his teeth ached for hours afterward.

"You don't need to tell me what they said," Angie murmured when they met later.

"Listen," Simon argued, "I've got everything worked out. We'll get married after my birthday."

"But you'll have left for college and…"

"I'm not going to the U."

"Simon, you've got to. Your father went there and his father before him."

"Marrying you is more important than some stupid tradition."

Angie's shoulders had drooped as she slowly, sadly, shook her head. "I won't let you do that."

"We don't have any choice."

"Your schooling is important."

"You're the most important thing in my life, Angie."

It had seemed crazy that the only serious rift in their relationship had been over getting married. Angie was adamant that Simon continue with his schooling in the fall. She wouldn't marry him otherwise. What she didn't know was that his father had already anticipated his son's defiance and had threatened to cut off Simon's allowance. Simon could never manage school while making a home for himself and Angie at the same time. As for college, he didn't care. Even when approached about a possible basketball scholarship, Simon wasn't fazed. All he cared about was Angie.

Not finding a happy solution to their dilemma, Simon had come up with a compromise. It wasn't the perfect answer. But when he said his vows in the church that night, he had meant every word.

Sweat poured off Simon from his long run just as effortlessly as the memories of Angie had filled his mind. He moved from the long driveway into the house and headed for the bathroom to shower. Stripping, he turned on the pulsating power spray and turned his face into the jet stream, letting water wash down on him. Even the pounding water whispered Angie's name. He felt like singing. The realization produced a smile. It had been years since he'd sung in the shower.

Stepping onto the bathmat Simon reached for a thick towel. A frown drove his dark brows together. His wet hair glistened as he eased his long arms into the starched dress shirt and fastened the top button. At seventeen he'd been more in love than at any other time in his life, he mused. A love that pure and good wasn't supposed to happen to a rosy-cheeked kid. Most people search a lifetime and never experience what he had those years with Angie. With a vengeance, he jammed the gold cuff link into place.

Dressed now, and ready for the office, Simon poured

a cup of hot coffee and glanced at his gold wristwatch. A thousand times he had questioned what a seventeen-year-old boy could know of love. Little, he admitted freely now, but enough to realize that if it wasn't Angie in his arms, it wasn't love. He emptied the coffee cup in the sink and moved to the garage. The turquoise convertible seemed to smile at him. This weekend he'd see about starting her up again. For now he had to hurry or he would be late at the bank.

He parked in his usual spot and jingled the car keys before putting them in his pocket.

Once inside the bank he began whistling as he walked across the large marble floor, drawing his secretary's blank stare.

"Good morning, Mr. Canfield."

"Morning, Mrs. Wilson," he repeated cheerfully. Five people in the bank gaped in surprise.

His secretary located Angie's business number in Charleston. Simon had lost her once, he wasn't going to make that mistake again. He loved Angie as much now as he had twelve years ago.

His heart was pounding as he punched in the telephone number. She answered on the third ring.

Five

The sharp corners of Angie's mind were crowded with a thousand niggling thoughts. She should be thinking of Glenn, not Simon. She was home now and engaged to a wonderful man who loved her. And she loved Glenn in return, only…only things in Groves Point hadn't turned out as she'd expected. She had hoped to find Simon married and happy with a houseful of rambunctious children. Instead she'd found a bitter, disillusioned man trapped in the same limbo that had held her prisoner all these years. She had traveled to Groves Point seeking release from the past. The trip had given her that and washed away the guilt that had plagued her from the moment she had accepted the money from Georgia Canfield. But with the release came another set of regrets. Simon.

Determinedly she pushed thoughts of him to the back of her mind and zipped up the soft pink smock that hung from a hook in the back of her shop, Clay Pots. It had been named for her father, and he was proud of her small business venture. She hadn't told Clay about her weekend trip. It was better that he never know. Her father had yet to learn that she had accepted Glenn's proposal. The three of them were having dinner together Thursday night. Glenn and Angie planned to tell Clay then. Not that he'd be surprised.

"Morning, Donna."

"Morning." Donna was busy placing the cut flowers in the refrigerated compartment in the front of the shop and didn't glance up.

Angie's one full-time employee worked the early shift and stopped on her way in to the shop to buy cut flowers direct from the wholesaler.

"Angie." Donna stuck her blond head around the glass case. "There was a phone call for you earlier. I left the name on your desk."

"Thanks." Absently, Angie leafed through the orders for the day, dividing them between Donna and herself. Donna manned the counter in the morning and Angie took over in the afternoon.

Her heartbeat came to an abrupt halt when she glanced at the pink slip on her desk. The note was brief: Simon Canfield phoned, will try again later.

Every time the phone rang for the next four hours, Angie stiffened and prayed it wasn't Simon. Everything had already been said. All Angie wanted to do was bury the hurts of the past and build a new life from the ashes of Groves Point. She couldn't think of what to say to Simon or how to explain to him her feelings. It would sound ridiculous to shout at him that it wasn't supposed to have happened this way. Erroneously, she had assumed him to be married and happy. She wanted to tuck him neatly into a private corner of her life, like a favorite book once treasured, but now outgrown.

"You're as jumpy as a bullfrog today," Donna complained early in the afternoon. "What's the matter with you?"

"Nothing," she lied. As she spoke the phone pealed. Something inside her, an innate alarm system, warned her even before she picked up the receiver that it was Simon.

"Clay Pots."

Simon chuckled. "Now where did you ever come up with a name like that?"

"Hello, Simon." She knew she sounded stiff and unnatural, but she couldn't help it. She realized that turning her back to Donna would only arouse her employee's suspicions. Her hand tightened around the receiver until the pressure pinched her ear.

"Hello, Angie. Is this a busy time? Should I phone back later?"

Briefly, she toyed with the idea of delaying this conversation. Even a few hours would help her compose her thoughts.

"Angie?"

"No...no, this is as good a time as any."

"I want to see you. I haven't stopped thinking about you since you left. There's so much we left unsaid, and more that needs to be made right."

Angie closed her eyes and measured her words carefully. "Simon, listen to me. What happened is in the past. We can't resurrect that now."

"Why not?" he argued. "I love you."

"You love a memory. I'm not a sweet, naive teenager anymore. I can't go back to being seventeen."

"Me neither, but I'm anxious to meet the woman you've become." His voice went low and seductive, as if he'd put his hand over the mouthpiece so not to be overheard. "I'm eager to show you the man I am now."

Angie's heart slammed to her knees. Her throat went dry and she discovered she couldn't speak.

The bell over the door chimed, indicating that someone had entered the shop. Angie was so grateful she could have cried. "I've got to go, a customer just came in."

"Angie, listen, I'll phone you later."

"Simon, don't. Please, don't." Angry with herself for being so weak, she didn't wait for his farewell, and replaced the receiver. With a forced smile, she turned toward the delivery man who was approaching the counter.

Simon stared at the auditor's report on his desk, knowing he couldn't concentrate on it when thoughts of Angie dominated his mind. His phone conversation with her earlier had been awkward. He should be in Charleston, not Groves Point. He needed to talk to her face-to-face and not try to carry on a serious conversation with customers walking in and out of her shop every few minutes. But with his father away from the bank so much of the time now, Simon couldn't pick up and leave. He rubbed a hand across his eyes to ease the growing pain that throbbed at his temple. The walls seemed to close in around him and he stood, jerking his suit coat from the back of his chair.

"Mrs. Wilson, I'll be back in an hour," he announced to his secretary on his way out the door.

"But Mr. C-Canfield..." she stuttered. "What should I do about your two o'clock appointment?"

Irritation furrowed his brows. "Reschedule it," he

snapped, then stalked from the room before she could comment further.

Georgia Canfield was in the backyard, pruning her rosebushes. A straw hat graced her silver head and was secured under her chin by a brightly colored scarf. Spotless white gloves hid her veined hands. At a glance, his mother looked like an aged Southern belle of the era of the War between the States.

"Hello, Mother."

"Simon." She spoke without turning. "I wondered how long it would take you to come."

"Then you know why."

Turning, she set the wicker basket filled with blossoms on the wrought-iron table. "Sit down and I'll ring for coffee."

Without question, Simon did as requested. The urge to hurl accusations at his mother seared his mind, and he clenched his fists with burning irritation.

The maid quietly delivered a tray with two cups of coffee. Resolutely, Simon glanced away, counting the interminable seconds before he could speak. At the sound of the retreating steps, he returned his attention to his mother. She sat across from him at the round ornate table.

"I understand that Angela returned the money," Georgia Canfield began without preamble. She offered no excuse or explanation, but added two lumps of sugar to her coffee and stirred it briskly. From her outward appearance they could have been discussing the unusually mild weather instead of the gross interference in his life.

Not for the first time, Simon marveled at his mother's aplomb. Sometimes the sheer bravado of her actions astonished him. From his youth, Simon had been taught to look upon his mother as fragile and delicate. At all costs she was to be protected from the cruelties of life. Now he felt as if he needed protection from her.

"Is that all you have to say?" he demanded in starched tones.

"I did what I thought was best."

"You interfered in my life."

A nerve near Georgia's eye twitched, and she set the china cup in the saucer. "Don't raise your voice to me, Simon."

It took everything in him not to cry out at the injustice of her actions. The hurt and betrayal must have shone in his eyes.

"I don't expect you to understand why I acted as I did, nor do I expect your approval," Georgia continued calmly.

Unable to sit politely in the chair, Simon vaulted to his feet. "If you think I've come to applaud your wisdom, Mother, you're wrong."

"No," she replied evenly, "I don't imagine you did."

"And what did Dad have to say about this?" Simon doubted his father's involvement. Not that he was incapable of this deception, only that ten thousand sounded like far more than Simon, Senior, would have parted with freely.

The slim hand shook perceptively as she sipped from the edge of the dainty cup. "He was in full agreement. Something had to be done. You were barely eighteen and on the brink of your college career. Angela Robinson was ruining that."

"I was in love."

"You were too young to know about love."

"And when I married Carol I was mature enough to know that kind of thing. Is that what you're saying?"

"At twenty-one, I would say so. Yes, you were."

"Do you want the real reason my marriage failed, Mother? The honest-to-God reason?"

"Simon, please, that was all a long time ago. Let's not drag up this unpleasantness."

"You handpicked Carol yourself, but you made one basic mistake, Mother dear. I was still in love with Angie. I married another woman because I'd given up the hope that Angie would ever come back. I didn't love Carol then, and God forgive me, I didn't love her the whole miserable year we were together."

Georgia Canfield went as pale as alabaster. No longer did she make the pretense of sipping her afternoon coffee. Her eyes became dull and lifeless. Simon's divorce had devastated his mother. Carol had become the daughter Georgia had never had, the one woman Georgia could mold into a replica of herself. The two had taken delight in the pointless avocations that filled his mother's life: bridge, the Garden Club and numerous charities. For months following Carol and Simon's separation and divorce his mother had held the hope that they would get back together. Not until Carol remarried did Georgia abandon the possibility of a reconciliation.

For Simon it had been only when Carol remarried that he was released from the guilt of having married a woman he didn't love.

Pulling the long white envelope from inside his jacket, Simon placed it on the table in front of his mother. "Unfortunately, the cost of sending Angie away was higher than you assumed."

"Simon?" A faint pleading quality entered her voice.

"Angie's repaid that now, but I doubt that you'll ever regain my respect."

Painfully, Georgia Canfield lowered her gaze to the envelope, knowing its contents without being told. "I'll ask only one thing of you, Simon. Your father's health isn't good. Don't mention this to him." She hesitated and added softly, "Please."

The air conditioner kicked on, and soothing cool air drifted into Angie's small apartment, relieving the intense afternoon heat. Barefoot, her hair swept up on her head, she filled the claw-footed cast-iron tub with water. Now that the money had been repaid, she could think about moving to a more modern apartment. The thought caused her to pause. No. Soon she'd be married to Glenn and they'd find a nice place to live. It bothered Angie the way Glenn escaped her mind. She did love him, she rationalized, she was confused that was all.

The tub was filled, and still Angie stood with her cotton bathrobe loosely tied at her waist. The urge to locate her high-school annual from her senior year drove her to the bedroom. She crouched down on her knees, and dragged out the narrow flat box from under her bed. Sitting cross-legged on the polished hardwood floor, she lifted off the cardboard lid. Memories sprang out and danced around her at all sides. On the top, in a sealed bag, was the crushed corsage that Simon had given her for the junior-senior prom when they were sixteen. Those were the first flowers any boy had ever given her, and Angie had treasured them more than riches. Even when Georgia Canfield had sent Angie away, she hadn't been able to part with these memories. Reverently she set the corsage aside and pulled out the yearbook she sought. With a sense of unreality she turned the pages and stared at the picture of herself as valedictorian of the graduating class. Had she really ever been that young and innocent? A sad smile touched her eyes. For someone so intelligent, she had been incredibly stupid.

She turned the pages one by one and a slow smile grew until it hovered on the verge of laughter. She wasn't the only one who looked young and innocent. Bob and Cindy were barely recognizable. And Simon, the gray eyes that stared back at her were so serious; his dark hair was several inches longer than the way it was currently styled. They'd changed, all of them. Without conscious effort, Angie realized that her index finger was brushing over the black-and-white photo of Simon.

The doorbell chimed and shook her from the deep retrospection. A moment passed before she realized what was causing the noise. Stumbling to her feet she tightened the sash of the thin housecoat and hurried into the living room. A glance through the peephole confirmed her visitor was Glenn.

Angie unlocked the dead bolt and pulled open the door. "Glenn, I apologize, I'm running a little behind schedule tonight."

His loving smile was filled with a warmth women dream of seeing in a man. "I don't mind," he said, taking her in his arms. His mouth claimed hers, parting her lips in a deep, languorous kiss. Angie linked her arms around his neck and tried to kiss him back and found she couldn't. *You'll learn,* her mind assured her, and Angie didn't doubt that she would.

Glenn's grip relaxed and his hand continued to hold her loosely. "I've had quite a day," he announced and kissed the tip of her nose. "I'm finding that I like being engaged, but I have a feeling I'm going to like marriage a whole lot more."

Tipping her head back, Angie smiled into his shining eyes. "I'm sure I am, too." This man loved her, and she wasn't going to let anything ruin that. "Pour yourself a drink while I hop in the tub."

"Are you sure you don't want company?"

Angie's laugh was light and breezy. "I don't know. That sounds interesting."

She'd been teasing and was surprised when Glenn followed her into the bedroom. He stopped short at the papers, books and pressed flowers scattered about the floor.

"What's this?"

Instinctively, Angie bit into her bottom lip. She'd rather not explain, but Glenn had a right to know. "I was looking through some things I saved from high school."

"In Groves Point?" His eyes met hers in a sober exchange.

Angie nodded, sitting on the edge of the mattress. "I can't believe I was ever that young."

Glenn bent down and retrieved the annual that lay open on the floor. Sitting on the bed beside her, he turned the pages to the senior pictures and grinned when he found hers.

"You go ahead and look while I take a bath," she suggested with feigned disinterest. Her back was to him as she took a sleeveless summer dress from the closet.

"Is there anyone else's picture I should look for?" Glenn asked in a bland voice that revealed all.

A tingling sensation ran up her spine, and Angie's fingers groped and bit into the wire hanger. Remov-

ing the dress gave her vital seconds to collect her
thoughts. She was marrying Glenn, he had a right to
know. "Simon Canfield's."

"And he is?"

"Was," Angie corrected. "Simon was the first man
I loved."

"Heart and soul?"

"And body." Angie didn't leave room for any misunderstanding.

A heavy silence fell over the room. When Glenn
made no response, Angie turned, her gaze seeking
his. For months Glenn had lovingly wooed her. He had
courted her in word and deed in the most romantic
of ways. Eventually his persistance had won her over
enough to encourage her to face the past head-on.

Sending her back to Groves Point had been a measure of how much he did love her. The hurt in his eyes
now revealed the pain her words had caused him. Angie
could offer no vindications or apologies. Nor could she
alter the circumstances of years long past.

Saddened, her eyes glistened with unshed tears of regret. The last person she ever wanted to hurt was Glenn.
He was the only man patient enough to peel down the
barriers she had erected about herself.

Closing the book, he set it aside. "He was the one
you went to see in Groves Point."

"Yes."

Their eyes were level now, unflinching. A minute
passed before he spoke. "Go ahead and take your bath
and I'll get myself that drink."

The questions in Glenn's eyes were shouting at her,
demanding some kind of explanation. But he asked for

none. The tension flowed from Angie until her knees felt weak with relief.

The bath water was lukewarm by the time she had settled in the bubbly surface and washed. Her mind was crowded, uneasy. She had agreed to be Glenn's wife. Maintaining secrets, even the most painful ones, was not the way to start their lives together. Before her resolve could weaken, Angie stood and roughly dried herself with a bath towel, rubbing her sensitive skin with unnecessary force. Hurriedly she dressed and moved into the living room.

Glenn was standing with his back to her, staring out the window to the parking lot below.

"Glenn."

"Angie."

They both spoke at once, then laughed nervously.

"You go first." He took a sip of the bourbon as if to brace himself, his dark eyes uncertain. Glenn was such a positive, forthright man that it was a shock to read the wavering doubts in him. He loved her, and heaven knew she didn't want to hurt him.

"You should know…" she began, then paused and gestured weakly with her hands. "The thing is, I don't know where to start."

"Will one of these help?" He held up his drink and the chunks of ice clinked against the rim.

"I think it would."

Angie so rarely drank anything stronger than wine that when she took a sip, the burning feeling sank to the pit of her stomach and stayed there like a red-hot coal. Grimacing, she handed the glass back to Glenn. "I'll do better without this."

"From the look about you, I think I may need it."

With a tumbler in each hand he sat across from her, resting his elbows on bent knees. White lines of tension bracketed his mouth. Playfully, he took a sip from each drink and found her eyes. "Go on, I'm ready now."

Angie knew what it had cost him to make light of this situation and appreciated him all the more. "I don't deserve you, Glenn."

"Just don't tell me you're married and have five kids waiting for you in Groves Point."

Her pain-shadowed eyes dropped to her hands. "There were no children," she whispered brokenly.

"But you were married?"

"Yes…no." This was the worst part. How could she possibly explain that through all these years she *felt* married?

"Which is it?"

"I was married to Simon, but the marriage wasn't legal."

"You'd better start at the beginning," he murmured after a lengthy pause, his voice aching and confused.

They talked nonstop for an hour until there was nothing Glenn didn't understand or know. When Angie was only a few minutes into the painful details, Glenn crossed the room and sat beside her, holding her close, lending her his strength. Angie was amazed that she could recount the events with such a lack of emotion. It was almost as if she were relating another person's story. Angie started the story when Simon and she were in high school, and ended with the bitter man she had found in Groves Point Citizens Bank and her confrontation with his mother the following evening. Sparing no particulars, accusing no one, she completed her narration and paused to study the grave look on Glenn's face.

"If you have any questions, ask them now," she requested softly, surprised at the dry, parched feeling in her throat. "After tonight, I want us to make a pact to never speak of Simon or Groves Point again."

Glenn was motionless beside her. "I don't think that will work," he said finally.

"Why not?"

"Because if I were Simon I'd be here right now. From everything you've said about him, I'm surprised he hasn't arrived already."

"Why?" Angie asked, unsure. She wanted to bury the past, not resurrect it. "No, he won't," she returned, sounding more confident than she felt. "I told him it's over and that he's dredging up a memory. I asked him not to phone again."

Angie felt the room temperature drop ten degrees. "He phoned?"

"Today...I told him it's over. We can't go back to being seventeen again."

"Is it really over, Angie?"

"Yes," she cried, her mind in turmoil. "Would I have agreed to be your wife otherwise?"

Naked uncertainty flashed across his handsome face as he clasped her hands tightly within his own. "I want to believe that."

"Oh, Glenn. My first instinct is to suggest that we go away and get married tonight. That would settle everything. But I can't. And I won't."

"I wouldn't do that." Glenn drew in a long labored breath. "Everything will be right for us and between us when I make you my wife." His voice was soft with tenderness.

Angie turned brilliant eyes to him and smiled her

thanksgiving. He was telling her that he understood
her need to do everything properly this time. Her marriage to him wasn't going to be a hushed affair, with
their vows whispered behind closed doors in the dead
of night. She wanted to stand before God and friends
and proclaim their love. With Glenn she would have a
maid-of-honor and bridesmaids and her picture in the
paper. This marriage was for a lifetime and there would
be nothing to make it sordid. In the years to come she
would look back and remember the joy in Glenn's eyes
when he slipped the wedding band on her finger. This
marriage would be a good one, and with it would come
the years of happiness that had been so elusive for the
past twelve years. The pain in her heart that had spread
like cancer into every facet of her life would forever
be healed.

Threading his fingers through her hair, he framed
her oval face between his hands and gazed into her eyes.
"I love you, Angie."

With a sublime effort, Angie forced herself to smile
and echo his words.

"The same man as yesterday called," Donna announced when Angie entered the back door of the
flower shop the next morning.

Angie dragged her gaze from her friend to the desk
and the offending telephone. "Did he leave a message?"

"No. Only that he'd phone back later."

Angie panicked, then became ice-cold as resentment
filled every pore of her body. "If he phones again, tell
him I'm not here. Better yet, inform him I've taken a
six-month cruise to Antarctica."

Donna stared at her with wide-eyed astonishment.

Angie instantly regretted her outburst, ashamed that she was crumbling because Simon Canfield had tried to contact her for the second time in two days.

The worst part, she thought, was that she couldn't chastise and berate him for interfering in her life. They shared a special bond of friendship, love, marriage and betrayal. Simon could never be just an old "boyfriend" in her life, and finding the proper place in which to fit him could be impossible.

Angie's eyes strayed back to the phone. She hardly believed the surge of emotion she was experiencing. Vividly she recalled the look in Simon's eyes as she had pulled out of the driveway on his property. His gray eyes had grown soft with confusion as if he wasn't sure if he should let her go or plead with her to stay.

The phone rang again ten minutes later. Donna's eye sought hers. "Do you want me to get it?"

"No." She shook her head as she spoke. "I will."

She drew in her breath and squared her shoulders as she walked to her desk in the rear of the shop. The area was small but granted her more privacy than if she were standing at the front counter.

"Clay Pots."

"Angie, it's Simon."

His voice was a gentle caress filled with the tenderness she had known from him in her youth. A surge of unexpected compassion spread over her, warming her. "Simon, before you say anything there's something you should know. Something important."

"Nothing could be more important than the fact I love you, Angie Robinson. Listen, I'm doing everything I can to make arrangements to—"

"Simon, please, will you listen to me?"

"Good. We need to talk. There are a few too many skeletons in our closets."

"I can't talk now," she insisted. "Not in the middle of the day."

"It's not even nine."

"That's the middle of the day to a florist. Are you going to argue with me long distance?" She nearly choked at how ridiculous that must have sounded. Simon Canfield drove a ninety-thousand-dollar car, lived on choice South Carolina soil and dressed in five-hundred-dollar suits. A phone call wasn't even worthy of a mention.

"I want to see you."

"No." It took all her restraint not to cry at him to stop pressuring her like this.

"Why not?"

Tell him you're engaged, her mind screamed. *He's got to know. It's the only thing that will get through to him now.* "I won't see you, it's too painful."

"Angie, I swear to you, I'll never hurt you again."

"Oh, Simon." Her voice became a throbbing whisper. "There's something you've got to know."

"Angie, please listen to me—"

"No," she cried shakily. Her hand pressed against her forehead and lifted the hair from her brow. "There's someone else who loves me now. He's a good man—" Her voice cracked, and she sucked in a calming breath.

A stunned silence echoed over the line.

"Please, Simon, don't phone me again," she begged. "I don't want to hurt you. Just leave me alone." Blind determination gave her the courage to sever the connection. Her hand remained on the phone, half expecting Simon to immediately call again. Hundreds of miles might be separating them, but it didn't take much to imagine the cold displeasure hardening Simon's face. Simon was a man who was accustomed to getting what he wanted. A full five minutes passed before she gave up the vigil. And it was another couple of minutes more before she realized that Donna was regarding her with a worried frown.

In a flower shop the phone was essential to run a profitable business. Angie learned that day to hate it. With every ring she cringed, fearing it was Simon. No day had ever lasted so long. She was out the door at ten minutes after five, relieved to have escaped partially unscathed.

This was the night she and Glenn were having dinner with her father. An evening to celebrate. Glenn was bringing his grandmother's ring to her and they were going to announce their engagement.

"This should be the happiest day in your life," Angie muttered out loud as she slipped her feet into delicate high-heeled sandals. "At least try to look the part." She checked her appearance in the mirror and groaned. Clay would take one look at her and demand to know who died.

She groaned and pinched her cheeks, hoping that at least would add color to her ashen features.

As usual Glenn was on time. His mouth caressed hers in a slow, undemanding kiss. "Are you feeling okay?"

Nodding took a monumental effort. "I'm fine."

The doorbell chimed in short, impatient bursts, and Angie tossed a stricken glance across the room. Panic filled her and her gaze flew to Glenn.

"Do you want me to get it?" he asked, almost tenderly.

"Please." Apprehension rooted her to the floor.

Glenn walked across the room and pulled open the door. "Hello, Simon," he said firmly. "I've been expecting you. I'm Angie's fiancé."

Six

Charleston had often been called the Holy City. Her skyline was punctuated with the graceful spires of churches, the symbols of man's faith in a merciful God. Angie's faith was at its lowest ebb as she sat beside Glenn in his Lexus. Silently, he drove to the elegant Philippe Million restaurant where her father was meeting them for dinner.

Angie's thoughts drifted to the scene they had recently endured. Simon and Glenn had faced each other like warlords defending their titles. At Glenn's announcement that he and Angie were engaged, Simon had turned his disbelieving gaze to her, demanding that she tell him it wasn't true. Instead, Angie had inched closer to Glenn's side. To her surprise, Glenn didn't place a proprietary arm around her.

"Does he know about us?" Simon directed his question to Angie, ignoring Glenn.

"Everything," Angie told him.

Simon continued to concentrate his fierce gaze on her. "We need to talk."

"As you can see, Angie and I are going out tonight," Glenn intervened, continuing to shock Angie even more.

Her thoughts drifted to the present as Glenn pulled to a stop at a red light and turned to her, laying his hand over hers. "Are you angry?" He looked as if he could stand fearless against the strongest enemy, but crumble under her distrust.

"Angry?" she echoed, and her graceful features scowled. "How can I be? Why, oh, why, do you have to be so noble? I don't want to see Simon again. I honestly want him out of my life."

Glenn's face tightened as he returned his attention to the road. "As much as I love you, as much as I want you to be my wife, I can't see us ever truly happy with the shadow of Simon looming between us."

"I went back to Groves Point," she argued. Already she had done everything he'd asked of her. More. The future stretched before her like an eagerly awaited journey, and for the first time this heavy load of guilt and unhappiness had been lifted. She was free. It wasn't right that Glenn was forcing her to turn around and go back.

A weary smile briefly relaxed the tight lines about his mouth. "Yes, my love, but you didn't bury the past, you simply stirred it up."

Smoothing an imaginary wrinkle from her favorite blue skirt, Angie spoke again. "But I don't want to see Simon." If Glenn harbored small doubts, then hers were giant mountains.

Glenn's hand reached for hers and squeezed it lightly, lending her his conviction. "He's only here for a few days. If you don't spend time with him then you'll always wonder. We both will."

Again Angie marveled at this man beside her. He loved her enough to risk losing her. And although he presented a facade of unwavering confidence, Angie recognized that he wasn't entirely convinced things would work out as he desired. "I don't want anything more than to be your wife," she said.

"Good."

The restaurant came into view, presenting another complication. "Glenn," she breathed, "what are we going to tell Clay?"

"Nothing."

"But…"

"My grandmother's diamond is in my pocket, but as much as I want to slip that ring on your finger, I won't. The time isn't right for you to wear it now. Spend this weekend with Simon. A few days will make all the difference in the world."

That was exactly what Angie feared the most. Another concern bobbed to the surface of her mind. Her father. "Clay mustn't know I was in Groves Point."

They exchanged meaningful glances. "Is it the money?"

"Yes."

"Whatever happened to it?"

She lifted one delicate shoulder, not wanting to say the words.

"Clay spent it?"

"It gave him the chance to follow his dreams. He's a wonderful musician," she said a trifle too defiantly. "He went to Nashville looking for a chance to sell his songs."

"And blew it." Glenn completed the sad tale in three simple words.

"I don't think he's ever forgiven himself. Although he never mentions the Canfields he hates them almost as much as he detests Groves Point."

Clay had followed his dreams and in doing so had shattered Angie's. With the money in his hands, he had become a stranger. He left Angie staggering with shock and grief in Charleston and bought a souped-up jalopy to drive to Nashville. The way to impress the powers-that-be was with money, Clay had claimed. He'd return, he promised, as rich as Rockefeller. Wealthier than the Canfields, at least. Within a month he was back, broke and broken. For a time he tried to convince Angie that she had sold herself cheap, and that the thing to do was to return to Groves Point and get more money. For the first time in her life, Angie refused her father something. Now he hated Groves Point and the entire population. His music would never be sung, and it was easier to blame the Canfields than to accept fault with his own actions.

"But he's going to wonder why we're celebrating. In all the time we've been going out, we've never taken Dad to a fancy restaurant. He's expecting us to announce our engagement. What are we going to tell him?"

Glenn grinned suddenly. "We'll simply have to make up something. Should I tell him you're pregnant?"

"Glenn!"

"All right, you come up with something."

In the end, they called it a belated Father's Day gift, until a sober, disappointed Clay reminded Angie that she had already given him a shirt and tie.

* * *

Friday morning, Angie must have glanced at her wristwatch fifteen times between eleven and eleven-thirty.

"You're doing your bullfrog routine again," Donna mentioned casually. "You sure have been jumpy this week."

Arguing with Donna would be useless, especially since she was right. In spite of herself Angie glanced at her watch again. Simon had said he'd be by to pick her up for lunch between eleven and noon.

The door opened and Angie looked up. Her breath froze in her throat, nearly choking her. Simon's smile was filled with a wealth of love. A slow, admiring grin crept across his features. He was dressed casually in an open-collared sport shirt and cotton slacks. Angie couldn't recall him looking more devastatingly handsome. Her eyes were glued to him, and for the life of her she couldn't speak or move.

Donna's gaze swung from the immobile Angie to Simon and then back to Angie.

"Can I help you?" Donna intervened, obviously confused.

"I've come to take your employer to lunch."

Angie's fingers worked furiously with the satin ribbon she was forming into a huge bow. With a dexterity that came with years of practice, she wove the ribbon in and out of her fingers, twisted it with a thin wire and set it aside for Donna to insert into a floral centerpiece.

"Are you ready?" Simon directed the question to her.

"Yes. Give me a minute."

Donna's face scrunched up with a frown. "You're the man who called earlier this week."

Simon's gaze didn't waver from Angie's. "Yes."

Flustered and eager to make her escape before Donna asked any more questions, Angie moved around to the front of the counter. "I'll be back at two."

"Make it three." Simon's gaze traveled to Donna as he flashed her a quick smile.

Once outside, Angie squinted in the sunlight of early afternoon. Simon strolled at a leisurely pace through the historic section of Charleston. Actually, Simon strolled and Angie followed, her arms crossed in front of her to convey her feelings about this arrangement. They drifted in and out of quaint shops along the way, browsing. Simon didn't seem to be in a hurry, but Angie had never been more willing to have an afternoon out of the way.

"Are you hungry?" he asked after an hour.

Her stomach was in tight knots. "Not particularly."

"You know, if you don't loosen up a bit someone might mistake you for a wooden Indian."

"Very funny."

Reaching out, Simon pressed a forefinger to the curve of her cheek. "None of this is the least bit amusing. Let's find someplace to sit and talk."

Simon chose the restaurant. Angie was too wrapped up in her feelings to notice the name. The hostess directed them to a table in the sun and handed them large menus. Angie couldn't have choked down soup let alone an entire meal. This meeting was awkward and unpleasant. Yet Simon appeared oblivious to it all. With the least bit of encouragement he looked as though he would pull her into his arms and kiss her senseless. Angie was determined that he wouldn't get that opportunity.

Simon studied the menu without reading a word.

This wasn't going well. He had spent the morning finding out everything he could about Glenn Lambert. The man had a good reputation as a stockbroker and investor and was coming up in the largest brokerage firm in Charleston. More important was the fact that Glenn loved Angie. They both did. Under different circumstances Simon would have liked the man. Lambert was an experienced gambler, but he was a fool to risk losing Angie. Now it was up to Simon to press that to his advantage. Too much was at stake to lose her again.

The waitress arrived, and Simon ordered the special of the day not knowing what it was. Angie ordered the same. Maybe they would both be surprised, he thought.

"When did you cut your hair?" Simon didn't know why he asked that, but anything was better than the tense silence between them.

Angie spread the starched linen napkin across her lap. It gave her something to do with her fingers as she composed her thoughts. She then lifted her gaze, looking directly into Simon's eyes. "A long time ago. I don't remember when."

He acknowledged her answer with a brief nod.

"When did you cut down the tree?" She had neither the time nor the patience to skirt around the issues.

His fingers tightened around the water glass. "Two years ago June seventh."

Their anniversary. In a flash Angie knew. She knew! Her breath jammed in her lungs as the knowledge seared her mind. He'd chopped down the tree because he couldn't endure the agony of having it in the clearing as mute witness to her betrayal.

She dropped her gaze, trying to find the words to

comfort him, afraid that if she stated her true feelings it would complicate an already uncomfortable situation.

"I don't think we need worry," she murmured, drawing in a long, quavering breath. "Our divorce wasn't any more legal than our marriage."

A shadow of pain crossed his features. "It's not that simple. I married you with my heart and discovered it was impossible to divorce you."

They each grew silent then, trapped in the muddy undertow of pain-filled memories.

By the time their lunch arrived, Angie's linen napkin was a mass of wrinkles from all the nervous twisting she had done. Simon had depleted his water glass twice.

Simon was annoyed with himself at being so unnerved by this encounter. Angie hadn't left his mind from the moment he had found her in the clearing last weekend. All week he had carried a clear picture of her in his mind. Now they sat like uncomfortable strangers not knowing what to say. It was obvious that she was uncomfortable. For that matter so was he. Silently he prayed; he didn't want to lose her. She was everything he had always known she would be: sweet, fresh, vital. He adored her frankness, her spirit, her capacity to love.

"How long have you known Glenn?"

The question came at her from out of the blue, causing the tight line of her mouth to crack with the beginnings of a smile. They had come to bury the past, and Simon was already challenging the present.

"We met two years ago when I invested the capital from the Petal Pusher."

"The what?"

Deliberately, she set the fork down beside the plate.

"For three years I had two businesses. Clay Pots and another I called the Petal Pusher."

"Petal Pusher? What was that?"

"I made weekly visits to restaurants, doctors' offices, or anyplace else that needed someone to come in and make sure their plants were healthy. It seems surveys prove that patients who wait in a doctor's office with dead and dying plants sitting in the corner lose confidence in their physicians."

Simon was enthralled. The idea was a marvelous one. "What happened to the business?"

Angie didn't hesitate. "I sold it for seven thousand dollars profit, invested that until I had the ten I owed you, plus the necessary interest."

"And that's how you met Glenn."

"Right."

"You always were the clever one," Simon said and a thread of pride laced his words.

For the first time that afternoon, Angie lowered her defenses. "I prefer to be thought of as intelligent. I simply found a need and filled it."

"Do you still play tennis?"

Simon had taught her the strenuous game and lived to regret it. Less than six months after he demonstrated the proper method of holding the racket, she was beating him at his own game. "Twice a week. What about you?"

"I've switched to racquetball. If you like I'll teach you that, too."

Glenn already had, but Angie preferred tennis. "No, thanks." She made a show of looking at her watch. "I should be getting back. A teenager comes in part-time on Friday afternoons, and Donna likes to leave a little early."

"It's barely two." He studied Angie and made a conscious effort not to argue. "Will you have dinner with me tonight?"

"Simon," Angie groaned. "It isn't going to do any good to continue to see me. We're different people now with nothing in common except a lot of pain. I'd rather we buried it and went on with our lives."

"Fine. I want that, too, but I also want you in my life. Now and forever."

Clenching her fist, Angie deposited her napkin on the table and pushed back her chair to stand.

"Tonight?"

Glenn's words echoed in the chambers of her mind. Neither of them wanted the shadow of Simon looming between them. "All right," she agreed reluctantly.

That evening, dressed in a short-sleeved Caribbean-blue linen suit, Angie nervously paced the living-room floor. She now regretted having succumbed so easily to Simon's wishes. Tonight was it, she argued silently with herself. She wouldn't see him again. Every meeting was a strain-filled confrontation that left her facing nagging doubts she preferred to ignore. Yes, she agreed, Glenn was right to force her into doing this, but she hated it.

Nervously she glanced at the wall clock. Clay had a habit of sometimes dropping by unannounced on Friday nights. The last thing she needed was to have him find her with Simon Canfield.

She stood by the window of the second-story apartment and gazed to the lot below. From her position, she viewed Simon's Mercedes pull into the parking lot. The vehicle looked incongruous with the cheaper models that filled the spaces. Unfolding his long powerful legs, he climbed from behind the steering wheel, paused and leaned over to retrieve a small box. Even from this distance, Angie recognized what it was. She should, she had seen others like it often enough. Simon, dear, wonderful, Simon, was bringing her a corsage. No one but him would think to do that for someone who owned a flower shop.

Opening the apartment door she stared at him, hardly able to believe what she saw and felt. Simon, who could afford to give her the most expensive orchids, had brought her a corsage of white roses and blue carnations, made in the very shape and color of the one he had given her for the junior-senior prom.

Their eyes met in silent communication as he walked into the apartment.

"Hello, again," he said, handing her the plastic container.

Numb fingers reached for it as unshed tears glistened in her eyes. "Thank you."

"You're most welcome." His look was full of warmth, and he smiled at her with gentle understanding. "A boy remembers things, too."

Her fingers fumbled with the opening as she struggled to avoid his knowing gaze.

"There are a lot of other things I remember, including this." He reached for her and slowly bent his head toward hers. She knew he was going to kiss her, but instead of pushing away, she lifted her face and met him halfway, seeking the proof that she needed. She loved Glenn and what she had shared with Simon was over. His kiss would confirm that.

Simon's mouth caressed hers in a long, tender exploration, and Angie's theory went soaring into space. Deepening the kiss, Simon shaped and molded her lips to his own. Angie realized that with the least resistance he would let her pull away at any time. Part of her was demanding that she do exactly that. Instead, she dropped the corsage and slipped her arms up and over his shoulders, her fingers seeking the patch of hair that grew at his nape.

"Angie," he groaned, weaving his fingers into the thick length of her hair. Then his hands cupped her face as he studied the doubtful, almost accusing light in her eyes. His slow smile was followed with equally unhurried, lingering kisses that caused her world to orbit crazily. Alternately, he tormented and teased her until she was only too happy to oblige him. His kisses became a sensuous attack that left her trembling uncontrollably and clinging to him with an unaccustomed helplessness. Fierce sensation shot through her as he repeated the assault. His hands roamed her back while he intimately explored her mouth. Her mouth broke from his. "No more," she pleaded.

In response he groaned and crushed her tightly to the hard length of his body. At the same moment his mouth came down on hers, silencing the forming protest. Simon groaned again, louder, his mouth leaving hers to explore her earlobe before blazing a path across her cheek, then covering her lips again. His hands released her and moved to the front of her, searing her heated flesh with every intimate brushing against the scented hollow of her throat. This newest intrusion penetrated Angie's senses and, drugged with passion, she battled desperately for reality by jerking free. Immediately, Simon relaxed his hold and Angie went stumbling backward.

Expertly, Simon caught her in his arms and hauled

her back into his embrace. "Okay, love, we'll stop." His voice was little more than a throbbing whisper, as he rubbed his chin across the top of her head until their labored breathing had returned to normal. Color invaded her face as Angie fastened the buttons of her silky blouse. She found it amazing that her fingers co-operated, they were trembling so badly.

Simon interrupted her, finishing the task for her. "Do you have anything to drink here?"

She answered him with a slow nod. His gaze followed hers into the miniscule kitchen.

"Sit down, I'll bring us both something."

Angie marveled at his control.

"What does all this tell you, Angie?" he asked as he sat beside her and handed her a drink. She stared at the ice cubes floating on the top of the amber liquid. Bourbon. Oh, no, bourbon reminded her of Glenn. Mortification flamed her cheeks all the brighter. She was engaged to Glenn and had allowed Simon to touch her like that. She could have wept with shame.

"Angie?"

"It tells me," she answered forcefully, "that I was a fool to let Glenn talk me into seeing you. I don't want this." Surging to her feet, she stormed across the room to the kitchen and dumped the contents of the drink in the sink. More than at any other time in her life she needed her wits. Being with Simon was enough to cloud her perception without adding alcohol. She thought she saw Simon's mouth twitch, but when she narrowed her eyes and searched his face, he willingly met her gaze.

"Something is funny?" she challenged.

"I find it amusing that your attitude toward alcohol remains the same. As I recall you were never angrier with me than the night Cal and I got drunk on moon-shine."

"You nearly killed yourself."

"I didn't know which was worse," Simon said chuck-ling, "your outrage or the headache I had the follow-ing morning."

"As it happens, I do have an occasional drink. Mostly wine." Her smile was involuntary.

"Good, I'll order a bottle with our meal. Are you ready?"

She hesitated and then said, "In a minute. I'd like to freshen up." Whole lifetimes could pass and she'd never be ready for Simon, not the way he intended.

It took far longer than a minute to repair the dam-age to her makeup. By the time she reappeared Simon was standing, his drink empty.

He drove to an elegant restaurant situated on a cliff overlooking the Charleston Peninsula. The specialty of the house was lobster, Angie's all-time favorite food. It astonished her that he remembered these minor de-tails about her.

"You remember how much I love lobster."

"There isn't a thing about you that I've forgotten," he answered as he closed the menu.

"Not everything," she said and lowered her gaze. He couldn't. It was impossible.

"I remember that you wanted to name our first daughter after your mother, and we decided on Caro-lyn Angela Canfield. And we both liked the name Jef-frey, so if it was a boy we'd decided on Jeffrey Simon Canfield. A second boy was to be named Clay. We had it all planned, remember? Two boys and a girl." His voice became low and thick as if it hurt him to recall the intimate details of their early marriage.

They sat across from each other at the narrow table, lost in each other's eyes. Angie didn't want to be sucked into the past and gestured irritably with her hand. "What about you and Carol? Why didn't you have children with her?"

Simon lowered his gaze. "I didn't know if you'd found out about her. I'm glad you did, I wasn't looking forward to explaining it. Marrying Carol was not my most shining hour. There was never any thought of children. We weren't in love."

"Never?" The thought of Simon making love with another woman produced a surge of jealousy that threatened to choke her.

"Never. What about you and Glenn?"

Angie knew instantly what he was asking, but decided to play dumb. "Yes, we're planning to have children. A houseful, if Glenn has his say."

Simon blanched. "That's not what I meant."

"It's the only question I'm answering."

The wine steward arrived and began removing the cork from an expensive bottle of Chardonnay. Simon's attention remained riveted on Angie. "Fair enough," he spoke at last. "We won't mention Glenn again."

The meal was the best that Angie could remember. When Simon decided to be charming no one could resist him. Least of all Angie, who had dreamed of shared moments like this.

From the restaurant they drove to a beach. Angie removed her shoes and they walked along the shore as dusk settled over the land. Fresh cool breezes blowing in off the peninsula cooled the evening. Simon attempted to take her hand, but she wouldn't let him. Neither spoke. Angie felt content and melancholy, pensive, and troubled, desolate and revived as contrasting emotions swarmed at her from all sides. She had to think, to plan. There had to be some way to sort through these emotions. But not now. Not when Simon was at her side and it seemed as if twelve years had fallen away and she was seventeen again and so much in love that all was right in the universe.

"My father has taken a turn for the worse," Simon murmured and looped an arm over her shoulder. She wanted to shrug it free, but discovered she enjoyed the warm, protected feeling it gave her.

Pleased that she let him, Simon paused to drink in the fresh fragrance of her hair and press his cheek to the crown of her head.

"I'm sorry about your father," Angie whispered. Clay, for all his faults, was her only family. If anything happened to him it would devastate her. Angie was uncertain how close Simon was to his father.

"He's been ill for several years now. I don't imagine he'll live another year. I've got to go back, Angie." The appeal in his voice pierced her heart.

"I know."

"Come with me."

"Simon, I can't...my life is here now."

"I love you."

Bitter despondency weighed her heart. "I love you, too." Her voice throbbed with the admission. "I don't think I could ever not love you. But that doesn't make things right."

Turning, Simon gripped her shoulders. "Angie, of course it does."

She was close to tears. "We can't go back."

"Why not?" he argued. "I love you, you love me and baby makes three."

"What?" she exploded.

Simon laughed and kissed her brow. "For the first time since I was eighteen, I'm aware of life. This afternoon I took a walk through the park near your shop. Children were laughing and playing and I stood watching their antics, thinking how much I want a child. Our child."

"Simon…"

"No." He pressed his forefinger to her lips, silencing her protests. "Hear me out. Two weeks ago if someone had suggested that I'd be talking about a family I would have laughed in their face. I'd given up that dream and a thousand others that we'd planned. I need you. My life is an empty shell without you there to share it with me."

Angie's smile was rueful. "What can I do? My home is here. Clay Pots is here."

"Glenn is here." Steel threads laced his words.

"Yes. You may dislike him, but it was Glenn who forced me to go back to Groves Point."

"You were planning to come anyway or else you wouldn't have wanted to return the money."

"I was going to mail it. Never at any time did I intend on going back."

"You went to see my mother, didn't you?" That was one thing that had troubled Simon. Georgia Canfield had known from the minute he stepped onto the garden patio the reason for his visit.

"No. She saw me."

"What did she say?"

"Nothing—she just wanted to be sure I wasn't planning on intruding on your life."

Resentment seared through Simon and he squared his shoulders. His jaw was set with implacable determination. "Is she the reason you—"

"No," she assured him quickly. "It's all of it. We accepted it twelve years ago even better than we do now. I'm from Oak Street and you live on Country Club Lane."

"Used to."

"It doesn't make any difference, you understand my point." She broke from his grip and crossed her arms, staring bleakly over the water. Her voice was flat and emotionless when she spoke. "It's time I went home."

Simon was silent on the drive to her apartment, and with each passing second Angie felt her confidence drain out of her. Simon was leaving and she wasn't sure she wanted him to go. And at the same time, with the same heartbeat, with the same breath, she wasn't sure she wanted him to stay.

Simon pulled into the parking lot and turned off the engine. His hands tightened on the steering wheel before he turned and draped an arm over the back of her seat. "I'm not going to pressure you into something you don't want. All I ask is for you to promise me you won't make any decision while I'm away."

They were saying goodbye, at least for now. She was astonished at the wave of bittersweet nostalgia that bordered on sadness.

Intently Simon's eyes were watching her. His face contained an uncharacteristic appeal that relaxed the firm jawline and faintly curved his mouth. She released an inward sigh of regret. He was, she mused, all the things a man should be.

Slowly his mouth moved closer to hers. "Promise me, Angie," he said softly, "promise me you won't make any decision when I'm not here."

Instinctively her arms reached for him, her lips parted to receive his kiss. Simon didn't disappoint her. His kiss sent a jarring jolt through her.

"Promise," he whispered.

"Simon."

His hand cupped the undersides of her breasts.

"I promise," she whispered, and the shock waves of his touch racked her.

Seven

Angie's dreams were filled with Simon. He satiated her senses until she woke feeling warm, secure and loved beyond measure. It was as though twelve years had been wiped out and she lay content in her bed, knowing Simon would come to her soon and take her to the clearing in the woods. Moisture formed tiny teardrops in the corners of her eyes and slowly spilled onto the pillowcase. When Simon had made love to her, it never failed to move Angie to tears. The experience had been so beautiful that she had cried with joy. Even the first time, when they'd both been innocent, it had been the most poignant experience of her life. Man hadn't created the words to describe the tenderness of that first time. Angie had thought it would be awkward and painful. Instead they had shared a love so ideal, so exquisite, that tears had flowed freely down her cheeks. She had gazed up at Simon in the moonlight and discovered that his face was as moist as her own. They had cried from happiness, their hearts swelling with joy, knowing the love they shared was perfect. It didn't matter what followed in her life, Angie would always treasure that first night in the woods with Simon. The thought of sharing that kind of experience with another man was intolerable. No man could ever reach so deep inside her that he touched her soul. No man could ever love her the way Simon had.

Wrapped in tranquillity, Angie pulled the sheet over her shoulder and snuggled contentedly into the warmth of her mattress. Simon loved her still, and together that love would overcome all the barriers that stretched between them like an impassable mountain range. Together they would forge a pass.

Drop by drop the dream drained from her consciousness, and reality intruded. Angie rolled onto her back and stared sightlessly at the ceiling. Moisture pooled in her eyes and slid haphazardly down her face. Only these tears weren't ones of joy. They had been born of heart-wrenching sadness. A love such as theirs was doomed to face many more difficulties. But Angie had learned long ago that love didn't make everything right. She stood to lose Glenn, and only heaven knew how her father would react. They'd talk soon and she'd find out. He hated the Canfields, his judgment tainted with the bitterness of his own weakness.

The cost to Simon for loving her would be just as great. His family would never accept her.

Tossing aside the covers, Angie climbed out of bed and reached for the phone. Glenn would want to talk.

A half hour later he was at her front door with a white bag in tow. "Warm croissants," he said, kissing her on the cheek.

"Coffee?" She rubbed her hands together to chase off a sudden chill.

"Please."

Glenn followed her into the kitchen and pulled out a chair. The look he gave her was long and penetrating, as if he could surmise her feelings with an exaggerated glance. Angie tried to ignore the questions in his eyes. He would wait until she volunteered the information, preferring not to pressure her. Angie didn't know how she could ever hurt a man as good as this one. And she was about to do exactly that.

She set out two plates and delivered steaming mugs of coffee to the table, then took a seat. The white lines of strain about his eyes revealed how tense he was. Waiting for her to tell him what had happened was killing him by inches. Her heart lurched with sadness. He cared for her, and she was about to repay that devotion and patience by crushing him. With a concentrated effort, Angie carefully composed her words.

"Simon and I had a chance to talk last night," she began haltingly.

"Good. I was hoping you would." He blew into the mug before taking a sip.

Angie stared into the black depths of her coffee. "We didn't settle anything. Apparently his father is ill and he couldn't stay."

"So he's gone?"

Angie nodded.

"But not forgotten," Glenn added.

"I don't know if I'd ever be able to forget Simon."

Glenn's hand reached for hers and squeezed it reassuringly. "Angie, I've known that all along. I wouldn't have insisted you see him otherwise."

Angie felt as if the weight of the world had come crashing down on her. "Why are you so good to me?" she pleaded in a low voice.

Glenn chuckled and shook his head. "Do you honestly need to ask?"

Angie swallowed, profoundly touched. "I don't want to hurt you."

His hand continued to squeeze hers. "Loving someone is a strange phenomenon. At least the way I feel about you has taken me by surprise. Your happiness is more important than my own. I'd be lying if I said I wanted to see you and Simon together again. The thought does funny things to my heart, if you want the truth. But I'd never stand in your way if you decided that you do love him and want to share his life."

"Oh, Glenn," she murmured miserably, on the verge of tears. "I don't deserve you."

"But I'm yours," he whispered, lifting her fingertips to his lips and kissing them gently. "No matter what you decide, I'll always be here for you."

A hundred fifty miles down the road, Simon stretched out his arms as he tightened his grip on the steering wheel. Within three hours he would be back in Groves Point. The six-hour drive would eat up most of the day, but he'd still have time to phone Angie once he arrived home. He felt seventeen all over again, happy and carefree. He had the world by the tail and this time he wouldn't let anyone destroy that happiness. Never again. Not after he'd realized just how much he loved her and always would.

The road felt good beneath him. Everything felt good. The sun was shining and the birds chirped from their lofty perch. For the first time in a lot of years, Simon thought, he was ready to look at life head-on.

There was time to appreciate the beauty of the world around him. He had Angie.

When Simon pulled into the driveway, Prince was sleeping on the back steps. Simon's wheels spit up gravel, and he eased his foot onto the brake, coming to a stop. The sleek, black dog was eagerly wagging his tail in greeting. Simon paused only long enough to affectionately scratch the dog's ears before rushing inside the house, taking the back steps two at a time.

The phone number was in his pocket and he dug it out with anxious fingers. Humming, he punched out the number with his index finger, thinking that even the rhythm of her phone number had a musical appeal. He closed his eyes and waited for the soft sound of her voice. Even after all these years it didn't fail to affect him. Heavenly angels couldn't sound more beautiful than Angie.

After several rings Simon hung up, disappointed. He had to hear her voice again, just to know this inexplicable feeling was real and he hadn't imagined it.

Pulling a chair from the kitchen table, Simon straddled it and smiled contentedly. Bringing her the corsage the other night wasn't a brilliant idea. For the love of heaven the woman owned a flower shop. But that wasn't the point. He'd wanted to take them back to the days when she had been his and life had been about as perfect as anyone could expect. The minute she'd seen the flowers, those brilliant eyes of hers had softened and he'd known the time was right to take her in his arms. At first he'd tasted her resistance, but hadn't been persuaded by it. She had probably felt disloyal to Lambert, but she hadn't held back from him long. Simon's spirits had soared and he had realized that without much difficulty he could have taken her right then. Only the time was wrong and he had known it. No need to rush. She'd felt so soft in his arms, so right. Her body had responded to him as freely as if the years apart had never happened. Simon didn't try to fool himself, he knew Angie hadn't been pleased about that. Just as he had tasted her resistance, he had also been aware of her surprise. She hadn't wanted to feel those things with him. She might even have been testing herself, thinking she would feel nothing when he held her. Instead, it had been like throwing gasoline on a small fire. The years apart hadn't dulled their bodies' instinctive message to each other.

Simon walked back down to his car and lifted the leather suitcase from the trunk. He deposited it in the bedroom and returned to the kitchen, and opened the cupboard. He should be famished, he realized, but a meal without Angie sitting across from him would always make him feel lonely now.

On impulse he tried her line again, holding the cell to his shoulder as he checked out the contents of the refrigerator.

"Hello."

Angie's soft voice caught him off guard. "Hello, yourself," he said, straightening. The refrigerator door made a clicking sound as it closed.

"Simon?"

"The one and only."

"Where are you?"

"Home." She had the most beautiful voice. She was relaxed, and none of the apprehension he'd heard in their previous phone conversations was evident.

"You must have driven like a madman."

"I got an early start."

She hesitated, and he could feel the tension crackle over the wire as if she were freezing up again.

"How was the drive?" she asked.

"Fabulous. Thinking of you helped pass the time. I told myself I'd play it cool and call you sometime this week. Then I walked right into the house and reached for my cell. I've gone without you for twelve years and suddenly eight hours is more than I can take."

Now she did freeze up. Simon prayed that the day would come when he could speak freely to Angie. But for now he had to be patient.

"Simon, please don't. It's difficult enough keeping everything straight in my head without you saying things like that."

"But it's true."

"I…know, I thought about you, too."

"See," he declared triumphantly. "You love me, Angie. When we're apart nothing is right. We were meant to be together."

She didn't say anything for what seemed an eternity. "Maybe."

This was wrong; he shouldn't press her. He knew Lambert wouldn't. The stockbroker would play his hand carefully and press his advantage when the time was right. Simon had too much at stake to bungle this now.

"I'll make the arrangements to come back next weekend. But this time I'll fly in. That way we can have more time together."

"Okay. By then I should know what I'm going to do. It's not fair to keep you dangling this way."

"I'd wait a lifetime for you, Angie, but don't make me. We've wasted enough time as it is."

Simon hung up, feeling frustrated and irritated with himself. He had to be more patient. Their conversation had started out well, but as soon as he started relaying his feelings, she had become uncomfortable. In future, he vowed, he'd be more careful about what he said.

The late-afternoon sun burst through the window as Angie replaced the telephone receiver. Her heart had soared when she recognized Simon's voice. Even when she'd spent most of the day with Glenn, her thoughts had been on Simon. The stupid dream that morning was the source of her discontent. Even now the memory had the power to disturb her.

Angie clasped her clammy hands together in her lap and stared at the light fixture on the ceiling, taking in several long, even breaths while she tried to clear her thoughts. Her simple life had taken on major complications and there seemed no one who could understand her dilemma.

When her doorbell chimed, Angie didn't need to guess who was on the other side. Clay almost always stopped in sometime on Sunday, usually around dinnertime.

His look was sheepish as he smiled at his daughter. "Hello, Angelcake." He was a tall man, thin and ungainly. His hair was mostly silver now and receded at the forehead to a sharp W at his hairline. The square jaw dominated his face.

Angie stood on the tips of her toes to lightly kiss his cheek. "I wondered if you'd be coming today."

"Been busy."

"I know." Clay was playing with a new band. For a while he had given up on his music, but his life seemed empty without it, and with Angie's encouragement he had gone back to playing weekend gigs. Although he was involved with music again, Clay had lost his dreams, having long ago abandoned the idea of making it big. He was content to play in taverns and for an occasional wedding. Fewer of those these days.

"I don't suppose you got supper cooking. It's been a powerful long time since I ate a home-cooked meal, you being gone last weekend and all."

Here it was. The perfect opportunity to tell Clay where she had been and whom she had seen, she thought. Her tongue swelled, and her throat went dry. The words refused to come.

"I'll check out the kitchen and see what I can come up with," she said finally. Emotions were warring so fiercely inside of her that for a moment Angie felt like blurting out the truth. Instead she turned toward the kitchen and took the leftover ham from the refrigerator. Cutting off thick slices she placed them in the frying pan.

Chancing a look from the corner of her eye, Angie noticed that Clay was engrossed in the Sunday paper. Misery washed over her and she squeezed her eyes closed.

"Clay."

"Yes?" He lowered the paper.

"I...I saw..." She paused. "I'm not sure where to start."

"For heaven's sake, girl, spit it out."

Angie braced herself for the backlash. "Simon Canfield was in Charleston this weekend."

Clay gave no outward appearance of having heard her. Angie knew by his look that he was struggling to control his outrage. "And?"

"And what?"

"Did you see him?"

Angie would have thought that much was obvious. "Yes, we had dinner."

With deceptive calmness, Clay laid the newspaper aside and stood. "You had dinner with that bastard after what he did to you?" A muscle leaped in the tightly clenched jaw.

Angie's fingers squeezed around the handle of the spatula, cutting off the blood supply to her fingers. She forced herself to relax and give the appearance of being calm. "Simon recently learned…we…we learned that the whole thing was a lie. Simon's mother made up the part about Simon finding someone else. He—"

"Of course he'd tell you that now."

"I believe him."

"Then you're a fool." Angie blanched and turned back to the stove, making a pretense of turning the meat and rearranging it in the pan. A brittle smile cracked her mouth. She hadn't even turned on the burner yet.

There had only been a handful of times in her life that Clay had raised his voice to her. In some ways it was as if their roles had been switched. Oftentimes it was Angie who did the parenting. Clay was the one who needed protecting. Angie forgave him for his weaknesses and loved him for his strengths. He was a rogue who had claimed her mother's heart thirty years ago. Carolyn Robinson had died when Angie was eleven, and Clay's world had shattered. For months he had drifted from job to job like a lost soul seeking his place in eternity. It had been Angie who had held them together, finding excuses for the creditors, smiling calmly at the landlady with the promise that the rent money would be there on Friday. Angie was the one who had insisted they move to Groves Point and settle down. Clay was running, chasing rainbows with his music. They couldn't eat dreams or pay the rent with good intentions. Clay had hated the job at the mill, but it had given them the stability they needed. Soon he had found other musicians and formed a small band. Within six months of settling on Oak Street, he was a semihappy man. At least as happy as he would ever be without his beloved Carolyn.

Clay's attention was riveted on Angie. "What other foolish lies did he feed you?"

"Dad, they weren't lies."

"I thought I raised a smarter girl than this."

"Clay," she protested. "I'll be thirty years old this year. That's old enough to know when someone's telling the truth."

Clay snorted loudly and crossed his arms. "Darn fool, that's what you are—a darn fool."

"Dad." Angie couldn't believe that this was her father talking to her like this. In many ways they were alike. All his life Clay Robinson had loved only one woman. As far as Angie knew he'd lived the past eighteen years celibate.

"I just hope to God that Glenn didn't hear anything about you and that Canfield boy."

"He was the one who encouraged me to meet Simon. In fact, he insisted upon it."

"I can't believe that." Clay continued to pace the confined area of the kitchen in giant, power-filled strides that ate up the distance in two steps.

"Glenn feels that we can't make a future together until we clear away the past."

Clay splayed his finger through his hair in a jerking movement. "Just how much does Glenn know?"

"Everything."

"Everything!" he exploded. "Only an idiot would have told him how you gave yourself to that rich boy."

"I don't have any secrets from Glenn."

"Well, you should have. You gave yourself to him like a shameless hussy."

Angie's head jerked back as if he had physically slapped her with the words. Her fingers tightened around the oven door as she fought to maintain her composure and hold back the tears.

"I'll just pray that you didn't tell Glenn about your so-called marriage."

"He knows that, too."

Clay turned on her with mocking disbelief. "He knows that you behaved like a common tramp and still has anything to do with you?"

"Dad." Angie reeled under the vicious attack of words. "Don't say that."

"Why not? It's true, isn't it?"

The words sliced into her heart like the serrated edge of a knife. This was Clay speaking to her, she reminded herself. But not the lovable roguish father she loved. This Clay was a stranger filled with rage and bitterness. One Angie didn't know or recognize.

"Glenn loves me."

"He must."

Angie's vision blurred until the tall stranger before her became a blurry haze. Somehow she managed to hold back the tears.

"I suppose Canfield claimed undying devotion. That sounds like something those greedy rich folks would do. He couldn't stand the thought of you loving another man." He rammed his hands deep within his pant pockets as he turned toward Angie. "I bet he's kept tabs on you all these years, just waiting for you to find another man. Then the minute you did he popped back into your life, claiming he's always loved you. Ha! The only things those Canfields love is greenbacks."

"I don't believe that." Angie's voice was little more than a hoarse whisper.

"I hope you told him a thing or two."

"No. In fact I'm seeing him next weekend."

Clay looked stunned. "You won't. I forbid it."

Angie's short laugh lacked humor. "It's a bit late for placing restrictions on me, Clay Robinson. I'm a woman now, not a child that you can order about."

Clay's hand gripped the back of the chair as anger contorted his features. "I can't believe my ears. This isn't my Angie talking. You'll do as I say or live to regret it."

"Just what do you plan to do? Lock me in my room or send me to bed without supper?" Angie didn't budge but boldly met his gaze. "You're talking to a woman now. Threats aren't going to intimidate me."

Clay was quiet for an exaggerated moment. "If you so much as speak to that rich boy, then you can forget you've got a father. You hear me, girl? I was fool enough to stand back and let you get involved with him the first time. No more. From now on you're on your own. Understand?"

The thoughts that swam through Angie's mind were ludicrous enough to bring a trembling smile to her lips. She recalled the last time she'd argued with her father. She had been twelve and afraid they were going to be kicked out of the small boardinghouse in which they were living. Clay hadn't paid the rent in two weeks, and no amount of sweet talk was going to persuade the landlady to extend their welcome without payment. At the time Clay was playing the fiddle on street corners, collecting dimes. Angie had been the one to sit her father down and tell him the time had come to look for a job that paid real money. In his usual jovial way, Clay had sung her a song and claimed that a band would come along needing a fiddler and they'd be in Fat City. Angie had shook her head and calmly explained to him that there wasn't any band. They needed money for the rent. She needed new shoes. Clay argued that all he needed was a little time. And twelve-year-old Angie, mature beyond her years, had told him time had run out. Clay had wept bitter tears, wetting her patched dress with his emotion.

"You hear me, girl?" Clay repeated.

"I'm seeing Simon." Composed now, Angie met his gaze without flinching.

"Then you've made your decision. You won't be seeing me again." He stalked from the apartment, slamming the front door as he left.

Crossing her arms to ward off the cold of Clay's departure, Angie slowly shook her head. This had been far worse than anything she would have believed. Clay hated Simon with a bitterness rooted so deep that it had choked off even the most basic reasoning. Given time, Angie was convinced that Clay would come around. She was his daughter, his only child. By tomorrow he'd be back to apologize, she reasoned. When he'd had time to think things through, they would have a reasonable discussion and everything would be made right.

* * *

Monday afternoon Angie called Clay before she left the flower shop. Her day had been miserable. The argument had hung over her like a storm cloud from the minute she had climbed out of bed. Even Donna had commented on how unusually quiet Angie was. Clay didn't answer.

Ten tries and five hours later, Angie broke down and drove to Clay's apartment. It was just like him to be stubborn enough not to answer the phone. Fine, she'd face him head-on. This whole affair had gone on long enough. All the family they had in this world was each other. She wouldn't be blackmailed by his demands, but the least they could do was talk things out reasonably.

No light shone through the window of Clay's residence and, after knocking for several minutes, Angie gave up. Reluctantly she returned home, weighted with despair and miserable.

Simon phoned her Tuesday evening, sounding happy and carefree.

"Angie, you won't believe what I did today."

Despite her mood, Angie felt herself drawn into his vivacious happiness. "Tell me."

"Are you sitting down?"

"Should I be?"

"That depends. No, on second thought you wouldn't completely understand this."

"Then tell me."

"I phoned the Y and volunteered to coach basketball next season."

He was right, Angie didn't know why this was such a monumental decision. Simon had always been a talented athlete. It seemed natural that he would share his gift. Maybe, she thought, she was supposed to be surprised that he chose something as common as the Y. "Congratulations."

"I didn't think you'd understand," he said with a chuckle. "Angie, I've holed myself up in my own little world for the past ten years. I've been little more than a recluse. Yes, I played tennis and racquetball and occasionally attended a social function, but it was only the motions of living."

"Simon—"

"Angie," he interrupted, "it's taken me all this time to realize that when you left, something vital in my life went with you: the reason for living."

"Oh, Simon." She felt the thickness building in her throat. When she left, all Simon knew was that she'd taken the money. All he knew was that she'd sold out. It was little wonder that animosity had dominated his life.

"Do you remember that I mentioned watching children play?"

"Yes." Her voice grew soft. Children were her weakness. Clay Pots kept her busy enough to make her forget about the family she'd planned with Simon. Glenn had talked about marriage long before Angie had ever considered it. Only when he mentioned children did he sway her.

"Angie, you have to understand that was the first time I stopped and noticed children. I couldn't bear to, knowing you and I would never have any."

She closed her eyes and placed a hand over her lips, afraid a sob would escape.

"Angie?"

"I'm here," she answered in tortured misery.

The line went silent. "Angie, what's wrong?"

"I'm afraid."

"Oh, love, I am too." For twelve years his life had been in limbo. Now he knew, if Angie chose to marry Lambert, he'd be condemned to hell.

Her throat felt hoarse, but she forced herself to go on. "With the past cleared you'd be able to find another woman to love. I did. Glenn and I were thinking of marriage. In time, you'd do the same."

Her use of the past tense where Glenn was concerned pleased Simon. "Yes," he agreed, not wanting to coerce her into a relationship. "I believe that in time I could. But I'm hoping I won't have to."

That night, Angie lay in bed sleepless. Charleston was hot and humid, and the night seemed the loneliest of her life. She tried not to think about Simon or Clay or the consequences if she turned away from either of them.

Unwillingly she remembered Cindy's words about Simon: an entity unto himself. Simon was independent, he needed no one. And yet he had built a house on the very property that they had once claimed as their own. A house that was little more than an empty monument to a marriage destroyed in its infancy. The house had become testimony to the stark loneliness of Simon's existence. The house had looked huge from the outside, and although she'd only been in the kitchen, it had obviously been built with a family in mind. Briefly she wondered if he'd built it when he was married to Carol. Pain shot through her. No, she reasoned, from everything she knew of his ex-wife the woman was a social butterfly handpicked by Georgia Canfield. Carol wouldn't have wanted to live outside the social circle of Country Club Lane. The realization eased her mind, but it quickly grew troubled again. The thought of Simon living in the huge house alone was enough to cause tears to gather in her eyes. A part of Simon had never abandoned the hope that she would come back. Knowing that made her decision all the more difficult. How could she ever turn away from this man?

By Wednesday Angie was frantic to know Clay's whereabouts. Every day she phoned the apartment. No one was there to answer, she discovered. Finally Glenn went with her to the tavern where Clay played to patrons who cared little for him or his music. The proprietor claimed that Clay hadn't showed up since Saturday night and that if Angie saw him first, she should tell him there wouldn't be a job waiting for him when he got back.

As he had always done when life became uncomfortable, Clay had run. The rascal, he'd done that to worry her, Angie knew. And succeeded!

"I wouldn't be too concerned. Clay will show up." Glenn placed an arm around her shoulder as they walked back to the car. This was a run-down section of town, poorly maintained. The street light had burned out and without Glenn at her side Angie would have been anxious. Yet Clay came here night after night.

"He's only doing this to punish me."

Glenn unlocked the car door and held it open for her. "From the look in your eye he's doing a good job."

"He's my father."

"Honey, I know." He took her hand squeezed it.

"We were both angry and said things we didn't mean." Angie waited for Glenn to comment about the argument. She'd given him a few details. Just enough for him to surmise what had taken place. Another man would have pressed his advantage, reminding her that if they married, Clay would bless that union. But Glenn remained silent, allowing her to form her own opinions.

They rode silently through the streets back to Angie's place. Glenn stayed only long enough for a cup of coffee. If Clay didn't show up by the weekend, they would look more seriously, he assured her. Glenn had connections. He kissed her lightly and left soon afterward.

Angie was anxiously watching the eleven o'clock news for reports of unidentified bodies, and hating herself for being so dramatic, when someone rang the doorbell.

Clay stood on the other side, pale and ragged. He didn't look as if he had a decent night's sleep since Sunday. For that matter she hadn't, either. Only Clay looked far the worse.

"Dad." Angie was so relieved to see him that she threw her arms around him and hugged him close. "I'm so glad you're all right."

He simply nodded and patted her back. "Can I come inside?"

"Of course."

He didn't take a seat but clasped his hands in front of him like an errant child. "I guess I've come to apologize for the things I said to you."

"Dad, it's forgotten."

"I'll always love you, Angelcake. But if you decide to have anything to do with the Canfields it'll ruin what we share. Glenn loves you. He's good to you, better than that rich boy ever was."

"It's not that easy." Her voice was low and pleading. She didn't want to rehash Sunday's argument.

"I can't decide for you. But I think you should thank

the good Lord for someone like Glenn Lambert. Don't ruin your life a second time."

Angie hugged her father.

"Now that I've said my piece, I'll be on my way. The decision is yours. I just wanted you to know I was sorry for the things I said."

"Thank you, Dad." Angie recognized what it had cost him to come to her like this. The argument was the first serious rift in their relationship. Long after he had left, Angie marveled at the depth of this man who was her father.

She tossed restlessly most of the night and waited until nine to phone.

"Angie." He sounded both pleased and surprised that she'd called. "I tried to catch you last night."

"I was busy."

"I know. It was nearly eleven when I quit trying."

"Was there something you wanted to tell me?" *Coward,* her mind screamed. *Tell him now. Get it over with.*

"Nothing in particular. I was going to tell you I chartered a plane and what time I hoped to arrive."

"Simon," she interrupted, her eyes closed and her back ramrod straight. "It would be better if you didn't come."

Eight

The force of Simon's shock could be felt through the telephone. "Not come?" His tone demanded an explanation.

"Dad and I had a long talk and—"

"What has your father got to do with you and me?"

Angie pulled out the chair at her desk and sat down, propping up her head with the palm of one hand. "Everything. He's been hurt. He doesn't trust the Canfields and when I told him that I'd seen you—"

"What's the matter, Angie?" Simon cut in sarcastically. "Did he think I could fix him up a gig at the country club? Maybe he wanted more money. My mother took delight in telling me how he came back looking for another handout."

Angie gasped, utterly shocked. She sucked in the oxygen so fast her lungs hurt. "That's not true," she cried. "Clay wouldn't do that." Yet in her heart she knew he had. He'd begged her to go back and demand more money and she had refused. So he'd done it himself. Angie's face burned with humiliation. "He didn't mean any harm," she said, her voice cracking. "I'm sorry...so sorry," she managed, struggling to keep her voice even. "It should never have happened...it won't again." Before she lost her self-control and burst into sobs, Angie disconnected the call. For a full minute afterward she sat frozen as abject misery washed over her.

Love wasn't supposed to be like this. Love should tear down barriers, build bridges and make everything rosy and wonderful. But in Angie's life it had erected barriers. Walls so high that even the purest forms of love couldn't conquer the granite fortress.

Tilting her chin proudly, she bit into her lower lip and sat unmoving until a reassuring calm came over her. She wasn't going to resort to tears. When she turned around and faced Donna, there would be a bright smile on her face.

Somehow Angie managed exactly that, but she didn't fool her astute employee.

"Things sure have been different around here lately," Donna commented as her fingers busily assembled a funeral wreath.

"Oh?" Angie did her best to disguise her feelings. "I can't say that I've noticed."

"Since most of the goings-on involve you, I don't suppose you have," she mocked.

"You're imagining things." Angie, too, found something to keep her hands busy.

"Hmph! Is it my imagination that you jump every time the phone rings, then run to the back of the shop if it's a certain low voice with a long-distance sound? Half the time you come into work looking like you're ready to burst into tears."

"You're exaggerating."

"Could be," Donna asserted, shaking her blond head,

"but I see what I see. I figure that I'm going to be making a wreath for you one of these days, but whether it's for a wedding or a funeral I can't rightly say."

Angie's light laugh was decidedly forced.

Later that morning, when she had a free moment, Angie called Glenn at his office to tell him she'd talked to Clay. When Glenn suggested tennis at his club and dinner afterward, Angie agreed readily. The thought of spending another humid night cooped up in the apartment was intolerable.

Simon closed his eyes, cursing himself for having blurted out the fact that Clay had returned to Groves Point wanting more money. His mother had taken delight in informing him of the event. She hadn't needed to elaborate; Simon could well picture the scene. Simon, Senior, had handled Angie's father and had made certain the man would never care to return again. It was little wonder Clay Robinson hated the Canfields. His father could be scathing when the situation called for it, and undoubtedly that one had.

He took another long swallow of his whiskey sour and rubbed a pensive thumb across his furrowed brow. He was going to lose Angie; he could feel it in the pit of his stomach. The acidic taste of the liquor extended all the way to his heart. She didn't want him to come this weekend and he knew why. That was the worst part. She loved him. But she was going to marry Lambert. After all these years she was unwilling to overcome the differences that separated them. Love wasn't enough for Angie. It didn't conquer the fear.

Another sip of his drink dulled the ache that came with thoughts of her. He remembered holding her in his arms and the way she had melted against him. Her lips had been filled with a sweet passion and although she'd refused to answer his questions about sleeping with Lambert, Simon doubted that she had. Angie was warmth and fire and sweetness and love all rolled into one. And he was going to lose her.

He slammed down his drink and called Prince to his side. Getting out of the house was paramount. Running, walking, anything was better than sitting here tormenting himself. He stood on the top step and looked into the woods. Their woods. A low-lying mist was coming in with dusk, covering the grounds until they resembled a graveyard. Without Angie this place would become little more than that.

His plane he'd chartered was scheduled to leave for Charleston tomorrow evening. He was going to be on it. If Angie was going to choose Lambert, then he wasn't going to make it easy for her. Too much was at stake.

Glenn worked out almost every night at the fitness center. Periodically Angie joined him as his guest. After they were married, he told her, he would add her to the membership. Angie wasn't looking forward to pumping iron and pretending she enjoyed it.

She'd gone inside to change clothes before meeting Glenn at the outside tennis courts. Glancing around the room at the Nautilus equipment and the trim, muscular bodies of the men and women working out, Angie was reminded that Glenn did indeed love her. If he could spend time each night in the company of these sleek, fine-tuned bodies and then come to her, with all her weak muscles, it had to be love. A set of tennis every week or so was all the exercise she wanted. Working in

Clay Pots tired her out enough as it was. The past two weeks had been the worst. Angie felt at her lowest ebb emotionally and physically. Her tennis game showed it.

"Are you sure you're feeling up to this?" Glenn asked her after she had lost the second match with nary a return.

Angie wiped the sweat from her forehead with a white hand towel. "I have played better tennis."

"My grandmother plays better tennis," Glenn teased. "Why don't we call it quits and get something to eat?"

Angie agreed with a short nod, although her appetite was practically nil.

The hour being early, the restaurant was nearly deserted. No sooner were they seated when a tall blonde waved from across the room and sauntered to their table. Angie self-consciously crossed her legs and ignored the glossily oiled body that claimed the chair next to her. The long-haired beauty had stopped off to say hello to Glenn and proceeded to drape her lithe build over him, making sure he was given the opportunity to admire her ample cleavage. Angie took delight in thinking catty thoughts. The blonde was at least ten pounds underweight. What did it matter if she looked fantastic?

Glenn's glance was apprehensive when the blonde left. "Sorry," he muttered under his breath.

"For what?" Angie's lips twitched with suppressed laughter. "You couldn't possibly believe I'd be concerned that Miss World would turn your head?"

A slow, appreciative smile worked its way across his face as he reached for her hand. "Her beauty pales when she sits next to you." He took her hands and clasped them firmly in his warm ones, his eyes smiling into hers.

"Then the saying that love is blind must really be true."

"Not in this instance. I'm a man who knows what he wants and I want you, Angela Robinson."

The words caught in her throat as she opened her mouth to reassure him that she was his. Instead she looked at him imploringly and miserably lowered her gaze.

"I would have introduced you as my fiancée, but..." He let the rest of the sentence fade.

"It doesn't matter," Angie murmured, picking up the menu and focusing her concentration on that. Good grief, did people honestly eat this stuff and live to tell about it? she wondered. A spinach salad was the safest item listed. Angie decided on that and set the menu aside. When she glanced up she discovered that Glenn was continuing to study her.

"You say your dad stopped by last night?"

"Shortly after you left." She reached for her water glass and took a long swallow. Even that tasted as if minerals had been added. Determinedly she set the glass aside.

"Is something else bothering you, Angie? You don't look relieved."

"I am, it's just that Clay didn't look well."

"The argument probably had him as upset as you've been the past few days."

"I suppose," Angie drawled, toying with the paper napkin.

"Have you heard from Simon?" Glenn's voice deepened and his eyes grew dark as their gazes locked.

The question caught Angie off guard. Glenn never brought up the subject of Simon. She knew it took great restraint and self-discipline for him to ignore her feelings with the other man.

"I phoned him this morning."

"You called him?"

Angie decided to ignore the implication in his voice. "I asked him not to come this weekend."

Glenn's eyes rounded with surprise, and when he spoke there was a quiet tenderness to his voice that touched her heart. "Does this mean that you're ready to accept my ring, Angie?"

Niggling doubts assaulted her, and she lowered her head as she wondered what madness had overtaken her even to hesitate. Yes, she was ready, as ready as she would ever be where Glenn was concerned. He represented love, security and all the things she'd lacked in her life.

"Glenn...I..."

"No." His hold on her fingers tightened. "That was unfair. Forgive me."

"Forgive you?" Angie felt a breath away from insanity. The most wonderful man in the world sat across from her and loved her enough to risk everything, placing her happiness above his own.

"I shouldn't have asked about Simon."

"You have a right."

"No." Slowly, he shook his head, his look thoughtful. "The only rights I have are the ones you give me."

Their conversation was interrupted by the waiter, who came for their order. The moment the man left, Glenn took pains to unfold his napkin and place it in his lap. "You realize he'll come anyway, don't you?"

Angie didn't need to ask whom Glenn was referring to; they both knew. "Yes, I think I do."

Almost immediately Glenn changed the subject, and to Angie's delight he began telling her about his misspent youth in San Francisco. During Glenn's first year of college, his father had been transferred to Charleston, but through the years Glenn had maintained the childhood friendships he'd made in California. With delight, he relayed several hilarious stories about his high school days and the crowd of young people who were his constant companions. Instantly, Angie's mood lightened. When he told her about his eccentric next-door neighbor, Muffie, she laughed outright.

"Her honest-to-goodness name was Muffie?"

"We called her Muffie because we wanted to muffle her mouth."

"She sounds wonderful. I'd love to meet her someday."

"You will. Some mutual friends of ours are getting married sometime in October. Muffie's the maid of honor and I've been asked to serve as the best man."

Angie liked the way he naturally assumed that she would be with him months into the future. He lent her the confidence she wasn't feeling. "I'll look forward to that."

By the time they left the club the sun was descending into a cloudless blue horizon. Since they had met at the fitness club, Glenn followed her back to her apartment in his car and accepted her offer to come in for coffee.

Angie made the pretense of fixing it for him, knowing it wasn't the coffee that had brought him inside. She filled the brightly colored red kettle with water from the kitchen faucet. A hand at her shoulder stopped her.

"I didn't come here for something to drink," he murmured, turning her into his arms.

Willingly, Angie yielded. Glenn had held her and touched her often over the past several months. Faintly, she recalled that he was taller than Simon and more muscular. Her heart pounded painfully. Why, oh, why was it when Glenn held her that her thoughts automatically went to Simon? Angry with herself, she looped her arms around Glenn's neck and fit her body intimately to his.

Apparently sensing her need, Glenn kissed her so long and so thoroughly that Angie could almost forget there ever had been a Simon in her life. Almost forget, but not quite.

Angie was struggling over the accounting books Friday afternoon when Donna came to the back of the shop.

"He's here again."

Angie's pencil froze as she glanced at the smiling round face of the yellow clock above her desk. Simon was earlier than she had expected. He must have left Groves Point early in the afternoon, she thought distractedly. Mentally she had prepared herself for this.

"He asked me to give you this." Donna set a small white box on top of the desk and returned to the front counter.

Angie's heart pounded so loudly her ears hurt with the hammering vibrations. Sluggishly and with extreme caution, as if she were handling something radioactive, Angie picked up the box. He wouldn't. No, please no, he wouldn't. Her fingers were trembling so badly she paused before removing the lid, biting her lip as she did so. The ring. Fleetingly she had wondered how long it would take Simon to play his trump card. The simple gold band with the tiny diamond had cost him far more than the money involved. He had saved for it out of the monthly allowance his father sent to him at the university. Simon had sacrificed to buy her the ring, going without the little things that would have made his life away from home more comfortable. The wedding band had been his Christmas present to her, and he'd made small monthly payments on it long after she had left Groves Point. The day Georgia Canfield had given Angie the money, she had handed his mother the small white box and asked that she return it to Simon. During all these years, Simon had kept the ring.

"Do you remember the night I gave you the ring?" His low, enticing voice came from behind her.

"No," she lied. It was unfair that he do this to her. No woman would forget a night like that. They couldn't be together Christmas Day because of Simon's family, so he had come to her late Christmas Eve with the box wrapped and hidden in his jacket pocket.

Angie had been so delighted that the lump in her throat had prevented her from speaking. Only that lump had been one of intense happiness.

"Don't you think it's time I gave my wife a wedding ring?" Simon had whispered in her ear. His gray eyes had filled with love and adoration as he slipped his class ring from her finger and replaced it with the small diamond. Later they had made love with an aching tenderness that stole her breath away. After so many weeks apart, Angie had assumed their lovemaking would be hot and urgent. Instead, Simon had loved her with a reverence, holding her so close Angie had been convinced that nothing could ever come between them. Not parents, not a whole town, not even God Himself. The beauty of their lovemaking was so profound that tears had shone in her eyes. With his arms wrapped securely around her, Simon had whispered the most beautiful words, his voice hoarse with tenderness. He murmured all the words a woman longs to hear, telling her of the unchanging love represented in that ring. He asked her to wear it proudly as a symbol of his devotion to her.

Clay had noticed the ring soon after Christmas, glee-fully assuming that Angie and Simon were engaged. In her innocent happiness, Angie had told her father about what she and Simon had done that summer in the church. Clay wasn't pleased and Angie regretted hav-ing told him anything.

"Angie," Simon spoke again. "You remember, just as I remember that Christmas."

"Why did you keep it?" She was amazed that the squeaky high voice was her own.

"You forget that for three years I waited for you to come back."

"But I didn't." She held her back rigid.

"Yes, you did, only it took longer than three years. You've come back to me now, Angie."

"You're forgetting something," Angie murmured tightly. Her fingers were clenched fast to the box, and she mentally ordered them to relax before she set it aside. "You're forgetting Glenn."

"I haven't forgotten anything." He placed his hand on her shoulder and his touch was like a slow fire that moved insidiously toward her heart, searing a trail as it traversed. "Angie, look at me," he requested on a husky murmur.

Slowly she turned the desk chair around, keeping her eyes focused on the tiled shop floor. Tenderly, Simon lifted her eyes to his and drew her gently to her feet, taking both her hands in his.

"I've been away for six long days." He wrapped his arms around her waist and brought her close. "Welcome me back, love. Tell me you missed me as desperately as I missed you."

Angie felt like a rag doll, powerless to resist Simon. She didn't want to kiss him and yet she knew that nothing on this earth would prevent what was about to happen. Very slowly she slid her hands over his chest and pressed her mouth to his. Immediately, Simon deepened the kiss. Simon groaned and leaned against her. Gently, Angie laid her slender fingers over his cheek and her mouth clung to his, moving back and forth in passionate surrender, aroused fully by the wildly erotic kiss.

Simon stroked her hair, weaving his fingers in and out of its glorious length as his mouth slanted over hers in a lingering kiss that left them both panting and breathless.

"Oh, love," he half laughed and half groaned on a long, unsteady breath. "That kiss was worth a six-day wait."

Angie buried her face in the open throat of his shirt and shivered with confused delight when he pressed her so close to his hard length that it felt as if their bodies were fused together. "Oh, my sweet Angie," he groaned into her hair. "I've gone twelve years without you, and a minute more demands all the restraint I can muster." There was an unmistakable quaver in his voice.

Angie was experiencing many of the same sentiments. Knowing that Simon had saved the wedding ring had pushed her over the brink.

"Please, Simon, this shouldn't have happened." It took a great effort to keep her voice steady. "Not here."

He lifted her chin and kissed her lightly on the lips. "All right. Your place or mine?" His eyes sparked with mischief.

Righteously she broke from his embrace, fighting back the sudden urge to laugh.

He took her hands in his and leaned back to study her, as if seeing her for the first time. Several electrifying minutes passed before either of them spoke.

"Have dinner with me tonight?"

"No." Angie shook her head and lowered her gaze. "I can't."

"Can't." His grip on her fingers tightened painfully. "Is it Lambert?"

"I asked you not to come this weekend."

"You honestly didn't expect that would keep me away, did you?" He was upset now and struggling not to reveal how much.

"Glenn knew it wouldn't...I guess I'd hoped."

"What exactly were you hoping?"

Angie had edged up against the desk so that the sharp rim cut into the back of her thighs. "I wish you hadn't come."

"You couldn't have proved it to me just now."

"We have...a physical thing." She tried desperately to play down the attraction between them.

"Is that a fact?" He gave a sad laugh as he said it. "And do you share this attraction with Lambert as well?"

"Yes," she lied, her heart throbbing painfully with the deceit.

Simon stiffened and held his body so tense that

Angie was convinced he couldn't breathe. The battle waging within showed plainly on his face. His eyes narrowed fractionally, and one side of his mouth twisted cynically. He didn't want to believe her and at the same moment didn't know if he dared not.

"I see," he spoke at last.

Angie's legs felt as if they were water, and she leaned her weight against the desk, praying it would keep her upright until she'd finished. "You asked me to make my decision," she began in a voice that trembled so hard she wondered if Simon could understand her.

"You promised not to until I was here."

"You're here now." She gestured weakly with her hand. "You will always be someone special in my life. You were my first love, and for a lot of years I didn't think I could ever love again. Glenn taught me that I could."

"Angie—"

"No," she cried desperately, "let me say what I have to, otherwise I may not have the courage to do it and the whole thing will drag out the agony."

Simon's eyes were so hard that they sliced directly into her. His jaw was clenched so tight that his face went white. Slowly, as if he couldn't bear to look at her another minute, Simon closed his eyes.

"Things would never work for us, Simon. I've thought it all out. That you could still love me is the greatest honor of my life. In the years to come I will always remember you with a fondness—"

"Fondness." His control snapped. "Save that weak, insipid emotion for your precious Glenn."

Her heart slammed against the wall of her chest at the pain she was inflicting upon them both. Her eyes ached with unshed tears, and she bowed her head unable to look at him. "Simon, I'm so sorry," she whispered and nearly choked, "...so sorry."

Angie wasn't sure what she expected. Her thought was that he would try to inflict the same kind of pain on her with bitter words or cruel accusations. The last thing she had thought he would do was laugh. Admittedly the chuckle was mirthless and devoid of amusement, but it caught her by surprise and she raised her eyes to his.

"I let you walk out of my life once and I'm not about to make that mistake again," he taunted.

"Simon—"

"You've had your say, now listen to me. More than anything that's happened in the past couple of weeks, you just proved how much you do love me."

"That kiss was—"

"Not the kiss, Angie, but your reaction to it. It scared you. You couldn't possibly love another man as much as you do me. I don't believe it's in you to marry a man you love less."

"I'll learn," she cried.

Simon was gambling and knew it. He struggled not to reveal his fear. "I know you. In some ways better than you know yourself. You wouldn't cheat Glenn by marrying him when you feel this strongly for me. And you do love me, Angie, so much it's nearly killing you."

"It won't work with us. Can't you accept that?"

"We'll make it work," he argued. "Go on—run away, marry Glenn if you think you can, salvage your father's pride, but I'll follow you. There won't be a minute of any day that I won't haunt you, because I'll be waiting for you, Angie, in Groves Point where you belong, where we belong."

"Simon…"

His mouth came down hard, silencing Angie. Her mind screamed a warning as her emotions reeled and waves of longing racked her. She tried to push herself free, but he wouldn't let her, holding her fast. His mouth softened, stroking hers with a gentleness until she mentally acknowledged that she had lost. Her mouth parted helplessly beneath his. The very hands that had pushed against his chest seeking freedom, now slid convulsively around his neck, clinging to him. Wildly she returned his kiss, on fire for him, loving the feel of his body rasping against her. Abruptly she was free. Reeling under the shock, Angie swayed until a hand at her shoulder righted her and she gained her balance.

"You think of me, Angie, waiting," he murmured, his voice raw with emotion. For interminable seconds he stood staring at her, as if studying every line of her pale face, drinking his fill before the self-imposed thirst.

Angie didn't move, didn't breathe. The four walls closed threateningly in around her, blocking her vision. Before she could utter a word to bid him stay or leave, Simon was gone.

Angie didn't know for how long she stood rooted and unable to move. Simon was right. She couldn't marry Glenn. To do so would be cheating him of the kind of wife he expected and needed.

With confused, sorrowful brown eyes, Angie stared ahead at the road that stretched before her. All she could see was a life of loneliness.

Nine

"You haven't seen that Canfield boy again, have you?" Clay asked a week after Simon had left Charleston. They sat around Angie's small kitchen table on a lazy Sunday evening, eating lemon meringue pie. Clay's favorite.

"No." Angie cast a pleading glance in Glenn's direction. His hand reached for hers under the table and held it firmly in a warm clasp.

"Angie won't be seeing anyone but me from now on," Glenn said, and his eyes glowed with a triumphant happiness.

Angie had spent long and difficult hours sorting through Simon's parting words. He was right, she did love him. Nothing could change that. The years hadn't diminished the intensity of her feelings and she realized she shouldn't expect time to ever gloss them over. But that didn't have to ruin her life. Glenn loved her, really loved her. Enough to accept the fact that her feelings might never be as strong as his.

Clay pushed his half-eaten pie aside and dabbed the edges of his mouth with the paper napkin.

Not for the first time, Angie examined her father's unnaturally pale features. "Are you feeling okay, Dad?"

He looked surprised that she would notice. "I've been having these funny pains lately. Nothing serious, but I've been thinking about seeing a doctor."

In twenty-nine years Angie had never known her father to admit he wasn't feeling up to par. Not once could she ever remember him visiting a physician. For years Clay had blamed the medical profession for her mother's death and claimed that all doctors were crooks.

"Would you like me to make an appointment for you?" She broached the subject carefully, not wanting to appear overly concerned.

"Maybe you should."

"I'll do that tomorrow then." Worried, Angie looked to Glenn for support and found his eyes studying Clay. Glenn's features were drawn with concern.

"I think I'll be headin' home," Clay announced, pushing against the table and scooting out his chair. "I'm feeling a mite under the weather."

"I'll go with you," Glenn offered, dumping his napkin on the table beside his plate.

"No reason for that," Clay scoffed. "What I'm really doing is giving you two young'uns time alone. A boy like you should be smart enough to see that."

"In that case," Glenn said with a chuckle, delivering his plate to the sink, "I'll put the time to good use."

Angie walked her father to the front door and felt his forehead. Annoyed, Clay brushed her hand aside. "I ain't that sick. Now you get back in the kitchen with Glenn and give me a call tomorrow, you hear."

But behind his words, Angie sensed an underlying fear. There was something wrong, and Clay was both worried and confused. Agreeing to a doctor appointment proved as much. "Yes, Daddy dearest," Angie murmured solicitously and kissed him lightly on the cheek.

"Have you two set the date yet?" Clay whispered, glancing into the kitchen. "I've been doing a lot of thinking lately. It seems time I was bouncing a grandbaby on my knee. I might even compose a lullaby or two."

Angie stiffened. The pressure was on her from both Glenn and Clay to set a wedding date. As it was, Angie had yet to accept Glenn's grandmother's ring. Her emotions were too unsettled to leap into a rushed engagement and marriage. She needed time and both Glenn and Clay were growing impatient. "Not yet."

"You aren't still hankering after that rich boy?"

Angie had been "hankering" after Simon Canfield since she was a high school junior. She shook her head. "No, Clay," she lied. "I'm over Simon Canfield."

"Good." His low hiss was filled with relief. "You won't be seeing him again?"

"No."

"He's not coming to Charleston?"

Angie felt like screaming. Why did Clay insist on dragging this inquisition out? "No."

Clay wiped a hand across his wide brow. "For all our sakes I hope so," he said and turned into the night. Angie stood at the door watching the dejected figure as he turned into the parking lot.

Glenn had cleared the dinner dishes from the table by the time Angie returned. She paused, deep in thought, and gripped the back of a chair.

"I'm concerned about Clay." Glenn spoke first. "I'd

bet you anything those little pains of his are a lot more than little."

Angie agreed with an abrupt nod, worried herself. "I'll make an appointment for him in the morning."

"I'd suggest he see an internist."

"What do you think it is?" Angie turned imploring eyes to Glenn, fear playing havoc with her composure.

"I don't know, honey. I'm not a doctor."

Angie nodded, fighting down a sense of panic. For all his weaknesses Clay was still her father and her only living relative.

"I've got the coffee poured," Glenn announced. "Let's sit in the living room."

"Fine," Angie agreed, following him into the room. They sat so close on the blue velvet sofa that their thighs touched. Relaxed, Glenn stretched his long legs out in front of him and crossed his ankles. He draped an arm over the back of the sofa. "Is there anything interesting on TV tonight?"

Angie flipped through the pages of the *TV Guide* and shook her head. "The usual."

His hand cupped her shoulder and moved slowly down the length of her arm. Angie closed her eyes, wanting desperately to feel the comfort of his touch.

"Dinner was wonderful," Glenn whispered and gently kissed her temple.

"Thank you, but I hardly think of fried chicken as wonderful. Wait until you taste my Shrimp Diane."

"I'll look forward to that."

Involuntarily, Angie stiffened. It was coming, she could feel it in every breath Glenn drew. He wanted to talk about getting married and her mind was devoid of arguments.

"Sitting here watching television after a big Sunday dinner seems natural," Glenn said, setting his coffee aside.

"Yes, it does," Angie agreed.

"Like folks who've been married for years and years."

"Yes." The lone word barely made it through the growing thickness in Angie's throat.

"You know how I feel about you, Angie. I've waited so long for you. I don't want to lose you now."

"You're not going to lose me," she argued, straightening. Turning, she looped her arms around his neck and pressed her cheek against his throat. "Be patient with me just a while longer." She paused to lightly kiss his Adam's apple.

Glenn's arms tightened around her. "How much longer?" Disappointment coated his voice.

"I...I don't know."

"Two weeks, a month, six months?" he pressed.

"I don't know." She squeezed her eyes closed, hating herself for doing this to someone as wonderful as Glenn.

"When will you know?"

"Soon," she promised. "Soon."

A finger under her chin lifted her face to his. For a long moment, Glenn gazed into the dark depths of her troubled eyes. His voice was deep and velvety as he spoke. "I want you, Angie." Slowly, enticingly, his mouth inched closer to hers and stopped just when she felt he could go no nearer without touching. "Don't hold back from me, love."

Angie saw the look in his eyes and a warning screamed along the ends of her nerves. Glenn wanted to love her completely. He was finished with having her so close and being denied what he craved most. For her own part she could see no reason to hold back from Glenn. She had shoved Simon from her life—oh, no, it was happening again, she groaned inwardly. Glenn took her into his arms and her thoughts flew to Simon.

Filled with self-loathing, Angie twined her arms around Glenn's neck and eagerly parted her mouth to his.

"Oh, love," Glenn groaned and hungrily devoured her waiting lips. Urgently, his hands moved down her shoulders and back, molding her to his upper torso. His kisses were insistent, thorough and seemingly endless. Angie's resolve to finally give in to Glenn splintered with every kiss, every caress. She longed to be warm and yielding, gifting him with the love he deserved. He had been patient with her, and soon she was going to be his wife. Yet she felt paralyzed with alarm, bewilderment and even shame, as if she were contemplating something as appalling as adultery.

"Glenn," she whispered, not knowing how to deal with these reservations.

He didn't seem to hear her, kissing her with flaming demand. Angie squirmed and jerked Glenn's arms free. Undeterred, he continued kissing her while fiddling with the buttons of her blouse.

Weakly, Angie submitted, not knowing how to stop him as he slipped the polished cotton cloth from her shoulders. Instantly his fingers sought to release her lacy bra.

"Glenn." She pleaded with him, but her voice was little more than a strangled whisper. "Don't, please."

When he finally drew back, Angie's forehead fell against his chest. Her hands were flattened against his

crisp shirt. She felt disoriented, frustrated and so bewildered. Tears filled her eyes and crept down her pale
face.

"Angie," he pleaded, "did I hurt you?"

He loved her, urgently wanted her to be his wife, and
she'd turned him away from the very things he should
expect. Yet he wanted to know if he had hurt her. She
buried her face in her hands and wept.

"Oh, Angie, I'm sorry." He wrapped his arms around
her, holding as if she were a child. He pressed a brief
kiss on the crown of her head and rocked her in a gentle swaying motion. "I wouldn't hurt you for anything
in the world."

"Glenn," she cried. "I'm the one..."

"Shhh." He kissed her again. "No, it was my fault, I
shouldn't have pressed you."

"But I don't think I'll ever feel differently."

"Yes, you will," he whispered confidently. "In time,
love. In time."

Angie couldn't get Clay an appointment for the internist until the middle of the week. She picked him up
at his place and was shocked at his drawn, ashen features. For half a minute she toyed with the idea of taking him directly to the hospital emergency room, but
the receptionist had gone to a lot of trouble to squeeze
Clay in for the last appointment of the day. Wordlessly
she drove to the doctor's office, chatting to keep her
mind off how worried she was.

The time in the waiting room while Clay was with
the doctor seemed interminable. Angie leafed through
the magazines with unseeing eyes and checked her
watch every few minutes. After an hour, she began

pacing the deserted room. What could possibly be taking so long?

The receptionist appeared moments later. "The doctor would like to see you in his office."

"Of course." Angie's stomach had coiled into a hard knot by the time she shook hands with the doctor and sat in his compact office.

"I'd like you to take your father directly to the hospital."

Angie scooted to the edge of the woven beige cushion. "What's wrong?"

"Don't alarm yourself. There are a few tests I'd like to run. Unfortunately, he seems averse to the idea."

"My...my mother died in a hospital." Angie knew how inane that sounded, but it was the only thing she could think to say. "Don't worry, Doctor, I'll get him there."

Saying she'd deliver Clay to Charleston General and doing so proved to be a formidable task.

"I'm not going to any hospital," Clay announced stubbornly.

"Yes, Clay," she agreed blandly.

"I mean it."

"Yes, Clay."

Angie started the engine of the car and eased into the evening traffic.

"This isn't the way to my house."

"I know."

"You're taking me to that hospital, aren't you?"

"Yes, I am. You can shout, scream and do anything else you want, but you're going to that hospital."

"Angie, don't. I'm begging you, girl. You take me there and I won't ever walk out. Mark my words. If I'm going to die I want to be in my own bed with my own things around me."

"You're not going to die, you understand," she cried, pressing back the growing fear. "I won't let you. Now quit your arguing."

"You're killing me as surely as if you'd stuck a knife in my heart. You're sentencing me to die."

"Stop it right now, Clay Robinson. The doctor said that he was only sending you there for a few tests. You'll only be there a couple of hours. Then I'll take you home."

"You promise me?"

The doctor had mentioned the possibility of admitting Clay, depending on the test results. "I promise that you're going for tests."

"But you won't let them keep me, will you?"

"We'll see."

"Angie." Clay doubled over in the front seat, gripping his stomach. "Oh, God, the pain. I can't take it."

Angie's hand tightened around the steering wheel. "I'm hurrying, Dad. We'll be there in a minute." Pressing on her horn, Angie wove in and out of traffic, driving at breakneck speed. She pulled into the emergency entrance and rushed inside for help. Two men with a stretcher raced to her car and jerked open the passenger door. By the time they arrived, Clay was writhing with agony. He tossed his head to and fro and flung his arms out like a madman.

"Angie," he cried pitifully. "Don't let them take me."

"Daddy." She gripped his hand. "You're sick, they only want to help you."

He squeezed his eyes shut. "They're taking me to my death."

The two attendants stopped her from going inside the emergency room cubicle. Angie came to a halt outside the room and leaned against the wall, needing its support to remain upright. Clay was right. He was going to die and there wasn't anything she could do about it. She wiped the tears from her face and smiled gratefully to the nurse who led her to a seat in the waiting room. What seemed like hours later, but could have been only a few minutes, a doctor approached her.

"I'm afraid your father will require emergency surgery."

"Why?"

"He has diverticulitis."

The word meant nothing to Angie. "Will he be all right?"

The doctor hesitated. "We'll let you know as soon as we do. If you'd like you can see him for a few minutes before we take him upstairs."

"Yes, please." Angie followed the doctor into the cubicle. Clay lay with his eyes closed on the stretcher-bed, his face as pale as the sheets and marked with intense pain.

"Clay," she whispered, reaching for his hand and kissing his fingers.

He rolled his head to the side and tried to smile. "I want you to remember that I always loved you, Angelcake. You were the light of your mother's and my world."

"Daddy, don't talk like this."

"Shhh…a man knows when he's going to die." He was so calm, so sure. "I'm ready to meet my Maker…." His voice faded. "…lots of regrets…loved you."

As the hours passed, Angie grew as certain as Clay

that this day would be his last. And with the certainty came the realization that there was nothing she could do. She prayed, pleaded, bargained with God to spare her father. Forcing happy thoughts into her troubled mind, she recalled the times as a little girl that he'd sung her to sleep and made up jingles just for her. He'd tugged her pigtails and called her his Angelcake. She remembered how desolate Clay became after her mother's death and knew she would feel the same without this roguish old man to love. He was a rascal, a scoundrel, a joy and a love, all in one. Life wouldn't be the same without him. He was her link to the past and her guide to the future. And he was dying.

Sweat outlined the greenish-blue surgical gown the doctor wore when he approached Angie several hours later. She could see from the disturbed frown that marred his face that his news wasn't good.

Linking her hands together, Angie slowly rose to her feet, bracing herself for the worst.

"I'm sorry," he said softly, "we don't expect him to last the night."

Angie's head jerked back as if the man had physically struck her. "Can I see him?"

"In a few minutes."

"Is there someone you'd like to call?" he asked her gently.

Blankly Angie stared at the exhausted man. Clay hadn't been to church in years. There was no one in all the world she wanted now, save one.

"Yes, please," she murmured, her voice barely audible. The card he'd given her was in her purse. The phone number was inked across the printed surface of the business card. For several exaggerated seconds she stared at the telephone dial, knowing what it would mean if she called.

He answered on the sixth ring. "Yes?"

"Simon," she whispered, trying to gain control of her voice. "Clay is dying. I need you."

Ten

The early light of dawn had washed away the dark, lonely night. Angie sat beside her father's hospital bed, pressing her forehead against the cold, metal railing, fighting off the enfolding edges of exhaustion. Clay remained unmoving, his head lolled to one side as he battled for each breath. Nurses moved in and out of the room with silent steps as they checked Clay's vital signs and marked their findings on the metal clipboards they carried.

Sunlight crept through the slits in the blinds, and the nurse quietly turned them completely closed. Angie yearned to tell her that she wanted Clay to die with the sun in his eyes. But it took more energy than she could muster just to speak. Instead she waited until the woman had left the room, and then she stood, intent on opening the blinds and flooding the room with glorious light.

"Angie." Simon's husky voice stopped her.

An overpowering surge of relief washed over her as she turned to him. They met halfway into the private room, reaching out to each other like lost souls released from a hellish trap. Simon's arms surrounded her, and he lifted her feet from the floor as he buried his face in her hair.

"Thank you," she whispered chokingly over and over. Her body shook violently as she clung to him with the desperation of a drowning woman.

"Angie," he answered. "Tell me what happened." Simon's gaze drifted to the unearthly pale face of the man on the bed. For all his differences with Clay Robinson over the years, Simon felt a stirring sense of loss. Angie and her father had always been close, and her grief affected him now more than he would have believed. Her softly murmured phrases were unintelligible and he could do little more than smooth the hair from her brow and hold her close to his warmth.

The doctor arrived, and Angie and Simon stepped outside the room while the middle-aged man with the serious, dark eyes examined Clay.

Angie's hand held Simon's in a tight grip as if she were afraid that he would leave her. If it were up to Simon they would spend the rest of their lives together, starting at this moment.

"Dad had diverticulitis."

Simon blinked and repeated the words. "What does it mean?"

"I'm not sure I know exactly, but from what the doctor explained the intestines have tiny sacs along the outside edges. When the diet doesn't include enough roughage these sacs can fill and become infected. That's what happened to Clay. His infection was so advanced that the sacs were filled and ready to burst. If they had, he'd be dead now. As it is…his chances aren't good." She paused and ran her fingertips along the hard, sculptured line of his jaw. "How did you get here?"

"Drove." He didn't add that he hadn't stayed under the speed limit the entire way. The desperation in Angie's voice had affected him like nothing he had ever known. Angie had always been the strong one in any crisis. People leaned on her. From the time they were in their teens, Simon had marveled at the way others sought her out with their problems. Now in her own grief, Angie had turned to him. Simon's heart pounded at the profound comfort he found in that. She hadn't called on Glenn, who was so close and who would have been so willing. She had reached out to him.

"Oh, Simon, I'm so sorry to put you through this."

"Don't be." He took her in his arms again, unable to keep from holding her. "I tried to book a charter but couldn't last minute like this so I drove." He didn't mention the fruitless time spent trying to locate a private plane and pilot. "I'm here now and I'm staying. That's all that matters."

"The doctor didn't think Clay would last the night, but he has. That's a good sign, don't you think?"

She was pleading with him like a small child, as if it were in his power to change the course of fate. Gently he kissed her temple. "Yes, I think it must be." The sight of the old man shook Simon. The Clay Robinson on the bed was barely recognizable as the man Simon had known. Clay had aged drastically in the past twelve years. His hair was completely gray now, and the widow's peak was more pronounced. His skin color was beyond pale, a grayish hue of a man just on the other side of death. Simon ached with compassion for Angie; his heart surged with the need to protect her from this.

When the doctor reappeared, Simon slipped his arm around her shoulder and held her protectively to his side.

"He made it through the night," Angie said eagerly, the grip on her emotions fragile.

The doctor's returning smile was tight. "Yes, he's surprised us all."

"How much longer will it be before we know?"

"It could be days. I suggest you two go home and get some rest. The hospital will contact you if there's any change in Mr. Robinson's condition."

Angie turned stricken eyes to Simon, communicating her need to remain at Clay's bedside. "Would it be all right if we stayed a while longer?" Simon asked.

"If you wish. Only I don't think it's necessary to continue a twenty-four-hour vigil. Mr. Robinson is resting comfortably now. I doubt that his condition will change over the next several hours. At this point I'd say we are optimistically hopeful for his recovery."

"Thank you, Doctor," Angie whispered fervently, her trusting dark eyes filling with tears of gratitude.

"No need to thank me. I can do only so much. The rest remains with God and your father."

Together the couple returned to Clay's room. With Simon on the other side of the bed, Angie sat across from him, her hand gripping the railing as if needing to hold on to something tangible in a sea of uncertainty.

Simon coaxed her once to get something to eat, but she refused with a hard shake of her head. Her hand clasped Clay's and she whispered soothingly as if her words would give him comfort. Gradually her head began to droop, and eventually she propped it up against the back of her hand as it gripped the metal barrier.

"Come on, Angie," Simon spoke softly, taking her by the shoulders. "Let me drive you home. You need your rest. We'll come back later."

Rubbing the sleep from her face, Angie yawned and slowly shook her head. She'd been awake for over thirty-six hours and was so rummy that she would have agreed to anything. Simon was here. She trusted him. Simon would take care of everything.

He helped her stand, and she leaned her cheek against his chest as he looped an arm around her shoulders, leading her to the parking lot and into the bright light of day.

The sun was shining and reflected off the hood of his sports car as Simon drove down the busy Charleston streets. Most of the traffic was heading for the downtown area, and since they were traveling in the opposite direction, toward Angie's apartment, they weren't hampered by rush hour.

Once inside the apartment, Angie flipped the switch to the air conditioner. Immediately a shaft of cooling air weaved its way through the apartment.

"You go ahead and get ready for bed. I've a few phone calls to make," Simon said softly. He wanted to contact the flower shop so they wouldn't worry about Angie not showing.

His words barely registered as Angie moved into her bedroom and began stripping off her blouse and slacks. She glanced longingly into the bathroom and decided to shower.

Simon heard the running water and paused to rub the exhaustion from his eyes. While waiting for Angie he discovered that the hall cupboard held an extra set of bedding. He'd get whatever sleep he could on the sofa when the opportunity presented itself.

Spreading the sheets for his makeshift bed, Simon felt a great weight ease from his heart. These past days apart from Angie had driven him to the brink of insanity. The agony of walking away from her with nothing more than a few parting words had filled him with regrets. His mind had ached like a throbbing bruise that didn't lessen with time, taunting him. Like Lambert, Simon had gambled. Clay's illness had hastened Angie's ultimate decision, but Simon had realized the minute he picked up the phone and heard her voice that she would never leave him again. She was his and would always be his alone.

The sound of running water stopped and Angie reappeared, standing just inside the living room. The thin nylon gown was lilac colored. Simon's breath stopped short, causing an aching shortness in his lungs. She was so exquisitely beautiful that he slowly straightened, unable to tear his gaze from her. Her breathtaking loveliness reminded Simon of the way she'd come to him in the clearing in the woods. The neckline of the gown formed a deep V to reveal the pale valley between her breasts, and she stood there waiting for him as innocent as spring. Simon recognized that he couldn't abuse her trust.

"Simon," she whispered and held out her hand. "Don't sleep on the sofa."

Briefly he closed his eyes to the gnawing ache in his loins. She couldn't possibly expect him to go to bed with her and not touch her. As desperately as he wanted to, he realized he couldn't take her now! Not with Clay on his deathbed and Angie distraught and confused. Yet he didn't know if there was anything he could refuse her.

"Here, let me tuck you in." He struggled to keep his voice cool and impersonal and crossed the room, not daring to look at her.

Her bedroom was small and dominated by the bed and dresser. Her slacks and blouse were neatly folded across the foot of the mattress. Simon turned back the covers and fluffed up the pillow. "There," he said, "your bed awaits you, my lady." Again he avoided looking directly into those soulful, dark eyes as she slipped between the crisp sheets. Wordlessly he pulled the covers over her shoulders and tucked them under the lip of the mattress as if he were putting a small child to bed.

Angie cast him a look of mild surprise and he noticed that some color had returned to her pale face. "Simon," she said in a low, husky voice. "Could you...would you mind lying down with me? I don't want to be alone."

Simon felt like gnashing his teeth. She had no conception of what she was asking of him. "Sure." He removed his shirt and trousers and slid between the sheets beside her. The narrow bed that forced her to scoot her thinly clad body close to him was an additional torture. He gathered her in his embrace, and closed his eyes to the agony of being so near her. Breathing in the fresh scent of her hair, Simon held himself completely still. He tried not to think of the satin feel of her ivory smooth skin and forced himself to concentrate on anything but the warm, vital woman in his arms.

Angie sighed contentedly, not completely unaware of what she was doing to Simon. Maybe it was selfish to use him this way, she thought sleepily, but she couldn't help herself. Today more than any time in her life she needed him. Dreamily, she smiled up at him and nestled in his embrace, pressing her face to the hardness of his chest. Her arm was draped over his lean ribs and she paused to murmur. "Thank you," she whispered, grateful for his sacrifice. Already she felt groggy, as if

she were floating away on a thick cloud. Her eyes felt
heavy, and Simon was warm and smooth and wonderfully masculine. Gradually she could feel the tension
drain out of him. After an exaggerated moment, he released a long, slow breath and curved an arm over her.

"I love you," Simon whispered sleepily as his hand
roamed down her back in long soothing strokes.

His voice sounded far away. "I know," she murmured
back and shifted her head so she could lightly kiss his
jaw.

"Be good, understand?"

"Yes."

Neither spoke again and Angie drifted into a deep
slumber, content to be in his arms.

Sometime during the morning, Angie's sleep became filled with resplendent, color-filled dreams that
were vivid with detail. Pleasant dreams of when she
was young and her mother was alive. Clay was handsome and happy, singing her his songs, and loving her
mother with everything that was in him to love. Their
trio was on a picnic by a clear, blue lake. The sun was
shining and the birds sang merrily from the flower-
ing trees. Clay and her mother and Angie were in a
long wooden canoe on the crystal-clear water. Clay
had brought along his guitar and was serenading them
with the silly jingles he loved to create. Angie clapped
her hands with delight and doubled over with laughter.
When she straightened, her mother was gone and Clay
sat across from her, old and gray-haired and in terrible pain. His hand was clenching his stomach and he
looked at her in such agony that Angie cried out with
shock. Clay begged her to get him to the hospital and

Angie reached for the paddle—only it was missing. If she didn't hurry, Clay would die.

Frantic, Angie cried out again, her voice piercing the still room. Weeping and thrashing about, she knocked aside the blankets and bolted upright.

"Angie." The voice was low and frenzied and Angie opened her eyes to find Simon standing above her.

"Oh, Simon." Her breath came in deep, uneven gasps. "I had a horrible nightmare." Blindly she reached for him, seeking his comfort. Simon was her closest friend, her most trusted love. Vaguely she recalled that he had been in bed with her, but now it was obvious that he had come from the living room.

"It was a dream." He bent over her, his hands folding around her back.

Angie's arms tightened as she clung to him. "Hold me, please hold me." She whispered the words against his throat as her hands clenched at him with fear and anguish.

Simon braced a knee on the edge of the mattress and pulled aside the blankets as he came onto the bed and lay beside her. Angie's arms remained locked around his neck as the full length of his hard body joined her.

"Hold me, hold me," she repeated again and again.

Simon did as she asked with a tenderness and love she had known from no other. His hands stroked her hair, her shoulders and her back. Angie buried her face in the hollow of his throat and drew in deep, shaking breaths as she closed her eyes. He didn't try to soothe her with words, but simply held her, his hands caressing her.

Gradually the fear subsided and in its place came another emotion so strong, so powerful that her senses clamored with the intensity. Her grip relaxed and the muscles under her exploring fingers flexed powerfully. This was Simon holding her so tenderly. Her husband of twelve years.

As if aware of what was happening to her thoughts, Simon's hands stilled and he tossed back his head. "Angie?" His voice was filled with question.

She answered by kissing the salty-tasting skin at his throat, darting her tongue in and out in a provocative action.

"Angie," he pleaded hoarsely, "are you sure?"

In response, she kissed his Adam's apple, her tongue teasing and challenging him as it explored the throbbing pulse point on his neck.

"Angie, dear heaven. It isn't in me to refuse you… I don't have the strength to turn you down."

"Love me, Simon. Please, oh please, love me."

Angie heard the sharply indrawn breath and opened her eyes to stare into the stormy, doubt-filled gray ones looking down on her.

Her hands slid over his shoulders and back again as their eyes continued to drink in each other. One palm slid down over his chest, and then lower, to the muscle-hard belly. "I want you," she whispered.

Simon groaned and positioned his hard body over hers. His breath was heavy, coming in deep pants as if he'd recently finished working out. He continued to hold her as he gradually lowered his mouth to hers, feasting on the sweetness of her lips with unhurried ease. He kissed her again and again until her mind was lost, incapable of any function beyond feeling the incredible sensations Simon awoke within her.

Simon's hands were unsteady as he pulled the nylon

gown over her head in an urgent movement, tossing it carelessly aside. "Simon," she moaned, her fingers digging into his hair as she arched her back to the exquisite sensations burning through her.

His lips found hers and she kissed him back greedily. Simon's fingers worked at removing the last barrier of his clothing that separated them. Free of the restricting material, he laid her back against the pillow. Mindless of anything but the taste and feel of Simon, Angie dug long nails into his shoulder blades. The pleasure that had been denied her for twelve years burst forth gloriously within her and sent her swirling to the heights of heaven. She gave a small whimper and clenched his neck, kissing him again and again as the tears slid down her cheek.

"Angie, my sweet Angie, I'll love you on my dying day."

Her hands framed his face and she kissed him, her mouth slanting over his. "Simon," she whispered, poignantly moved by his lovemaking. "It's even better than I remember." She sniffled, smiling up at him. Lazily, his thumb wiped the moisture from her face.

"Yes," he agreed. He didn't move, kissing her again and again. "Am I too heavy for you?"

"Never." She closed her eyes, drinking in the warmth of his body sprawled over hers. "Don't leave me again."

"I won't," he murmured, close to her ear. "Never again."

Angie didn't know how or when it happened, but she fell into a deep slumber. She stirred once and felt the dead weight of Simon's arm over her waist. He was cuddling her, spoon fashion, in the narrow bed. The sound and feel of his even breathing assured her he was asleep. She nestled closer within his arms and returned to a contented, blissful sleep.

When she woke again it was to the warm sensation of someone kissing her earlobe.

Caught in the delicious sensations that shot through her, Angie rolled onto her back. "What time is it?" she asked, not bothering to open her eyes.

"Almost dinnertime."

Her eyes flew open. "That late?" She sat up, pulling the sheet with her. "I've got to…"

"I've already called the hospital. Your father is showing definite signs of improvement. He's not out of the woods yet, but he's in better shape than last night at this time," he told her, sitting beside her, fully dressed. His hands were positioned on the delicate slope of her shoulders and his gaze was filled with fierce tenderness.

It didn't seem possible that it was less than twenty-four hours ago that she had been sitting in a doctor's office with Clay.

"Are you hungry?" Simon questioned.

She smiled at him with all the love stored in her heart these past years. "Starved."

"Good. I took the liberty of snooping through your kitchen and fixing us something to eat."

Angie leaned against the headboard and stretched her arms out in a long yawn. "I feel wonderful."

Simon leaned forward and kissed her lightly. "You cried."

Self-conscious, Angie lowered her gaze. "I always did."

"I know," he said in a husky, low voice. "Angie…" He paused. "There hasn't been anyone else, has there." It was more a statement than question.

"No. I couldn't."

He gathered her in his arms and buried his face in her throat. "I don't deserve you."

"I love you."

"I'm going to spend the rest of my life letting you know how much."

"Do you honestly think that'll be long enough?" she teased.

Clay's eyes were closed when Angie moved into the hospital room an hour and a half later. The nurse standing at his bedside glanced up as Angie entered the room.

"He's been comfortable," the woman whispered, answering Angie's question before she could ask it. "He's showing signs of improvement."

Angie felt a rush of intense gratitude flow through her. "Good."

The nurse left a few minutes later, after charting her findings. Angie pulled out a chair and sat, taking Clay's hand between hers.

"Hi, Dad," she said softly. "Simon and I are back."

Simon stepped forward and placed a hand on Angie's shoulder. "I don't think he can hear you."

She turned around and smiled up at him warmly. "Maybe not, but I feel better talking to him."

Simon located a chair and scooted it beside Angie's. "How is Clay going to feel about us?"

"I...I don't know." Some of her happiness dimmed. "Once I talk to him and explain how much I love you, then he'll come around."

"He's hated me for a lot of years."

"Simon, Clay doesn't hate you."

His hand squeezed her shoulder. "That's something we'll find out soon enough."

"Yes, I guess we will."

They sat, both caught in their doubts for a long half hour.

"Clay never says your name," Angie murmured. "He calls you 'that rich boy' or 'the Canfield boy.' He'll be surprised when he sees you to note that you're far from a lad."

Simon's soft chuckle was interrupted by a low strangling sound. At first Angie didn't hear it. Only when the amusement drained from Simon's eyes did Angie pick up on the soft sound. Standing, she stood over her father. "Daddy?"

"Angelcake." His voice was incredibly weak.

"How do you feel?"

"Like hell...should be dead."

"No," she protested.

Quietly, Simon stood and moved to the back of the room, out of Clay's line of vision.

"You did wonderfully well," she continued.

Clay scoffed at her with a small mocking sound. "Do the doctors expect me to kick the bucket?"

"No one's given up on you yet," Angie murmured softly and brushed the hair from his temple. "Least of all me."

"I may prove you right yet."

"Good."

Clay closed his eyes. The effort of keeping them open this short length of time had apparently drained him of all strength.

"Go back to sleep."

"I dreamed..."

"Shhh." She placed a finger over his lips. "We'll talk later."

Within minutes, Clay returned to a peaceful slumber. Angie tossed a triumphant glance to Simon, her heart soaring. Her greatest fear had been that Clay would never wake up.

A jubilant sensation filled her breast. "He's going to be all right," she announced confidently, holding her hand out to Simon. "I can feel it in my bones."

Simon's arms slipped around her waist and he held her close. "I don't doubt that Clay Robinson will be seeing his grandchildren."

Angie and Simon left the hospital after visiting hours. Night was settling like a restless cloud over the land. The sky was dark and threatening, promising an imminent rainfall.

Simon followed Angie into her apartment.

"Angie." His voice was a husky caress. "Come here, love."

Obediently she walked into his embrace, sliding her arms around his waist and tilting her head back to smile at him. "You wanted something?" she teased.

"If only you knew."

"I think I do." She undid the first button of his shirt.

"Just what do you have in mind?" he asked with mock surprise.

"Let me show you, Mr. Canfield." The second button followed. She smiled a little and arched a suggestive brow. When the shirt was unfastened, she eased it from his shoulders and let it drop to the floor.

Hesitant at first, she reached out a hand and touched him, trailing her fingertips over the hard muscles of his naked torso. Simon closed his eyes and grinned. Angie's exploring hands paused at his belt buckle.

"You aren't going to stop now, are you?" he challenged.

"No." Her voice was shallow and low. Her hands resumed their task, and she stopped breathing completely. "Simon," she whispered, a little afraid. In their lovemaking he had always been the initiator.

Apparently understanding her hesitancy, he opened his eyes and kissed her lightly. "It's my turn now." He captured her hand and kissed her fingertips.

Seconds later her cotton blouse slid soundlessly to the floor and was soon followed by her slacks, so that she stood before him in only her bra and bikini panties.

"Oh, Angie," he moaned. "You are so beautiful."

She bowed her head and her dark hair fell forward, wreathing her face.

"What's wrong?" He raised her eyes to his. "You don't believe me?"

She couldn't answer him with words. Instead she stood on her tiptoes and kissed him. "Thank you," she whispered reverently. "Thank you for loving me."

"Oh, Angie." He picked her up and carried her into the bedroom, stopping every few steps to press a thick, seductive kiss to her eager mouth.

He laid her on the unmade bed, his mouth feasting on hers while his hands fumbled with the tiny hook of her bra. Once it was free, he tugged it from her arms. "Oh, love," he breathed. "I want you so much."

Long afterward, Angie lay in his arms, her head cradled in the crook of his arm. Lazily her fingers toyed with the short, dark hair that grew at his navel. Words weren't necessary. They were completely and utterly content. The living room light dispersed its golden shadow into the bedroom, and when Angie lifted her head she was surprised to note that Simon was asleep.

Easing herself from his embrace, she kissed him lightly on the forehead and reached for her robe, wrapping it around her nakedness. As ideal as their few moments together had been, there were still many roads they had yet to traverse. Gazing down at him, Angie's heart swelled with love. Together, she knew they would cross any bridge that was necessary. As long as they were together, nothing else mattered.

Angie was in the kitchen putting on coffee when the doorbell rang. Her hand froze and she looked frantically toward the bedroom. There was only one person who would visit this late. Dread settled over her as she toyed with the idea of ignoring the bell. But Glenn would only ring again and wake Simon. That thought caused her to hurry across the room and open the door.

"Angie." Glenn stepped past her into the room. "Where the hell have you been? I've been trying to get you for the past two days." He paused as if taking in her appearance for the first time. "I didn't get you out of bed, did I?" He checked his watch. "It's barely ten."

"Clay's in the hospital."

Glenn raked his hand through his hair. "I feared as much. What was wrong and why didn't you call me?"

"I…" She struggled for the right words. She didn't want to hurt Glenn.

"Angie?" Simon staggered into the room, his hair in disarray. His hastily donned pants left little to conjecture as to his whereabouts. He stopped cold and straightened when he caught sight of Glenn. The two men eyed each other with shocked disbelief.

Eleven

Glenn's mouth twisted up at one corner as he regarded Angie with shock and embarrassment. "How long has this been going on?"

"Glenn, please, I'm so sorry…" Angie's eyes pleaded with him.

"Angie's been under a lot of stress," Simon intervened, as he stepped into the room.

Angie glanced at Simon and murmured, "Let me have a few minutes alone with Glenn."

His nod was filled with understanding. He returned to the bedroom and was back a minute later fully dressed. He paused by the front door, his eyes warming her as he murmured that he'd be back in fifteen minutes. The door made a clicking sound as it closed.

She smiled her appreciation and turned back to Glenn. His thick brows were bunched together to form a single intense line. His eyes were cold and angry; they looked as if they had frosted over. The clenched jaw was white and a muscle twitched warningly. Angie had never seen Glenn like this.

"Glenn," she began haltingly, "I can't tell you how

sorry I am that you found out about Simon and me this way."

"Tell me one thing," he ground out savagely. "How long have you been sleeping with him?"

Angie struggled to keep her voice calm, but her eyes pleaded with him for understanding. "Today was the first time…I would have let you know only…"

"Only what, Angie? Only you thought you might be able to hold on to me a while longer, is that it?"

"No," she wailed loudly.

"I've always been honest with you. But I was a fool to expect that same kind of integrity from you."

"Glenn," she begged, "it's not like that."

"Then what was it like? You made a fool out of me. Couldn't you have had the common decency to let me know about Clay? At least then I wouldn't have worried and shown up here like an idiot."

She struggled to find the words. "You have been the most wonderful, patient man in the world."

"I'm not St. Thomas Aquinas," he barked. "Don't try to pin those saintly virtues on me. I loved you. I wanted you to be my wife. But most of all I respected and trusted you."

"I know what this must look like—"

"It looks like exactly what it is: a sordid affair with an old lover."

"No." Angie recognized that Glenn was lashing out at her with his pain, but she couldn't allow him to distort the love she shared with Simon. "I won't have you talk to me like that. I've loved Simon all my life. You knew as well as I did that…that if I'd married you I could never have given you the love you deserved."

Glenn's reply was a low, mocking snort. "Do you

want me to give you a medal because you gave Simon the love *he* deserved?"

"Oh Glenn, you've twisted everything."

"I don't know," he argued. "It seems that for the first time in six months, I'm finally seeing everything clearly. You used me to get Simon back. That's what you really wanted—your old lover."

Angie could see that arguing was useless. "You have been extremely patient and dear. I'm so sorry everything's turned out like this, but when…when Clay became deathly ill I knew I couldn't face losing him without Simon. He was the one I reached out to."

Glenn grimaced and his clenched jaw tightened all the more.

"I wouldn't want to hurt you for the world. I can't tell you how sorry I am."

"Sorry. You're sorry?" He glared at her explosively.

"I owe you so much. It pains me to do this to you."

"I was the fool," Glenn barked. "A hundred times I could have had you. We should have been married weeks ago and you wouldn't have any choice but to stay with me."

His words were cruel and mocking and with every minute he looked more enraged.

"I don't think there's any way to make this up to you. But I want you to know there will always be a special place in my heart for you."

"You used me."

Angie couldn't deny it. "Please try to forget me, Glenn, and forgive me if you can. A thousand women would count themselves lucky to be loved by you."

"But you're not one of them."

Her gaze dropped to the floor. "I'm sorry…so sorry."

"Don't waste that emotion on me." The air between them was as tight as a hunter's bow stretched to its limits, ready to spring. "I can see there's no need to waste my time here. Enjoy your lover, Angie."

She kept her eyes shut until after the door was viciously closed. The harsh sound reverberated around the room.

A few minutes later, Simon knocked lightly against the front door. Angie hurried across the room to let him in. Instinctively she reached for him. He folded her to his embrace, his hands running soothingly down her back.

Gratefully she accepted his comfort, pleased that he had given her this time alone with Glenn. It hadn't been easy for him, she'd known that by the troubled look in his eye.

"What did he say?" Simon asked.

She shook her head hard. "It isn't important."

"He was hurt and angry."

"I wish I could have spared him the pain of finding us like this. I blame myself for that. I should have called him."

"He'll recover," Simon said confidently.

"I hope so," she whispered, tightening her grip. They slept in each other's arms, content just to cuddle close. It surprised Angie that after all the years of sleeping alone her body would adjust so easily to sharing a bed. Somehow she knew it wouldn't have been that way with another man. Only Simon.

She woke to find him grinning at her beguilingly. "Morning," he whispered and kissed her warmly.

Angie looped her arms around his neck and smiled

into his eyes. "I could get used to waking up next to you."

"You'd better. I don't plan to sleep without you."

"Good." Her index finger wove around his curly chest hairs. "Have I told you lately how much I love you?"

"No." Simon's voice was deep and resonant.

"Yes, I have." She giggled. "You simply weren't listening."

"Hmm, I was listening," he said and buried his face in the rounding slope of her shoulder to tease her unmercifully with small, biting kisses. "But I'm a man of action. Shall I demonstrate just how much I love you?"

"Oh, yes," she whispered, her leg sliding provocatively up and down his. "But I feel I should warn you, it may take a lifetime to prove it to me properly."

"You drive a hard bargain, Angie Canfield," he growled before hungrily lowering his mouth to claim hers.

The morning was half spent before they ever left the bedroom.

After a leisurely brunch Angie dressed and prepared herself for a visit to the hospital.

"You've gotten quiet all of a sudden." Simon stood behind her, his hands cupping her shoulders as she rinsed off the breakfast dishes. "Are you worried about your father?"

Angie had phoned the hospital twice and each time received an encouraging report. "No," she whispered unconvincingly.

"You're frightened of what he's going to say about us, aren't you, love?"

"I'm afraid it's all going to happen again." She turned

around and gripped his waist, pressing her cheek to his chest. She was comforted by the even, reassuring sound of his heartbeat. "Dad hates Groves Point…"

"And the Canfields," Simon added.

"Yes."

"But he's forgetting something important. Something that we'll need to remind him today, if necessary. You, Angie, are a Canfield. You have been for twelve years."

"But, Simon…" she argued and lifted her head to meet his gaze.

He pressed a finger to her lips, silencing her. "Today we'll make it clear that we have no intention of ever being separated again."

"But he's ill."

"Good," Simon argued, "there won't be much fight in him. He'll simply have to accept what we say."

Angie didn't feel any of the confidence Simon apparently did when they drove to the hospital. She hesitated outside Clay's room. "Maybe it would be better if I talked to him first," she suggested, her eyes seeking his approval.

Simon hesitated. "You're sure you don't want me with you?"

She answered him with a short nod, laid her open palms on his hard chest and kissed him briefly on the lips.

Clay was awake when Angie entered the room. He didn't make an effort to greet her. From the disapproving look in his eyes, Angie wondered if Glenn had come to Clay. As quickly as the thought came, Angie rejected it. Glenn would never do anything so petty. Clay looked so incredibly pale that her steps faltered. The hospital had assured her that her father was out of immediate danger, but she knew that the road to a complete recovery would be long and difficult.

"Hi, Dad." She leaned over and brushed her lips to his forehead.

"What took you so long? I've been waiting for you all morning. The least you could do is visit a dying man who happens to be your only living relative."

Feelings of guilt immediately assailed her. "I...woke late. When I called the hospital they said you were resting comfortably."

"Ha! That just goes to show you what they know."

"I'm here now." She clenched his hand in hers and held it close to her heart. "How are you feeling?"

"How do you expect me to feel? The pain would have killed most men. I nearly died. Do you think those doctors were gentle with that knife?"

"No...you suffered terribly."

"It ain't much better now."

Angie sighed miserably. This wasn't going well. Clay was like a demanding, unreasonable child. She lowered her gaze to the hospital bed and the white sheets. "I have something to tell you." Her voice nearly failed her and her resolve wasn't much better. If Simon hadn't been standing on the other side of the door, Angie wouldn't have had the courage to continue. "When you were so deathly ill and I didn't know if you were going to live or die, I was so afraid. I was terrified of losing you."

Clay patted her hand impatiently. "You nearly did lose me. That's why I can't understand the reason it took you so long to get to the hospital." He looked at her empty hands. "And the least you could do is bring me the newspaper."

Angie felt like gritting her teeth. "Clay, let me finish.

I…I thought you were going to die and I reached out to someone I've loved forever…someone I knew would comfort me." She swallowed against the tightness forming in her throat. "I called Simon Canfield." Not waiting for a reaction she quickly moved to the door and stepped outside the room and took Simon's hand. He smiled encouragingly at her and squeezed her fingers.

By the time they entered the room, Clay had half risen from the bed, lifting himself up on one elbow. His face was contorted with rage and fury. "Get out," he hissed. "I won't have Canfield scum in my room."

"Clay," Angie cried.

"And you get with him. If you don't know any better than to bring him here when I'm dying then you ain't no daughter to me."

The color drained from Angie's face. "Don't say that."

"I'll say that and more." He fumbled with the button to summon the nurse and fell limply against the pillow, his face twisted with pain. "Get out."

"Maybe you have reason to hate me," Simon said, fighting to control his temper. "But I love Angie and I won't allow you to come between us, old man. So understand that here and now."

The nurse with the crisp white uniform entered the room. "Get them out of here." Clay pointed a finger accusingly at Simon and Angie. "Leave me to die in peace." His voice shook, he was so weak. The pale features were filled with angry color as he glared accusingly at Simon.

The nurse's face was grim as she turned to Angie. "Maybe it would be best if you came back another time."

Angie blinked back the scalding tears that threatened to spill.

"Just get one thing clear," Simon said in a low, hard voice. "I'm marrying your daughter and nothing on God's good earth is going to prevent that."

Clay lay on his back and stared at the ceiling, his features void of expression. "I ain't got a daughter."

"Daddy," Angie cried.

"Leave him to sulk," Simon whispered, gripping her elbow.

The nurse followed them out of the room, closing the door behind her. She hesitated and cleared her throat. "I don't want to become involved in family squabbles, but I feel you should understand that at this point your father's condition is extremely delicate. It would be best if you didn't do or say anything to upset him. If coming here is going to provoke him, then I suggest you stay away."

"But…" Angie couldn't bear the thought of having Clay step back from the brink of death only to lose him to stubborn pride.

"Any one of the staff would be happy to report his condition to you," the older woman continued.

"You don't think I should come at all?" Angie was aghast at the thought.

"Not if it's going to drain his strength. Your father is going to need all the fight he can muster just to recover properly."

"Come on, Angie." The pressure of Simon's hand at Angie's elbow increased. "Let's get out of here."

She nodded and smiled her appreciation to the nurse who had spoken so freely. On the ride back to her apartment, Angie didn't say a word, her thoughts dragging her spirits lower and lower with every mile.

Simon pulled into her parking lot and turned off the engine. For a long minute they didn't move. "What are you going to do?" he asked finally.

"What can I do?" she choked and covered her face with her hands. "Simon, he's my father."

"I'm your husband."

Angie felt as if the two men were waging a battle over her. Each was pulling on an arm, driving a wedge between Angie the daughter and Angie the woman, placing her in an impossible position.

Simon looped an arm around her shoulders and breathed into her hair. His voice was a gentle whisper close to her ear. "Let's go inside. We can talk there."

They made two cups of strong coffee and sat next to each other on the sofa. Simon's shoulder supported Angie's head as they became lost in the tangled web of their disturbed thoughts.

"With my own father so ill, I can appreciate your position," Simon began hesitantly. "The best solution would be for us to separate ourselves from family altogether. I could leave Groves Point and you could leave Charleston and we'd start a new life."

"We can't do that," Angie protested.

"I know, love." Wearily, he leaned his head back and let his eyes slip closed. "With my father sick, it'd be impossible for me to leave Groves Point."

"And Clay needs me in the same way."

"If you think I'm going to suggest the noble thing, you're wrong," he said quietly. His hand gripped her in a punishing hold. He'd endured too many miserable years without Angie. A hot anger surged through him at the thought of facing more of the same. He couldn't part with her when he'd come this close.

"What are we going to do?" Angie whispered, close to tears.

"About the only thing we can do for now. Wait. When Clay is back on his feet, we'll face him again. Only next time we won't back down. Agreed?"

Angie didn't hesitate. "Agreed."

Simon returned to Groves Point three days later when he could no longer ignore the commitments awaiting him. Clay Robinson was released from the hospital sixteen days after being admitted. Angie had visited him daily. At first he refused to speak to her. That was fine, she did most of the talking, chatting with him about little things that went on at the flower shop. She brought him the afternoon edition of the newspaper, his mail and a daily supply of fresh-cut flowers. After a day or two Clay started asking her about Simon. Angie ignored his questions.

"You aren't seeing him, are you?" Clay had demanded.

Angie opened the blind and stared into the sun. "I can't ever remember a more glorious afternoon. The sun is brilliant."

After two or three days of that type of response, Clay quit asking.

Because his condition remained weak and he would need someone to care for him, Angie drove her father to her apartment when he was released from the hospital. "You're to stay here until you're completely well, understand?" She didn't expect much of an argument. Clay knew a good thing when he saw it.

The situation wasn't ideal, but it soothed Angie's conscience.

With Clay at the apartment, Simon, who phoned daily, was forced to contact Angie while she was at Clay Pots. Their conversations were often short as she was interrupted by customers and the usual hectic activity of running a flower shop.

"Simon." She drank in the sound of his voice after one particularly bad morning. "I'm so glad to hear your voice."

"How's Clay?"

"Demanding."

"In other words he's running you ragged."

"Nothing seems to satisfy him," came her trembling reply. "Yesterday he called me three times with different requests. He wanted me to pick up his mail, which I do every night anyway. Then he didn't like what I'd planned to cook for his dinner and wanted me to shop at the grocery store and pick up something that wasn't on his diet. I don't know why he bothered to ask. He knew I wouldn't."

"Angie, this can't go on much longer."

"I know," she agreed with an exaggerated sigh. "He's playing the deathbed recovery to the hilt. He makes it sound as if each request is his last."

"If I got hold of him it would be."

A slow smile touched her tired eyes. "Simon, just let me complain. I need someone to sympathize with me."

"I'm willing to comfort you as well." His voice went low and suggestive.

"Are you now?"

"Eager even."

Angie giggled. "I bet you're not half as eager as me."

"Angie, for the love of heaven don't say things like that. Three hundred miles never seemed so far. I'm dying for you."

"It shouldn't be much longer," she promised. "Clay's going to the doctor tomorrow afternoon. I'll ask about having him move back to his own place. As much as I love my father, he's driving me crazy."

"Another minute without you is too long," Simon argued. "I'm coming this weekend."

"Simon." She breathed his name, pushing the hair back from her forehead with one hand. "Do you think you should?"

"I'll go crazy if I don't."

"Me too," she admitted.

"You are going to marry me, aren't you?"

Her smile was filled with contentment. "I've been your wife in my heart for twelve years. I'd say it was time we made it legal."

"More than time."

Donna glanced to the back of the shop and Angie straightened. "I've got to go."

"Me too."

But neither hung up. "Bye, love."

"I love you, Simon Canfield."

"You better. I'm counting on collecting on that promise this weekend."

Saturday morning, after being assured by the doctor that Clay would be with her for another two weeks and perhaps longer, Angie was as nervous as a teenager about Simon's visit. Simon's flight was due to arrive shortly after noon. From the airport he was checking into a hotel, where she was meeting him for lunch.

"What's the matter with you this morning?" Clay snapped. "You're as jumpy as water on a hot griddle."

"Sorry."

"You should be sorry to leave a sick man on a Saturday."

"That can't be helped," she said and swallowed down the guilt.

"Where did you say you was going?"

"To a meeting."

"You're dressed up mighty pretty for a simple meetin'."

"This one is with someone important."

Clay snorted. "You just remember what that fancy doctor said. I ain't out of the woods yet. I could have a relapse any day."

"You're getting stronger by the minute," she countered. Checking her watch, Angie brought Clay the television guide and kissed him briefly on the cheek. Dutifully, she tucked the blanket around his waist.

"What time will you be back?"

"I…don't know."

"The least you can do is give me my cell so I can reach you in case something terrible happens while you leave me."

Angie froze, making a pretense of checking the insides of her purse. "I'll have to call you."

"The person you should be calling is Glenn."

Glenn's name had been mentioned at least five times every day. "How come he ain't been around lately? I would have thought Glenn would stop by to see me. It's the least my future son-in-law could do." He paused and Angie could feel the heat of his gaze as he studied her.

Angie decided the best thing to do was ignore him.

"Bye, Clay." The minute the door was closed, Angie released a pent-up breath and relaxed. This was worse than anything she'd endured in her secret meetings with Simon the summer they were seventeen.

The drive seemed to take forever; Angie was anxious to get to him. She was afraid of wasting a single minute, afraid Clay would demand an accounting of her afternoon.

Simon was waiting for her in the hotel lobby. Their eyes met from across the width of the room. At the intense emotion shining from his deep, gray ones, Angie paused. He seemed to be digesting everything about her as if he couldn't determine if she was illusion or reality.

The tension eased from Angie and she offered him a trembling smile of happiness. They met halfway into the room.

"Hi," she whispered, as their eyes drank in the sight of each other.

"You are so beautiful." He stopped himself from taking her in his arms and kissing her in front of a lobby full of people. Impatiently he glanced around. "Are you hungry?"

Shyly, Angie lowered her lashes. "Only for you."

"Room service?" he asked with a chuckle, tucking her hand in the crook of his arm.

"I think we'd better."

The minute they were inside Simon's suite, he took her in his arms and kissed her with a hunger that had been building inside of him for three interminable weeks. They undressed each other with trembling, eager hands, pausing only long enough to kiss. Their bodies were on fire for each other, their mouths clinging, twisting, yearning. Their hands paused only to explore

with awe and promise. When they were both completely
nude, Simon's head drew back to look into her dark
eyes. His thumbs lovingly brushed the high arch of
her cheekbones.

"Oh, my sweet love." He dropped his forehead
against hers. "I love you so much I think I'd die without you now."

"I'll always be yours," she whispered emotionally,
then surrendered to the exquisite agony he inflicted
upon her with his hands and mouth. Angie thought she
would die from the sweet torture before he carried her
to the bed. He took her then with a savage tenderness
that was unlike anything she had ever known.

When they had finished, Simon drew her into his
arms and kissed the trail of tears that ran down her
cheek. Nestled in his embrace, she laid her cheek upon
his chest and breathed in even, contented breaths, thinking that nothing this side of heaven could be more wonderful than being loved by Simon.

"Are you asleep?" he whispered after a long moment.

"I don't want to waste a moment of our time together by sleeping." Each second was precious. Angie
didn't know how long it would be before she could see
him again.

"In some ways I think I'm going crazy. I'm still
warm and content from loving you and already I'm
worried about how soon it'll be before I can have you
again."

She smiled and kissed his neck, letting her tongue
tease his Adam's apple. "Any time, Mr. Bank President."

His arms tightened around her. "Angie, I've thought
of a way to bridge the gap between our parents."

He sounded so serious that she lifted her head and

turned onto her side, supporting her head with the palm of her hand. "You must be more of a genius than I give you credit for."

"A baby," he whispered reverently, placing a hand on her trim stomach. "The best thing that could happen to us is to get you pregnant as soon as possible."

Angie closed her eyes to the tenderness in his voice.

"My mother would give anything for a grandchild. I can think of nothing better to make us acceptable to the other's parents."

Angie recalled Clay's words about wanting to bounce a "grandbaby" on his knee. "Jeffrey Simon Canfield," she responded dreamily.

"Or Carolyn Angela Canfield." His hand traveled from her smooth stomach to capture her breast. "Only I think we should think about getting this marriage made legal and the sooner the better."

Tears of happiness brimmed on Angie's eyelashes. "Yes," she said and gave him a watery smile, "I think we should."

"Next weekend?"

Angie shook her head. "I don't ever expect Clay to give me his wholehearted approval, but I'd rather wait until he's at least well enough to be on his own."

Simon's hand caressed her shoulders. "As soon as possible, though."

"Yes," she agreed.

Long after Angie had left, Simon lay staring at the tiled hotel ceiling. A feeling of dread he couldn't shake settled over him. He didn't usually have premonitions, but the fear continued to grow in his chest until he couldn't bear to stay still. Jerking to a sitting position, he sat on the edge of the mattress and buried his face in his hands. Angie was so close to being his. He could think of no reason that this fear should assail him now. She loved him more than he dared hope, more than he deserved. They had talked of making their marriage legal and starting a family. There were twelve years of wasted time to make up. Years of love and laughter.

He glanced at the phone, more than half-tempted to call her. These past few weeks he had lived for those few minutes each day when they spoke. It was never enough time.

The irony of their situation caused a frown to mar his brow. Twelve years ago, his family had stood in their way. They'd been forced to meet secretly then. They had been married twelve years and the first time he'd spent the night with Angie had been when Clay was in the hospital. Now they were compelled into that same kind of clandestine meeting, only it was her father who was keeping them apart. Their relationship, he thought pensively, was only a sad reflection of yesterday.

Angie let herself into the apartment and painted a smile on her face. Her heart was heavy. In some ways it would have been easier not to have seen Simon. It hurt so much to say goodbye.

"How are you feeling, Dad?"

"I thought you were going to call?" He didn't take his eyes from the television.

"I'm sorry, I forgot." Angie knew immediately that she'd said the wrong thing.

Angrily, Clay tossed the television guide to the floor. "Your own father is near death and you run off to some all-important meeting and completely forget about him."

"I didn't mean it that way." She flushed guiltily.

"It'd serve you right if I was to up and die."

"Good grief, I was only gone three hours."

"And ten minutes. I'm bored. Did you bring me my mail? I wasn't hungry at lunchtime, but I could eat something now. You can bring it in to me."

Gritting her teeth, Angie stepped into the kitchen and took the lunch she'd made for him earlier out of the refrigerator. She carried it out to him on a tray. "Do you want anything else?"

He ignored the question. "The way you snuck off like that one would think you were hurrying to meet a lover."

Angie's step faltered, causing her to nearly drop the lunch tray. "Stop being so dramatic," she chastised in her sternest voice. She set the lunch on the coffee table and straightened.

"That's exactly what you was doing, wasn't it?"

Angie returned to the kitchen, her composure rapidly disintegrating. "The subject isn't open for discussion."

"You're a fool, girl."

"And you're interfering in my life."

Clay pushed the tray aside, disinterested. "Tell me somethin'. What makes you think that those highfalutin Canfield folks is going to want you any more the second time than they did the first. Can you see Mrs. Canfield inviting you to the Garden Club? Not hardly."

"I'm not talking to you about it."

"Sure you're not, 'cause you can't answer me. Nothin's changed in twelve years that will make you more acceptable to those rich folks."

"Clay, you heard me. I refuse to discuss this with you."

"All these years I thought I was raising me a decent

girl," he mumbled as he crossed his arms and leaned back against the pillows supporting his shoulders. "You ain't no better than a common…" He hesitated, apparently thinking better of his choice of words. "You're making a big mistake, little girl. I'm begging you to reconsider having anything to do with the Canfields."

"Dad. Why do you have to do this to me? I love him. If Mom had come from a rich Atlanta family would you have loved her less? Would you have decided not to marry her?"

Clay's cheeks expanded until he looked as if he were about to explode. "I won't have you dragging the good name of your mother into this. You hear me, girl?"

"I hear you," Angie said, her voice coated with defeat.

Twelve

At five-thirty Angie closed up Clay Pots for the night. She had finished counting the money from the till when there was a knock at the bolted glass door. Glancing up from behind the counter she was shocked to see Glenn standing on the other side.

"Glenn," she murmured, turning the dead-bolt lock.

"Hello, Angie." He regarded her sheepishly. "I apologize for stopping by unexpectedly."

"Please come in." She resecured the lock. "Is something wrong?" He didn't look right. He was darker, tanner, as if he'd spent lots of time in the intervening weeks working outside. As always he was meticulously dressed in a three-piece business suit and silk tie. Glenn had always been a stickler for neatness.

"I've come to ask you to forgive me for the things I said the last time I saw you."

"My forgiveness," she gasped. "Oh, Glenn, don't make me cry." He was such a wonderful, dear man and she had hurt him immeasurably, and then *he* came to apologize.

"What I said that night was unforgivable."

"You were only reacting to your anger. I don't hold any of it against you. We've been good friends for a long time. I knew you didn't mean it."

"I've felt bad about it for weeks. In thinking it over, I realized that the only thing to do was to come back and tell you that I wish you and Simon every happiness. I'll always love you, Angie, but I know that you belong with Simon. The only thing I want is to be certain that my anger didn't hurt you in any way."

"It didn't. I understood."

"I thought you might, but I wanted to be sure." An uncomfortable silence followed. It was so good to see Glenn again; she had missed his friendship, especially now that Clay was recovering and being so difficult.

As if reading her mind, Glenn asked, "How's Clay?"

"On the mend. Why don't you stop by and visit him sometime? He's at my apartment and I know he'd love to see you. He's bored and out of sorts and would welcome the company."

"Would you?"

Angie lowered her gaze, ill at ease. She didn't want to give Glenn any reason to hope there was a chance they could get back together again.

"I didn't mean it that way," he amended. "I only wanted to make sure that you didn't mind if I came by."

"I wouldn't have asked you otherwise." Briefly her hand touched his in an assuring action.

"You don't look happy, Angie. What's wrong?"

How like Glenn to look past his own troubles to recognize and comfort her. "Clay has strong feelings about Simon and me. He doesn't want me to have anything to do with the Canfields, let alone marry Simon. There's a continual cold war waging between us that

is wearing me down." It felt so good to talk to someone about Clay. Someone who would understand. Any
mention of her difficulties with her father would have
only added to Simon's problems. And he'd been having
plenty of those lately.

"In other words he's constantly nipping at your
heels."

Glenn had a way of describing it perfectly. "Yes."

The worst part was that Simon's father had died
suddenly and Simon had been tied up in Groves Point
for the past two weeks. Angie's heart had gone out
to him in his grief, recalling her own overwhelming
emotion when Clay had been close to death. Simon
had explained that he'd known for several months that
his father was extremely ill. The two had never been
close and although he gave no outward sign of op-
pressive sadness, Angie knew that the death had affected him greatly. Many times in the past weeks she
had wanted to be with him, to offer what comfort she
could. Simon had assured her that he understood the
reason she couldn't. He was fine. Just knowing that she
loved him and wanted to be with him was enough for
now. The demands on his time from his mother, settling
his father's affairs and those of the bank had prevented
him from coming to Charleston. But he would be there
as soon as circumstances would allow. Angie lived for
their daily telephone conversations.

For the funeral Angie had sent an elaborate floral arrangement, but Georgia Canfield hadn't acknowledged
the gift. Angie comforted herself with the knowledge
that it was too soon to expect a note of appreciation.

Only when Clay continued to harp on the differences
between the two families, the Robinsons and "those rich

folks in Groves Point," was it difficult to dismiss the doubts. Simon was sure that their love would construct all the bridges necessary. If not, fine. They didn't need anyone else, they had each other. Angie's confirming echo grew weaker every day. She needed Clay, and as much as she resented his intrusion into her life, he was her father. Clay had been her staunch supporter when she started in the flower business and now it was her turn to stand by him. Clay's unfailing belief in her had helped Angie at a time in her life that she'd needed it most. As far as he was concerned there wasn't a thing in this world that she couldn't do. Even though she'd bragged to Simon about Petal Pushers, Clay had often helped her. Some days he had spent more hours than she had, taking her assignments until Angie found her feet with Clay Pots. Unwittingly Clay had worked to repay the Canfields all those thousands. Although Simon might not readily agree, he relied on his mother, too. Especially now. In death Simon's father had healed the gap between mother and son. They shared an emotional bond and as the days passed it became all the more evident that Georgia Canfield needed Simon for moral and mental support during the difficult days.

"Maybe you'd like to come tonight," Angie suggested to Glenn. "Make it a surprise for Clay."

The handsome male features broke into a smile. "I'd like that. I'll follow you."

A couple of times Angie checked her rearview mirror on the way home. Glenn had been stopped at a yellow light at a major intersection so she was about three minutes ahead of him when she came through the door.

She greeted Clay with a warm smile and kissed his cheek. "How was your day?"

He grunted and threw back the blanket that covered his legs. "About as good as you can expect a man to feel who's been cooped up in a stuffy apartment for the last month of his life."

"But, Dad!" Her voice rose indignantly. "I've begged and pleaded with you to get some fresh air. It's not good for you to sit around all day and do nothing."

"You're just looking for a way to kill me off so you can marry that rich Canfield boy."

Angie's fingers curled around the leather strap of her purse as she battled down the rising irritation. Clay had been living with her for almost a month now and every day the atmosphere grew more strained.

"I've got a surprise for you."

"Don't want no surprises."

"I think you'll like this one," she said confidently.

The doorbell chimed and Clay's eyes flew to the front door. "Why don't you get that? The exercise will do you good." Not waiting for an argument, Angie disappeared into her bedroom where she changed into a cool pair of shorts and a sleeveless knit pullover. She paused and smiled when she heard Clay's happy exclamation of surprise.

Slipping her feet into sandals, she returned to the living room to discover Clay sitting on the sofa, his shoulders shaking with huge sobs. "She's going to marry him. I know it in my heart, and he'll ruin her for decent men just the way he did twelve years ago."

"Clay!" Angie gasped. She couldn't believe that her own father would talk about her this way.

"See what I mean," Clay said and leaned closer to Glenn. Tears ran unrestrained down his face. "Already he's turned her against me. You've got to do something."

Clay's hands gripped Glenn's forearm as he regarded the younger man with pleading, sad eyes.

"If anyone's turned against anybody, it's you against me."

"Angie." Glenn stood and crossed the room, taking her by the shoulders. "Listen, it's easy to see that you've worn yourself to a frazzle taking care of your father. Let me stay with him tonight. Go do some shopping or take in a movie. Anything. Just leave for a while and relax."

"But I've got to fix his dinner."

His finger lazily wiped a lone tear from her cheek. "I've cooked before."

"He's on a special diet."

"Clay knows what he can and can't eat. Now, don't you worry. Just go and enjoy yourself."

She placed her hand in his and squeezed it with all the appreciation in her heart. "Thank you."

She left without saying a word to Clay who sat regarding her mutinously. His eyes were slightly red as he glared at her angrily.

In the mood for a peaceful ride, Angie drove to Sullivan's Island and walked along the sandy beach for what seemed like hours. A gentle breeze ruffled her hair and the tangy scent of saltwater followed her as the waves crashed against the peaceful shore. Her thoughts weren't profound. She was too run-down, mentally and physically, to deal with any of the problems that plagued her. She didn't want to think about Clay or Simon or anyone. The beach had often offered her solace she couldn't find elsewhere. As if not to disappoint her, the sky turned a vibrant shade of pink and the warm sand welcomed her bare feet. Granules of the wet beach squished between her toes as she sat and stared out over the swelling rolling waters, at peace at last with her world.

It seemed ironic that the one to rescue her from another night of bickering with Clay would be Glenn, the man she had rejected. Intuitively, it seemed, Glenn had known when she was at her weakest point, struggling to maintain some semblance of sanity. Glenn Lambert was a rare man, she realized anew.

After a peace-filled hour, Angie called Groves Point.

"Yes." Simon's answer was abrupt and impatient as if he, too, was stretched to the limits with the demands and pressures made on him.

"Hello, Simon." It was so good to hear him that the effort to keep her voice steady was monumental.

"Angie." Her name was issued on a rush of air that sounded like a warm caress. "Is anything wrong?"

Nothing was right, but Simon didn't need to hear that. He was under enough stress as it was. "No," she answered softly, "I just needed to hear the sound of your voice." She could almost feel the tension drain out of him as he began to speak.

"Where are you? I can hear a strange noise in the background."

"Landlubber," she teased affectionately. "Don't you know the sound of the ocean when you hear it?"

"The ocean?"

"You won't believe this."

"Knowing you, I'd believe anything," he said, chuckling.

"I'm on Sullivan's Island. Here, listen." She opened the door to the small pay-phone cubicle and pointed the telephone receiver toward the beach. "What do you think?"

"I think I'm going to go crazy if I don't see you soon."

"This weekend?" she asked, trying to disguise how anxious she was.

Simon hesitated, his voice filled with angry frustration when he spoke. "Honey, I can't. There are a thousand things I have to do with Dad's estate."

"Don't worry, we've got the rest of our lives. Another week or two isn't going to matter." She tried desperately to hide her disappointment.

A long moment of silence stretched between them.

"How's Clay?" Simon asked finally.

Angie forced a light laugh. "Cantankerous as ever. He seems to be recovering, but he refuses to do any exercise." Angie had come to believe that he was purposely making himself an invalid to prevent her from marrying Simon. Only she wasn't going to allow him to do that. The next appointment with Clay's doctor was the following week. Once Clay was given a clean bill of health, she was moving him back to his own place so fast it'd make his head swim.

"How are you?" Simon asked next.

"Cantankerous as ever," she said with a light laugh. "I miss you, and I wish I was pregnant so Clay would insist that you make an honest woman of me and fall right into our plans."

Simon chuckled. "My thoughts toward you at the moment are completely dishonest. Angie, I love you. I can hardly wait to show you how much."

"Believe me, I'm just as eager to prove my love." Where Angie had felt cold and tense before, she now felt warm, loved and utterly secure.

They talked for an hour of silly inanities and ones not

so silly. It was the most time they'd had together since Simon's one-day visit to Charleston two weeks before.

Even when she replaced the receiver, Angie felt the warm glow of contentment that covered her with its serenity. Times were difficult for them now, but they would be better, and soon. It was vital that she didn't look down at the mire she was standing in, but raise her line of vision to the long and happy life that stretched ahead of her with Simon.

After talking to Angie Simon twined his fingers behind his head, balancing his chair on two legs as he leaned against the kitchen wall. Without Angie these past two weeks, he would have been driven to the edge of insanity. He had known and accepted that his father was gravely ill, but his death had still caught Simon unprepared. He had heard that from others but hadn't recognized the truth until his own father had gone. Maybe if he hadn't been so involved with Angie he would have seen to his father's business affairs sooner and they wouldn't be in this mess now. What did he know about all these legal matters? Darn little. His father had known he was close to death, Simon was convinced of that, and yet he had done practically nothing to get his affairs in order, leaving Simon with the distasteful task.

His mother was little help. She appeared totally ignorant of their financial affairs and was content to have Simon sort through the legal hassles.

A frown drew his thick brows together as Angie filled his mind. By all that was holy he loved that woman. It seemed a miracle that their love had endured all these years and they were back together. He'd lost her once. Heaven and hell would pass away before he'd let that happen a second time. The pressures on her had been difficult these past several weeks, with her father underfoot night and day, making constant demands. The phone call tonight had come as a surprise, a pleasant one. They'd needed that, both of them.

Somehow, some way, he'd get to Charleston this weekend, even if it was only for a few hours. Angie needed him. Snickering softly, he shook his head; who was he trying to kid? He needed to see her. Not since his early college days had he felt like this. He was supposed to be a serious businessman, yet every spare thought revolved around a wisp of a woman who had claimed his heart so completely that he would never be the same without her. He didn't just want to sleep with her, although that was a part of it. He wanted to care for her, ease her burden with her father and protect her from Clay's angry words. He wanted to laugh with her and hear her laugh in return. And if she needed to cry, then he wanted her to do it in his arms so that he could comfort her as well.

His resolve tightened. He was going to Charleston. Nothing was going to keep him away from Angie. Not ever again.

Glenn was sitting on the sofa waiting for her when Angie returned to the apartment. "Hello." At her anxious look around, he quirked his head toward the bedroom. "Clay's asleep." He smiled then, his mouth rueful. "I can see why you're so worn down. Clay has a way about him."

"I suppose he talked your ear off," she said with mock seriousness.

"And then some." He paused and chuckled. "There's coffee on if you'd like a cup."

Angie moved into the kitchen and automatically poured two mugs, carrying both into the living room and handing Glenn one. "I don't even know how to thank you for tonight." She felt better than she had in days.

"By having dinner with me tomorrow."

Angie hesitated before sinking into the thick sofa cushion. Seeing Glenn again would serve no useful purpose. He was kind and good, but she wouldn't take advantage of that.

"As friends," he inserted quickly. "I realize that you're involved with Simon now, but I've missed your friendship. There's nothing that says we can't be friends, is there?"

"Nothing," she agreed. If anything she needed a friend now more than at any other time in her life. Only she didn't want to hurt Glenn, and a prolonged relationship, even a friendly one, could do exactly that. "As long as we understand each other." She paused to wipe a weary hand over her tired eyes. "I have a feeling I'm going to end up feeling guilty about this. I don't want to use you as an escape from my troubles."

Glenn ran his index finger along the rim of the coffee cup several times, seemingly unconscious of the action. "I told you this once, but perhaps now it bears repeating. Loving someone means accepting them as they are. I know you love Simon. I'm not saying that doesn't hurt and that I regret the fact you can't love me in the same way. I should have known from the minute you returned from Groves Point that I'd already lost you. Blindly I chose to believe otherwise."

"Glenn…stop, please. I feel guilty enough already."

"No, let me finish. I want you to be happy, Angie. I wish I could say all the bitterness is out of me, but I can't. That will come with time. The two of us having dinner is as much for me as you. Say you'll come as a gesture toward the friendship we once shared."

Angie studied him for a long time before speaking. "All right," she agreed reluctantly.

"As friends," Glenn reiterated.

"As friends," she echoed softly.

The following morning Clay was much more himself. When Angie woke she found her father dominating the lone bathroom, humming softly to himself as he shaved. The round mirror above the sink was fogged up with steam from his recent shower.

"Better wipe that mirror off or you'll cut yourself," she quipped.

"I been shavin' a lot more years than you been livin'. I know what I'm doing."

Angie laughed, and tightened the cinch of her housecoat. "Yes, Daddy dearest." She was halfway into the kitchen before she realized that this was the first morning in weeks that they'd had a teasing, loving conversation. Usually Clay lingered in bed, claiming that he was in terrible pain and accusing Angie of being no better than those uncaring nurses who didn't give a hoot if he lived or died as long as his medical bill was paid. Angie had given up arguing with him for being so wrong and unreasonable.

She dressed in a simple two-piece skirt and blouse outfit of pale pink colors and returned to the kitchen to cook Clay breakfast.

"You're looking might pretty today," Clay commented. "Are you doing anything special tonight?" The intonation of his voice told her instantly that Glenn had discussed with Clay the fact that he was going to ask her to dinner.

"I might."

"Might?"

"Glenn offered to take me to dinner tonight." She decided to play Clay's game and busily cracked two eggs against the side of a dish.

"Always did like that young man. A smart girl would know what she was turning down. All my days I thought I was raising me a smart girl, but..." Abruptly he stopped. "You goin' to dinner with Glenn or not?"

"How could I possibly leave you? A loving daughter would never leave her father alone when he's been so sick and near death."

"Bah, I can take care of myself." He dismissed her concern and sliced the air with a heavy hand for emphasis.

Holding back a laugh was nearly impossible. "You've been telling me for weeks that you've got one foot in the grave."

Clay looked flustered, his impatience growing. "I feel better today."

Angie studied him skeptically. His doctor's appointment wasn't until Monday, and at that not a minute too soon. Until Clay moved in, Angie hadn't realized how much she treasured her privacy. This togetherness was slowly driving her crazy.

"I'm glad to hear that you're more chipper today. Why don't you take a nice walk this morning before it gets too hot and muggy?"

"I might," Clay answered noncommittally.

"And I *might* go to dinner with Glenn."

Clay's fiery gaze clashed with hers. "Then I'll go on that walk you've been pestering me about for the last few weeks."

"Which means I'll probably be late tonight."

"Good." Clay's boyish smile went from ear to ear.

As it turned out, dinner with Glenn was the most relaxing night she'd spent in weeks, maybe even months. He could have taken her to an elegant restaurant and impressed her with wine and song. Instead he chose a Mexican place that was close to her apartment, where the food was fabulous and the atmosphere didn't cost a dime.

"I'll have you know that my agreeing to this dinner has gotten Dad out of the house for the first time since he left the hospital."

One side of Glenn's mouth lifted with a dry smile. "I thought it might. Your father's quite a character."

"I can imagine the things he told you about me last night."

"He's frightened, Angie. Frightened of losing you to Simon. Once you're married, you'll move to Groves Point and he'll be left in Charleston alone. Losing you is his greatest fear. I don't think he can bear the thought of being separated."

"He can move back to Groves Point with me."

"I know that," Glenn replied calmly.

Warming to the subject, Angie clenched her fists. "Dad's got some twisted emotions that need to be sorted through," she declared hotly. Clay's attitude on the subject of the Canfields was relentless. They never openly discussed Simon anymore. Yet the subject loomed between them like a concrete wall they each stepped around and couldn't ignore. "Dad seems to think everyone in Groves Point knows what went on between Simon's family and us. I'm confident that simply isn't so."

"I'm sure you're right."

"Honestly, Glenn," she returned angrily. "Quit being such a yes-man. It isn't like you and I don't like it."

Glenn burst into laughter as he placed his napkin beside his plate, his eyes avoiding hers.

Recognizing that he was simply letting her blow off a little steam, Angie felt sheepish. "I'm sorry. I didn't mean that."

"Don't worry about it."

"Quit being so nice," she snapped playfully.

Shaking his head Glenn rolled his dark eyes at the revolving ceiling fan. "It's little wonder Clay complains. There's no satisfying you, is there?"

It felt so good to laugh again that Angie's heart swelled with appreciation for this man who was more friend than she had ever known or deserved. She wasn't completely sure of Glenn's motives. In that respect he worried her. No one was that wonderful. There had to be something that he expected in return for this. Quickly, Angie discarded the thought, disliking the cynical meanderings her mind had taken lately, and concentrated on having a good time for the rest of the evening.

The following day she sent Glenn a basket of fruit and a brief note as a thank-you for their evening together.

Glenn stopped by the apartment Thursday after work and took Clay out for a walk. Clay didn't look pleased when Angie declined the invitation to join them. Instead she took a leisurely bath, painted her nails and phoned Simon. The evening was young and she wasn't surprised that she didn't catch him.

When he phoned her at the shop at their regular time the next morning, she mentioned her call.

"Believe me, I could have used a sweet voice to clear away the insanity," Simon murmured. "Has Clay moved out? You seem to have some free time in the evenings of late."

"Monday," she whispered, purposely avoiding his question. "His appointment with the doctor is the twenty-fifth."

"Believe me, love, the minute he's given a clean bill of health I'm coming to get you. We're going to get married as fast as I can make the arrangements."

"My head is swimming just thinking about it."

"Honey, listen, I'm not making any concrete promises, but I'm doing everything I can to clear Saturday."

Angie felt ridiculously close to tears. Even a few hours in his arms would be enough to wipe out several days of bickering with Clay. "I'll ask Glenn to keep Clay occupied so we can spend more than an hour or so together."

A heavy, stone silence stretched over the line.

"Glenn?"

How stupid she'd been to mention him. She didn't want to hide the fact she was seeing him, but she would rather not have discussed it with Simon over the telephone. "Yes, he's the one who's responsible for—"

"You've been seeing Glenn?"

The ice in his voice sent chills up Angie's spine. "Not the way you're implying."

"Then just what is going on?"

Slowly, Angie mentally counted to ten before answering. "He's been helping me with Clay."

"I'll just bet."

Angie's temples began to throb and she pressed two fingers to them to ease the pounding ache. "A customer just came in...I've got to go."

"Angie," Simon breathed impatiently. "I didn't mean anything. I think we're both going a little crazy."

"You might be able to come Saturday?"

"I'm coming." He didn't leave any room for speculation. He was going to be there and her heart throbbed with anticipation.

"You'll phone me when you get into town, then? I'll be in the shop until noon."

Simon hesitated. "I'll phone."

If Angie felt guilty about going out to dinner with Glenn it was nothing to what she felt when she asked him if he'd mind keeping her father occupied while she met Simon Saturday afternoon.

Simon hadn't contacted her by the time she left the shop Saturday, which meant he'd probably catch her at the apartment. Normally this would have been a cause for concern, but Glenn and Clay were going for a long drive and would be leaving shortly after Angie arrived back to the apartment.

Their mood was light and teasing when she sauntered in a little after one o'clock.

"Beautiful day, Angie girl. Are you going to join us this time?" Clay asked her on a cheerful note. "Can't see you wasting away in a stuffy apartment when two handsome men are eager for your company."

She was pleased to note the color in Clay's cheeks.

"Another time, Dad." She shared a conspiratorial smile with Glenn.

"We'll catch her another day," Glenn interjected.

"But I thought she'd want to come along today." Clay pursed his lips like a discontented child who had been outwitted by his parents.

"I'll join you another day," Angie promised.

"But what are you going to do that's so all-fired important that you can't come with us?" Clay insisted.

Angie looked imploringly to Glenn, but was saved from answering by the doorbell.

Clay stood closest, and swung open the door. Angie couldn't see who it was since Clay was blocking her view. But her father's body language gave her all the clues she needed.

"Hello, Angie." Simon stepped around her father and gave her a phony smile. His gaze went from Clay to Glenn. "I hope I'm not intruding on anything important," he said sarcastically.

Thirteen

Simon recognized immediately that by arriving unannounced to the apartment he'd done the wrong thing. The hurt and confused look in Angie's eyes sliced into him. His gaze clashed with Glenn's as he avoided looking toward Angie. Earlier, he'd tried her cell, but it had gone directly to voice mail. He was dying for the sight of her. For weeks he'd dreamed of taking her in his arms and loving her until they were both sated and exhausted. Every minute apart these past weeks had been torture. Yet Angie had gone back to the apartment without even waiting to talk to him and that rankled.

"Simon," Angie said, her dark eyes round and imploring. "What are you doing here? I thought…"

"Sneaking behind my back." Clay's pale face turned to his daughter with a hurt look that went far deeper than words. "You two were going to sneak behind my back."

Glenn took the old man's hand and lowered him into the cushioned chair. "Maybe this is the time for the three of you to sit down and talk things out."

Angie's bewildered gaze went from her father's pale

face to the intent look marking Simon's features. She stood defenseless between the two of them, knowing that she was about to be forced into taking sides. To one she was a puppet, pulled by the strings of guilt and duty. To the other, impatient in his way, she was a love long-lost.

Clay crossed his arms over his chest and looked straight ahead with stony eyes. Anger and bitterness emanated from every pore. "There's nothing left to say."

"Dad, stop acting like a two-year-old," Angie said, looking desperately to Simon. "Why did you come here now, like this? Couldn't you have waited until Clay was well?"

"I believe I'll leave this to the three of you to settle," Glenn murmured, heading toward the front door. "Good luck."

Simon watched the other man's departure with a sinking feeling. Glenn did indeed love Angie. Far beyond what Simon had suspected. He would like to hate the man but discovered that he couldn't. Instead, a grudging respect came, and he wondered if he could have been half as decent over this situation as Glenn. With that realization came another. Glenn wasn't coming around Clay and Angie for his health. Obviously, the man thought there was still a chance he could win Angie. Glenn wasn't a masochist, nor stupid. He was standing ready to pick up the pieces. And now in his impatience, Simon had fallen directly into the other man's hands.

"Simon, maybe it would be best if we sat down. We should be able to reach some kind of understanding." Angie's words helped clear the fog in his mind.

"All right." He moved into the room and took a seat

on the sofa. For the first time he studied Angie and was mildly shocked to see how tired and run-down she looked. The faint purple smudges under her eyes were artfully camouflaged with makeup. Her mouth drooped just enough for him to recognize that she was struggling with her composure. By forcing the issue today, he'd done nothing but increase the pressure on her. Silently, he cursed himself.

"I owe you an apology for showing up like this." Simon directed his words to the stiff, motionless man who sat across from him.

Again Angie turned questioning, hurt eyes to him, and Simon could see talking would do no good. "Then why did you?"

"I want to marry you, Angie. I'm tired of sneaking around and meeting in hotel rooms. We're consenting adults. There shouldn't be any reason in this world to keep us apart any longer, and if that means forcing Clay to accept certain truths, so be it."

Clay gasped and his eyes narrowed into thin, accusing slits as they centered on his daughter. "So you've been giving yourself to him. Again."

Angie dropped her face to her hands and again Simon realized that every time he opened his mouth, he was only making things worse for Angie.

"Is this the way I raised you, daughter?" Clay asked in a choked voice that was barely above a whisper. "Your mama, God rest her soul, was a lady. I tried my hardest to raise you to be just like her. Until now, I didn't realize how miserably I've failed."

"It isn't like that." Angie moved from the sofa and took her father's hands in her own. "I don't know why Simon is doing this, but—"

"I'm doing this because we shouldn't need to hide our love. From the time we were kids we belonged together. As long as I breathe, nothing's going to stand in the way of our happiness."

"Simon…" Angie ground out his name. "Don't say anything more. You're only making things worse." Could he be so blind not to see what he was doing to her? She was Clay's daughter, and although he was playing on his recent illness to keep her apart from Simon, that wasn't any reason to drive a wedge between her and her only relative.

Frustrated, Simon rolled to his feet and buried his hands in his pockets. "Listen, maybe it wasn't such a great idea to show up like this. Maybe I should have been patient and played it cool. But for how much longer?"

"Only a few days. A week at the most," Angie cried, not bothering to disguise her hurt.

"Just who are you trying to kid?" Simon asked, watching her closely. He hated to see her on her knees, groveling at her father's feet. "Do you honestly believe that Clay's going to let us find any happiness together? I can guarantee that there'll always be another reason to prevent our marriage."

"You don't know that."

"Angie, look at him. He's never going to give his approval."

Angie shook her head as if to clear her thoughts. "Yes, he will," she cried. "In time."

"I'm through waiting," Simon said on a cold, sober note. "I'm tired of waiting. I want us to get married now."

"It'll only be a little while," she pleaded.

Simon released a low moan of frustration. Angie was living in a dream world. "The doctor will gave Clay a clean bill of health soon, and immediately after that something else will magically appear to delay our marriage."

"That's pure conjecture."

"That's fact," he shouted in return. "We're nearly thirty years old. I'm through with living my life to satisfy parents. I want us to get married and I want it now. Are you with me or not?"

Angie hesitated, slid her eyes closed and inhaled deeply. Here it was. She'd known from the minute Simon stepped in the doorway that it was coming. With everything that they'd shared, she would have thought he'd know not to do this. The impatient frustrated man standing over her wasn't the Simon she loved. This was a man driven to the limits of his patience, irrational and demanding.

"You can't ask me to do this. Not now."

Simon paused. "When?"

"I...I don't know."

In a blinding flash he knew that he was right. Angie was tied to her father and the bonds were far stronger than he'd realized. In pitting himself against the old man, Simon would lose the very thing he treasured most in life. He had to reach Clay.

Simon took a seat across from Angie's father and swallowed down his pride. "Can we lay aside the hurts of the past? I love Angie and I'll spend every second of my life proving just how much. We want your blessing. We need it. Can you overlook everything that's happened and give us your love?"

A full minute passed before Clay spoke. "No words

could ever undo the embarrassment and pain your family caused mine."

Simon realized that he should have known the old man would demand blood. "What is it you want then?" He fought back the building anger, clenching his hands so tight that his fingers ached with the effort.

Clay didn't respond.

"What do you want from me?" Simon repeated.

Silence.

"More money, is that it?"

"Simon," Angie cried. "Don't do this."

"If you don't want money, maybe I could—"

"All I want from you is to leave my Angie alone. You hear me, boy, leave my daughter alone."

Simon expelled a ragged breath. "That's the one thing I won't do."

"Dad." Angie's voice was so weak that Simon could barely hear her. "Simon and I need to talk."

Clay grunted and crossed his arms. "I suppose you're going to do your talking in that hotel room."

Knowing it was useless, Simon stood and took Angie's cold, limp hand in his. "Let's get out of here. We don't have to listen to that kind of garbage."

Angie stared up at him undecided, her look rotating from Simon to her father. "I...don't think I should leave Dad like this. Not now."

"Yes, you can," he argued fiercely, shouting.

Angie pulled her fingers free of his grasp and shook her head, placing her hands over her ears to blot out any protest. "No."

"All right." Simon murmured. He had brought this on himself, by coming to the apartment, forcing her into this dichotomy. He was pressuring her to choose between a lifetime of love and loyalty to her father and the reclaimed love she and Simon shared. She couldn't choose one and not betray the other. The crazy part was that all he had ever wanted to do was love Angie and cherish her, protect her, give her his children and love them with the same intensity that he loved their mother. Instead he had set her up for more anguish. Very gently he placed his hands on her shoulders, cupping them. He leaned forward and kissed her lightly on her cheek, shocked at the chilled feel of her skin.

"You know where I'll be," he whispered. It could have been his imagination, but Simon thought he felt her stiffen as if to pull away. His heart plummeted to the very depths of hell. He was so close to losing her, and powerless to reach out to her now. Angie Robinson was the only woman he ever truly loved, and he had somehow managed to louse up their relationship...a second time.

"I'll talk to you later," she whispered in return.

For two hours Angie wrestled with her emotions. The more she thought about what Simon had done by coming to the apartment the more upset she became. Maybe he was right. Maybe Clay would always find an excuse to keep them apart. But now wasn't the time to catapult her into making a decision. For days she had eagerly anticipated being with Simon, looking upon his visit as a time for renewal and rejuvenation, mentally and physically. Their time together was to be a brief oasis in a life whose route had taken her deep into the arid, lifeless desert. In the past weeks, they'd both been taxed to the limit of their endurance with family pressures. They'd needed this time for their sanity.

Clay sat so motionless that for an instant Angie wondered if he'd stopped breathing. When Simon had gone she'd half expected her father to blast her with a fiery tirade of insults. In the past he'd done exactly that, knowing how much it hurt her. Instead his eyes revealed a deep, bitter pain that words wouldn't easily erase. So they didn't speak, but sat like strangers, yearning to reach out to each other and not knowing how.

When she could endure the agony no longer, Angie stood and reached for her purse.

"I...need to think," she whispered. "I don't know when I'll be back."

"You're going to him," Clay said with cruel certainty.

Angie's jaw sagged, prepared to argue. Dejected, she closed her mouth. She hadn't given thought to where she was going, only that she couldn't tolerate another minute in the tension-filled apartment.

"Don't lie to me, girl. You're going to him."

Clay was right, that's exactly where she was going. "I'll be back" was all she said.

The ride across town took her through heavy traffic, giving her plenty of time to think. She loved Simon, had loved him nearly all her life. When she'd taken the money and left Groves Point twelve years ago, something keen and vital had died within her. For a long time she couldn't look at men without experiencing a deep, harrowing pain. After a while, more for Clay's sake than her own, she'd started dating again. If her date was tall, Angie decided she preferred someone shorter. If her date was quiet and introspective, she found him boring. If he was intelligent and opinionated, she wished for someone dull. After a while, Angie gave up dating completely. Until Glenn...

The front desk at the Hilton connected her with Simon, who gave her his room number. She marched across the lobby, her indignation building. She loved him, but she couldn't allow him to pressure her this way.

She'd hardly had time to knock when the door was opened. "Thank goodness you came," he whispered.

"Why?" The word barely made it through the tightness in her throat. "Why did you come to the apartment? Didn't you stop to think what would happen?"

"Angie, listen—"

"No," she cried, "you listen. I want to marry you. All I'm asking for is a little patience. My dad is lucky to be alive. I'm not prepared to do *anything* to endanger his health and that includes upsetting him the way you did this afternoon. You...you may have blown everything. I can't understand you."

Simon pushed the hair off his brow and splayed his fingers through his thick hair. "I think I went a little crazy when I learned Glenn was coming around."

She couldn't believe that he could possibly be jealous of Glenn. "He's been wonderful." She said this to imply that Simon hadn't been.

A grimness tightened his face. "Of course he has. Glenn loves you. Why else do you think he's been hanging around."

Angie struggled with the building discontent. "Glenn came to apologize for that last scene... He saw the toll that nursing Dad was having on me and offered to give me a break."

Simon heard this with a frown of distaste. "You don't really believe that, do you?"

Angie raised angry, stricken eyes to him. "Of course I believe that. It's exactly what happened."

Simon's snort was filled with disgust as he stalked to the far side of the room. "Are you so naive as to believe that your father didn't have a hand in that? I don't doubt for a minute that Clay was responsible for Glenn's sudden appearance."

Angie stared at him in shocked disbelief. She thought she knew Simon so well but discovered that she didn't know him at all. Together they owed a great unpayable debt to Glenn Lambert. Glenn's love and patience had given her the courage to face the past and go back to Groves Point. Even after she'd returned to Charleston, he had loved her enough to step aside until she'd sorted through her feelings for Simon. Angie didn't try to kid herself. None of this had been easy for Glenn, but he had acted with a patience, love and understanding that was, at times, almost superhuman.

A frozen, deadly silence iced the room.

"You may be right." Angie's words shattered the cold quiet. "But we both should thank God for Glenn."

Simon lifted one dark brow at her, assimilating her words. "I didn't realize your feelings were so intense."

"Stop trying to make something sordid out of Glenn's affection for Clay and me. He at least had the common decency not to pressure me into—"

"Choosing between your father and me."

"Yes," she finished, her voice quavering.

"That's the beauty of the situation," Simon returned with heavy sarcasm. "With Glenn there would be no decision to make. Clay would love to see you married to him."

"I've already agreed to be your wife. What else do you want?" Swallowing down her irritation Angie sank onto the side of the queen-size mattress, struggling against the rising hysteria. She had so looked forward to this weekend with Simon. She couldn't believe that they would waste this valuable time together fighting.

"Where's the ring I gave you, Angie?" His slicing gaze fell to her bare fingers.

One hand curled over the top of the other. "With Clay feeling the way he did I couldn't wear it. Surely you can understand that."

"No." Simon's voice was deadly calm. "I'm afraid I can't."

"All right, I should have worn it," she cried, knowing he was hurt and hating herself for being so weak. The ring, the most precious piece of jewelry she owned, was locked in a desk drawer at Clay Pots. A hundred times she'd thought to slip it on her finger and decided against it, knowing the sight of it would cause an argument. She'd been so tired lately and hadn't wanted to battle Clay at every turn.

"What's in a ring? Right?"

Her head snapped up, positive she hadn't heard him correctly.

His eyes narrowed on the soft rise and fall of her breast.

"Simon," she whispered pleadingly. "Your ring is a symbol of your love. I'm sorry I haven't worn it."

"Not sorry enough." He sat beside her impatiently and tugged at the buttons of her blouse, jerking it open and off her shoulders. Shocked and appalled, Angie was stunned.

"If you love me so much," he taunted, "I'll let you prove it."

"Simon, what are you doing?" she cried, attempting to cover herself.

In answer he stripped off his shirt and slacks, his eyes avoiding hers.

"I love you," she murmured in a choked voice, "only don't do this to me. This isn't making love."

He was a stranger whom she didn't recognize.

Tears swam in her eyes as she slumped onto the mattress. "Simon, what's come over you?"

"You keep saying that you love me so much." He leaned toward her. "I want you to show me how much." Angie was numb with disbelief. This couldn't be happening to her. Not with Simon. He'd always been such a gentle, kind lover. He had given of himself, never taken. Their lovemaking was special, a sharing of their intense joy of each other.

"Why are you doing this?" she begged, her hand stopping his.

"Why?" he echoed cruelly. "Because it's clear to me now that you don't love me enough," he said. Harshly, he took her mouth, grinding his lips over hers until Angie pushed herself free.

"You think I should have been more diplomatic with your father."

"Yes," she cried. "He's ill."

"The time for diplomacy is past. Either you want to be my wife or you don't."

"Oh, Simon," she whispered, needing his tenderness. "I do love you." She turned her face to him and hesitantly laid her fingers over his rigid jaw. He was angry and hurt and lashing out at her in a way she'd never expected.

Momentarily, his steely eyes softened. "Then marry me. Today. Now." Again, his mouth claimed hers, parting her lips with a deep, languorous kiss. Angie locked

her arms around his neck and kissed him hungrily in
return. He burned a hot trail of kisses down the scented
hollow of her throat to just above her bra-line. "Simon,"
she whispered, "please."

"Do want me?" he taunted in a low voice.

"Yes," she pleaded.

"Enough to come away with me today for the rest
of our lives."

Angie's eyes flew open and she went limp against
the mattress. Simon raised his head, his eyes boring
into hers. "Today," he repeated starkly.

"I…can't. Don't ask that of me."

"I just did."

"All I want is your love." She raised her head and
tried to kiss him, but he held himself stiff and unyielding, avoiding her touch.

"I won't settle for what's left over when Clay takes
advantage of you," he said harshly.

"But I'm offering you everything," she said desperately. "Everything. If you'll only be patient. I love you
so much." The last was offered on a soft sob that erupted
from her parched throat.

A long moment of tormenting silence passed as his
expression clouded over with bitterness. "Words no longer satisfy me," he ground out. His mouth came down
in a kiss that was devoid of tenderness. She tore herself from his grasp when he tried to reach for her and
bring her back into the comfort of his arms. Grabbing
her purse she rushed to the door. Her fear was that she
couldn't escape fast enough. She prayed that he
wouldn't try to come after her. Her throat was burning
with the effort to suppress the tears. She hesitated as
she turned to look back and found Simon was sitting

at the end of the bed. His face was buried in his hands; his shoulders hunched over, giving a profile of abject misery. As she opened the door Simon raised his head, his eyes pale and haunted.

"Angie, wait."

She didn't hesitate, but briskly stepped across the room.

"Please."

Her hand tightened around the doorknob and she paused. "Clay always said you were a spoiled rich boy," she whispered through her pain. "I never believed him until today."

Dejected and utterly defeated, Simon didn't try to stop her as she pulled open the door and walked out of his life.

In the long days that followed, Angie had plenty of time to think over their last meeting. In many ways she understood why Simon had behaved the way he had. That didn't excuse his actions, but granted her the time to be more forgiving. In the beginning she decided that when he phoned she'd treat him aloofly, with mild contempt. A miserable week passed and she realized she would have given her soul to hear from him. Another week and she recognized that Simon never planned to contact her. He'd given her the option either to marry him then or it was over. She had made that choice.

Not knowing what had transpired, Clay watched her guardedly for several days. The second afternoon following the doctor's appointment, he moved back to his own place and showed up only at periodic intervals. They never mentioned Simon.

Glen called once a week to chat and ask how she was

doing. Their conversations were brief and one-sided. He didn't ask her out, intuitively recognizing, she supposed, that she'd turn him down. In many ways Angie would always be grateful to Glenn. He had been a good friend when she needed one most, but she had abused that friendship and was paying dearly for it now. She didn't know if Clay had asked Glenn to visit her or if he'd come of his own initiative. It didn't seem to matter and she didn't inquire.

When she realized that she wouldn't be hearing from Simon, Angie prayed fervently that she would become pregnant, and wept the morning she learned she wasn't. For a time she thought he might contact her if only to ask if that last time together had given life to his seed. Angie didn't know if her tears were from bitter disappointment that she wasn't going to have his child or that Simon didn't seem to care enough to find out.

Slowly, each day a test, Angie began to gain her perspective again. She had a good life, a meaningful one. Her business was profitable, and she made casual inquiries into opening a second shop on Calhoun Street near Marion Square. At the end of the third week, Angie discovered that she could smile again and occasionally even laugh.

The hottest days of summer came in late August and the muggy afternoon heat was unbearable. Angie took long walks along the beaches, watching the children play in the sand. The world seemed full of children and young mothers. In a month she would be thirty. Simon would be thirty-one. Friday afternoon, a half hour before closing time, Angie was working in the back of the shop when she heard the small bell ring, indicating that someone had entered. She set aside the centerpiece she was constructing from dried wildflowers and approached the counter. Her eyes met the elegant ones of Georgia Canfield and she faltered slightly. Quickly regaining her composure, Angie braced her hands on the counter.

"Hello, Mrs. Canfield."

"Hello, Angela."

She looked calm, but out of place in something as common as a flower shop. "It's a lovely place you have here."

"Thank you."

"I understand you named it after your father."

"Yes." Angie didn't feel all that comfortable with this woman. She couldn't understand what Simon's mother would be doing here unless something had happened to Simon. An instant of panic filled her mind, but she dismissed it quickly. Knowing Georgia Canfield, she was sure the woman would tell her soon enough the reason for her unexpected visit.

"I never wrote to thank you for the wreath you sent for Simon's funeral."

"I understand that you were very busy."

"Yes." She hesitated. "My husband's death was a shock."

"I'm sure it must have been."

The phone rang and Angie excused herself to take an FTD order from Boston. As she wrote it out, she noticed that Georgia sauntered around the shop as if she hadn't a care in the world. The woman was amazing.

Replacing the receiver, Angie cleared her throat softly. "Was there something I could do for you, Mrs. Canfield? I'm sure this isn't a social call." Angie wanted to fill this order before closing time and there were only a few minutes left. She didn't know what kind of game the woman was playing, but she wasn't in the mood to go along.

Georgia Canfield sighed appreciatively. "Charleston is such a lovely city."

"Yes," Angie agreed, letting her eyes drop to the FTD order. "Mrs. Canfield," she said, breathing heavily, "I don't mean to be rude, but if you have something to say, I wish you'd say it. I don't have time to play cat and mouse with you."

The older woman paled slightly. "If you insist on being direct then I shall. I'd like to know what happened between you and my son."

Angie's smile was bittersweet. "You'll have to ask Simon that."

"My dear girl, I would hardly come three hundred miles to quiz you if I wasn't forced into doing so." Her voice was calm and even. The only outward sign that she was angry was the drumming pulse in her neck.

In spite of herself, Angie smiled anew. "No, I don't suppose you would."

"My son is deeply in love with you."

Angie walked briskly past the woman to the flower case. Opening the refrigerated cabinet, she withdrew several long-stemmed roses and a variety of other flowers she would need for the arrangement.

"Doesn't that mean anything to you?" she demanded.

"Yes," Angie admitted with an uncomfortable feeling of guilt. "It means a great deal."

"Do you love him?"

"I don't believe that's any of your business."

A small, admiring smile twitched at the corner of the older woman's mouth. "I strongly suspect that you do."

Angie's fingers tightened around the unstripped stems in her hands. The thorns cut unmercifully into her hands. "If you'll excuse me."

"No," the woman barked.

Angie turned, surprised at the uncharacteristic rise in the older woman's voice. "Twelve years ago, I paid you ten thousand dollars to leave Groves Point," she said in a low, controlled voice. "Today I would offer you everything I own if you'd agree to come back."

Fourteen

"I promised myself I wouldn't intrude on Simon's life a second time," Georgia Canfield continued, more subdued now. "But my son needs you." Her gloved hands were folded primly in front of her creaseless linen suit. "I thought at first it was my husband's death that had affected him so greatly. But now I believe it's you."

"Mrs. Canfield, if Simon loves me as much as you say then he would have come back for me."

"And if you love him as much as you say," she fired back, "you'd make the effort to go to him. Listen, Angela, you're not the woman I would have chosen for Simon, but I've already had my chance at handpicking one wife. All I want is my son's happiness, and if that means you then I'm willing to accept you as a daughter-in-law."

"Maybe we should understand each other, Mrs. Canfield," Angie shot directly back. "I don't play bridge and have no intention of learning. I don't want to have anything to do with the country club and I plan to be far too busy to join all the charities that interest you. Furthermore, if I come back to Groves Point I plan to bring my flower shop with me and work in it until the babies come."

The frown that drew the delicately lined eyebrows into one stiff curve relaxed at the mention of children. "You do want children?"

"A houseful."

"And you wouldn't restrict me from seeing them?"

"Mrs. Canfield, we've all made mistakes. I don't hate you. I couldn't. You're Simon's mother, and the very things I love about Simon are the best parts of you. You would be the only grandmother our children would have. They would need your love just as much as Simon and I would."

The older woman's tight mouth relaxed and trembled at the corners. "My dear," she whispered so softly that Angie had to strain to hear, "perhaps you would consider being a guest speaker at the Garden Club someday."

Angie's own voice was soft and quivering. "I'd enjoy that very much."

Mrs. Canfield opened the clasp of her purse, took out a dainty lace handkerchief and dabbed the corners of her eyes. "Believe me, I didn't expect to resort to tears, but I've been terribly distressed about Simon."

"What's happened?" A niggling fear invaded her happiness.

"I think it would be best if you saw for yourself. Do come soon, Angela."

"I'll be there within a week."

"Thank you."

"No, Mrs. Canfield," Angie whispered through the emotion blocking her throat. "Thank you."

* * *

Saturday morning, after furiously making arrangements with Donna regarding the flower shop, Angie packed her bags. Her first stop on the way out of town was at Clay's. Apprehensive, she sat in her car an extra minute to compose her thoughts. This was the moment she dreaded. She was going home to Simon, to where she'd always belonged, but in doing so she was pulling away from the loving, protective arms of her father. Long ago Angie had recognized that Clay's actions had been motivated by love. Fear and pride had played a large part in his actions, too, but mostly there was love. He had used his health as a means of emotional blackmail so that she stood torn between the two men she loved the most in the world. Clay thought he'd won.

He opened the door and gave her a look of mild surprise.

"Angie." He glanced at his wristwatch. "It's barely eight. What are you doing up so early?"

She gave him a kiss on the cheek and raised her eyes to his. "I'm leaving, Dad."

The smile drained out of Clay's face inch by inch, leaving him pale and deadly sober. "You're going to him."

Angie nodded. "It's where I belong."

He smiled a little sadly and hunched his shoulders forward as he slumped onto the sofa. "I guess I've always known you would."

"Thank you for not trying to stop me."

"I wouldn't," he said, and his low voice was edged with pain. "You go to him, Angie girl, and tell him for me that he's the luckiest man in South Carolina."

Sitting beside her father, Angie took him by the

shoulders and gently laid her soft cheek to his jaw. "I'll be moving Clay Pots with me."

Clay nodded and closed his eyes. "You've done well for yourself. I've been proud of you from the minute your mama laid you in my arms for the first time. No matter what I've said to you, I've always been proud you are my daughter."

"Dad…do you remember how Groves Point gave us a second chance after Mom died? It'll do that again. I want you to move back…"

"That's impossible, Angie." He lowered his head and studied his clasped hands for a heart-wrenching minute. "I've never told you how deeply I regret taking that Canfield money."

Angie laid her hand over his. "I was the one who took it."

"No," he argued. "Not only did I convince you to accept that money, but I took the chance of giving you the college education you deserved. I wasted all those thousands on a pipe dream."

"Dad—"

"No, I want you to listen. I've got some money saved, not much, a few thousand. When you go to Simon I want you to give him that with the promise that I'll repay him the rest of the ten thousand when I can. I realize it's a little old-fashioned, but I want you to think of this as your dowry."

"Oh, Dad," she whispered hoarsely, fighting back tears. "I should have told you."

"Told me?"

"Remember when I sold Petal Pushers?" She gave him a moment to absorb the meaning of what she was saying.

He looked puzzled, a deep frown narrowing his brow into three thick lines as he studied her.

"That was our business, yours and mine. You worked as many hours as me. Often more. I sold it, invested the profit and returned the ten thousand dollars to the Canfields with twelve years of compound interest."

Clay's puzzled frown turned to one of amazed stupefaction.

"We don't owe the Canfields a penny."

"Why didn't you tell me?"

She shrugged one shoulder. "I wish now I had."

Clay hugged her close, squeezing her head with his long arms. "Go to him, Angie. With my blessing and with my love."

"Thank you, Dad," she whispered through a heart pounding with happiness.

The drive took the better part of seven hours. Angie stopped twice. Once for gas and another time to grab a sandwich and something cool to drink. As her car ate up the miles, Angie grew more content. She felt as if she was going home, really going home after a long time away.

She didn't stop in town, but drove directly to Twenty Acres and Simon's house. Their house, her mind corrected, with its four spacious bedrooms, office and family room.

Prince barked when she pulled into the long driveway, but stopped when she climbed out of the car and gave him her hand to smell. The short-haired black dog seemed to recognize her and wagged his tail in greeting. Laughing, she found a stick, threw it into the woods and watched him scramble after it.

The back door was jerked open, and Angie turned

to see an angry scowl on Simon's face disappear into one of shocked disbelief.

"Angie," he whispered as if seeing an illusion. He rubbed his hand over his eyes. "Is it really you?"

Unexpectedly, she felt shy. It took everything within her just to meet his gaze. "Hello. The real estate man said I might want to look at this place as a possible home for a family."

Slowly he came down the concrete steps, measuring her words as though he couldn't believe that she had come back to him a second time. Every instinct in him urged him to pull her into his arms and thank God for giving him another chance with this woman. A crippling thought paralyzed him on the bottom step. No woman would return to him after the way he'd abused her body and spirit. Not unless there was a good reason. Angie had every right to hate him.

Immediately he wondered if Angie could be pregnant. She just said she was looking for a family home. After all the weeks that he had prayed she would conceive his child, the thought that she had given life to his seed when he had treated her savagely tore a hole straight through his heart. A gnawing fear froze the smile on Angie's face as she watched Simon. The happiness that had filled her heart left as quickly as it came. He didn't want her. "Simon," she whispered achingly, "please say something."

"Why did you come?" He wanted to hear her say the words, telling him what he already knew. From the way she spoke, he'd know her feelings on the matter. He studied her face, praying he'd find some clue that she didn't hate him though she had every right.

"Why?" she repeated, dropping her gaze, her mind

discounting his mother's visit. So this was to be Georgia Canfield's ultimate revenge. She'd persuaded Angie to return to Groves Point when Simon no longer loved or wanted her. "If you need to ask, then you don't know." She felt sick with defeat and failure. Her stomach heaved and she placed a calming hand on her abdomen.

He stiffened, his body tensing into a rigid line as her hand moved to her stomach. He closed his eyes and groaned inwardly. The hurt, betrayed look told him everything. His eyes flickered open. No matter what her feelings were, Simon realized, he wanted that child enough to fight her in every court in the land for the right to raise him. It didn't matter that his son had been conceived in anger and pain. The child was a part of Angie he had never dreamed he'd have. His gaze narrowed menacingly, and, frightened, Angie took a step in retreat.

"I shouldn't have come," she whispered miserably.

Her fear sobered him and he drew back slightly. She would be a wonderful mother, gentle and caring. Tender and nurturing. No man in his right mind would tear a child from her arms. She'd die before she would let it happen. If she wouldn't have him, then, by God, he'd give the child his name. Some way, somehow he'd make her marry him.

"I'll make the arrangements for the wedding as soon as possible."

She swallowed and stared at him. "Don't you think we should discuss things first?"

"No," he barked, taking her by the elbow and escorting her into the house. He pulled out a kitchen chair and sat her down. Pacing the area in front of her, he threaded his fingers through his hair angrily. "Maybe I should get you to the doctor first. Who have you seen?"

"Seen?" Good heavens, Simon wasn't making any sense whatsoever. "The only person I've talked to was your mother."

"My mother," he raged furiously. "You went to her and didn't have the common decency to tell me? I wondered, God knows I wondered, but I thought you'd contact me first. I never dreamed you'd go to her."

"I didn't go to your mother," she shouted back on the verge of tears, her voice shaking. "She came to me."

"How did she know?"

Angie blinked twice. "She must have guessed.... Simon..." She paused, drew in a deep breath and shook her head. "What are we talking about?"

"The baby," he told her evenly. He knelt beside her and took her hands in his. Shocked eyes met tender ones and Simon smiled at her with a fierce gentleness that robbed her lungs of oxygen. "After everything I've done and said to hurt you, can you find it in your heart to forgive me and marry me?" He drank deeply from her eyes and continued. "I love you more than life itself. These past weeks have been a living hell."

He thought she was pregnant! She laid her hand on his smoothly shaved cheek and smiled. When she spoke her voice was filled with tears. "You may not want to marry me when I tell you something."

"I've wanted you from the time we were sixteen. Not once in all those years has that changed."

She dropped her forehead to his and closed her eyes. "Simon," she whispered brokenly. "I'm not pregnant."

The words went through him like a bolt of lightning. "You're not?"

"No. I wanted to be so badly. Every day I prayed that I was." Shyly, she closed her eyes. "If I was pregnant, then I'd have an excuse to come to you."

"Come to me? Oh, my sweet, darling Angie." He couldn't believe that this incredible woman loved him after all he'd put her through. He'd suffered the agonies of these damned weeks without her, knowing that after what he'd done he couldn't go back to her. Pleading for her forgiveness wasn't enough to take away the pain of their last meeting. "Oh, love, I don't deserve you. You're far too good for me."

Through joy and tears and an immense relief, her arms sneaked around his neck and she smiled at him through the watery haze. "Simon, dear Simon, I love you so much."

His arms came around her, crushing her. His eyes were dark with emotion as his mouth found hers with all the aching longing of this last separation. "I hope you're sure," he whispered against her lips, "because I'll never have the strength to let you go again."

"I'm sure. Very sure." She kissed him in all the ways he'd taught her until she was faint with joy and longing.

Simon's mouth and hands moved over her with a fierce tenderness until their breaths became mingled gasps of pleasure. They strained against each other wanting to give more and more.

When Simon stood, lifting her in his arms, Angie tossed back her head until her radiant gaze met his. "Where are you taking me?" she teased, finding his earlobe and sucking it until she felt the shivers race through him.

"Who said you weren't pregnant?" he asked and

traced the delicate line of her chin with his forefinger. "After today I can guarantee you that will change."

And it did.

* * * * *

REQUEST YOUR
FREE BOOKS!

2 FREE NOVELS
FROM THE ROMANCE COLLECTION
PLUS 2 FREE GIFTS!

YES! Please send me 2 FREE novels from the Romance Collection and my 2 FREE gifts (gifts are worth about $10). After receiving them, if I don't wish to receive any more books, I can return the shipping statement marked "cancel." If I don't cancel, I will receive 4 brand-new novels every month and be billed just $6.24 per book in the U.S. or $6.74 per book in Canada. That's a savings of at least 22% off the cover price. It's quite a bargain! Shipping and handling is just 50¢ per book in the U.S. and 75¢ per book in Canada.* I understand that accepting the 2 free books and gifts places me under no obligation to buy anything. I can always return a shipment and cancel at any time. Even if I never buy another book, the two free books and gifts are mine to keep forever.

194/394 MDN F4XY

Name _____ (PLEASE PRINT) _____

Address _____ Apt. # _____

City _____ State/Prov. _____ Zip/Postal Code _____

Signature (if under 18, a parent or guardian must sign)

Mail to the **Harlequin® Reader Service:**
IN U.S.A.: P.O. Box 1867, Buffalo, NY 14240-1867
IN CANADA: P.O. Box 609, Fort Erie, Ontario L2A 5X3

Want to try two free books from another line?
Call 1-800-873-8635 or visit www.ReaderService.com.

* Terms and prices subject to change without notice. Prices do not include applicable taxes. Sales tax applicable in N.Y. Canadian residents will be charged applicable taxes. Offer not valid in Quebec. This offer is limited to one order per household. Not valid for current subscribers to the Romance Collection or the Romance/Suspense Collection. All orders subject to credit approval. Credit or debit balances in a customer's account(s) may be offset by any other outstanding balance owed by or to the customer. Please allow 4 to 6 weeks for delivery. Offer available while quantities last.

Your Privacy—The Harlequin® Reader Service is committed to protecting your privacy. Our Privacy Policy is available online at www.ReaderService.com or upon request from the Harlequin Reader Service.

We make a portion of our mailing list available to reputable third parties that offer products we believe may interest you. If you prefer that we not exchange your name with third parties, or if you wish to clarify or modify your communication preferences, please visit us at www.ReaderService.com/consumerchoice or write to us at Harlequin Reader Service Preference Service, P.O. Box 9062, Buffalo, NY 14269. Include your complete name and address.

DEBBIE MACOMBER

32988	OUT OF THE RAIN	___ $7.99 U.S.	___ $9.99 CAN.
32918	AN ENGAGEMENT IN SEATTLE	___ $7.99 U.S.	___ $9.99 CAN.
32858	HOME FOR THE HOLIDAYS	___ $7.99 U.S.	___ $9.99 CAN.
32828	ORCHARD VALLEY BRIDES	___ $7.99 U.S.	___ $9.99 CAN.
32798	ORCHARD VALLEY GROOMS	___ $7.99 U.S.	___ $9.99 CAN.
32783	THE MAN YOU'LL MARRY	___ $7.99 U.S.	___ $9.99 CAN.
32743	THE SOONER THE BETTER	___ $7.99 U.S.	___ $9.99 CAN.
32702	FAIRY TALE WEDDINGS	___ $7.99 U.S.	___ $9.99 CAN.
32569	ALWAYS DAKOTA	___ $7.99 U.S.	___ $7.99 CAN.
31624	ON A CLEAR DAY	___ $7.99 U.S.	___ $8.99 CAN.
31598	NORTH TO ALASKA	___ $7.99 U.S.	___ $8.99 CAN.
31587	A MAN'S HEART	___ $7.99 U.S.	___ $8.99 CAN.
31580	MARRIAGE BETWEEN FRIENDS	___ $7.99 U.S.	___ $8.99 CAN.
31535	PROMISE, TEXAS	___ $7.99 U.S.	___ $8.99 CAN.
31457	HEART OF TEXAS VOLUME 3	___ $7.99 U.S.	___ $8.99 CAN.
31441	HEART OF TEXAS VOLUME 2	___ $7.99 U.S.	___ $8.99 CAN.
31426	HEART OF TEXAS VOLUME 1	___ $7.99 U.S.	___ $9.99 CAN.
31413	LOVE IN PLAIN SIGHT	___ $7.99 U.S.	___ $9.99 CAN.
31395	GLAD TIDINGS	___ $7.99 U.S.	___ $9.99 CAN.
31357	I LEFT MY HEART	___ $7.99 U.S.	___ $9.99 CAN.

(limited quantities available)

TOTAL AMOUNT	$ _____
POSTAGE & HANDLING	$ _____
($1.00 for 1 book, 50¢ for each additional)	
APPLICABLE TAXES*	$ _____
TOTAL PAYABLE	$ _____

(check or money order—please do not send cash)

To order, complete this form and send it, along with a check or money order for the total above, payable to MIRA Books, to: **In the U.S.:** 3010 Walden Avenue, P.O. Box 9077, Buffalo, NY 14269-9077; **In Canada:** P.O. Box 636, Fort Erie, Ontario, L2A 5X3.

Name: _____
Address: _____ City: _____
State/Prov.: _____ Zip/Postal Code: _____
Account Number (if applicable): _____
075 CSAS

*New York residents remit applicable sales taxes.
*Canadian residents remit applicable GST and provincial taxes.

MIRA®

www.MIRABooks.com

MDM0115BL